RIVERS RAN RED

The Last of the Romans Trilogy

RIVERS RAN RED

The Last of the Romans Trilogy

J.A. GRIERSON

CLOUD
INK

First published in 2019
Published by Cloud Ink Press Ltd, Auckland
P.O. Box 8988, Symonds Street, Auckland, 1150
www.cloudink.co.nz

ISBN: 978-0-473-48748-5

Book design: Craig Violich (CVD Graphics)
Printed by Ligare Ltd, Glenfield, Auckland

To lost heroes who wanted their stories told.

Contents

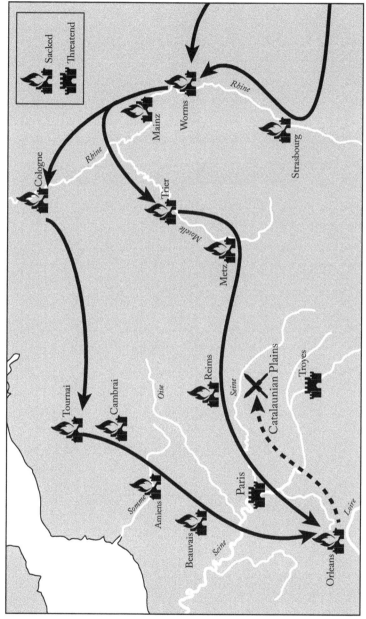

Map i – ATTILA IN GAUL, 451 AD

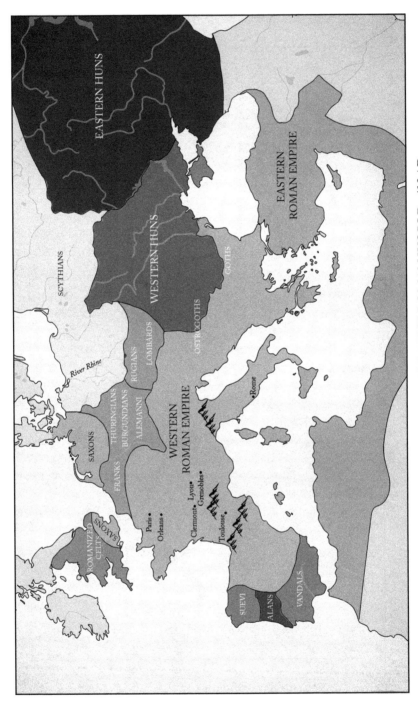

Map ii – BARBARIAN TRIBES IN THE ROMAN WORLD, 410AD

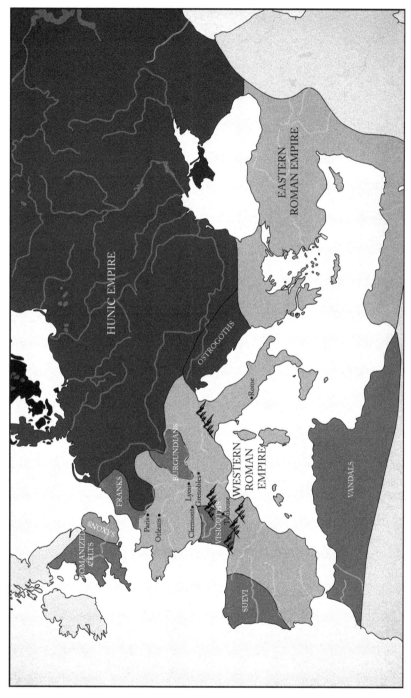

Map iii – BARBARIAN TRIBES IN THE ROMAN WORLD, 451AD

Prologue

The Goths Cross
Northern Gaul
New Year's Day 410 AD

It had been a bitter winter. Even the most ancient men and women in the village agreed that they'd never known another like it. Snow choked the roads and cut off the grain dole. Flotillas of skiffs, plying their trade along the River Rhine, panicked and flocked south. White drifts turned a row of hauled up Roman patrol boats into burial mounds.

Half a mile back from the river, in a stone-walled house only six paces square, Diana helped her five-year-old daughter to dress. With numb fingers, she sectioned Sola's curls into three long tresses. Clumsy with cold, she wove them into a plait and thought back to the day a fur trader had smuggled her family from barbarian to Roman shores. A sallow man, he'd poked a blunt finger through a handful of bronze and silver coins.

"No gold?"

Diana shook her head.

He looked her up and down. "I'll need your amulet as well then."

"It belonged to my grandmother."

"D'you want to cross or not?"

The year of her wedding, Diana's home had been burned to the ground by the Goths. Her brothers rebuilt it but the following spring the Sueves had raided and left them all dead. Only Roman territory was safe from tribal wars. She wriggled her amulet off.

The boatman scowled at her pregnant stomach and the little girl clinging to her hand. "Lie flat in the bottom and keep that child quiet."

Diana levered herself down, curling her body around her daughter's while the ferryman buried them under layers of uncured deer pelts. Sola wrinkled her nose at the smell. The sudden darkness frightened her but she knew she could not move.

Midstream, a Roman river patrolman ordered the boat to heave to. The trader wiped a sweating palm on his tunic then proffered it to steady the soldier aboard. Diana didn't breathe as she heard him plant his foot on the gunnel. She listened to water rippling along the flat-bottomed hull. A deck-board creaked; metal-toed boots clacked towards her head. With the tip of his spear the patrolman flicked back the top deerskin.

"Pwah!" he took a step back from the reek of a hide crawling with maggots, "nothing else to declare?"

"Nothing but pelts this time of year."

"No wonder all you barbarians stink," he sniggered, stepping back on to his own craft. "Move on."

What relief Diana felt as she swung her toddler over the last yard of water and saw her daughter leave tiny footprints in the gravel sand; what joy when she watched Tallus, the girl's father, step out from behind the bush where he'd been waiting and scoop his child up into his arms.

Diana sold the silver scabbard of her husband's sword and the last of her mother's jewellery to pay a stone mason to help build a house. Each morning she listened out for the donkey braying as the mason arrived, walking alongside a cart laden with slabs to cut to shape on site. The chime of hammers on chisels brought a smile to her lips. Her husband's hands grew calloused as he learned the stonemason's trade. Despite her expanding belly, Diana helped the men lay out the blocks to build a wall. It was heavy work and she wasn't used to it, but each stone she levered into place with a long iron rod brought *hope*. The windows covered with cowhide shutters couldn't keep out the cold but, at the end of each week, imperial waggons rolled into the village forum and dished out the grain dole. Her neighbours, Roman citizens, shared their quota with the newcomers.

Weaving her daughter's hair in their freezing home, Diana huffed over memories, so recent yet so distant, in this winter where not one cart had made it through snow-buried roads. Her husband hunted farther afield each day only to come home at nightfall, blue-lipped and empty-handed.

Diana twisted the last blonde curl at the end of Sola's plait around her finger, too cold to tie a ribbon, and looked up. A dim shaft of light edged between stone and shutter and picked out the face of her weather-beaten mother-in-law as she stirred melted snow and the thrice boiled bones of a rooster in an iron pot. Grizzling on empty bellies, two small boys huddled next to her. White puffs of breath painted hunger in the air.

Starvation drove Diana to the frozen river. Gritting her teeth to stop their chattering, she tucked her daughter's plait down the back of a fine-woven cloak that had been hers as a child and was a reminder of better times. She wrapped a rabbit skin scarf around Sola's neck, pulled up the hood and brushed her forehead with a kiss, then passed her a satchel and helped her wriggle her arms through the straps.

The aged woman looked up from her fire. "I'll feed the boys enough to get them settled and save the rest for when you get back. Good luck."

"Thank you," said Diana, pulling on mittens. She cupped her sons' cheeks. "Be good my darlings".

Diana listened to her daughter's footsteps smooshing in the snow behind her as they waded in muffled silence to where she hoped the river would flow.

For a glacial hour, Sola tailed her mother down a dug-out track with banks as high as a man's waist. She could only just peer over the top of them. Her lips and chin were too frozen to speak and her eyes and nose watered from the cold. When the track petered out, mother and daughter were forced to high-step on numb feet through last night's powder. Diana carried a sharply pointed shaft of wood and a stone-headed mallet to break the ice for a fishing hole. Sola carried rough twine lines with pebble sinkers and bone hooks in the small leather pouch across her back. She didn't mind the straps cutting into her shoulders; she felt grown up and important.

If it were not for the Roman frontier watchtower, as sharp and threatening as a brandished spear, neither mother nor daughter could have told where solid land ended and frozen water started. As they passed by its foot, Sola tilted her head back to see if the soldiers were watching. Against a looming sky she glimpsed armour moving. Winter sliced at her exposed throat. She tucked her chin back into her rabbit skin and glued her eyes to her mother's hem.

Diana led her a furlong past where the banks would normally be in search of the middle of the river. She knelt and pushed the sturdy stick through the snow. Her mittened hands made a hollow and twisted its point into the surface of the ice. She told Sola to hold the base steady. Diana stood up, raised the stone mallet above her shoulder and prepared to strike.

Horn blasts split the frozen air.

Three short. Two long.

Diana's head snapped backwards in the direction of the Roman sentry post. Her first thought was that the noise was an admonition intended for her, but she quickly realised otherwise.

A shriek of alarm rushed up her body. Her eyes seared the slow sweep of the Rhine. One after another, the brush bales of warning flares atop the watchtowers shot up, red against the grey-white sky. Diana grabbed her daughter's hand, held it tight and stared into the frozen expanse behind the Roman defences but saw only blank whiteness. The river rumbled beneath her feet. Unable to make sense of what was happening, she looked down at the patch of ice she'd cleared in fear that it was about to cave in, but it was solid and opaque, without the tiniest crack.

Roman trumpets blasted the call to action stations down the line.

Her heart galloping against her ribs, Diana looked up and squinted towards the far side of the river. It was only then that she saw horned heads appearing through the icy fog. Barbarian boots kicked up clouds of snow before them. The advancing warriors could have been mistaken for oxen were it not for the long pikes and the edges of double-headed axes that spiked the mists.

She and Sola were an isolated black speck in the whiteness.

Sola's bottom lip quivered and she started to cry. Diana dropped her mallet and stick, hitched up her skirt and dragged the child behind her as she bolted in the opposite direction to the encroaching hordes. The balls of fishing twine and sinkers bounced out of Sola's bag and trailed behind her then the strap slipped off her shoulder and the pouch fell to the ground. Her plait unravelled and her hair flew loose.

Woman and girl ran until their limbs were so deprived of air that they had to stop, doubled over, their stomachs heaving. Diana barely dared to look behind her. Although she had put distance between herself and the advancing men, the situation was hopeless. There were too many of them, her village was too far away and Sola couldn't run any farther. She scanned the stark landscape for cover. A few mounded bushes, buried in snow along the river bank, were the only hope. Panic pumped her limbs as she dragged her daughter towards them. When they came to the largest she threw herself to her knees and, her hands a flurry, dug out an entrance way. She shoved Sola into the heart of the thicket then, insensate to the claw of twigs, scrambled in after her. Her stomach churned. Had the barbarians passed through the copse where her husband went hunting?

* * * * *

A horse reared and whinnied behind the stable-gate at the bottom
of the Roman watchtower. Impatient for the order to ride, a youth
called Avitus, pulled hard on the bit. A decurion clad in a chainmail
tunic ducked the horse's hooves, slid two greased bolts from their slots,
and looked over his shoulder. On his officer's signal, with all his force,
he threw the door wide. Hit by the brightness of the snow outside,
Avitus' blue eyes flinched as he spurred the horse into hostile space.
The decurion slammed the gate shut and rammed the bars back into
their sockets.

From his vantage point on top of the watchtower, the captain of
the Roman guard riveted his eyes on the horse as it bounded across
the snow. Lips thin and face rigid, he waited to see if the barbarians
would give chase. With grim satisfaction he watched just long enough
to see that a burst of pace had put Avitus out of reach of the hordes,
who wallowed in comparison.

But there was only a moment of hope to be found in his horseman's
alacrity. The captain took the measure of his enemy and clenched his
jaw. He would not waste the lives of his men by sallying out into a
sea of barbarians that bled into the mists in the distance. Instead, he
positioned a spindly row of archers around the top of the watchtower.
With bows at the ready and faces blanched they waited for the order
to fire, but the invaders skirted out of range. The captain commanded
the rest of his skeleton force to defend the tower stairs. Nine men
drew up in rows of three and made ready to fight until they fell.

* * * * *

Diana stared out aghast from her hiding place. Her footprints looked
black, enormous and obvious. She huddled with her whimpering child
tucked under her shoulder and moved her lips in silent prayer. As if in

18

answer, snowflakes fluttered down like feathers and blurred the marks that betrayed their presence.

Barbarian boots crunched through knee-deep powder. Sola's eyes were wide and glassy with terror. Her mother put her finger over her lips to signal silence and the child held her breath.

First came the warlords mounted on horses, behind them warriors of all ages, wearing little armour apart from their helmets, but coated with as many weapons as a hedgehog's back. Tribes of Goths, Alani, Sueves, Franks and unrecognizable others appeared from across the water as if conjured by a sorcerer's spell. Mother and child kept still and waited for what seemed an eternity for the first wave to pass. With a long twig Diana worked a hole through the thicket and watched. It was only as daylight faded to a washed-out gloom and she had seen no movement for an hour that she dared to enlarge the hole and stick her head outside.

The barbarians had cut a swathe twenty times wider than a Roman road through the snow. The hollows of her footprints had been tramped into oblivion. She pulled back into the bush, trembling violently, retched then wiped her mouth and sat up. Sola was crying. Diana pulled her into her chest to muffle her sobs, stroked her hair until they stopped then kissed her brow and mouthed, "Don't move".

Her knees trembling, Diana pushed her way right out of their hiding place, stood up, listened and looked in every direction. All was still; she heard nothing except the soft plush of an armful of snow as it slipped from an overburdened bush.

She knelt and took her daughter by the hand to lead her out but Sola pulled back. Smothering her urge to shout at the girl, Diana coaxed and tugged in whispers. All she could think about was her two baby sons and their grandmother as she dragged Sola onto the track flattened by the barbarians. It led to their village.

Diana didn't hear the rear-guard approaching until their leader kicked his horse into a canter fifty strides behind her. With an iron grip on Sola's hand she burst into a sprint. The Goth drew his sword and gained ground on them. A full-grown woman could cause trouble and slow his men down but a small child would sell well in the slave markets.

Only the tips of Sola's toes were touching the ground when she felt the swoosh of a blade pass over her head; her mother's hand went slack. Through a spray of blood, she saw her neck split sideways on its shoulders. The body crumpled. In the moment that Sola's arms shot out to gather the pieces and put mother back together, the barbarian grabbed a fistful of the girl's hair, yanked her off the ground and threw her face down over his horse's withers. With one elbow nailing her spine to the pommel of his saddle he spun the beast around and trotted back to his men on foot.

Two of them stepped forward. One held a length of rope while the other grabbed Sola by the waist. The horse skittered sideways as the child swiped at the rider's eyes as he lurched out of reach. The man on the ground tightened his grip on Sola's waist but she lashed out with all four limbs. He cursed and held her at arms' length but she drew five streaks of blood across his cheek.

The rope man laughed and threw a punch into her jaw, not quite hard enough to break her neck, and Sola's white world went black.

* * * * *

Granules of ice stung Avitus' eyes as he spurred his horse along the river bank. Breath blew like smoke from its nostrils, but it found its rhythm, heaving and steaming twelve miles to the next staging post. Leaping from one saddle to the next without rest, Avitus gave staccato orders to the troops to make ready to defend themselves.

A week of mountains and rivers later, he glimpsed a smudge of smoke from the hearths and bakeries of the world's largest city in the distance. Under an arch of the Claudian aqueduct he slowed to a canter, a prayer of thanks to Mercury on his lips, then crossed a dry moat. Wiping the grit of the road from his brow, he arrived at portcullised gates built high enough to let elephants pass. With a perfunctory salute, the sentries ordered him to dismount and wait.

Avitus paced the confines of the guardhouse courtyard, his eyes narrowing with derision at the sight of off-duty soldiers seated on mats, playing dice or buffing their breastplates.

An hour passed before a slave-born litter deposited an over-fed senator on the parade ground. The starch in his purple-striped toga announced in advance of a word being spoken that the barbarian invasion of Gaul was a matter of little consequence.

"It was an act of the gods that the Rhine froze over," said the toga, "we have no help to offer the provinces. There are barbarians at our gates."

Avitus drew himself tall, hands balled into fists at his side. He glanced round at the guardsmen lounging off duty. "With respect, sir, I saw no sign of enemy troops outside your walls."

The senator's lip twitched at the insolence of a boy, not yet a man. But the intensity of Avitus' stare, the wolfskin strapped across his shoulders and his hand on the hilt of his gladius made the toga glance round for his guards. Seeing them at hand, he puffed himself up and wielded words that cut – "Barbarians pose a constant threat to Rome. Gaul will have to deal with the invasion without the Emperor's help. Now, young equites, there are affairs of state to which I must attend. Find your own way out."

Rage burning in his gut and injustice welling his eyes, Avitus glared at the senator back as he walked, faster than he should have, to his litter. At the click of their master's fingers, slaves knelt to help the fat man up.

Avitus called for his horse. This time, as he spurred it through the gates, the guardsmen held a long salute and, when the stallion's hooves had thundered past, the eldest sentry said to his juniors, "One day

Rome will march for that young man."

With each milepost Avitus passed, he grew more resolute. The pompous indifference of the Senate deserved no allegiance and an emperor who could not defend his territories must be deposed. Crossing into Gaul, Avitus rode from camp to camp summoning the legions to arms. They rose with a roar, united with their cohorts in Britain and proclaimed their general, Constantine, Emperor of Rome.

* * * * *

Sola's father comes home from his hunting to the blackened ruins of his home. Flakes of snow twist in a wailing wind while he sifts ashes through his fingers. Two little ribcages, barely bigger than those of a chicken, are unearthed. The skulls and legs are there. The body of his mother is hidden under a fallen rafter. He levers the log off. No sign of his wife or daughter. With the iron head of a spade whose handle burned away he scrapes a shallow grave and lays out the skeletons. Tears blind him as he joins together what is left of the bones of their hands. He makes no sacrifice to the gods who robbed him. He offers them anger and anguish, the only things real to him.

Tallus discards the broken spade but puts his hammer and chisel into a sack on his back. His search spirals wider but he finds no trace of Sola or Diana. He waits a frozen week, then he gives up and falls in with a band of refugees. Tossed and spun like dead leaves in a winter wind they head south towards Lyon, the Roman capital of Gaul.

In 418, at last, they find peace when Constantine buys a truce with the Goths, allowing them to settle under their own king around Toulouse. Deep in the belly of Roman Gaul, barbarians take root.

Avitus

Alone stallion, its mane and tail flying, clattered past the last milepost to Narbonne then disappeared into the canyons of shadowed streets. A warrior in a blood-red cloak reined the horse to a halt at the foot of limestone walls one hundred feet high. It reared then planted plate-sized hooves squarely onto echoing stones.

From under the shadow cast by his general's helmet, Avitus' cobalt eyes scaled the implacable ramparts to where their crenellations stabbed at the belly of a dazzling sky. Black wisps of smoke rose into the blue. They whispered of death and burning but the iron-bound gates of the fort were intact and shut. *Taken by sea*, thought Avitus with grudging admiration.

At the sight of Gothic spears bristling on the Roman ramparts above him, his blood surged with indignation. A guttural order rang out and archers nocked arrows to their bows. They took aim at his throat but Avitus did not flinch. With exaggerated slowness, he took off his lion-embossed helmet. A sea breeze lifted sweat-drenched locks from his scalp and his cloak gusted like dragon's breath behind him.

The weather-beaten creases at the corners of his eyes deepened as he squinted up and stared out his enemy then, with a wry grin, winked at the horned heads leering down at him. "You'll have to do better than that if you want to oust Rome from Narbonne."

Their fingers trembled on their bowstrings as the archers glanced towards their officer for the order to fire, but dark circles spread under the captain's armpits and he remained mute.

"Bring me Theodoric, your king!" bellowed Avitus at battlefield volume.

The Goth captain wiped a hand over dry lips.

"Only a dead man hesitates!" boomed Avitus.

The captain stood staring at him, panic blinding him to his next move.

Avitus locked eyes on him. "My death would cost Theodoric more than his kingdom."

The Goth's knees turned to water but he squeaked out to his bowmen – "Fire on my command."

Avitus shook his head in disbelief. "A fatal mistake."

"Thus say you!" bellowed a new voice, thick and nasal from the blood of a broken nose, but familiar to Avitus. Theodoric, King of the Goths, pushed aside his archers on the battlements and leaned down to stare at his old friend and new enemy. On each shoulder of his mantle snarled a dead, fanged wolf.

A sure shot with a ballista had knocked Theodoric's helmet off as he had stormed the walls in the hours before dawn. The Gothic king had taken delight in avenging himself by having the boy crucified as soon as the fortress fell. The lad hung dead alongside his officers, a few still moaning, in a row of crosses at the foot of the bloodstained walls.

"About time you got here," said Avitus.

Theodoric studied the general sitting square-shouldered and calm in his saddle then lifted his head and strained his ears for the clang of legions on the march. All he heard was the snorting of Avitus' horse, still breathing hard, and the caw of circling gulls. Their raucous calls goaded him to murder the most respected Roman in all five provinces of Gaul.

He grabbed a bow from an archer, pulled the string taut and aimed at the Roman's jugular. "You're a dead man, Avitus!"

"Come to your senses, Theodoric." Avitus raised his shield to protect his neck nonetheless, "and if you plan to kill me, at least come down here and do it like a warrior, in hand-to-hand combat."

Theodoric looked up from his target. Through eyes swollen to slits he scanned the horizon for legionary banners. "Where's your army?"

"At my back."

"Not today, they're not."

"You can gamble your life on that if you like," said Avitus. His horse shimmied as he slid his helmet back and tightened the strap under a jutting jaw. The cheek plates clasped Avitus' face, leaving nothing in sight but two diamond-bright eyes and an eagle-beaked nose. "But you know that if you kill me, the magister militum himself will cross the Alps with ten legions to avenge me."

Theodoric searched the horizon again. If Flavius Aetius, the supreme commander of all the Roman empire's troops, invaded Gaul, his own chance of survival would be nil. A chill ran through his blood as he caught sight of a bird in the distance, nothing but a thin black line in the sky, rising on a thermal wind, like an eagle. He swallowed and did not reply.

Avitus shook his head in sadness. "I'm disappointed in you. I strung your bow for you when you were but a boy. Taught you the ways of a Roman warrior so that we might fight side by side, allies, not enemies.

The Goth looked back down at the man in the gleaming imperial breastplate, whose greaves were grimed with dust from the road but whose voice was deep and unhurried, then he shook his fist. "I'm a king now, Avitus. Save your lectures for someone who cares what you think."

"I offered you the friendship of almighty Rome," boomed Avitus' baritone.

Theodoric wondered how the Roman, a man of only moderate height and one hundred feet below him, seemed to tower above him, but snarled back, "And what does friendship with Rome bring besides taxes and death?"

"It brought *you* your kingdom and peace! D'you choose to live – a friend to Rome – or meet your death?"

Theodoric's ears were ringing from his injuries and Avitus' words reverberated in his head. He breathed roughly through his mouth and searched again for the bird on the horizon. He caught sight of its feathers' tips shimmering in the wind and took it as an omen. With a thick, dry tongue he tried to lick his lips then let out a coughing sigh.

"Why'd you ride down here? I made sure you were in Lyon before I attacked. Even you can't cover 250 miles in under a day!"

Avitus gave a wry smile. "You can't attack the capital of Narbonensis and expect me to let you get away with it."

"But why d'you come alone?"

"To save your miserable life, you fool! Give you the chance to evacuate. But if you won't – " slowly, finger by finger, Avitus pulled a red gauntlet from his hand and raised it above his head – "I swear you'll die."

Theodoric's face blanched behind its bruises and the thicket of his blood-matted beard. His eyes flicked towards the bird he was sure now was an eagle, a portent of a coming invasion and his own destruction.

Avitus raised the gauntlet in his fist and pierced him with his eyes. "Ally or enemy, dead man or king – which is it, Theodoric?"

The Gothic king slammed his bow on the edge of the battlements and stepped back from the abyss. "Alright! Come in and parley!"

Avitus grunted. He tucked his gauntlet into his belt and drew his spatha.

Theodoric's eyes widened at the sight of the gleaming blade, and fear coursed through him. Was it too late to sue for peace?

"Not before I've run a sword through those men," said Avitus, nudging his horse towards the row of crosses at the foot of the walls.

Cuckoo in the Nest

Villa of Avitacum
Province of Auvergne, Gaul
444 AD

Three boys were practising their swordplay on a lawn that sloped from the doric façade of Avitacum down to its lake. With a flick of his wrist Ecdicius, Avitus' fourteen-year-old son, sent Graecus' sword spinning end over tip. It was the fifth time in as many minutes that he had unsworded him. Sidonius, son of the Praetorian Prefect of Gaul, bit his lip to hide his grin but Ecdicius guffawed. Graecus' throat bobbed as he swallowed back tears and watched his blade arc through the air then land point first, upright and quivering, as if it too were laughing at him.

Across the lawn, in the shade of a giant fig tree on the western side of the villa, Avitus leant forward in his chair. His forearms, hard as ironwood, were at ease on bronzed thighs; his chest and shoulders were broad and square. His bright eyes glanced up from under grizzled brows, but he said nothing. The boys were old enough to sort out their differences.

Graecus, his pustulent acne comically obvious, yanked his weapon from the closely scythed turf, floundered up the lawn and slashed out wildly at Ecdicius who swerved and sent the sword hurtling through the air again. Crimson with humiliation, Graecus lunged for his throat.

Avitus' growl drowned out the scuffle. "That's enough."

Despite his urge to knock Graecus' legs out from under him and rub his face in the dirt, Ecdicius backed off and looked up at the general, but Graecus kept his puff-adder eyes fixed on his rivals.

"Ecdicius!" Avitus summoned. Honorius, Sidonius' father, signalled for him to come too.

Ecdicius feinted with his dagger at Graecus then walked, in step with Sidonius, to face the two most powerful men in Gaul.

With a wave of his hand Honorius invited Avitus to discipline both boys. Without rising from his seat, the general thrust a pile of wax tablets into Sidonius' hands. "Copy these requisition orders onto parchment –" Ecdicius rolled his eyes behind his father's back – "In triplicate. You have one hour." Seeing both boys slump at the prospect, Avitus added, "Work together. Dismissed."

"I swear he's got eyes in the back of his head," grumbled Ecdicius as soon as they were out of earshot, "and why does Graecus get special treatment? He started it."

"We'll pay him back."

From the shade of the giant fig tree, Avitus' face mellowed as he watched Ecdicius and Sidonius stride off. Their quick wits and fine horsemanship would make them fine field officers. Then he looked at Graecus, who showed no such potential, and his features became sharp as a hatchet. There was venom in the way Graecus stared after the other boys and, not for the first time, Avitus wondered if Tertius – a favourite field-officer who'd bled to death in his arms – was really the boy's father. Avitus' last promise to the dying man had been that he'd raise his son as his own, but sometimes he regretted it. "Graecus, clean yourself up, get your marching boots on and report back, on the double." Avitus turned back to Honorius. "That boy wouldn't last a day in the army."

The weight of managing the Empire's affairs in Gaul had ploughed parallel furrows between the Praetorian Prefect's brows. He didn't want to be distracted. "You know the Goths better than any of us, Avitus, will they stick by their treaty or rebel?"

"The Goths are always unpredictable," Avitus ran a hand over the half-day stubble on his chin, "took years to make that treaty work. But Theodoric'll honour it or I'll have his head."

Honorius cleared his throat to broach another awkward subject. "The Emperor has ordered another round of military cuts."

"Another!" exploded Avitus, "ever since the Vandals took Carthage that's all I hear from you. Cuts?! We must raise an army and kick the barbarians out of Africa!"

"You know that the Vandal occupation has blocked the grain supply and broken our tax spine. We can neither feed nor pay our standing army – let alone raise an invasion force."

"Pah! Where there's a will there's a way." Frowning, Avitus scratched the back of his neck with a frown. "Has Rome ever had an emperor more useless than Valentinian III? When Galla Placidia was regent the army came first, but her son's a spineless wastrel."

Honorius glanced around the lawn and lowered his voice. "I agree my friend. Valentinian isn't half the man his mother is. He's weak, vacillating. Rome would be stronger if . . ."

Avitus raised a hand to cut him off and shook his head. "Such talk is treason."

"Would it really be treason to give the Empire a decent leader?" hissed Honorius. "Galla ruled for the good of Rome, but since Valentinian attained his majority. . . ." the Praetorian Prefect raised despairing hands "and we can expect worse. Since his fourth attempt to assassinate her –"

"*Fourth*? It's hard to keep up with them! What happened this time?"

"He sent her to sea in a ship then had it sunk," said Honorius. "Sat drinking on the terrace of his palace in Capri, staring out over the bay in his ghoul-eyed way, sending messengers to the coast every half hour to keep him apprised of progress. When he heard that the ship had gone down with all hands, he punched the air for joy. But the next morning a courier ran up with the news that there had, in fact, been a sole survivor and Valentinian fell into a morass of apprehension."

Avitus slapped his thigh and chuckled. "True to form, the old battle-axe managed to swim ashore, did she? Who'd have expected that! That's a rugged bit of coastline too, nothing but cliffs and rocks."

"Galla did rule the Empire for nigh fifteen years."

"She's as tough as the girth of my saddle," said Avitus, "and as sharp as the tip of my gladius, but even she could never have lasted that long without Aetius' support."

"Be that as it may," said Honorius, "yet again Galla Placidia's shown her son to be blundering, cruel and inept and he's in a frenzy to be rid of her. He's retained the world's top poisoner to assassinate her and threatened him with a slow and excruciating death if he fails."

"Poison – just what you'd expect from a fop who's never lifted a sword in his life."

"Shrewd though she is, Galla's in mortal danger, and when she's gone, a fool will rule." Having said more than he should have, Honorius clamped his mouth shut.

Avitus rubbed calloused fingers over his creviced brow. "The Empire has survived worse emperors than Valentinian, but you, my friend, *you* must be careful. To have such thoughts is one thing, to speak them aloud another." From under his brows, Avitus looked round. "Even here, in my own home, the trees may have ears."

With consummate discretion, Honorius scanned for spies. Empty lawn stretched out from the ancient fig tree in all directions. He looked up into its branches and noticed a cuckoo. It called, as if on signal, then flapped loudly skywards.

In the moment of stillness it left behind, Honorius asked, "Avitus, if the day ever comes where you have to choose between loyalty to the Empire and loyalty to the Emperor, what will you do?"

"Speak no more of this," said Avitus, "I don't aspire to be Emperor. Those who wear the diadem are cursed. Give me battle tactics, not politics."

Avitus turned his shoulder to the governor and watched Graecus' ungainly progress across the lawn towards Avitus' dark-haired daughter, Papianilla. She was reading in a bower where a fountain played but snapped shut her book and hid it in the folds of her chiton when she caught sight of the intruder. Avitus smiled wryly. He'd noticed that Plato's *Apology* was missing from the men's end of the library and Graecus would be quick to tell tales to Papianilla's mother, Sedulla, if he caught her reading it.

Last summer, on sweltering days like this, Papianilla would swim in the lake with her brother and Sidonius but the passage of four seasons had transformed her body from girl to woman and Sedulla had put a stop to that. While Graecus ran water through his clammy hands and slicked down his kinky hair, Papianilla abandoned her alcove and sought refuge inside the villa.

Drumming his fingers on his kneecap, Avitus tried to mask his impatience with the way the day was turning out. When Graecus finally sorted himself out and came back, he thrust a roll of papers into his hands and snapped, "Take these drawings to the stone mason in charge of works at my church."

"Yes, Sir."

"Give my greetings to the priest and be of use to him for the rest of the day." *Stay away from my daughter and out of my sight.*

Graecus dismissed, Avitus turned to Honorius.

The Praetorian Prefect was shaking his head. "You're building a church? Your money would be better spent on bucellarii."

"Every estate is expected to have a church these days, and I don't need a private army."

"You have the biggest temple of Mercury in Gaul on your doorstep."

"Mercury isn't Christian but the Emperor is. I used to think this new religion was a passing cult but it's sprouting like weeds around us."

Honorius shrugged. "Has Valentinian ever heeded the teachings of the prophet from Nazareth?"

"I doubt he even knows what they are." Avitus stared into the distance. "How am I to feed my cavalry horses after all these budget cuts?"

"Yes, we need to keep your horses," said Honorius.

Avitus cocked an eyebrow at his friend. "That's the first time I've heard you defend the cavalry. Usually you complain they cost too much and tell me we must cut them first."

Honorius' furrows deepened. "I heard this morning that Attila has murdered his brother, Bleda, and taken sole control of the Hunnic Empire. The crippling tribute he exacted from the Emperor of the East after the defeat at Constantinople last year won't satiate Attila's appetites."

"You fear Attila will turn against us?"

"He lusts to rule the world, including us. Bleda was rational but his brother revels in blood."

Avitus sat back in his chair, chewing on a blade of grass. "While Rome weakens, the Hun strengthens."

"A diplomat returning from the Hun camp told me that to meet Attila is to stare into the face of the devil." Honorius shivered and leant closer to Avitus. "Attila *ate* four of his own children."

"That may be true, or it may just be one of the myths Attila weaves." Avitus ground the stalk of grass between his canines then spat it out. "The Hun's a fearsome adversary but he's still a distant threat. He'll attack Persia next."

Honorius wiped his brow. "You're right. He'll devour the rest of the East first, but then he'll come for us."

Avitus picked up a stylus and wax tablet. "Give me precise figures for your budget cuts, Honorius. I must work out how to feed my cavalry and where the infantry can lose some flesh – there's no fat left."

A Suitor for Papianilla

Avitacum
Roman Province of Auvergne, Gaul
448 AD

In the sitting-room overlooking his favourite fishing lake at Avitacum, Avitus struggled to make himself comfortable on a sofa plumped up with goosedown cushions. Despite the fact that Honorius was married to Avitus' favourite cousin, Andromeda, and that they'd been friends for over twenty years, he'd had come to dread the Praetorian Prefect's visits. Honorius was a pessimist, his news always negative, and today he'd told Avitus that Galla Placidia had succumbed to Valentinian's poisoner and was close to death.

Avitus had always had a soft spot for Galla. She had intelligence and guts and had been a friend to the army and Gaul. Although she was the daughter, wife and mother of Roman emperors, when Avitus had first met her she'd been a barbarian queen. Ataulf, King of the Goths – 'Father Wolf'- had taken her prisoner during his sack of Rome in 410 then married her.

When Avitus met her in Toulouse, the Gothic capital in Gaul, Galla had been young, beautiful and madly in love. Dark-haired and dark-eyed, she'd been quick to smile. Yet only two years later both her husband and her infant son were dead. Her husband's assassin had humiliated Galla by making the newly-delivered mother march twelve miles in his victory procession. But his reign was short-lived. Only seven days later he too was murdered. Avitus smiled wryly.

Sudden and unexpected death was often the consequence for those who opposed Galla Placidia. Avitus admired her, for, in the years that followed Athaulf's death, Galla had risen above her grief to rule Rome. After a second marriage ended in the death of another husband, she claimed the throne for her six year old son, Valentinian III, and held it for him against usurpers and barbarians alike. After decades of division and decline, Galla and Flavius Aetius had put the Empire on its feet again.

Avitus sighed. After all she'd survived, Galla didn't deserve to be murdered by her own son – Emperor in name but not act. Valentinian wasted his days playing with his bow and arrows on the Campus Martius and his nights with his eunuch, Heraclius, debauching honest men and women. He financed his excesses by ordering the army to tighten its belt but it was pulled so tight already that tugging it in another notch would emasculate the Empire's fighting force.

Seated on a sabre-legged chair opposite him, Sedulla, Avitus' wife of more than twenty years, looked up from her study of St Paul's epistles to assess his mood. His forehead was creased and his lips a down-turned crescent on a wide, square chin. She closed her book. It was no surprise that Galla Placidia was dying and it was time he cheered up. Sedulla missed his deep belly laugh. Perhaps the prospect of a suitor for Papianilla would soften the crags in his face. "It's time we talked about our daughter, dear."

"What, again?" Avitus looked out to the terrace where, in the shade of the purple wisteria that tumbled in clouds down the walls of the villa, Papianilla was poring over a book. She looked as graceful as a swan but he could tell that she was fuming at her mother who had insisted she wear a pale pink palla and remain at home.

"She's nearly eighteen," said Sedulla.

Resigning himself to a long discussion, Avitus asked a slave to bring him some figs and a pitcher of sparkling water from his mineral springs.

"Marcus Aurelius Pontius," said Sedulla, "has been widowed again and is looking for a new wife."

"Pontius?" Avitus knew that a marriage to a local dignitary would never satisfy his wife's ambitions but he couldn't bear the thought of his only daughter being sent far from home.

"You remember him, don't you? At the forefront of senators. Extremely rich. With Pontius' support and a skilled throw of the dice, Rome itself could be within our reach."

Avitus tapped the flat of his palm on the arm of the sofa and tried to summon an image of Pontius forward from the rear ranks of his memory. It came to him: tall, with a purple-veined snout betraying his drinking habits and brown-grey hair that had receded from his pate and relocated to his nose and ears, out of which it protruded with unseemly vigour. "Isn't Pontius older than I am?"

"There are few men more ancient than you, my dear, but Pontius is, indeed, one of them."

"I'm not about to marry off my spirited young daughter to a man who's older than her father and has hair sprouting from his nostrils."

"Since when has nose hair been a criterion for the eligibility of a suitor?"

"Since the beginning of civilised time," said Avitus. "You'd never have married me if I'd been ungroomed."

"You were in the army, dear, you had no choice but to keep yourself tidy. Pontius sent you some gifts while you were away, generous gifts, and invited us to stay with him in his new palace near Narbonne."

"Money means nothing to Pontius," said Avitus. "Send his gifts back."

"That'd be rude. He's just trying to show that he's serious about Papianilla. A man with his connections could advance your prospects."

"My prospects? How often have I told you that Rome doesn't interest me? I'm a soldier, Sedulla, a fighting man. The army is all I know, all I care for, and I don't need to sell off my daughter to advance my military career. My victories speak more loudly than money or connections ever could."

The corners of Sedulla's lips tightened. Whilst it was true that Galla Placidia had always rewarded her generals well, under the reign of her son Valentinian their victories counted for nothing. "Pontius' money could help fund your household guards or Ecdicius' cavalry unit. Besides, I've already accepted Pontius' invitation."

"You should've deferred to me before doing that! And to suggest that I'd let someone else pay for my bodyguards or my son's horses is ridiculous."

Sedulla attempted a disarming smile; it had worked in her youth but was less effective now. Decades of keeping the estates running during her husband's long absences on campaign, never knowing if he would return again, had hardened her features. "You would have agreed anyway, my dear. You've always wanted what's best for Papianilla and a man with a fortune like his is not to be ignored. Quite tragic for Pontius that his wife died just before the palace he was building for her was completed, but that poor woman's loss may mean a windfall for our daughter."

"Opportunity arises from tragedy, eh?" Avitus was not fond of his wife's scheming, although she saw it as one of her better points. The slave returned with the wine and figs. "Put them in my library."

With a nod to Sedulla, Avitus took his leave. "Saving my soldiers from that capricious idiot's military cuts takes precedence over our social life."

Sedulla frowned. "Hush, Avitus – you know one mustn't speak of the Emperor like that."

* * * * *

The next afternoon Papianilla was chatting to her maternal grandmother, Nona, in the old lady's sitting-room. In a world where

Papianilla's parents were often absent, and even when present were usually distant, Nona nurtured Papianilla.

"I heard your parents talking yesterday evening." Cataracts had clouded Nona's eyes, but she had the knack of hearing everything important.

Papianilla's stomach tightened. "Are they trying to marry me off again?"

Nona nodded. "Your mother has found a suitor."

"Is he young, handsome and rich?"

"Rich, old and ugly, I'm afraid."

"Not again! I bet he's fat as well."

Nona made a curious sound that was not quite a tut-tut but expressed both sympathy and disapproval. "Remember your manners, Papianilla."

"Everyone talks about me as if I were a lump of meat to be sold off to the highest bidder."

Nona couldn't deny it. "This time your mother's serious."

"I'm not going to do it."

"You'll have no choice if your father tells you to."

"My father wouldn't make me marry a man I don't like."

"You can't go on living here alone all your life, reading books. No man will want to marry you if you're too clever." Nona's gentle eyes smiled out from under crinkled-silk lids. She feared her words were wasted on Papianilla. The girl loved learning, more than her brother did. Give Ecdicius a sword and he was happy, but Plato bored him.

"I need to read," said Papianilla, "there's nothing else to do around here. Since Ecdicius left home, none of his friends visits anymore."

"I didn't think you liked his friends."

"Graecus is the only one who annoys me. The others are fun."

Nona noticed that Papianilla avoided mentioning Sidonius by name, although he was the only friend of Ecdicius with whom the girl had spent much time. "Your mother should take you back to Lyon.

There are plenty of young people from good families there."

"I don't want to go to Lyon. All that matters there is who you know, what you wear, whom you're going to marry. All the girls are in their groups already and I don't belong."

"That's because you choose not to. You're the best connected of all of them." Nona felt her granddaughter's sense of isolation. Papianilla's intelligence, hip-length tresses of hair so black that it reflected blue in the sunlight, amber eyes and watermelon lips made her too beautiful for her own good. She was the daughter of the most powerful general in Gaul. Unless she married and had her own family, she would remain a threat to other women and the object of jealousy. "You should talk to your mother about what she has in mind. You've been invited to visit this man in his palace in Narbonne."

"I don't want to go."

"Papianilla, I'm afraid you have no choice this time."

A Trip to Narbonne

Gaul

448 AD

The lesser vehicles on the journey from Clermont to Narbonne melted off the road to make way for Avitus' shining black carriage drawn by four perfectly matched black stallions. On each corner of its roof a gilded lion rampant reared up with claws extended. The horses' polished hooves flashed in an elongated stride as they clipped past the highway markers. They were so fit that Avitus skipped every second staging post and changed teams every fifty-two miles instead of twenty-six. This was private business, not an imperial trip, but Avitus could never stand to move slowly when he could move fast.

Papianilla's excitement rose as she counted down the mile-markers. Through the carriage window the landscape changed from volcanic plateau to tumbling fields. On hilltops at all strategic points Roman fortresses stood stern-walled and alert. On the approach to Narbonne the land became more verdant before shaking off all cover and exposing its rich, red flesh. Lines of ploughed fields and row upon row of trimmed vineyards heralded the outskirts of the thriving capital of the province of Narbonensis.

When the carriage approached the forum, the coachman reined his horses to a walk.

A fountain with three open-mouthed lions as spouts cascaded crystal water into a pond in the central square. In the cool of vaulted alcoves either side of the footpath, handcarts and pedestrians jostled for space and merchants showed off their wares. Slaves dressed in dun-coloured linen carried baskets brimming with rust-red and lupine-yellow spices on their backs. The fragrance of cloves, verveine and frankincense competed with the reek of sweat. Matrons ran gossamer-thin organza, dyed pink and blue, between bejewelled fingers.

A gust of wind caught the edge of a bolt of apple-green silk carried on the shoulder of a passing merchant. Papianilla let out a wistful gasp – "Can we stop, Mama – can we please stop?"

Sedulla and Avitus shared a smile as their daughter leaned out of the carriage window and watched the silk float tantalisingly past.

"Of course, we can," said Avitus. "I'd like to look in on the garrison."

"Looking in" on the garrison was a characteristic understatement. The garrison would greet him, their hero, in full parade formation.

Papianilla glanced at her father then up at the hundred-foot walls of the fortress. She had heard the story of how he had single-handedly evicted the Goths from the city but found it hard to believe.

"Shall I accompany you on your inspection?" Sedulla asked her husband.

"Just come in long enough for the commander's wife to say hello then take your leave and amuse yourselves. We'll spend the night in the fort. It's a comfortable journey along the Via Domitia to Pontius' palace, no need to rise early tomorrow."

"Our daughter needs new robes for our visit."

"That's understood, my dear," said Avitus with a wink.

The carriage pulled to a smooth stop in front of the arched gateway leading into the fortress that guarded the port. The garrison commander had called up a cohort of five thousand men in parade formation and only the plumes of their helmets stirred in a warm sea wind. Twenty trumpeters blasted out a series of rising notes and sustained the last until their lungs nigh burst. Sunlight bounced off polished helmets and dazzled the crowd who jostled to get a glimpse of fabled General Eparchius Avitus, the Roman who had saved their city from the Goths. With majesty, Avitus returned the salute and inspected the ranks.

Pontius' Palace

The visit to Narbonne was a great success for Papianilla. The apple-coloured gossamer was hunted down, a fair price negotiated, and a palla made to order. Draped in her finery, she readied herself to play the role of the virgin bride about to meet a powerful future husband. The weight of her hair, piled up and fixed with solid gold pins, made her neck ache but she held her head high. Her stomach fluttered as the carriage suddenly turned off the Via Domitia, slipped between the tallest corinthian pillars she'd ever seen and headed up a driveway shaded by plane trees. Their branches made a tunnel of the road, hand-sized leaves waving the visitors on towards the palace. Papianilla felt that the moment the carriage passed the trees would lower their branches and form a wall to prevent her escape and her mouth went dry. Pontius, like her father, had a church under construction but it was at least four times the size – would he want to marry her under Roman or Christian rights?

The stallions huffed and jangled their bits as the coachman slowed them to a walk and the palace façade loomed at the end of the tunnel of trees. With each step it became ever more enormous until the coach pulled to a halt and a bevy of slaves leapt forward to take the horses' reins. Papianilla looked round for the master of the palace but he remained out of sight.

Pontius was hidden by the deep shadow of a pillared portico. He allowed his guests a long moment to descend and be impressed by the view over his fields to his harbour where the fingers of his oyster farms stretched into the distance before giving way to navigable water. He let them admire his sailing ships, laden with his wine, as they plied his blue waters on the way to his warehouses in Rome. Mt Julius, hovering in the background on the far side of Pontius' horseshoe-shaped bay, formed the back-drop to his magnificence.

Sedulla stepped down from the carriage first. With the grace of a dancer, Papianilla followed her mother. The girl's eyes, enhanced by a smudge of Egyptian kohl Sedulla had insisted she wear for the first time, took in the height of the portico and opened wide. Thick, white, fluted columns towered along the façade of the building. The ornate plasterwork of the coffered ceiling had been picked out in gold and green against a background the colour of oxblood.

Pontius stepped out from his portico into the blazing light of day. Manners stopped Papianilla from staring at him but, from under lowered eyelashes, she analysed every detail of his appearance. He was gigantically tall, with an ogre-like belly hanging over a gold belt. He had not quite dressed himself as an emperor but had created the same effect by draping a red cloak on top of a blue one, creating a shade of Tertullian purple. Like a snorting bull, he strode towards Avitus with his right hand extended.

"Welcome, my old friend!"

Avitus did not care for word "old", given that Pontius was years his senior, nor for the word "friend" given that he had barely met him before, and his square shoulders stayed rigid. Pontius tried to pull him into an embrace. The result of Avitus' unflinching posture was that Pontius, who was a head taller, looked as though he was collapsing onto his shoulder and sobbing. For an awkward moment he hung there, patting Avitus on the back, and Papianilla noticed that black and grey hairs crawled like spiders across the back of his hands.

When Pontius raised his head, her eyes homed in for a closer look and the polite smile fell from her lips. Her prospective husband had a cobweb of purple veins across his bright pink splodge of a nose and Papianilla suspected his proboscis maintained its colour by his constant sampling of his stock. She noticed the corrugations running in ruts across his forehead then a wave of revulsion overtook her as she imagined that his nose and ear hair might have lives independent of their host.

Then Pontius pulled himself to his full height, his dynamic energy came to the fore and his exaggerated gestures drew all eyes towards his dominating presence. When he looked at Papianilla his eyes had the intensity of molten iron in a blacksmith's crucible.

He could be a bully, she thought, glad her father was with her. Yet even while these words ran through her head, Pontius' charisma started its work of compelling her to please him.

Pontius ushered his guests into a salon forty feet square with walls clad from floor to ceiling in sheets of blue-grey marble. The floor was covered with a myriad of mosaics laid to create the illusion of protruding then receding when guests stepped over them. They made Papianilla feel dizzy and vaguely sick.

Pontius bragged, "This floor is laid with 100,000 stones per square metre, not the normal 30,000."

"Remarkable," said Sedulla, unimpressed.

Slaves led Papianilla to a bedroom furnished with a tall cupboard, a double bed, and a dressing table on which three mirrors had been set up so that she could see both sides of her head as well as her face all at once. The floor mosaics were black ribbons laced round red rosettes. Papianilla got down on her knees, counted the chips and calculated that they were laid in only the normal density. The pattern was slightly off centre and it looked as if Pontius had tried to hide the error under the plethora of furnishings.

Rather than risk encountering the pot-bellied Pontius naked in his bathhouse, the virgin bride washed in cold water in her room. Sitting down before the three-faced mirror she took a long hard look at herself. She had a sense of what was expected of her, but Pontius was so old, fat and ugly. Did her parents really believe she could go through with it?

Papianilla wanted nothing more than to hide in her room but a slave-girl summoned her to join the other guests in the atrium. Two dancing girls, twirling saffron veils and striking tiny brass cymbals, led them into a banquet hall sixty feet square. Each wall was perforated by a domed alcove where dining couches fanned out around small, round tables. Slaves carrying platters of steaming dishes wove their way through musicians, acrobats and singers of all shades of colour and gender. Pontius had placed Papianilla in the alcove opposite his and, although the floor between them was never empty, through it all she could feel his tentacles reaching out to her.

To make matters worse, she knew she couldn't refuse to sample the platers he sent over to her. While she did manage to nibble at the sows' udders stuffed with giant African snails not even Sedulla's disapproving stare could force her to taste the stuffed dormice with singed ears.

Wine, served warm or chilled on snow, flowed ceaselessly from silver pitchers. Papianilla put down her fork and lifted her glass to the light, for as much as the food repulsed her, the sight of glasses of every hue made her catch her breath. Some were tall and pale blue, others garnet or cobalt almost as dark as black. Some were clear, others speckled. The most intriguing had finely twisting spirals rising through the centre of their stems and splintering the light.

Pontius, lounging on his dining couch with his belly flopping to one side, was pleased with himself. He made a habit of marrying high-born virgins. Although he was over fifty, his last wife had been only seventeen. He had seen her, wanted her, spoken to her father and acquired her. It had taken only two days to negotiate the marriage contract. A shame the girl had died but Papianilla was both beautiful and aristocratic and would be a most satisfactory replacement. Her long neck, the poise with which she held her head and her cupid's lips lit his loins. He decided to negotiate with Avitus for her hand in the morning. With that in mind, he levered himself to his feet to address the banquet. "Gentlemen, ladies! Unaccustomed as I am to public speaking, I propose a toast to my honoured guest, Avitus, the man to whom we owe everything."

The room fell silent. Avitus dipped his head in embarrassment.

Pontius encompassed the full magnificence of his domain with an expansive wave of both arms, warming to his theme. "Fellow Romans, do you know the story of how Avitus liberated Narbonne?"

Everyone in the room had heard some version of it but all remained quiet.

"When Theodoric the Goth broke his treaty and seized the capital of Gallia Narbonensis, did the Emperor send an army to evict the invaders? No!" said Pontius, oblivious to the folly of criticising Valentinian III in public. A sober man would have been more circumspect. "Avitus alone saved Narbonne and were it not for him, my palace, my vineyards, my oyster farm would not exist. Citizens of Rome, I raise a toast to the man whom one day, might rise to be emperor – Eparchius Avitus!"

The room sat in open-mouthed silence for a moment, not sure how to respond to the treasonous toast, then Avitus rose to his feet. "I thank our host for his amusing joke. We all know that I'm a soldier, plain and simple, and have neither the ambition nor the ability to meddle in politics."

To murmurs of approval, Avitus sat down while Pontius again raised his glass – "To Avitus!"

"To Avitus!" the crowd chorused.

A slave helped lower Pontius back down into the prone position on his dining couch and the banquet continued.

Papianilla turned to her mother. "Did father really save Narbonne the way Pontius said he did?"

"Not exactly, my dear, but near enough," said Sedulla. Thankfully, none of the slaves had ever dared to talk about the spectacle she had made of herself clinging to Avitus' booted leg as he sat astride his stallion, begging him not to set off alone to challenge Theodoric. "You must ask your father to tell you about it some time."

"And when will he ever have time for that, Mother?" Papianilla's eyes lost the lustre of pride the story about her father had lit. If she married Pontius, Avitus would be far away and she would rarely, if ever, see him again. She looked over to where her corpulent suiter was gorging himself, and her courage failed her. Then her eyes strayed in search of Sidonius.

Pontius had not neglected to invite Honorius, the Praetorian Prefect, to his banquet but the governor of Gaul had more important things to do and sent the eighteen-year-old Sidonius in his place. Sidonius had grown tall and broad-shouldered but still had the lean torso of an athletic youth. His thick, dark hair fell in waves either side of a noble forehead and aquiline nose, the lips were full and his eyes profound and passionate under level brows. But it was Sidonius' hands that Papianilla noticed first, as eloquent as his voice, while she watched him talk, and then his smile that revealed straight white teeth. She watched his mouth moving and wondered what it would be like to kiss. When he looked up and caught her staring at him she blushed.

My Papianilla, thought Sidonius, *how much you've changed, how regal you look with your hair all pinned up.* But then she poked out her tongue to hide her embarrassment and it made him laugh. She laughed back as if she'd been joking all along, but Sidonius had seen the pink rise to her cheeks. Their eyes met and the colour deepened until they both broke away. But as soon as he thought she wouldn't notice, he looked back and his eyes swept down her neck, past the gentle nexus of her clavicle, to the gossamer silk draped between her breasts. *My Papianilla*, he thought again, then noticed Pontius was looking at her too, *why is that lecherous old man staring at you?*

Sidonius had found it odd that women had been invited to this banquet, but now the reason was becoming clear. *I'm imagining things –*

he tried to convince himself – *and it's none of my business who her parents marry her off to.* His eyes darted from Papianilla's beauty to Pontius' salivating face, and logic was swamped by the instinct to protect her. *They can't marry you off to him – he's a hundred years old!*

The young man lying to Sidonius' right interrupted his thoughts by proffering his hand. "Gaius Marius Antonius, at your service."

"Sidonius Apollinaris."

Antonius knew already that Sidonius was the son of the Praetorian Prefect of Gaul and making a name for himself as a poet. "What did you make of Pontius' speech?"

"It had the virtue of brevity," replied Sidonius, still distressed by his realisation that Papianilla was destined for Pontius.

"Yes, at least that can be said for it!" said Antonius. "I hope you don't mind my asking, but who's that pretty, dark-haired girl you keep staring at?"

"Papianilla, the daughter of Avitus."

"Agricola's sister? I had no idea she was such a beauty."

"You know Agricola?" Sidonius looked at his neighbour for the first time. Agricola, Ecdicius's virtually invisible elder brother, had been eclipsed by his sibling's military exploits. It was a surprise that Antonius had heard of him.

"Agricola and I studied under the same grammarian in Narbonne for a couple of years; he was a pleasant chap, quiet back then. Graecus was there at the same time. I've lost touch with them both. Do you have news of them?"

"Agricola manages his father's largest farming estate, has married well and has two children. Graecus is studying at the monastery on the island of Lerins, the one that Salvian made famous."

"That will suit Graecus – he's more academic than athletic."

Sidonius' eyes gravitated back to Papianilla.

"Do you know Avitus well?" Antonius asked.

"Yes, his father and mine are friends. I grew up with Ecdicius',

Agricola's brother. We spent summers together at their villa, Avitacum. I'm surprised that you and I didn't meet there."

"You know what it's like when we are young, a few years' difference in age keep boys apart, but now that we're grown men our circles widen." Gaius cleared his throat. "Do think you could introduce me to Avitus?"

Sidonius unglued his eyes from Papianilla. "I imagine so, if the opportunity arises. Do you have any particular reason for wishing to meet him?"

"If you must know, I rather like the look of his daughter," Antonius answered, "although, judging by the way my uncle keeps drooling over her, my interest in her may have no future."

Sidonius reddened. "Your uncle?"

"My cousin was Pontius' third wife."

"It's bad luck to outlive three wives."

"I'm not sure about that," Antonius laughed.

"Does Pontius have heirs?"

"Sadly, not. My cousin and her baby were lost at sea when Pontius sent her ship to sea too early in the season. It was overladen and went down in a storm."

"What happened to the two previous wives?"

"Both died in childbirth. Pontius is a big man."

Sidonius glared over at Pontius. A slave girl in a transparent saffron tunic was dropping stuffed dates into his gaping mouth while Pontius undressed Papianilla with his eyes. Pontius waved away the slave and lumbered to his feet. "Avitus, my friend, do you think that your wife would do us the honour of leading the ladies to their sitting room?"

The word "friend" still grated on Avitus but he leant over to Sedulla and repeated the request.

Pontius summoned a giant Nubian slave, whose arm sagged under the weight of a twelve-stemmed candelabra, to lead the women away. Papianilla followed the blaze of candlelight away from the clamour of the dining hall into a vaulted room with a raised alcove at one end. As she stepped up into the alcove, light pooled on a floor mosaic idealising Pontius in chips so fine that there must have been even more than the 100,000 per square yard. Opposite Pontius' portrait, the blind eyes of a long-necked beauty, her head adorned with a weighty crown of spring blooms, stared up at the coffered ceiling. *His dead wife, no older than I am now.*

The ladies safely escorted from the banquet hall, Pontius ordered up a troop of dancing girls. As the lead performer gyrated her buttocks at the tip of his ruddy nose, he asked Avitus, "Do you like her, or is she too fleshy for you?"

"Your excellent wine and food have completely satiated my appetites," said Avitus, "I think I'll retire for the night."

"What? Going to bed already? But the fun's just beginning."

"I'll leave the fun to younger men."

"Really? It surprises me that a man like you would lack . . . energy."

Avitus laughed. "My men grumble I'm too fast for them on a forced march."

"Really," drawled Pontius, "I'm pretty energetic myself, although it's more often women than men who comment on it." He jabbed a stubby finger in the direction of two more of the dancing girls, "Hoy – you two, over here!"

Avitus groaned inwardly – *is the old goat about to start an orgy with our wives and daughters in the room next door?*

Pontius licked drool from his lips. "Enjoy your slumbers gentlemen; I've other things in mind."

All eyes followed him as Pontius rolled his legs off the dining sofa and a slave levered him to his feet. Hanging a porculent hand over the shoulders of one dancer, he slapped another on the buttocks. Her face stiffened but Pontius neither saw nor cared.

Proposal

South coast of Gaul
448 AD

When Avitus woke up in Pontius' exuberantly furnished guest room the next morning, his head was pounding. Slaves opened the shutters and bright sunlight shot shards of pain behind his eyes. He lay on his back and pulled a pillow over his face.

Wine, by custom, was served watered down – only the gods could drink it undiluted – but the unceasing pressure to compliment his host on his vineyard had led to far too much of it being consumed.

Sedulla took in her husband's jaundiced appearance. "Did things end well last night?"

Avitus didn't remove the pillow to speak. "Don't ask." The inside of his mouth felt as if it had grown scales during the night. "Will you bring me some water, or do I have to ask a slave?"

"Don't fret, I'll get it, dear."

Slowly, Avitus rolled up onto his elbow and took a few gulps, shook his head like a dog, then pushed himself up and planted both feet squarely on the floor. "Pontius was keen to show off what money can buy. It may have been in the effort to convince his prospective father-in-law that he could still sire children or perhaps he'd eaten too many of his own oysters."

"That sounds rather distasteful."

"I told you not to ask." Avitus shaded his eyes as he stood up. "How many days have you told Pontius we're staying here?"

"Three."

"Ye gods! Can I survive another two days of his hospitality?"

"We have to give the man a chance to make up his mind about Papianilla."

"I hoped that you'd forgotten about that."

Sedulla need not have been concerned, Pontius was a man who charged like a bull at what he wanted.

Just before noon, he hunted down Avitus, who was stretched out on a divan nursing his hangover under the shade of a pergola profuse with jasmine blossom. Bees buzzed lazily about their work as if slowed down by the torpor of mid-summer.

"Avitus, my friend – " Pontius' voice bounced around Avitus' head – "what did you think of my banquet last night?".

"It was an exceptional evening." Avitus propped himself up on one elbow and inwardly cursing the man for bellowing instead of speaking in a civilised morning-after tone.

"Good! Good! We do our best to be hospitable. You must visit me in Rome next time. D'you mind if I join you?" Avitus minded very much but the question was rhetorical. The legs of the divan squealed as Pontius collapsed onto it at Avitus' feet. "There's a matter we need to discuss."

Sharing the bed with Pontius did not appeal to Avitus. He got up and paced, his hands clasped behind his back. Pontius delivered his proposition as if he were speaking from the rostrum and concluded his address with the promise of enough gold coins to fund Ecdicius' cavalry unit for the next five years.

Feeling somewhat sick, Avitus weighed in the balance his daughter's and his son's futures.

* * * * *

While her father and prospective husband bargained over her fate, Papianilla slipped away from the prattle of the ladies' sitting room and headed off down to a paddock. She was watching a snowy Arab mare prance and toss its mane, as if flaunting its beauty, when an unwelcome bulk arrived at her side. Like a slab of raw steak, Pontius' hand landed on her shoulder.

"Do you like her?" he asked.

Papianilla's throat was dry but her posture remained as rigid as a soldier's. "It's a lovely horse."

"She could be yours. I bought her for my poor, deceased wife." Pontius' clammy digits squeezed Papianilla's neck, sending a wave of revulsion through her. She took a step sideways. He noticed but wasn't disconcerted. Lifting his slab of hand from her shoulder, he leant his elbows on the six-by-six-inch top rail and scoured her face.

Papianilla kept her eyes focused on the white mare on the far side of the ring. Etiquette had been drummed into her since birth, but she couldn't stop herself from flicking her fingertips over the shoulder that Pontius' hand had just vacated as if she were brushing off dandruff.

Pontius wasn't blind to the rejection but it would take more than that to discourage him. She was young and inexperienced, unused to the touch of a man. So much the better, at least he knew he would be her first and only lover. He'd break her in, just like a horse.

Papianilla could feel the rumble of an approaching earthquake and was bracing herself against the impact. *What am I going to say to this man when he asks me to marry him?*

"Do you like my palace, Papianilla?" his deep brown eyes fingered her profile.

"It's most impressive."

"That too could be yours. I've many others like it, including one on the Palatine Hill in Rome. The emperor and I are almost neighbours." Pontius paused as if waiting for a round of applause. Papianilla didn't dare to look towards him for fear that he would plaster his slimy lips on hers.

"I've spoken to your father about you and he supports my plans."

Papianilla stayed dumb.

"D'you understand me, Papianilla?" Pontius waited for a smile or a flutter of her lids, but she was motionless, inscrutable. "I'm asking you to marry me."

In her moment of need, centuries of breeding didn't desert her. As if from a distance she heard her own voice answering her suitor with awe-inspiring composure. "Sir, I thank you for the great honour you do me, but I must decline your most generous offer."

Like air suspended just before a clap of thunder, nothing moved for a second as Pontius' brain processed a response he had never anticipated. *No one* had ever said 'no' to him since he had become rich, over twenty years ago. He concluded that the girl must be slow-witted. "You don't understand me, I've just asked you to become my wife."

Again, Papianilla had the sense that her voice was disembodied. Impressed by the clarity of her own diction she answered, "I have understood you perfectly, sir, and am most sensible of the honour you do me, but I'm afraid I cannot consent to be your wife."

The storm broke. "What!? What d'you mean you won't marry me? Why not? You don't know what you're saying! You have no choice in the matter. I've already arranged it with your father."

The meaty slab grabbed her shoulder again and turned her forcibly to face him. He locked his eyes into hers to bend her will to his. His voice became slow and sinister as he pronounced every syllable, "You will do what your father tells you to do."

* * * * *

Back under the shade of the jasmine bower, lying on his divan, Avitus was finding it hard to get any rest.

Sidonius appeared, striding towards him at a purposeful pace. "Excuse me for interrupting, sir; may I speak with you?"

"Does no one have respect for my hangover?" Avitus grumbled as he sat up. "Is it important or can it wait until tomorrow?"

"It is important to me, sir, but if now is not a good moment I can come back."

"Spit it out then, son, my day's already been ruined."

Sidonius' stomach lurched and his knees shook but he went straight to the point. "I would be most grateful if you would grant me the honour of asking for your daughter's hand in marriage."

Avitus' eyes bored through Sidonius for a second before he burst out, "Why couldn't you have asked me that yesterday? You've left it too late!"

Sidonius' face blanched. "Do I have your permission to speak to Papianilla or not, sir?"

Avitus hesitated. He hadn't given his word to Pontius, he had simply told him that he would not stand in the way of his daughter's happiness. Seeing the look of anguish on Sidonius' fresh young face, he realised Papianilla's happiness might not lie in the direction he had thought. "Alright then, boy, but be quick about it!"

Pontius did not come out to farewell the Aviti when they left the palace early the next day. The rampant lions on each corner of Avitus' lacquered black carriage glared out at the empty portico with bared fangs. The stiff-backed Aviti stepped up in silence and a slave shut the door behind them. The axle turned so sharply it squealed against the wheel hub and Avitus made a mental note to speak to the coachman at the first change of horses.

To compensate for his too hasty turn, the coachman made sure the carriage rocked as gently as a cradle while the horses headed back down the driveway of hushed leaves. When he reached the gate, he clicked them on to a trot and Papianilla took a last look at the monstrous church where she would never be married.

"I wonder if Pontius has actually ever read the teachings of Christ," mused Avitus. The word "obstinate" used by Pontius in relation to his daughter was still rankling in his ears.

"I doubt it," replied Sedulla.

Half a mile beyond the gate, Avitus rapped on the partition between him and the driver as an order to halt. "Go and sit up front with the coachman," he told Papianilla, "I'd like a few words in private with your mother."

Papianilla leapt out, only too pleased to escape the close-lipped atmosphere. The wind would blow the fog of shame out of her hair.

When she'd gone and the horses moved into a comfortable trot again, Avitus said to Sedulla, "I suppose you're angry with me."

His wife shrugged. "Not really, I think we can do better for our daughter. To tell the truth, I didn't warm to Pontius. He lacks not only taste but judgment. There are some things that even his unimaginable fortune won't protect him from. He's rash. On top of that, the hairs that protrude from his ears and nose are positively vulgar."

Avitus laughed. "I'm relieved to hear that. You seemed so set on him."

"I'm set on doing what's right for the family. Besides, I don't like the idea of Pontius becoming the father of my grandchildren. He would have made Papianilla miserable. She's much more sensitive than she appears and to have to face his attentions, coupled with a stream of nubile dancing girls, would have ruined her over the years."

"You can be blunt for a woman of breeding, one could even say 'coarse'." Avitus teased his wife and she rose to his bait.

"Coarse? No one could ever accuse me of being coarse."

Avitus let the coach rock on gently for a few minutes. As land and seascapes unfolded around them, he watched boats with comfortably puffed up sails – white as a freshly laundered chiton – leave foam trails on the turquoise bay beyond the vineyards. Cool green leaves contrasted with ochre earth under the mounting heat of late morning. Leaning forward, he told the coachman to walk the horses, there was no point in hurrying, he wanted to enjoy the scenery. They passed half a dozen mile posts before Avitus broke the silence. "Another possibility for Papianilla has presented itself."

"Anyone we know, or know of?"

"Yes, someone we know very well in fact," Avitus looked casually out the window, "young Sidonius."

"Sidonius? But he's still a boy."

"He had the courage to ask me for her hand despite competition from one of Rome's richest senators."

"But he hasn't even finished at the school of rhetoric yet. And the Apollinarii have no real money. They're amongst the handful of officials in Gaul who haven't used their tenure of public office to line their own pockets."

"They may have more means than you know of, my dear, and simply be discreet," said Avitus. In truth he suspected his wife was right about Apollinari fortunes but to him money counted less than good character when it came to choosing a husband for his daughter.

The moment was right to stay silent. Avitus leant an arm on the window-sill and waited for the sound of the carriage's steel-rimmed wheels honing the stony road and the reassuring clop of horses' hooves to do their work.

"On the other hand," said Sedulla as they passed the next milepost, "I've always liked Sidonius. He's a handsome boy, intelligent, and infinitely more refined than Pontius. Papianilla likes him too, I know it, although they've always been more brother and sister than sweethearts."

Avitus' lips split into a grin, exposing a straight row of yellowed teeth. "I knew you'd come around! When you think about it, he's part of the family already. He's a good lad and will make an even better man."

"That's all very well, but where will they live?" Sedulla was already running through the practicalities, imagining her daughter with garlands of flowers in her hair at the wedding ceremony and seeing herself cradling the couple's healthy and handsome babies.

"I thought that we could give Papianilla Avitacum as her dowry."

"*Avitacum* – that's exceptionally generous of you!"

"I can afford it. We let Agricola have our largest estate when he married. You still have the properties you inherited from your mother. Avitacum suits Sidonius. He's a poet; it's a restful place. Both he and Papianilla have spent their happiest summers growing up there."

"It's your decision, my dear." Sedulla adjusted the pins in her hair then sat back in her seat and looked over at her husband. "I'll miss being mistress of Avitacum but Papianilla loves the estate as much as I do. She and Sidonius must have a long engagement though; he must establish himself before they marry."

"Don't worry about that, dear, Sidonius will amount to something in this world, I'm just not quite sure what yet," said Avitus.

"Will you discuss this with Papianilla before Sidonius asks for her hand?"

"Sidonius has already spoken to her, with my permission, which I had to give as a matter of urgency before Pontius tied Papianilla up in a marriage contract. If she wishes to marry Sidonius, I take it that you will not stand in their way?"

"She's lucky to be given a choice in the matter," Sedulla raised an eyebrow, "but of course I want only her happiness."

The general smiled to himself then leant forward and rapped out a new beat for the horses. The coachman flicked the reins and the stallions' hooves struck out in unison.

The carriage rolled past villa after comfortable villa, their white walls glistening in the middle of open fields or surrounded by neat rows of apple trees. Avitus noticed, as always, the complete absence of defensive walls. This world – his world – so beautiful but fragile, where people believed themselves safe, protected by far-distant fortresses in colder climes with foreign names that they had never heard of. But Avitus had been there, where they had not, to borders stiff with ice and bathed in blood.

He cricked his neck, suddenly stiff, and glanced over at his wife where she sat, smiling enigmatically and scheming, no doubt. Then he looked back out the window, to the fluttering apple blossoms and the straight rows of vines and thought *how different the world would be if it were not for Aetius, my oldest friend, a man without equal.* Then, comforted by the thought that Flavius Aetius, the illustrious magister militum, patrolled the borders of this world, Avitus closed his eyes and let the carriage rock him to sleep.

Rising Storm

Sky Hawk, A Scythian herder of goats who scrabbled on stony ground to eke out a living, watched a dust-storm rising on the plains beneath him and took it as a portent. He pulled out the dagger he wore on his belt, cut the heel of his hand till blood dripped into the dry earth, then swore an oath to follow the rising storm west.

Vowing to return to his village when he had booty enough to make himself headman, he mounted his wiry pony and picked his way down saw-backed ridges in search of the Hun.

"Attila" meant "Little Father" and Sky Hawk expected to discover a prophet or munificent king but found instead a warlord who lived for blood, power and plunder. The further he rode, the more cities and villages they sacked, the larger grew Attila's nomadic force.

Settling nowhere, building nothing, they lived on loot and plunder. Soon Sky Hawk's saddlebags were packed with enough booty to buy his village ten times over but he never looked back.

On a windless day in the summer of 451, Sky Hawk reined in his pony on the peak of a hill midway between two Roman relay stations. In the distance behind him smouldered the city of Amiens, which Attila had sacked the day before, and out of sight, down a long, straight road, cowered the cathedral city of Reims.

The sun had reached its zenith. Although Sky Hawk's foraging party of six men on horseback had been out since first light, all they had caught was the single hare dangling on a rope from the pommel of his saddle. Desperate to avoid Attila's wrath, Skyhawk narrowed his eyes and scoured the plains for prey.

Palls of smoke marked the path he and his men had ridden through abandoned villages that morning. On hearing that Attila had crossed the Rhine, the villagers had bundled their meagre possessions onto carts and fled, but Skyhawk burnt their homes to the ground out of spite.

He was about to swing his horse back down the ridge when he heard a far away metallic ring of shod hooves on paved stone. Cupping his ear, he peered in the direction of the sound and waited. When a lone Roman courier rounded an ochre bluff in the distance, Sky Hawk's lips turned up. He raised a fist to signal two of his men to gallop with him to the next ridge to head off the Roman and the others to cut off his retreat.

Down on the naked stretch of road, the Roman imperial courier saw columns of smoke rising in the distance and kept pressure on his spurs. His cut-down version of the cavalry helmet protected his neck but left his peripheral vision open and the instant Sky Hawk's men began to plummet towards him, he dug his heels deeper into his horse's flanks. The mare flattened her ears to her skull and her legs became an invisible blur. Sky Hawk hurtled onto the road behind him, but the courier horse out-paced his pony.

At full gallop, the bandit took six arrows in one hand, drew his bow and fired them off in just five seconds. The volley whizzed past the Roman's ears but Sky Hawk reloaded from his quiver and fired again. This time an arrow thudded into the back of the Roman's thigh.

Raw iron sent a scream of pain through the courier's body, but he clung to his horse's neck. The distance opened further between him and his hunter but his body slid inexorably round his horse's belly. His armour struck sparks off the stones as he crashed onto the graded strip alongside the road. The courier rolled through his fall and came up on one knee with dagger drawn but couldn't find his feet before Sky Hawk, with an exultant whoop and vicious grin, sprang down from his pony.

Sky Hawk slashed his scimitar through the courier's neck. The blade clanked against the inside back of the helmet and sent the head bouncing back up onto the road. Skyhawk wiped the blade, sheathed it and drew a dagger. Clambering onto the road after the decapitated head, he cut off both its ears to take back to Attila as proof of his kill.

Looking up from stringing the ears onto his belt, he saw his men chasing the courier's riderless horse. The mare was getting away from them and the metallic gold of her coat and her long, lean build told him she could run forever, jump a river at a gallop without pausing for breath and stand strong in the face of a cavalry charge. He'd always dreamed of owning a horse like that – an Akhal Teke. His men gave up the chase and turned back. Sky Hawk cursed and scrambled down from the road to take all he could from the courier's body before they came back.

The riderless mare galloped on towards Reims.

Troyes

Northern Gaul

451 AD

Avitus sat stony-faced on a sorrel mare outside the gates of Troyes. The horse flicked her flaxen tail, free of all cares, but the praefectus castrorum, on foot at Avitus' side, was sweating under the helmet he'd polished to its brightest when he'd heard that Avitus was coming to inspect his garrison.

The general's previous visits had made the commander proud but this time Avitus was stern. Instead of making jokes and giving praise for a job well done Avitus had marched him round the perimeter walls – thirty feet high and fourteen thick – not once but twice. Eyes sharp as a whetted blade had scoured the tightly knit brick and stone in search of the slightest weakness.

A refugee, locked out by the curfew last night, had lit a fire to keep himself warm and Avitus was scowling at the fingers of soot it had left on the walls. Neither thoughts of Attila's rolling siege towers nor his battering rams bothered Avitus, but the ghost of flames clawing up the side of the fort gave him a premonition that Attila would besiege and burn this town. He looked down at the camp commander, whose shoulders hunched the moment he felt Avitus' gaze upon him, and ordered, "Scrub off that soot."

The soldier's shoulders relaxed. He saw no sense in the order but was passing it on to a decanus when a cry went up from the northern watchtower. "Courier!"

Avitus looked up in the direction of the spear a guardsman pointed towards the approaching rider, then touched his heels to the sorrel's flanks and cantered through the gates to the praetorium in the centre of the forum.

Inside, Sidonius' dark head and the short-cropped scalp of a Tribune were bowed over a map of Northern Gaul but on hearing the hobnails of Avitus' boots striking the flagstones both men straightened up and saluted.

"At ease," said Avitus, "a courier's on the way in and I need your report before he gets here."

Sidonius sat down at a campaign desk and took out a wax tablet and stylus to record proceedings. The Tribune cleared his throat. A single line hung like a dagger between his brows as he spoke. "Metz and Trier have fallen. The Rhine cohort has insufficient force to engage Attila and is falling back on Troyes. They're three days' march away."

Avitus balled his fist. "To Hades with the Hun!"

In the pause that followed his outburst, a sentry looked in, "The Paris courier is here, sir, do you want to see him now?"

Avitus nodded. A tall rider entered and saluted. Sweat had streaked the dust on his forehead and Avitus saw the beat of his pulse in his throat.

"Report."

"Attila has razed Tournai and Cambrai. They resisted. He burned them to the ground and massacred the citizens. There were almost no survivors, but I passed refugees on the road to Troyes. I don't know where they were fleeing from."

Avitus swallowed the expletives that burned on his lips. "Paris?"

"Attila has not yet attacked Paris, but its garrison requests immediate reinforcement."

Avitus turned away and paced, hands clasped behind his back. Sidonius sat with his stylus poised above his wax. "Don't write," snapped Avitus. "Courier, wait in the guard-house. It may be some time before I have an answer for you." The rider saluted and left.

Avitus turned to his Tribune. "What of Amiens and Reims? Has the courier from Reims arrived yet?"

"No, sir."

"He was due last night." Avitus returned to his pacing, raising an eyebrow at his son-in-law. "What do you make of that, young equites? Has Attila sacked Amiens and Reims as well as every other town in the north of Gaul?"

Sidonius' frowned. *Was the question rhetorical?*

Avitus leant over the desk and stared the boy in the eye – "But of course he has! Burned every blade of grass between here and Constantinople, slaughtered every man, woman and child who stood in his way. Attila was born to shake our nations! He's a scourge and a plague. While we speak, he crows his victories like a carrion beast, strutting on bandy legs over mountains of our dead. Rolls his eyes back in his head and shrieks out his battle cries. If Attila drained every drop of blood in Gaul he'd still thirst for more – slave to war that he is!"

Avitus fell silent and put a hand to his jaw. A sudden pain had shot into his head from a tooth he had no desire to pull out. The pain ebbed and he bent his head over the map again. "Ye gods! Where will Attila burn next? East, west, south? There's not a village left to the north he hasn't already sacked."

Sure that the question was rhetorical this time, Sidonius didn't attempt an answer but waited, watching Avitus brooding over the vellum map. A long minute passed before the general looked up and fixed a sharp eye on his son-in-law. "What news of Aetius?"

"The magister militum is still raising an army in Italy."

"As soon as he can, he'll march," said Avitus. *But even then, what hope have we against Attila's half million?* "And Heva, the Burgundian?"

"Northwest of us, sir, recruiting auxiliaries to fight for Rome."

"The Burgundians march at the pace of slugs," said Avitus, "if Heva doesn't turn back now he'll be swallowed by Attila's advance."

Another shaft of pain shot from Avitus' molar into the depths of his cranium but he stared doggedly at the map then shook his head. "No, it won't be Paris. Paris isn't rich enough. Nor Troyes. The Hun will drive deep into our gut – Lyons, the capital." He looked over at Sidonius. "Send an order to Heva to fall back to Lyon."

Sidonius scribbled down his command, shocked that Avitus' proposed line of defence was so far south, so close to his home in Auvergne, to Papianilla and his father and mother.

"What about Orleans, sir?" ventured the Tribune.

"Orleans's limp-wristed Alani governor would sooner open the gates to Attila than put up a fight – put that stylus down!" Avitus growled at Sidonius who was still writing, "That's not for the record. If we can regroup in time, we'll defend Orleans, but we need reinforcements before we pit our army against half a million Huns."

"And Paris, sir," Sidonius worried for his best friend, Felix, who lived there. "It's in Attila's path if he heads south."

"The Hun lacks logic. Who knows where next he'll attack?" Avitus paced again, chewing his lip, a hand on the side of his jaw. "Write this order on parchment for the commander of the Paris garrison: There will be no reinforcements. Evacuate and march south towards Lyon."

Sidonius, blinking back tears that blurred his vision, reached for a sheet of vellum. When he had finished writing he blew on the ink and handed it to Avitus. "Do you really think Attila would march past Paris without slaughtering her citizens?"

"It's a calculated risk to withdraw our garrison," said Avitus, "I can make no promises, but yes, I believe that Attila may by-pass Paris. It's neither strategically important nor rich enough for him. He wants to wipe us out before the campaign season's over, loot our capital and quarter in the south for the winter. Or that's what I'd do in his position. Doesn't mean that madman will – Attila guzzles blood and fights in all seasons."

"And Troyes, sir?" The Tribune was concerned for his home town. "What orders do you have for Troyes?"

Avitus fixed solemn eyes on him. "If Attila comes this way – and I pray to all the gods that he will not – defend the crossroads. We must keep them open for our supply chain from Italy. When you can hold them no more, barricade yourselves behind your walls. Hide all non-combatants in your cellars to save them from the fire. Then fight till the last man falls." Avitus wiped the creases from his brow.

"Yes, sir."

"Send a courier to Aetius. Tell him that I've ordered all troops except the Troyes garrison to muster in Lyon. I won't be joining them."

Sidonius and the Tribune stared at him, their mouths agape.

"The Goths," said Avitus. "I'll be in Toulouse, trying to convince Theodoric that instead of splitting Gaul with Attila and wrangling over Rome's carcass, he should abandon his kingdom and march a thousand miles to face certain death at my side." Avitus glanced at the Tribune whose face was a portrait of doubt. "Dismissed."

When the Tribune had left and Sidonius was alone with his father-in-law he said, "Theodoric will never do what you ask."

Avitus let out a long breath. "Theodoric's obdurate, but without the Goths we have no hope of turning Attila's tide. Even with them . . . " Avitus shook his head.

"But Theodoric's our enemy."

"Only from time to time," said Avitus wryly, placing a hand on Sidonius' shoulder. "Now, do me a favour, son, and find me a physician who can see to my tooth. If you do, our march to Toulouse might be slightly less agony for me and my wife might stop recoiling from my kisses." Avitus' eyes crinkled and he winked. "What d'you think? Are my chances better with Theodoric or Sedulla?"

Sidonius smiled knowingly. "Sometimes, I think I'd rather face Attila than either of them."

All humour dropped from Avitus' face. "If you'd seen a town where Attila had been, you wouldn't jest like that."

Sidonius hung his head, embarrassed that his joke had fallen flat.

New Recruits

On the road from Latium to Genoa, Italy
451 AD

"Life in the legions . . ." Brutus hurled the tip of his spade into hard clay, "isn't what it's cracked up to be!" Brutus, who had shoulders as wide as three pick handles laid end on end and weighed 220lbs, put his boot on the spade and thrust it a foot into the ground.

Without putting down his shovel, his friend and cohort, Quintus, used a forearm to swipe globules of sweaty grit from his forehead. "You mean, you don't enjoy marching twenty-four miles in the sun all day w'a hundred pounds of kit on your back?"

"Not saying I like the marching, but it's the digging that gets me, how they make us wear full armour while we do it. Same routine every day, 24-mile slog then build a bloody palisade! Who's going to attack us here in Italy?"

"Bandits – bagaudae – I guess."

"I've got pain in bits of my body I didn't even know I had." Brutus turned over splayed hands and looked at the puckered and ripped skin on every phalange. "My hands are bleeding."

"You've always been useless with anything with a handle," said Quintus. "You grip the shaft too firmly – that's why you've got all 'em blisters."

"I could plough a field faster than you any day!"

"Not likely!" said Quintus. "Enlisting was your stupid idea: *It's the only way to escape the downtrodden misery of our peasant lives. Free food, regular pay*. As if you 'ad the first idea of what you were on about."

" . . . a pension and your own plot of land when you retire," Brutus smirked.

"You're not as smart as you think you are," said Quintus, "it's twenty years before we get to retire."

"You're just a runt, Quintus. You had to stand on your tippy-toes to make the minimum height."

"Get away with ya! I'm as tall as you are!"

"Only if you jump."

"I can jump higher than you can, 'n all."

"Prove it, let's see how high you can jump in full armour!"

Quintus heard the grind of a scabbard on chainmail behind him and sped up his shovelling.

"If I hear another word out of you two herd animals tonight," said an approaching decanus, "I'll order you to be given restricted rations."

"Yessir!"

The decanus set off in the direction of another slacker.

"Power's going to 'is head, that one, sees himself climbing up the ranks over our backs." Brutus gave his spade another kick. He dug in silence for a few minutes then stood up and stretched. "We're marked men," he shook his head in mock sorrow at the black VII XII etched on Quintus's arm, "branded for life."

Brutus looked down at the stigma on his own forearm. Being accepted to the legion had marked his transition from boy to man and was the culmination of his mother's years of sacrifice. She'd scraped together enough money to get him lessons to pass the compulsory reading and writing test and buy him his sword and armour. Brutus grinned at the thought of adventures ahead, booty to win, barbarians to kill.

Paulus, a recruit with three days' seniority to them, was digging just down the line from the pair of new boys. He looked up and said, "Well, that's bloody brilliant, you've got an officer marching back over here now. We'll be set to digging the latrines next."

As a set of reticulated shoulder armour and a red horsehair-crested helmet marched past in the recruits' peripheral vision the boys tightened up their formation, but the officer passed them by. Paulus let out an awed breath. "That was the aquilifer, the eagle-bearer for the legion."

The boys all kept digging but their eyes followed the aquilifer until he disappeared from sight. The new recruits hadn't met up with the other cohorts yet and therefore hadn't ever seen the carved and gilded standard, for the eagle left camp only when the whole legion followed it.

The nightly fortifications built, the men ate their fill of corn and bacon stew, sopped up with freshly baked bread, then brought out their dice and played games of chance around the campfire.

Brutus had started on again about his blisters when the decanus stepped out of the shadows into the circle of firelight. He stood above them, legs astride and arms crossed. "You lads still complaining?"

The boys put down their dice and leapt up to salute.

The decanus looked them up and down. "You need to toughen up. You're in for a spot of on-the-job training. We march before cock-crow." Wind buffeted the fire and his shadow loomed large. "There's a purpose to everything we do, no matter how senseless it may seem to you. When an order's given, never question it." The wind battered the flames and the decanus' features softened for a moment. "Pack up and get some sleep, you're going to need it."

When their equipment had been squared away for the night, the guy ropes tightened against the wind and the sentries of the first watch set, Quintus pulled his blanket up under his chin. "Where d'you think we're headed?"

"How'd I know?" said Brutus, "they never tell us nothin' except what we need to know."

"It's only three weeks since we joined up. We haven't even finished basic training. Why'd the decanus talk to us like that?"

"Won't be nowhere too dangerous first time up," said Brutus, "probably just some drills with another cohort or something."

"No, that's not it," whispered another new recruit. "I was standing sentry outside the praetorium when a messenger came in – can't tell you what I heard or they'll flog me."

"What's the point of saying anything then?"

"Just to tell you all to get your last good night's sleep while you can."

Brutus lay on his back, listening to his tent mates' breathing slow down as, one by one, exhaustion overcame them. The wind was rising, howling like a wolf in the valley, but their tent was pegged so tightly the canvas barely flapped. Brutus wondered how he could be so physically exhausted and still be wide awake. "Quintus?"

No answer. Suddenly Brutus felt an urge to wake him up and say, "You know that I've always loved you," but he didn't in case the other men heard and took it the wrong way. Instead, he lay awake in the dark, feeling the cold come up through the groundsheet and longing for the bed of fresh straw he slept on in a safe corner of his mother's home.

The orders in the morning were brief. There would be no additional training. The rest of the legion was already on the road from Genoa to Turin. The new recruits would march at the double to catch up with them.

Although nothing official was said, as the men shouldered their packs in the grey light before dawn a rumour swept down the ranks that they were marching to Gaul.

"Nah," said Brutus, "they wouldn't send us there, what for?"

"I 'eard the centurion say it myself," said Quintus, "an' you'll never guess what – the magister militum 'imself will lead the march over the Alps."

Brutus' jaw dropped. "Never! Not Flavius Aetius."

"Mars' balls, I swear it, 'magister militum,' that's what I 'eard."

Brutus scratched the back of his head. "If the Field Commander of the Western Empire 'imself is marching us over the Alps . . ." his stomach lurched and his groin tensed up, "then we're headed for . . ."

Quintus' eyes shimmered with fear. "Attila?"

Lone Rider

North Eastern Gaul
451 AD

Two days' ride beyond the safety of their own territory, a Burgundian cohort was sweeping the countryside in search of recruits to fight under Aetius' command.

Not far north of Troyes, just off the road to Reims, they pitched their faded crimson, green and ochre tents. With pointed spindles at the top of their centre poles, the tents stood in a cluster between two stands of straight-trunked trees. Although each tree was slender, grouped together they had enough ballast to disperse a cavalry charge. Sentries stood guard round the camp perimeter.

From amongst the flock of tents the smoke of cooking fires rose in discreet wisps, white against the darkening woods but grey against the last green-blue of evening sky. The men had already eaten and either made their way to their tents or unrolled blankets and furs under shelters made from cut boughs of aspen. A few sat yawning around the fire, singing somnolent songs of old-time heroes. A courier had tracked them down and given them Avitus' order to withdraw to Lyon and they'd all turn south in the morning.

"Lone rider! Approaching at the gallop!" a lookout yelled.

The singing stopped. Soldiers reached for their weapons and leapt to their feet.

"Another Roman courier?" the captain of the first watch asked.

"I can't see yet, sir," the sentry reported. The dusk had smudged out the rider on the purple plain.

"I see him!" shouted another. "Trappings of a courier, but the rider's out of uniform."

The captain frowned. "You two, ride out and intercept him, and you –" he pointed at a boy, "awaken Prince Heva. The rest of you, arms at the ready!"

The outgoing riders blurred into the fug of falling night. Just when it seemed that they'd been gone too long their flapping cloaks came into sight. At the camp perimeter, they slowed to a walk and picked their way between the tents to the clearing round the fire.

The courier's horse was slathered in sweat from the rims of its flaring nostrils to the tip of its tail. Its ribs blew like bellows, its mouth foamed as it strained to draw breath and steam rose from its flanks.

The Burgundians slid from their mounts then disentangled the legs of what appeared to be a bundle of rags from the four-pommelled Roman cavalry saddle. One pulled the rider from the horse and the other caught him before he hit the ground. A waif of a person struggled to find his legs, but his knees buckled.

"Bring him here," the captain ordered. The Burgundians slung the rider between their shoulders and carried him into the firelight. As they drew up in front of the officer, one volunteered, "It's a girl, sir."

The captain's eyes widened as he ran his eyes over girl and steed. Were it not for the long mass of dust and sweat-covered hair that hung over the rider's back and chest, she could have been a boy. "Get her water and a seat. No hope for the horse, it's all blown out," but a young groom ran forward with a bucket of water and the horse drained it.

Two older men brought forward folding stools, set them up by the fire and helped the girl down onto one of them. The captain closed her hand around a gourd of water and her arm shook as she lifted it to soot-covered lips. She gulped faster than she could swallow and water drew white tracks down her neck.

At the rattle of scabbards, all eyes turned towards Prince Heva who strode out of the half-light towards the fire. The golden hilts of his swords were studded with garnets and he wore a burgundy-red tunic bordered with white. A woven leather circlet held back thick blond hair from his forehead. A pair of hunting hounds, one silver-grey, the other tan and white, followed at his heels.

Heva's aqua eyes lit with curiosity as he sat down opposite the bedraggled rider. His whippets twitched their ears at distant sounds then sat with paws crossed at his feet. "Summon the surgeon," Heva ordered in the Burgundian tongue before addressing the girl slowly in Latin. "Where do you come from?"

Her mouth shaped the word *Reims* but no sound came out. The swelling around her eyes had reduced them to slits and she had a sooty streak down her left cheek. In a wave of unexpected tenderness, Heva put his hand to the side of her head and tried to wipe it away with his thumb.

She swallowed back tears and croaked out, "Reims. Attila sacked it this morning."

"This morning? But Reims is sixty miles away. You rode from Reims – alone?" He wouldn't have believed her were it not for the state of her horse.

She nodded.

"What's your name?"

"Leonida." Her face crumpled. "Attila murdered my father, Marcus Ruricius. He was a town councillor." She wiped her tears with her sleeve, smudging the soot on her cheeks.

"I'm sorry to hear that, Leonida."

The surgeon put a basin of water on the table. Heva dipped a cloth in it, wrung it out and wiped the soot from her cheeks then handed it to Leonida who pressed it over her eyes. She didn't want these barbarians to see her cry. Her breathing juddered for a few minutes, but when she found her self-control she raised her chin. "I have a message to give to the magister militum, Flavius Aetius."

Heva's brows shot up. "You're carrying a message for Aetius?"

"Is he here?"

"No, but we're allies of Rome, marching to join him. If you give me the message, I'll ensure he receives it."

Leonida frowned. "How do I know you won't forget?"

Heva smiled. She looked and sounded so young. "I give you my promise, Leonida."

"Alright, then." Blushing, she fumbled at the clasp of her cloak then slipped her hand down the front of her tunic, pulled out a square of folded paper and passed it to Heva.

He read the message in silence. "This is important, Leonida. Thank you for bringing it; Aetius will be grateful." Turning to the doctor he said in Burgundian, "Give her my tent, I'll sleep by the fire tonight," then repeated the instructions in Latin.

"You don't have to translate for me," she said, "I understand a little of your language."

Heva's eyes lit with interest. "You speak Burgundian?"

"No, I don't speak it, but I understand the meaning. My mother speaks it sometimes."

"She's Burgundian? Would I know her?"

"I don't know if she really is Burgundian. She was stolen by the Goths and sold as a slave when she was little."

"She remembers her childhood?"

Leonida shook her head, struggling with another wave of tears.

Heva leant towards her and brushed the hair back from her temples this time. "I'll post a sentry outside my tent so you can sleep."

Leonida's eyes circled the bearded faces of Heva's soldiers, leaning on their homemade weapons, slack-jawed with amazement. They looked as barbarian as the Huns who had murdered her father. "I'd rather have the dogs guard me than any of those men," she said in Latin.

Heva looked down, caressing the heads of his hounds for a moment to hide his smile at her childish turn of phrase, but when he looked up again there was a crease between his brows. He surveyed the faces of his troops, lit by the campfire. Old men and young boys – all that was left to fight Attila. The professional soldiers had long ago marched to meet their fate, joining their warlords or Roman auxiliary units. He shook his head. "The surgeon will take you to my tent, Leonida. You will be safe there."

Leonida studied the prince, whose blond hair was edged with gold by the firelight, then let the surgeon lead her away.

When she had gone, Heva asked the riders who had brought her in to tell him all they knew of the girl, but it was nothing more than she had told him herself.

"She's coughing up smoke," reported the doctor after settling her in the tent, "her legs are chaffed and bruised, her hands raw from the reins but they will all heal. I can say nothing for the wounds to her soul."

"Triple the sentries on watch," Heva ordered, "then dismiss the troops for the night."

When his orders had been executed, he sat on the ground next to fire. A breeze whispered through the aspen leaves and the sounds of tiny nocturnal animals ruffled the air. Twigs crackled into flame. All else was quiet. He sat alone for an hour then lit a taper, called his dogs to heel and made his way to the tent.

Moonlight washed out the faded red canvas to silver-grey. Silently, he turned up a corner of the door flap, listened to Leonida's rough breathing for a moment, then stooped and entered. In the flickering light of his taper he watched her lips trembling, as if she were about to cry in her sleep, then she rolled onto her side and he slipped back out into the night.

The grass was covered with dew, but his men had laid a deerskin not far from the tent and stacked wood for a fire. Cupping the flame of his taper in his palm, he crouched and lit the twigs under the logs.

They sparked into flame and gave him light and the beginnings of warmth. He sat, cross-legged, unsheathed his sword and laid it across his knees – it was not only a duty but an honour to defend Leonida. While he watched the gold, red and pink of the growing flames, a sense of elation rose in him. He didn't hear her open the canvas door over the fire's crackle and spark, but felt a gust of warm air as she sat down at his side.

"I was having bad dreams."

Heva put out an arm and encircled her with a blanket. She smelled of stale ashes and fear. "Would you like to talk?"

She drew a deep breath and, in a voice that barely rose above the rustle of night, spoke slowly. "Before dawn, shouting and screaming woke me up. Fire was raining from the sky. Hard clay balls flew over the city wall then hit the ground and splattered into flame." She brushed away tears. "My father was standing in the doorway, struggling to fasten his sword belt in the doorway. When he saw me, he put his hands on my shoulders and told me to hide in the cellar. His hands were shaking and, when he kissed my forehead, his lips were cold." Leonida drew a shuddering breath. "He told me that he loved me then ran out the door and the smoke swallowed him up, leaving me alone, completely alone. The slaves had run away as soon as they'd heard that Attila was coming, and my mother had gone to visit a newborn baby in a faraway town."

"What did you do when your father had gone?"

"I ran out after him but I couldn't see through the smoke and my eyes stung. The roof of a burning house collapsed and spat flames across the road so I couldn't turn back. Over the roaring blaze, I heard clashing swords getting closer so I sprinted down the street, through the smoke, to the church. When I banged on the door, Father Nicasius opened it."

Leonida took a long breath and rubbed her eyes. "Inside, mothers held their children wrapped in their arms and were rocking them, praying out loud when the banging of a battering ram started on the doors. The doors starting to bend and split, so I ran to the altar and hid underneath the cloth covering it. Each time the ram hit, the wood cracked. Children were screaming. The door split off its hinges and short, ugly men with wispy beards and pointed helmets rushed in. Mothers threw themselves over their children but the Huns pulled them off and . . . and . . . did dreadful things to them, then stabbed them, right in front of their children."

Leonida put her hands over her face. Tears streamed down the sides of her nose. Heva tightened his arm around her shoulder and stroked her hair. "You don't have to tell me more."

"But I do – it got so much worse!"

He put a hand over his forehead and shook his head. "How could it get worse?"

Leonida took a shuddering breath then steadied herself. "The priest was standing on the altar steps, just a few feet in front of me with his arms outstretched. He was praying – *my soul cleaveth to the dust, quicken me according to thy word* – but the Huns hacked him down. One of his hands fell back under the altar cloth and a pool of blood spread towards me. I squished back as far as I could . . ."

Heva took her frozen hands in his and squeezed them. Her whole body was trembling.

"The Huns snatched the candlesticks from the altar" said Leonida, "then piled up rush-seated stools in the aisle. A baby was crying somewhere but I couldn't see where. A Hun went over to a pile of bodies on the floor, pulled back his leg and kicked and kicked and kicked until the crying stopped."

The muscles in Heva's jaw clenched.

"The Huns struck sparks from their fire-flints and set the seats afire then jumped up and whooped with glee. Smoke filled the church. I lay my head on the floor, next to the priest's blood. My eyes were stinging but I saw the Huns ran out then heard them nailing the doors shut."

Heva's eyes turned arctic. "How could you escape?"

"My mother and I used to polish the silver. The incense burners were too high for us to reach so she made a ladder from birch saplings and the priest let us stow it in between the wall and the altar. There were three windows, not much wider than watchtower slits, high up. When I was at the top of the ladder, I could just reach the windowsill with my fingertips. I don't know how, but I pulled myself up, squeezed out and jumped. My ankles felt as if they were breaking when I hit the ground but I rolled onto the grass then lay there listening for danger. When I was sure the Huns had left, I ran through the necropolis to the wall that follows the towpath. I hid behind it and waited to see if anyone else would escape but no one came. The screaming stopped before the roof caved in."

Heva pulled her head to his shoulder and held her there but after a minute she pushed herself up and away from him. "I followed the towpath to the eastern gate. In the guardhouse courtyard I saw the bodies of Romans who had died fighting back to back. The only living creature was a horse, standing in a corner, all by itself. It had a shiny, golden coat and was drinking from a trough, as if everything was normal, but its saddle was halfway under its stomach."

"The courier horse you rode in on?" asked Heva.

Leonida nodded. "I crept over and took the bridle, then pushed up the saddle and tightened the girth. The horse nuzzled me. As soon as I was on its back, I felt brave again and I rode to the cathedral, where I hoped I would find my father."

"Was he there?"

Leonida shook her head and stared into the fire. "The cathedral doors were hanging off their hinges. Blood dripped off the big cross outside. I didn't want to leave the horse next to such a frightening thing, so I led it up the cathedral steps. Dead men were laid out in rows on either side of the aisle. My father was one of them."

"I'm sorry," said Heva, "you were brave to look for him."

She tilted her head to one side, her eyes looking into the night. "I found one man alive, a centurion, with blood flowing out from under the eagle on his breastplate. He was clutching his helmet over his stomach. On the ground next to him lay the body of an old man with holes through his wrists and his feet.

That's the priest, said the soldier, *Attila crucified him. I cut him down from the cross outside. Despite his wounds, he did what he could for the injured before he died.*

Where are the rest of your men? I asked.

I ordered them out, to fight to the last. Did you see anyone alive on your way in?

I shook my head.

His lips went tight but there was pride in his eyes. *Can you get me some water, girl?*

My steps echoed, past all the dead men, down the aisle to the font. I filled his helmet but he managed only a few sips then said, *Give the rest to your horse.* When I did, he tried to laugh but coughed up blood.

Why are you laughing, aren't you dying? I asked. I didn't mean to say it out loud. I thought he'd be angry, but he smiled so I took his hand and told him that I'd stay with him until he went to the next life.

I got cold, sitting there with him. He didn't speak but his breathing was rattling, with longer and longer gaps between each breath. I wondered if he was dead but suddenly he lifted his chest and neck from the floor and looked straight over my shoulder, as if he'd seen someone standing behind me. I looked round, but there was no one there.

My name is Johannes, he said quite clearly, *a free-born Roman. Find Aetius. Tell him we never surrendered. Tell him I die strong in the knowledge that he will avenge me.* Then his head fell back to the floor and his eyes rolled up."

Heva opened his arms to Leonida and this time, instead of pushing away, she buried her head in his chest. There was a long silence while he stroked her back then he said, "I'll make sure that Aetius gets Johannes' message."

Leonida looked up through bleary eyes. "Thank you. Johannes deserves that."

"So do you," said Heva. "What did you do after he died?"

"I closed his lids then went to say goodbye to my father. His body had gone yellow, like lemon rind, and didn't look like him anymore. It wasn't as hard as I expected to leave him behind. I covered the body with the altar cloth, made the sign of the cross and led my horse away down the aisle without looking at the dead either side.

I've never been so grateful to be alive as when we got outside, into the light! The sky was vivid and birds were chirping. The air stank but I was still breathing when none of the men inside would ever breathe again. I galloped away and didn't stop till I reached your camp."

Heva cradled her, waiting a minute to make sure she'd finished before asking. "How did you know we were friends, not enemies?"

"I didn't know, but there were no signs of Attila south of Reims. He must have gone in the opposite direction, to Paris." Leonida's chin crumpled again.

"Where's your mother, Leonida? I can help you find her."

"She went to see my aunt's new baby . . . in Paris."

"Oh . . ."

Heva picked the broken girl up and carried her into his tent. There he laid her on his bear-skin bed, wrapped her snuggly in a rough woollen blanket, and lay down next to her. She settled her head on his shoulder and wept. Her hair was acrid from the fires of hell, but he pulled her into the warmth of his body and held her until her sobbing ceased.

＊ ＊ ＊ ＊ ＊

Leonida woke to dappled sunlight playing over the faded rose canvas roof. For a moment she couldn't remember where she was or how she'd got there, then her breath caught in her chest. Memories of her father's corpse in the cathedral and fires roaring through Reims shook her body and she threw out her arm for Heva, but he was gone. Leaping to her feet, she rushed out in search of him.

The air was fresh and the sun bright but it hadn't yet risen high enough to warm the clearing. A breeze shuttered through the aspen leaves and she could hear a brook tripping through the woods nearby, but her heart raced and her eyes were wild. Then she saw him, stretched out on his side next to the ashes of the fire, sleeping the deep sleep of the young and strong. She would have run to him but his hunting hounds leapt up, growled and raised their hackles. Crouching low, she extended her hand but they skittered from side to side. "Come on," she coaxed and one then the other loped over, sniffed and licked her fingers.

Without opening his eyes, Heva stirred and Leonida felt a rush of self-consciousness. He rolled onto his back and his blond hair fell away from the flawless skin of his forehead. Lit by sunlight, the stubble on his chin only made him appear more angelic. She slipped back into the tent but there was nothing to groom herself with except the flannel and pitcher of cold water that the doctor had left the night before. Her fingers snared in her hair when she tried to smooth it, so she bundled it up into a loose knot at the nape of her neck. Swishing water round her mouth, she realised she'd have to go back outside to spit it out and raised the corner of the tent flap – only to be met by the sight of Heva's lips.

"I was coming to wish you good morning," he said as she gulped down her mouthful. He leant forward, put his hand lightly on the back of her neck and kissed her cheek. His fingers drifted down her arm to the warmth of her hand and he gathered it in his. "Is there anything you need?"

Leonida was immobile, scared to leave her hand in his but too nervous to rip it away. Yet, when he closed his fingers more firmly around hers, a feeling of safety enveloped her. "New clothes please, mine are disgusting. They stink of smoke and blood." She longed to take them off and burn them. "Ghosts cling to the folds of these rags."

Heva rummaged through his bag inside the tent and emerged holding a cream tunic of light wool out to her. It was three times wider at the shoulders than Leonida and the arm-holes would gape half way down her ribcage. "What do you think of this?"

With the first hint of a smile, she tilted her head to one side. "Perhaps it would work if I wore it with a belt."

"The whole camp will be talking if you emerge from my tent wearing my clothes."

"I hadn't thought of that! Perhaps we should look for someone the same size as me and borrow clothes from him?"

Heva frowned. "I'd gladly do that but none of the men travelling with me has anything but what he stands up in."

"Oh! I'm sorry. I should have thought of that."

Feeling their fragile moment of joy disperse, Heva put a hand in the small of her back and guided her towards the centre of the camp. "Tomorrow afternoon we'll arrive in Troyes. It still has a Roman garrison and I know a magistrate there – if he and his family haven't fled already – who has daughters about your age. You'll be able to have a hot bath and wash your hair. Now, let's get you some breakfast."

Rubbing sleep dust from their eyes, the rustic soldiers had congregated around a newly lit campfire. A blackened pot hung from a bowed iron spear that was propped up at either end by forked branches. A boy, no older than Leonida, stirred the contents with a long metal spoon, not letting them spill or burn. Steam and the smell of barley tinged with cinnamon evaporated over the brim. Leonida's stomach rumbled but the aroma made her think of her mother and her eyes filled with tears again. Heva saw them and distracted her by introducing her to his officers. The common soldiers gawped.

Seeing that Leonida was feeling better, he left her in the company of the surgeon and disappeared for a few minutes. When he returned he was grinning from ear to ear. "Your horse wolfed down her oats this morning and looks fit to ride."

For the first time since her father had disappeared into the fires of Reims, she smiled with parted lips. She would have thrown her arms around Heva's neck but knew that the men were staring. "We'll have to give her a name."

"I know it's not original," said Heva, "but, given her speed, I suggest 'Lightning'."

"That's not original at all! But it doesn't matter. It suits her. My horse shall be called Lightning from now on. What's your horse's name?"

"Thunder," Heva said with a flash of white teeth.

"You tricked me! Now everyone will think I called her Lightning on purpose to be like you."

"Do you mind?"

Leonida tried to pretend she was annoyed but in truth she was flattered that he'd chosen to couple the names of their mounts. "Do you think I'll have to give her back to the imperial courier service when we find Aetius?"

"If the Romans make a fuss, I'll buy her for you."

"That would be too kind!"

"Not at all, you and your horse have been through a lot together." A shadow passed over Heva's face. "Leonida, 'we' aren't going to find Aetius, that's a job for me and my men."

Leonida felt the ground sink. "Why can't I come with you?"

"We're marching to war. I would never forgive myself if anything happened to you."

"Where are you heading?"

"The courier despatch in your saddlebags told us to join the allied forces in Lyon. You can read, can't you?"

"Of course!" Leonida tossed her head, "but I'm a magistrate's daughter and don't read confidential documents."

Heva grinned. "What a correct little lady you are!"

"I'm not little – I'm fourteen and a half years old and tall."

"Fourteen is still very young." Heva was barely twenty.

"How long before we part?"

"Twelve days. Aetius would do the march in less than ten and consider himself to be strolling but my men aren't legionnaires. They're raw to war, our last reserves, if you could even call them that." Heva fell silent, watching young boys and old men roll their blankets and tighten up the girths on the pack mules. Most of them had lived their lives under the protection of Avitus and *pax romana* and had no idea of what they were about to face. Some were armed with only pitchforks or other farm instruments.

"Lyon is hundreds of miles away," said Leonida, thinking that by the time they reached Lyon Attila would have sacked Paris.

Heva turned back to her. "We'll regroup with the rest of the Burgundian army in Dijon first. I'll present you to my father, the king, and my brother Gundobad. I have the feeling that you will know them for many years to come." Then he turned abruptly away to give orders to his men, leaving Leonida wondering what he'd meant by that.

When he returned, Heva found her stroking Lightning's velvet nose and invited her to join him and his handful of mounted men to hunt in the forest. Using her teeth, Leonida tightened up the knot in the linen the surgeon had used to bind her blistered hands and a groom, called Marco, gave her a leg up onto Lightning's back. Never more than a length behind Heva and joyful in his presence, she raced with the hunt and began to believe that, no matter what trials life threw at her, she would be able to overcome them as long as he was at her side.

Heva drew the string of his bow, sat back in his saddle and let an arrow fly into the neck of a twelve-pointed stag then dismounted so that his men could strap the deer over Thunder's back. Four of them hoisted the carcass over the horse's flanks. Thunder whinnied and shied as a careless shove drove one of the tips of the deer's antlers into his flank. When the hunting party returned to camp, Heva called for Marco, who hid a face that had been kicked in by a mule behind a thick black beard, to salve the wound.

"When we charge into battle," said Heva, "Thunder fights alongside me."

"But he doesn't look fierce," said Leonida. The chestnut horse had a cream mane, tail and feathers and a white blaze down the front of his face. His eyes glowed, deep brown and gentle.

"That depends on what I ask of him," said Heva.

Marco handed him the halter and the prince stroked the soft fur behind the horse's ears.

"How many battles have you and thunder fought in together?" asked Leonida.

"Not many."

Leonida saw his eyes darken and wanted to make them shine again. "I like your name, does it mean something?"

"It means 'life' in our tongue. And you must be named after King Leonidas of Sparta, who led the three hundred against the Persians at Thermopylae."

"You're clever to think of that, but my mother chose my name for a different reason," Leonida looked up at him with pride in her voice, "she was the last of the female gladiators."

"Female gladiators were outlawed two hundred years ago," said Heva his eyes soft and sad for her.

"They were," admitted Leonida, lowering her lashes, "but my mother was still one of them. She won't be afraid of Attila. She'll search for me."

"What's her name?"

"Sola."

Heva was too young to have heard of her. "I see." *You can't face the truth but I'll let you keep your fantasies.* "What's the matter? Your face has gone pale."

Leonida shivered. "I was thinking of Attila. Will Troyes be on fire, like Reims?"

Heva looked ahead, in search of smoke, but the sky was fresh. "No, it's not burning. Look, there're Roman sentries patrolling the battlements." He ordered his men to form a phalanx and march in unison into the city. Untried and untrained, they formed a shaggy column and rambled towards the walls, their baggage waggons rocking behind them.

The Troyes garrison saluted and quartered their allies then Heva presented Leonida to their commander and his wife who whisked her away to the magistrate's house.

When Leonida returned the next morning, the gaggle of Burgundian troops milling around waiting for orders turned as one and stared at her flowing white gown and royal-blue travelling cloak. The magistrate's daughter had sacrificed her second-best chiton along with a new pair of boots that had not quite fitted but which she would have preferred to keep all the same. Slaves had woven sky-blue cornflowers and tiny buds, blushed with pink, into Leonida's waist-length plait. The family had refused any form of payment for their gifts and services.

Heva's breath caught in his throat. Washed and struck by the sun, Leonida's hair shone with a metallic lustre, just like Lightning's golden coat. As she drew close to him, he caught the scent of roses and myrtle with an undernote of hay. That she could be immaculately presented and still smell of horses filled him with tenderness. He quenched an impulse to lean down and kiss her in front of the crowd.

"The garrison commander recognised Lightning's coat," said Heva, "and came over to check her brand. He tells me she's the fastest horse in the imperial courier service."

"Did he take her?"

Heva smiled. "He came back with a squad of eight and tried, but I told him that he could have the horse or the thousand men who march with me, but not both."

Leonida laughed. "What did he reply to that?"

"He blustered about giving Caesar back his property but calmed down when I explained that you'd lost your father in the defence of Reims and had escaped Attila on Lightning's back. A good thirty of my men had gathered round and were keen to defend your claim so he thought the better of starting a fight. You've made many admirers amongst us."

"Then I can keep her?"

"You may." Heva smiled too, but then thoughts of news he didn't want to share with Leonida shadowed his face.

"What's the matter?" she asked.

"Tournai, Cambrai and Amiens all lie in ashes."

All colour fled from Leonida's face.

Heva took her hand in his and held it tight. "Paris will not be reinforced."

Leonida's whole body started trembling and her hand went cold. She saw Paris looted, like Reims, and her mother, like her father, lying dead, or worse – raped, like the women in the church then burned alive.

* * * * *

For ten days after leaving Troyes, the Burgundian entourage ambled through rolling hills swathed in forest. The hounds hunted and Leonida discovered that Lightning could jump over logs and rivers on the same breath as she galloped.

With Leonida and Heva at their head, the infantrymen forgot their woes. War was just a phantom that should not be feared. The troops smiled over the couple's nascent love and joked as they followed their

89

prince. But when the last full day of the march arrived they realised that this interlude of peace was about to end.

On the evening before they arrived in Dijon, Heva and Leonida climbed through dew-covered grass to the top of a rounded knoll. Nestling together under Heva's cloak, they sat on a log in the lee of its crest and watched cumulus clouds catch fire in a coral sky. The sinking sun collided with the prow of a purple mountain.

A breeze blew up the bronzed skin on the back of Heva's neck. He studied Leonida's face in wonder at the finest of lines at the corners of her heart-shaped lips and the flecks of sunset reflected in her blue-green irises. The wind drifted strands of her hair round her head and the sun made a halo of them. Her beauty, courage and innocence commanded his heart. He went down on one knee before her, his noble profile bowed. Cradling her right hand in both of his, he turned over her palm and ran his thumb over its mounts and valleys, feeling through the softness of her newly healed skin to the strength of her bones.

"I would do this properly, but your father is gone and we know not if your mother lives. Tomorrow we part and battle lies ahead." He raised his eyes to hers. "You're too young to marry, Leonida, but old enough to be betrothed. If I searched till the end of my years, I could never find another maiden like you. No soldier can ever promise that he'll come back from war, but I will do my utmost to return to you. My love, will you wait for me?"

Leonida's pupils dilated. She closed her left hand over his and placed both over her heart. "I will wait a lifetime for you, Heva."

The Illustrious Aetius

T he supreme commander of the combined forces of the Western
Empire, the illustrious Flavius Aetius, chose to live with his troops
in a temporary camp, laid out on flat land beyond the walls of Gaul's
capital city, rather than inside its fortified citadel. Behind newly dug
ditches and stiff palisades, eight-man bivouacs marched in taut canvas
rows towards the forum. At its centre stood Aetius' personal tent, the
praetorium, which he used as his headquarters. He had too many troops
to accommodate in the garrison barracks. Too many, but so terribly few
compared with the hordes of his enemies.

Sidonius camped down on the plain, under canvas like any other
soldier, as Aetius had refused him permission to reside in the Governor's
house with his family. Despite Sidonius' junior rank of equites, Aetius
put his name on a pared-down list of guests to attend dinner in the
praetorian villa. He wanted him to forge diplomatic bonds with the
sons of allies, or potential allies, sent to attend the banquet by fathers
who preferred to keep a safe distance from their long-standing enemy. If
there was one man alive whom none would dare to cross, it was Flavius
Aetius.

It was a muggy, midsummer evening and Sidonius' mother,
Andromeda, deemed that her guests would be more comfortable
eating under the stars in the atrium than in the banquet hall. No breeze
dispelled the heat from torches that branched out from the horseshoe of

walls protecting the villa from the outside world.

Two sets of dining couches, one for the senior officers and the other for younger men, fanned out on opposite sides of an ornamental pool. Euric, third son of Theodoric the Goth, sat between Sidonius and Ecdicius who separated him from the princes of the Bretons and Franks lest a fight flash between the rival tribes.

Andromeda had made sure that the courtyard fountains played just high enough to stifle any possibility that the princes would overhear the generals' discussion. One could never tell in advance which ally would turn out to be a spy. She hoped to give her newly-wed son and his bride the chance to say goodbye before he followed the eagle into battle and had placed a table and chairs in the obscurity of the portico for Papianilla and Sedulla, the only other women present. As hostess, she had kept the dishes simple – with Attila drawing ever closer, no one was in the mood to savour their food.

At the apex of his arc of dining couches Aetius was sombre, but even in this subdued state the very air around him crackled and stood to attention. His thick hair had silvered but that was the only discernible sign that he had reached middle age.

"What news from Avitus?" he asked Honorius.

The Praetorian Prefect put down his wine glass and the furrows between his brows deepened. "Not good. He's still in Toulouse trying to persuade Theodoric to join us, but the Goth is obdurate."

"Continue."

"Theodoric asked him what forces you command. Avitus told the truth, that you march with twenty thousand auxiliaries and a handful of new recruits. Attila has half a million mounted warriors. Theodoric won't join your suicide mission. Even Avitus hasn't been able to make him change his mind."

"Damnation!"

"It's frustrating, to say the least." Honorius picked up his glass again, tilted it and watched light travel up the spiral in its stem, then leant forward and hissed into Aetius' ear –"I don't understand why our esteemed Emperor, Valentinian, hasn't given you the legions."

"He's keeping them for his own defence," said Aetius, with an ironic lift of his lip.

"You can't tell me that mother-murdering fool . . ."

Aetius raised a hand to cut him off.

"You're right," said Honorius, sitting back, "I should not speak ill of our Emperor – but if her son hadn't poisoned her, Galla Placidia would have given you Rome's army."

Aetius put a hand on his shoulder and looked him in the eye. "We will build an alliance of our enemies."

Honorius nodded, but his lips were sour. "If the Burgundians agree to fight under our banner, so will the Bretons, the Saxons and Franks, if only because they know Attila will crush them in an instant otherwise."

"Theodoric feels no such pressure?"

"Theodoric has larger numbers and Toulouse is nigh impregnable." Honorius studied the angles of the Field Commander's face. No point in mincing words with Aetius. "Attila has offered half of Gaul to Theodoric if he will take the field against us. And if he does nothing but stay within his city walls and leave the Huns to finish us off, Attila has pledged that he won't make war on the Goths."

"All obvious posturing by Attila! His every word's manipulative lie."

"I'm sure that Theodoric puts little weight on Attila's 'promises' but the numbers speak. Once Attila has annihilated us, Theodoric knows he will have to fight him over who scavenges what from Rome's carcass, but Attila will have put an end to our Empire and Theodoric is ambitious to expand his own territories. He's always resented the way we've confined him to Aquitaine. This time, he's betting we'll lose; it's as simple as that."

Aetius thumped the couch with his fist and silver plates leapt then clattered to the ground. "Does he not understand that the future of the whole world is at stake? We win or we face oblivion – all of us – including the Goths."

From the far side of the fountain, Sidonius looked up and saw his father wince, but couldn't hear what was being said. Aetius shook his head then started talking again just as Heva the Burgundian leaned towards Sidonius' ear and asked, "Could you make sure that Aetius gets a message for me?"

"Of course, but why don't you take it to him yourself while you're here?"

"This isn't the moment, look at how preoccupied they are."

"Better give it to me in writing then and I'll put it in with his despatches."

"It doesn't belong amongst the despatches," said Heva, "it's a personal message from a centurion who died defending Reims. I promised someone I love that I'd give it to Aetius."

Sidonius rasied his brows and Heva leant closer, but the crunch of spiked boots marching across the courtyard arrested his words. All eyes followed two armed sentries who were advancing at double-time towards Aetius. Andromeda rose to her feet, as if to throw herself between her guest and his assailants but, barely raising four fingers, the magister militum signalled that there was no reason for alarm.

"Sir!" the sentries saluted. "An ambassador bearing a gift from Attila is at the gates and seeks leave to enter."

"Denied."

"Our orders concerning the gift, sir?"

"Have you inspected it?"

"No sir. It's a small coffer with holes in it, as if to allow an animal to breathe."

"A snake perhaps?" said Honorius. "That'd be a clumsy assassination attempt. Or perhaps its the head of a common enemy?"

"Attila and I share not a single foe," said Aetius, "any enemy of his is an ally of mine."

Honorius' frown cut deeper. "It worries me that Attila knows we're meeting here tonight."

"We need to trace his source immediately." Aetius ran flint-sharp eyes over the barbarian princes yet, despite his concern as to who the informant might be, he was curious to know what Attila had sent him. "Bring the coffer in, under guard, and open it before me. Hold the ambassador at the gates."

The sentries saluted and withdrew. The guests murmured amongst themselves until four guards carrying a metal-bound box hung from two long wooden bearer poles entered the atrium. While a squad of eight men stood with weapons at the ready, a decanus smashed apart the padlocks with the hilt of his sword then held out his hand for a spear to prise open the lid. But just as he extended the spear's point towards the coffer, with no apparent human intervention, the lid flew open.

The guests had expected some spring mechanism to be the force behind this trick and gasped when a tiny black man leapt up and out of the trunk, cartwheeled across the floor and onto his feet with arms outspread as wide as his shaky grin. In the dark of night his bright teeth and the whites of his eyes seemed to float, disembodied.

The dwarf seemed to expect applause but found instead that he was at the centre of a chrysanthemum of spears. His smile stayed pasted to his face while his features took shape in the firelight and he awaited his fate.

"What are you, little man, spy or assassin?" asked Aetius, his hand on the hilt of his dagger.

The performer answered in accented Latin. "Neither, my lord, I'm a gift."

"Any gift from Attila comes at an exorbitant price," scoffed Aetius.

"I'm a jester, an acrobat in a small way, my lord, not a spy. I'm not big enough to be an assassin!" the dwarf quipped, attempting to inject humour into a high-pitched voice that trembled and squeaked.

"Size is irrelevant. Poison and deceit are the weapons of the physically weak." Aetius turned to his lieutenant. "Optio, inform the ambassador that the gift isn't welcome and will be returned as soon as it's had a chance to stretch its stubby little legs and been fed. Order the ambassador to wait outside until summoned to escort the dwarf back to where he came from. What's your name, little man?"

"My name is Xerkon, Sir." The dwarf made a courtly bow.

"Well, Xerkon, do you have anything further to tell us?"

"I have a message from the almighty Attila, Emperor of the Huns, lord of my world and soon to be the master of yours." Xerkon shook in the face of Aetius' thunderous brows. "The Emperor of the Huns demands that you return the gold platters from the church of Amiens that a Roman priest stole before his highness raided the sacristy."

"Ha!" snorted Aetius. "Attila expects me to hand over the treasures he would have stolen from the church if the priest hadn't been quick-witted enough to send them to safety in Rome? His self-delusion never ceases to amaze me! Why would I do that?"

The dwarf stared glumly back at Aetius, certain that at any instant he'd be run through by one, if not all, of the spears that clustered ready to pierce every vital organ in his body. Attila would kill any messenger who brought him such an insolent demand.

"My master told me to tell you that if you do not agree there will be a contest of arms."

"Indeed, you must be a jester, if you think any contest of arms could be avoided by caving in to Attila's endless lust for booty and power!"

Xerkon dropped his smile, fell to his knees and looked over his shoulder to make sure that Attila's emissary couldn't hear him. "Your lordship, I was sent here against my will, I beg you, spare my life and return me to my wife and children."

"So be it," said Aetius with a dismissive flick of his wrist. "Take him to the kitchen."

"No! No!" screamed Xerkon, "I beg you – don't boil me alive!"

"Be quiet, please!" said Andromeda, as the guards steered the blubbering dwarf towards her and she led him away. "You're going to be fed, not eaten."

"What d'you make of that?" Honorius asked Aetius once the hubbub had settled.

Aetius shrugged. "It's an insult, Attila's way telling me that I'm insignificant – a small, dark dwarf."

"Quite," said Honorius, sharing a rueful smile.

The evening resumed. Aetius appeared more than usually composed but, beneath his frigid exterior, blood roared through his arteries.

From the time that Aetius had been a child-hostage in the Huns' camp, he and Attila had been rivals. The Hun had plundered, murdered and burned his way through the East until the Emperor had paid him a bankrupting tribute to leave Rome alone but gold was never enough for Attila. He hewed down entire forests to build rafts and cross the Rhine into Gaul. Sweeping towards her heart, he was annihilating every creature and stalk of grass in his path.

Aetius pushed his plate away and sat up on his dining couch, scanning every inch of his surroundings and every face in the atrium from under glowering brows. Who was the traitor who'd told Attila where to find him? His eyes pierced the women then quickly passed to the barbarian princes.

Half-hidden in the shadows of the portico, Papianilla shivered as Aetius' gaze brushed over her, but every ounce of her being was focused on Sidonius. Her pride was full but poignant at the sight of her new husband. The glow of torch light on his thick, dark hair led her back to their wedding night, only four weeks earlier, when, for the very first time in their lives, they'd been left alone together. He'd lifted her across the threshold of her childhood home then set her down in the long colonnade that flanked the atrium. Together they had passed through a doorway wreathed with Aphrodite's myrtle, the eliptical leaves crumpled by slaves to release their perfume, and into their bedchamber at Avitacum.

The night had been warm and the room glowed with the steady flames of ten dozen beeswax candles. Sidonius had swept away the long, flame-coloured wedding veil from her face and, with both hands, had lifted the amaracus leaf crown, entwined with jasmine, from her head. She had stood motionless, a virgin, wondering what would come next. Heat rose up her neck as his fingers unravelled the ceremonial wedding knot in her belt. When the sash had fallen to the floor, his eyes had darkened and locked with hers while he ran his hands, ever so slowly, up under her white muslin gown.

Tonight, watching him talk with animation, the high bridge of his nose and his noble forehead gilded in turn by the flames of torches, her lips thickened at the memory of his kisses. She hoped he'd find a reason to come over and talk to her but only three times during the night's events had he so much as glanced in her direction. Over the fountain's tumbling water, she watched him play his role of diplomat. He was clothed in a crisply pleated, snow-white toga that exposed his thoroughbred frame. Movements of his hands, both masculine and sensitive, punctuated the elixir of wit and attentive pauses with which he charmed the barbarian princes.

But Attila's gift had brought the stench of evil into their midst and the evening was tarnished. Aetius retired early. When he rose to his feet and Sidonius followed, Papianilla was stricken by a rush of impending loss. She drew in her breath. Were there to be no farewells? No tears, no caresses? No lingering kisses? Could Sidonius not hold her in his arms? Would he come back from the wars with Attila?

As Andromeda prepared to descend the short flight of stairs to bid the guests farewell she slipped her arm through her daughter-in-law's. "Come and stand with me. It'll be your last chance to say good-bye before they march. Aetius allows no exceptions when it comes to camp discipline."

Papianilla looked towards Sedulla, her mother, aware that she'd be left alone at the table but Sedulla shooed her on with a long-fingered hand that wore only one simple, gold band. "Don't worry about me. Go say goodbye to your husband."

Aetius' face was stern as he thanked his host and hostess. He eyed the barbarian princes up and down as if he could see right through them, bid them a cursory good evening, then turned peremptorily on his heel. Square shouldered and decisive, he marched towards the gate.

It was visible only to those who knew and loved him deeply how heavily the fate of the world weighed on his back. Aetius felt the Hun's remorseless choke-hold around the Empire's neck as if it were cutting off his own air supply. Without the Goths even he, who had always found an answer to every problem, could see no solution. His army was outnumbered ten to one and if Avitus couldn't convince Theodoric to join him, no one could.

Sidonius fell in with the other officers and marched in time to Aetius' beat to the gate but when the sentries saluted the realisation that he was about to be cut off from Papianilla – perhaps forever – stabbed his heart. His feet marched forward but his head turned back at the moment the impenetrable gates of the villa thudded shut and cut the cord between him and his wife.

Trapped inside the villa, Papianilla put her hand up to her neck as if to capture the ghost of a kiss. Andromeda led her back up the stairs of the portico and the bride's face crumpled.

"Don't worry," said Andromeda, "Sidonius will come back safely. Avitus has told the magister militum that he expects Sidonius to give him intelligent grandchildren. Between them, he and Aetius'll make sure he's kept back from the front line and away from any serious fighting."

* * * * *

On the steep streets beyond the villa gate, Aetius was setting the pace. Without looking at Sidonius, he addressed him. "I hear from your father-in-law that you've taken it upon yourself to preserve the culture of our race. He tells me you are erudite."

Sidonius pulled his shoulders back, proud to be spoken to. "Not at all, sir, Avitus flatters me."

"But you write, don't you?"

"A little, sir, poems and letters, but they're of no consequence."

"Somebody has to write it down or it'll all be forgotten."

An unfamiliar pitch in the Field Commander's voice, a tone not quite vulnerable but no longer invincible, unsettled Sidonius. It rang out sharply against the crunch of the body-guards' boots.

"What will you write about Attila?" asked Aetius.

"Sir, I don't intend to compose anything about the Hun. Whatever I write will focus on the heroic deeds of our army under your command. Attila himself doesn't merit great mention."

"You're wrong about that. The future will never know what we stood for unless it knows what we stood against."

Aetius' comment hit Sidonius. He walked in silence, digesting it.

Aetius seemed to need acknowledgement. "Avitus told me you are intelligent, but you appear naïve."

"I apologise, sir, if you find me dull," Sidonius inclined his head, "it is an honour that you speak to me at all."

"I notice everything about every person in my presence." Aetius turned his slate-blue eyes towards Sidonius for the first time. "In common with many highly intelligent people, you appear to be stupid sometimes, but my estimation is that you do that in order to dissimulate your intentions. You were the epitome of charm with our barbarian guests tonight but while you spun your jokes you missed nothing. Your focus on the princes was professional, just as your thoughts for your bride were human. I'm glad to see that you care for her; Avitus is an old friend of mine."

"I hadn't realised that I was so transparent, Sir." Sidonius' cheeks grew hot.

"Transparency is a point in your favour. In return for your honesty I'll humour you by asking you one simple question, but in two parts. Tell me, young Sidonius, when you look around you and see Rome depart from her former dominions, what does she leave behind her?"

"Aqueducts, roads, Latin, sanitation, granaries, sculpture, poetry, a legal system . . ."

"Enough! You needn't be prolix. Now, the second part, and keep the answer brief. What does Attila leave behind him?"

Sidonius thought a moment – was there a trick? – then answered. "Nothing; nothing but ashes."

"Exactly. Do I need to say more about Attila?"

"No, sir. I've heard people fleeing him say that the grass will never grow again where Attila has been." Sidonius hung his head as he walked. The word prolix was stinging him. He'd just published his first volume of poetry and some critics had accused his style of being overly elaborate when all he was aiming to do was preserve the highest register of the Latin tongue.

Aetius' voice shifted down an octave. Tension sank its fangs into his shoulders. "Now is not the time for writing history; we're in the thick of making it. We must defeat Attila or millennia of Greek and Roman culture will be obliterated. You've heard the priests call the Hun *the scourge of God*?"

"Of course," said Sidonius, more confident on a subject he knew something about. "I've read what Salvian, the monk from Lerins, writes: that God has sent Attila to punish the Romans for having turned our own people into slaves with our burdensome taxes. He says that Attila's victories over us are to teach us to repent and prepare for the second coming of Christ. . ."

"Yes, yes, all that – we're familiar with Salvian. My view is simpler. Attila isn't the scourge of God; he's *the devil incarnate*. There will be no second coming. It is *our* job to defeat him."

With that the squadron arrived at the gates of the temporary Roman camp. It was surrounded by a double row of V-shaped ditches. Each of the first pair of trenches was twenty-feet wide and ten-feet deep. The first row was filled with "lilies" of upright, sharpened stakes hidden under brushwood and set out in a quincunx pattern. The second appeared deceptively clear but the crease at the bottom hid an ankle-breaking slot. The third had a relatively easy slope on the inward approach but was nearly vertical on the side nearer the camp. It invited invaders to slide into it and either face a steep climb up, under fire from the walls above, or turn their backs on the defenders and scrabble out against the influx of their own men. The fourth trench repeated the shape of the third but with the addition of three rows of stakes in the bottom. The inner wall was made from the packed tailings of the trenches, its base reinforced with closely cut stone, and was surmounted by a twenty-foot high palisade.

The fortifications were lit up by moonlight. Sidonius tilted his head back to see the top of the wall as they crossed one of the bridges over the earthworks and passed through the heavily armed gates. None of this had existed a week ago.

Inside the camp they marched up the main thoroughfare, itself sixty-feet wide, past the stables and rows of tents set out legion by legion, into the forum and towards the heart of the camp – Aetius' tent, the praetorium. Before it the eagles of eight legions were grounded in a glittering row. Behind them stood the standards of each century, barely breathing in the sultry night. For the first time ever, the flags of Frankish, Breton and Burgundian regiments hung with them, inside a Roman camp, all under Aetius' command.

On either side of the entrance to Aetius' tent stood two of his most trusted bucellarii, Optila and Thraustila, their armour gleaming and their bearing upright despite the lateness of the hour. They saluted and Aetius smiled. They'd seen hard battle together and he considered them brothers-in-arms rather than subordinates.

"An imperial messenger is waiting for you, sir," said Thraustila.

"Order him to report."

Thraustila marched off to rouse the messenger who'd been permitted to sleep while waiting.

"How've our allies been behaving inside our camp?" Aetius asked Optila.

"Better than they do on the battlefield, sir."

"Glad to hear it," Aetius smiled again, "or the camp would be chaos."

The courier and Thraustila marched back, saluted and presented Aetius with a scroll. Aetius unrolled and read it. Attila was marching on Orleans and Sangibanus, the Governor of the Alani garrison who held the city as Roman allies, had offered to open the city gates to the Hun.

Aetius' smile faded, but it was no surprise that Sangibanus had failed to put up a fight. His face inscrutable, Aetius read the rest of the despatch – a litany of Attila's atrocities and massacres – then dismissed the courier and his guards.

Orleans is as good a place as any to face the Hun. Tomorrow we'll start the 300-mile march to put an end to him. Without the support of the Goths. Tonight, I must work.

He entered his tent, alone.

His jaw locked and a knife-like line appeared between his brows. He let out a deep breath and undid the leather straps that held his polished silver breast and back plates together. They were beaten into an idealised sculpture of a hero's torso but, when he hung them on a hook and pulled his tunic off over his head, his own flesh outshone the armour. His muscles were knitted in perfect proportion, the product of thirty relentless years of physical warfare. Few were the scars and all well healed. He was so used to the nagging tweak in his right kneecap, smashed countless times by the impact of bone on bone as he rode off enemy cavalry, that he was unaware of it. He bent and deftly undid the intricate lacing of his greaves, his mind far away.

He was reflecting on the column the grateful people of Rome had erected in his honour at the door of the Senate house back in 439. It thanked him for "saving the Empire". When that column had been raised, he'd already spent half his life saving the empire. For him the battle to save the empire had never had a moment's respite. Would he be remembered for it? Or would Attila's name be passed down through the generations?

Aetius didn't like the answer he gave himself, but nor did it matter, he'd made his choices long ago. He bent over an opaque glass bowl of cold water on a tripod table, filled his hands with crystal liquid and splashed it over his face, keeping his eyes open. Turquoise drops coursed the sinews of his neck, less viscous than blood, more like tears than sweat.

He looked up into a mirror that hung above the bowl and thought of his father, a great Scythian warrior, who'd ruled the plains but had chosen to exchange his high-peaked chieftain's hat for a Roman horse-hair-crested helmet. His father, who'd traded horn-scale armour for plate. The warrior-chieftain, who'd ridden out to war with his face painted red or black or white. His father, primitive, but courageous and effective, who'd married a Roman woman. Together they gave their son to the empire that recognised his talent and made him one of her own.

Across his cheekbones, Aetius drew stripes of water, as if they were paint, then wiped them away and wrung out the cloth. Water coursed down his back. Behind the polished façade of the Roman magister militum, a savage drum still beat in Aetius' heart, and Attila knew it. The Hun's hatred for his rival was visceral, personal and tribal.

The night was hot and close. Clothed only in a linen loincloth, Aetius sat with his elbows propped on his campaign table, the fingers of one hand spread across his brow, lips set. He must stay awake and concentrate. The last of the cold water rolled down the canyon of his spine. His eyes focused on a stack of blank paper before him, he picked up his pen and wrote, his mind moving faster than his hand.

No wind whispered as he worked, ears alert to every sound. The sentry watch changed three times. Night drew in its breath and became its blackest. The Field Commander of the Western Empire wrote a final command for the Lyon garrison, which would be left behind once the eagles had flown, to demolish the camp after the legions had marched to face the Hun.

This army would never come back.

Love Defies Obedience

Lyon, Roman capital of Gaul
1st – 2nd September 451 AD

Surrounded by his snoring tentmates, Sidonius stared at the diffused light of the moon through the canvas roof. At dawn, he'd march to face Attila and his half-million Huns but he wasn't worried about that. He was trying to work out how to escape Aetius' camp and make love to Papianilla. He wanted her so much it hurt, but he would be stoned for desertion if caught.

In his mind's eye, he worked his way backwards over the top of the spiked palisade and down the twenty-foot drop the other side into the closest of the camp's three defensive trenches. How would he stop himself from sliding onto the rows of upright, razor-sharp spears in the bottom? He imagined squeezing his way through and climbing up the other side. The next trench would be easy, just a quick slide down and a scramble up the opposite slope, but he'd have to watch out for the ankle-breaker hidden in its crease. He frowned at the thought of the last trench. Even if he could weave his way through the razor-petalled 'lilies' in its depths, the sentries would hear him crashing through the bushes that hid them.

He thought of trying to bluff his way past the guards at the gate on the pretext that the Field Commander had ordered him to take a message to his father, the Governor of Gaul, but he knew they'd check his story before letting him out.

With a sigh, he rolled onto his side, realising that Aetius' defence system was just as effective at keeping soldiers inside the camp as it was at keeping them out. But the more he tried to forsake the idea of seeing Papianilla, the more his body ached for her.

As quietly as he could, he crawled towards the door and untied the lowest knot fastening it to the tent pole.

"Uhh?" one of his sleeping cohorts stirred.

"Need the latrines," Sidonius whispered.

He slipped out, tied the tent flap back down behind him then drew in a breath of night air and looked around to see if the sentries had spotted him. Up on the wall he could see the recognisable outline of one of the biggest men in camp, a gregarius called Brutus, who had a fierce reputation for fighting both on and off the training ground. Sidonius watched as Brutus stood still in the moonlight for a moment then turned away. A tethered horse whinnied gently and shifted its weight. The rhythm of boots marching along the creaking boardwalk behind the palisade became regular again. Only one light burned, in the praetorium at the centre of the camp, where the almighty Flavius Aetius worked alone through the night.

Sidonius was watching that steady glow of light when the sentries stopped pacing. His pulse notched up, but he feigned nonchalance and forced himself to walk over to the wooden benches with cut-out holes that covered the communal sewer. He picked up a sponge on a stick and took a seat near the end of a row.

Suddenly, out of the dark, one of Aetius' bucellari, marching like an aquilifer leading a legion into battle, headed in his direction. *Christ*, thought Sidonius, bending his neck so that his hair fell forward and hid his profile. The officer picked up a clean sponge on a stick from a stand at the end of the row, dipped it in water, and settled down on the seat four holes to his right. From behind the shield of his hair, Sidonius glanced sideways at him and, seeing that it was none other than Aetius' body-guard, Optila, wished he could sink into the sewer.

"Evening," grunted Optila then yawned widely. Sidonius nodded, still hiding his face. Optila made himself comfortable, chucked his sponge into a bucket of water that the slaves would empty in the morning, then got up and strolled towards his tent.

Sidonius let out a long breath and whispered a prayer of thanks. But time was running out. If he didn't move now the guards would soon be down to investigate. He splashed his own sponge into the bucket loudly enough for all the sentries to hear and walked over to where a bronze pipe nosed through the fortress wall at shoulder height. Fresh water spouted into an open ditch that flushed out the latrine trench. He stretched out his hands and made a loud show of washing them. The water licked silver tongues around his fingers in the moonlight while, out of the corner of his eyes, he watched for the moment Brutus would turn and march away along the palisade.

As soon as Brutus turned his back, Sidonius hoisted himself up onto the waterspout and from there onto the internal walkway. Although the inside of the palisade was as high as his head, he found a footing on the timber framing and sprung up and over the top. By the time Brutus turned back towards the latrines, Sidonius had disappeared.

Out of sight on the far side of the wall, he dangled from his fingertips above the spikes of the innermost defence trench. Dropping, with a painful thud, onto the bronze water pipe he locked his arms and legs around it and lay on his belly, waiting for the agony between his legs to subside. As soon as he could, he started dragging himself forward, in the direction of freedom, smiling victoriously – he had outwitted Aetius.

When he reached the flat stone top of the main aqueduct he stood up, ran the last twenty yards and jumped down to the safety of solid ground. But when he looked back along the pipe towards the palisade to make sure that no one was watching him, his smile disappeared. The wall was sheer on the exterior side; he wouldn't be able to return to the camp the way he'd got out.

But it was too late now to change his mind. The thought of being court-martialled and put to death in the morning made him even more determined to make the most of his last night with Papianilla, so he set off at a run uphill towards the Governor's mansion.

Avoiding the gates of his father's home, where the guards would certainly recognise and turn him in, he skirted round the outer wall and darted from the shadow of one tall cypress tree to the next until he came to the side of the villa. Three pairs of long, shuttered windows looked down from a height of nearly thirty feet. The limestone walls were bathed in moonlight so bright that he could distinguish the colour of the shutters, a blue-grey-green. These, he knew, were the windows of the best guest bedrooms and his beloved would be sleeping in one of them.

Gathering a handful of pebbles and selecting the heaviest, he took aim at the middle window but the stone hit just shy of the shutters and bounced back to the ground, landing with a thud that raised a wisp of dust. He put more muscle into the next throw and the stone clattered loudly against its target.

As the middle pair of shutters began to open, a warm rush of blood rose up his body, but it froze instantly when pewter light hit the hard angles of his mother-in-law, Sedulla's, face. She leant right out of the window, peering deeply but – Sidonius hoped – blindly into the darkness of the row of cypresses into which he'd shrunk. Her undressed hair bushed about her shoulders in snake-like ringlets that reminded him of the Medusa. *I'm done for now,* he thought and flattened his back against one of the trees until he heard the creak of shutters closing. Risking an upwards glance at the window, he took a deep breath and resolved that it'd be better to go round to the front gate and throw himself on his father's mercy than be caught by the guards.

Just as he was about to step out from the cover of the cypresses, he heard not one but two pairs of shutters opening above his head. Looking up again, he fancied that he could see Sedulla roll her eyes as she banged her pair shut. His heart danced at the sight of Papianilla, framed by the other window, leaning towards him with her arms outstretched, her smile shining bright in the moonlight. A shiver of delight made the hairs on his arms and legs stand on end as she signalled for him to wait then disappeared back into the darkness of her room.

With glacial slowness, five minutes passed before he saw a tall, slender wraith appear around the corner of the building. Moonlight painted the folds of her gown in silvered whites as she flew towards him, her quick footsteps scrunching tiny pebbles on the dusty summer ground. Without pausing, she reached out her hand and pulled him through the row of cypresses towards a walled orchard. At its rusty iron gate, she took out a key and unlocked the chains. Sidonius put his hand around her wrist and led her into a quadrangle that smelled of summer then locked his lips to hers. Rows of trees greeted them, ripe plums and figs hanging on bowed boughs, waiting for the harvest.

Together at last, they savoured the taste of desire, made urgent by the fear of discovery and death. His hand reached up and cupped her breast, his thumb and finger caressing the nipple. They broke off to breathe. Neither spoke as they walked hand in hand to an apple tree, whose branches curved close to the ground under the weight of the crop, and he laid her down under its bower. Papianilla's raven hair mermaided around her shoulders. The whole world floated while Sidonius fathomed her widening pupils, ran his hand up under the gossamer of her chiton and pushed it aside. Unable to wait a moment more, he entered her and her eyelids closed.

The full-faced moon, peaking through the apple leaves, was the only witness to the gleaming muscles of his back, dewed with sweat, as his breathing quickened. Papianilla opened her eyes and watched as his abdomen tautened. Her body arced to meet his thrust and a cry escaped her lips, then the world shifted. He collapsed into her embrace and his breathing slowed. Worried he would be too heavy on her breasts, he rolled off, lay at her side and wove his fingers through hers.

With a gentle smile, she lay on the dew-laden grass, holding him as if she could never bear to be apart. A rare breeze stirred the leaves above their heads and cooled their skin. Her cheek on his shoulder, together they looked up and tried to pick out the stars, now outshone by the risen moon. Time seemed infinite, but a humble biting insect pulled Papianilla back to earth. "You'll be stoned to death if Aetius finds out you escaped camp."

"He'll never know, not unless your mother informs him."

"My mother?" laughed Papianilla, "she won't betray us. When she saw you under the cypresses she woke me up. My parents have been married for over twenty years and every one of them she's sent her husband off to war not knowing if he'd survive another campaign season. She understands our agony."

Sidonius smiled and rolled onto his side to look at her. "That's impossible," he brushed a tendril of hair from her cheek, "no one has ever loved like this before."

He placed gentle kisses the length of her neck, across the fine bones of her clavicle and down the soft skin of her belly. She put her hands in his hair but didn't stop him as he moved lower. Pleasure coursed through her body. He rose above her again. Wrapping his hand in the waves at the nape of her neck, he lifted her up and turned over so that she was on top of him. Moonlight caressed the curves of her body as he put his hands around her waist and urged her to move to his rhythm. Just before their passion peaked again, they turned so that it was Papianilla who could see his torso outlined against the stars in all the power and glory of youth. This time, afterwards, they slept.

But a jealous sun, driving away the watchful moon, turned the sky green and prised open Sidonius' eyes. "I need to get back to camp before it's light."

"I know." Papianilla was already on her feet, brushing leaves and dirt from her chiton. They walked hand-in-hand back to the orchard gate without speaking. They knew that this might be the last time ever they could be together. When they'd stepped out of the haven of the old stone walls, Papianilla locked the gate, the orchard, the night and all it meant, behind her.

"The words 'I love you' are inadequate," said Sidonius, searching her face, seeking to memorise her features in the way that only a soldier going to battle must.

Papianilla looked up at him and quoted her wedding vows. "*Ubi tu Gaius, ego Gaia.*"

"*Ubi tu Gaia, ego Gaius,*" replied Sidonius, "where you are happy, I am happy."

He left her then, with one last kiss, and sprinted off down the line of cypress trees so that she wouldn't see his brimming tears.

By the time the camp palisade came back into view, the sky had turned grey. He followed the aqueduct down to the perimeter wall, searching in vain for a potential foothold. Panic rose in his stomach as he walked back along the top of the aqueduct, jumped down where it neared the ground, and set off towards the main gate. He had no choice but to surrender and face the consequences but, even if that meant death, it had been worth it to show Papianilla his love.

Inside the fortress, Aetius had risen from his habitual shallow sleep and was walking along the palisade path, greeting each sentry by name as he passed. Infallible instinct drew his eyes to the form of a single man, out of uniform but distinctly Roman, approaching the main gate through the half-light. Aetius focused, then raised an eyebrow in amusement and surprise. Before the guards on watch could call out a challenge to the approaching figure, he ordered the gate to be opened and the son of the Praetorian Prefect to be escorted directly to the praetorium.

By the time Sidonius arrived, Aetius was seated with his legs outstretched on a cross-framed chair to the side of his desk. Sidonius and his captors saluted and Aetius ordered the guards to withdraw.

Sidonius stood stiff, his face crimson with shame, aware that he had disappointed the greatest of men and ready to be told he was going to be court-martialed for desertion.

Thin-lipped, Aetius drafted orders on a wax tablet and let the boy appreciate the gravity of his disobedience for a full three minutes before speaking. "A man has never been stoned for returning to camp, Apollinaris."

A wave of relief swept through Sidonius, but he braced himself for an alternative punishment to stoning. The magister militum rose to his feet and walked around him, a mixture of disgust and amusement on his face. "You're lucky this morning, I've no time for distractions and can't afford to lose a single fighting man. I know where you've been and why. What I want to know is how you escaped my camp."

While Sidonius explained, Aetius put on his armour and tightened the straps between his back and breastplates, a quirk at the corner of his lips. "Your antics show determination and initiative," he said, thinking *I hope you got the girl pregnant.* "Dismissed."

To Brutus, who had failed in his duty as a sentry, Aetius showed no such mercy and ordered the errant gregarius to be flogged with a nine-headed whip.

Attila Takes Orleans

Orleans, Gaul
15th September 451 AD

The somnolent River Loire nestled the city of Orleans in the crook of her elbow. Pale and delicate, like a girl too pretty for her own good, Orleans turned an elegant face towards languid plains – Attila's favourite terrain – with nothing to protect her but the long white petticoats of her limestone walls.

The Empire had granted federal status and the right to settle Orleans to a barbarian race, the Alani, on condition that they protect her on Rome's behalf. But as soon as Sangibanus, the limp-wristed Alani governor, heard that Attila was coming he sent out a stream of panicky messages offering to throw open the gates – if only the Hun would spare him.

Attila replied with a series of escalating threats that ended with, "Open all the gates or I'll cut off your balls, force you to swallow them in front of me, then strangle you with your own guts". Sangibanus' bowels emptied on hearing this.

One of the effects of Rome's army cost-cutting was that a supply of career officers became available to her allies and the Alani had recruited one of them, a bear-like praefectus castrorum named Ursus, to command the Orleans garrison. When Sangibanus sent a page to give the order to open the gates, the youth found Ursus directing a group of soldiers and civilians demolishing buildings near the forum and piling the rubble up into makeshift barricades.

While the page shouted to be heard over the blows of pick-axes on rock and timber, Ursus tipped his helmet back, wiped sweat from his brow and stood drumming his fingers on the hilt of his sword. By the time the messenger had finished reciting the order to capitulate, a sneer had spread over the Roman's face.

"Must be something wrong with my hearing," he said to his centurion, Silvanus, "no one in his right mind would invite the Hun to torture, rape and kill our citizens, now would he?"

"No sir."

"You got the message wrong, laddy," said Urus to the page, "so I'm ignoring it. Now run on back and tell that yellow-livered governor of yours that he needs to give his orders like a Roman – from the front line – or we can't hear'em."

"Boy could make himself useful digging a ditch," said Silvanus, "I'll find 'im a spade."

The page's eyes darted over the hustle of civilians ripping buildings apart with their bare hands then he stripped off his tunic, grabbed the spade and joined them. Ursus gave Silvanus a nod then swung his pick into a fragment of frescoed wall and it crashed at their feet.

With grim determination, Ursus hacked away, knowing that the ultimate outcome of a battle where a defending garrison of only five thousand faced a blood-lusting foe of half-a-million could never be in doubt. But Attila hadn't yet brought up rafts to cross the Loire and if Ursus could hold the bridge it'd be an escape route for the noncombatants. The ground sloped down towards the river so he'd be fighting on the back foot every inch of the way but he'd hold up with his back to the water for as long as he had to, or as long as he could, whichever came first. A priest had told him that St Genevieve's prayers had saved the people of Paris but Ursus had no time for saints. He put his trust in his sword and Roman generals like Avitus and Aetius.

Horn-blasts from the watch towers straightened Ursus' spine. Protecting his head with his arm, he squinted up into a hail of clay incendiary grenades as they flew over the city wall, shattered on rooftops and roads, and splattered into flames. Tandem battering rams pounded at the gates facing the plains. "Fall back to the first barricade!"

With debris crashing round them and their eyes smarting from smoke, the squadron bolted for cover behind the barricade. Ursus stared out between the top of the stacked-up rubble and his shield. Huns in pointed helmets were scuttling like scorpions over the ramparts and, despite being covered by soaking wet cattle skins, the roofs of the buildings in the forum were ablaze. But, oblivious to the flames, a lone figure in a cassock was walking across the forum towards a church. "What's that madman doing?"

"He's the priest of that church, sir," said a young gregarius, "shall I try to save him?"

"Too late."

"I can do it." The youth's eyes judged the distance between the barricade and the dark doors that had swallowed up the priest.

"Go, and be quick!"

Smoke enveloped the soldier while battering rams thundered in Ursus' ears. He was regretting sending the boy to his death when, a few minutes later, coughing his lungs out, the lad scrambled back over the barricade. "The priest won't come, sir. I tried dragging him, but he held onto the altar, praying for a miracle."

"Fanatics, all of 'em Christians," said Ursus, his eyes on the northern gates as they splintered, cracked, let out a final groan and fell from their hinges. Ursus glanced over his shoulder to the second barricade, but it was too late to pull back. In a torrent of flashing scimitars, Huns surged through the gap and across the forum.

"Form up!!!" yelled Ursus over their shrieking war-cries – "Lock shields and make a stand!"

The Romans slammed their scuta into a wall of steel, but the attackers' weight pushed it back, back and back . . .

Blood trickled down the gutters towards the last refuge by the river.

* * * * *

Five miles outside the city walls, under a sky of relentless blue, Aetius scoured the plains for Attila. The summer drought had brittled the grass and it puffed into powder under his horse's hooves as they advanced at a quick trot. At the smell of fire in the distance, the horses, except for Aetius' mount, Achilles, pricked forward their ears and flared their nostrils. Achilles held one ear forward and the other back, as if listening to the generals.

Avitus rode at Aetius' side. He too searched the plains, but not for Attila, for Sidonius. He'd told his son-in-law never to volunteer for anything in the army – it was almost always fatal – but when Aetius had called for a rider to go behind Attila's lines Sidonius had stepped forward. To Avitus' surprise, instead of ordering him back, Aetius had said something cryptic about how Sidonius was suited to the mission and let him go.

Avitus saw no sign of Sidonius, but a pall of black smoke rose on the blue horizon. He raised his red-gauntleted hand and pointed. "The city's ablaze."

Aetius looked the image of the eagle for whom he was named as his eyes pierced the distance. "Attila's breached the walls. Gives us the chance to catch the rat in a trap of his own making."

From a distance, with tongues of fire flicking in and out of its window-slits, the slender watch tower of Orleans was the silent personification of a ravaged woman screaming for help. While Avitus stared at sheets of flame rising from the foot of the walls, Aetius lifted his chin in the direction of a flare of dust kicked up by a galloping horse. "Looks like Sidonius is on his way back."

Avitus peered at the approaching horseman long enough to confirm who it was, then a smile raised his lips and he started humming a tune.

"What're you singing?" asked Aetius.

"An old song but with my own lyrics – *it's a nice day to burn a city* were the words that came to mind. Have you noticed that a wind's come up and is blowing the flames in the direction of the river? The whole city will be ablaze by the time we get there."

"I've always enjoyed your optimism, Avitus, and your gift for stating the obvious. The wind just means we must ride faster. The only way to boost our ranks is to rescue what's left of the Orleans garrison."

"I s'pose it'd be too much to hope that Attila will burn himself to death," mused Avitus.

Aetius was in no mood to laugh. "The day we rely on the vagaries of the wind as a strategy, we're finished."

Avitus' eyes sparkled with mischief under the shadow of his helmet. "I wasn't proposing *let's wait and see if Attila accidentally burns himself to death* as a tactic when your alternative of *lead a charge into a wall of fire* is clearly superior."

In a flurry of dust Sidonius reined up beside them. Clouds of steam rose from his horse's flanks and he smelt of singed hair.

"Report," ordered Avitus.

"Attila controls Orleans but the garrison's fighting a street by street defensive action and holds the Loire bridge. They can't last long. Flames are leaping the firebreaks."

"Who's leading the defence?" asked Aetius.

"A Roman praefectus castrorum, Ursus."

Aetius glanced at Avitus. "D'you know him?"

Avitus nodded. "Career soldier, worked his way up through the ranks. He'll hold out till the last."

"Four miles to the gates," said Aetius. "Enemy numbers?"

"The plains are black with the Huns and their allies, sir."

"How many, I asked."

"An Alani decanus told me half a million. He'd tried to keep count when Attila manoeuvred into position for the attack, but it was impossible because the enemy stretched out of sight."

Aetius' face was expressionless but a dark flicker crossed his eyes.

"Fall in, equites."

When Sidonius had taken his place amongst the other young officers, Avitus said, under his breath, "At this morning's muster, we numbered 39,891 men fit to fight."

"You think I don't know that? Let's hope your friend Theodoric doesn't swing his army against us when battle engages."

"Every Gothic man or boy who can walk and carry a sword marches with him, including his own three sons," said Avitus. "There's no rear guard in Toulouse. This isn't about plunder for Theodoric, it's about the survival of his race." Avitus judged that the moment wasn't right to remind Aetius that, as part of his negotiation to get Theodoric to fight for the Romans, he'd promised the Goth half of whatever booty they recaptured from Attila.

"A Goth's a Goth," said Aetius, "but you've taught Theodoric a thing or two, including how to march every man in his nation 1,000 miles in the heat, in good order and a respectable time. The Burgundians, Franks, Bretons and Saxons are all lagging behind."

"I've known Theodoric since he was a boy. Trained him in the art of Roman warfare, but it's to his credit that he's with us today." Avitus became pensive for a moment then added, "I'd venture you won't have to fight the Goths as long as I live."

"Then I hope you live long."

"That's always been my intention."

Both fell silent as smoke made them sniff and their eyes started to water. The horses whinnied and snorted. Aetius raised his hand to summon Avitus' son, Ecdicius, and Thorismund, Theodoric's heir. "Ride forward – two columns, flanking movement. Rout the Hun rear ranks."

The young commanders raised their banners and galloped off at the head of two phalanxes of cavalry.

When the horsemen had disappeared into the clouds of dust kicked up by their horses, Aetius took a moment to scrutinise Avitus. His lifelong friend rode square-shouldered at his side. Decades of battle had carved a history of courage, resilience, power and unexpected mercy on Avitus' face. It was craggy, the skin leathered and deeply lined, but his blue eyes still danced. "D'you think you're still up to hand to hand combat in narrow city streets, old man?" Aetius asked.

"When I order my men to charge into a burning inferno, they expect me to be in front of them."

"Stay mounted. You won't be able to run fast enough to keep up with them."

"I never said anything about getting off my horse, I'm not senile you know."

Aetius smiled. "What d'you think – attack directly or wait for the Gothic infantry to march up?"

"No time to wait."

With an imperceptible clench of his muscles Aetius increased the pressure on Achilles' flanks. The horse pricked both ears towards the flames and lengthened his gait. The magister militum's eyes locked on his target. "Sound the order for battle positions."

The rallying call of one hundred trumpets blasted the order down the line. Hearts pumping, the troops jostled into formation.

"Weapons at the ready!"

Aetius' standard-bearer raised a scarlet banner on which a golden eagle swooped ready to strike.

"Charge!"

The battle cry of ten legions in unison surged like a tidal wave over the plains and echoed back off Orleans' limestone walls. The horses flattened their ears to their skulls and thundering hooves drummed up storm-clouds of dust.

Two miles behind, Theodoric the Goth heard the roar of war and trebled his pace.

The Chase Begins

Attila, lost in the ecstasy of a gush of blood from the throat of the kneeling priest, nonetheless noticed in his peripheral vision that his accomplice, in the process of shovelling gold candlesticks and a crucifix into a saddlebag, had frozen. In the momentary silence caused by his transfixion, Attila heard the bellow of Roman horns. Blood dripping from his dagger, he stood up and cocked his head. The rousing bray sounded like the rallying call of at least eight legions and that surprised him as his spies had said that Aetius marched with less than twenty thousand men. Attila cursed profanely, his mind whirling, then ordered a retreat. He wouldn't risk being caught between the remnants of the Alani garrison and that ubiquitous kill-joy, Flavius Aetius – a hex on his name!

Confident that his army still outnumbered Aetius' twenty to one, Attila was more annoyed at being interrupted while taking his pleasure than he was worried by the Roman's arrival. The plains around Orleans lent themselves to his forte, the sweeping cavalry charge, and he had more than enough numbers to wipe the Roman out. The prospect of sticking a sword through the neck of the man he hated above all others made him salivate.

With a sneer on his face, on short, bandy legs Attila jogged out of the church, swung up into his saddle and cantered past sooted walls, crackling with flame, to the plain. But as he passed through the gates the sight of his men in full rout kicked the breath from his lungs. Even worse, one of the two phalanxes of cavalry scything their way through his Huns was not Roman but Goth. While shock travelled down his gullet to his belly, a thundering roar assailed his ears. He twisted his torso and his jaw dropped. Behind red, legionary banners, twenty thousand Roman infantrymen were charging straight towards Orleans' walls of flame.

Flashing his scimitar around his head, Attila shrieked a blood-curdling cry and bared the whites of his eyes. The stench of his tribesmen's panic told him that he couldn't stop their rout so he whipped his horse till it bled and led their flight.

The Coward Sangibanus

Orleans, Gaul
15th September 451 AD

Aetius, wearing body armour that fitted like a second skin, took the marble steps up to the governor's palace two at a time. His bloodstained cloak billowed behind him. Optila, Thraustila and a steel-clad squadron of eight clanked in his wake. Gates swept wide to let them pass then slammed shut as white-faced Alani made way for their rescuers.

Aetius called a halt in the centre of Sangibanus' audience chamber. The flames of torches reflected in his shoulder plates, as if his armour burned with its own fire. He stood with arms crossed and legs astride.

"Magister militum," intoned the Alani governor, prostrating himself at his feet, "I'm at your service."

"Save your grovelling for someone who's impressed by it, Sangibanus, we all know you gave the order to open the gates for Attila."

"I had no choice –"

"Don't waste your breath!" Aetius snapped. "Get up. I'm here to talk about tomorrow, not what happened today. Muster your troops for my inspection – parade ground formation, half an hour before sunset. Able-bodied and walking wounded, no exceptions. We march at dawn."

Sangibanus' face turned puce. "You intend to pursue Attila?"

Aetius raised level eyebrows at him. "Not only do I intend to pursue him, but you will too. You'll honour your treaty with Rome and march beneath my standard."

Sweat broke out along Sangibanus' upper lip. He dipped his head and studied the cyclamen toes of the soft-kid slippers peeking out from under his robes of office, then raised his eyes to Aetius and summoned his most persuasive tone. "I can understand that you expect the Alani to give you assistance . . ."

Aetius barely resisted snorting at the suggestion that the Alani were helping him rather than the other way around.

" . . . but the fact is there's little point in pursuing Attila now. He's already destroyed every town and city north of Orleans. He fled from the field of battle today as fast as his horse could carry him. Victory is yours, magister militum, you saved our city."

Aetius didn't deign to speak.

"There's nothing to be gained from chasing Attila!" spluttered Sangibanus.

The curl of a sneer raised the edge of Aetius' lip.

Sangibanus wrung his sweaty hands and tried to calm himself. Emotional outbursts wouldn't alter the resolve of the Field Commander of the Western Empire. Taking a deep breath, he changed tack. "Attila has burnt every blade of grass in Northern Gaul. Even he can do no worse. The campaigning season's almost over. He's in full retreat and won't be back till spring next year – if at all! That gives us time to develop a more considered strategy."

"Sangibanus!" The words on Aetius' lips were "cowards disgust me" but he held them in check. The Alani were federate allies, not under his direct command, and he couldn't assume that Sangibanus' troops would mutiny against their governor and march with the Romans now that they'd saved Orleans. "We're here in force with the entire Gothic nation, Bretons, Burgundians, Franks and allied tribes. The Saxons have sailed from Britain to fight at our side."

Sangibanus stood, staring glassy-eyed at Aetius' stern jaw and eyes afire with purpose, his knees shaking and his mouth went dry. Sweat trickled down his forehead while his mind raced through the host of unpalatable alternatives. Aetius had already stationed divisions of Goths within the city walls. Like the wolves they were, they would loot and massacre if Aetius let them off his leash. And if he didn't comply with Roman orders, Aetius would have him arrested and executed for treason. All in all, the least terrifying of the miserable options he faced was to submit to Aetius and march in the general direction of Attila. With any luck, the Romans would never catch up with the Hun and the Alani would be sent home without having to fight.

Aetius, standing straight, the muscles of his back flaring out from his waist and his legs tensed with unleashed power, watched Sangibanus deliberate. Derision danced in his eyes as they flickered over the Governor's gold-embroidered robes. "Get yourself out of that dress and into some armour. Report as ordered. You have only one choice, fight under my command, or die."

Sangibanus folded into a grovelling bow and his bejewelled rings scraped the floor. With the barest nod Aetius acknowledged his abdication, posted sentries to make sure he didn't attempt to flee overnight, then marched out.

* * * * *

Seated on a cross-framed chair in the praetorium, Avitus was waiting for the magister militum. He held his helmet on his lap, running gnarled fingers up and down over the tips of the horsehair crest. Sidonius was standing duty outside with the rest of his bodyguard and Avitus heard their salute then Aetius' broad-shouldered outline appeared in the doorway. Avitus' knees cracked as he rose from his seat then thumped a fist to his chest. Aetius returned the salute and the moment of formality passed.

"Everything in order with Sangibanus?" asked Avitus.

"I left him trying to find his suit of armour." Agile as a panther, Aetius took two strides across the tent and poured himself a glass of water. "How goes it here?"

"Good news from the advance cavalry," Avitus' face beamed with silent pride, "they've destroyed Attila's rear-guard."

"Excellent. Hun casualties?"

"Ten thousand dead."

"Our losses?"

"Light. All cohorts are still at battle strength. I've ordered both Roman and Goth cavalry to rest while we bring up the infantry and artillery."

"On that positive note, old man," said Aetius, "let's go and see what we've rounded up in Orleans."

Avitus put on his helmet and tightened the strap under his jutting jaw. Shoulder to shoulder, the generals marched out. Avitus gave Sidonius' uniform a reproachful look as he fell in behind them. Sidonius hadn't had time to wipe splattered blood off his armour since he'd joined the charge against the Huns.

They marched past smouldering buildings and rounded a corner into the forum where ranks of soot-covered wounded saluted in unison. Sidonius struggled not to cough as smoke rasped fingernails down his throat. Through stinging eyes, for the first time in his life, he beheld the slaughterhouse of war. At the far end of the forum, next to neatly stacked rows of allied dead, hacked off limbs were piled high. A single hand had tumbled from its heap and lay alone on the ground. Black hairs crawled like spiders' legs across its waxy back. Sidonius felt an absurd urge to pick it up and put it back with the rest. He clenched his jaw and swallowed hard, blaming the smoke for the tears in his eyes.

The dead numbered more than the living, but, as if that meant nothing, his father-in-law was quipping to Aetius, "Sangibanus' armour looks a little tight on him."

Aetius eyed the roll of fat protruding between Sangibanus' breast and backplates. "It's been a long time since he's worn it. But look how prettily he sits his horse." Aetius ran his eyes along the line of troops.

"That beaten up old wreck standing next to him in the praefectus castrorum's uniform must be your Ursus."

"I guess he must be." Avitus struggled to recognise him. An open gash ran from Ursus' forehead to his chin and had closed one eye, perhaps forever. His jaw was broken and his right arm, not yet in a sling, hung at a sickening angle. Blood seeped through a bandage on his thigh, spiralled in uncongealed stripes round his leg and pooled beneath his foot. Yet, despite his injuries, Ursus stood upright.

"I think he's done his bit," said Aetius through gritted teeth, reluctant to let go of a single fighting man.

"He wouldn't make it through the first day's march," said Avitus, eager to save a brave warrior from a senseless death, "better get his men used to taking orders from someone new before we engage battle."

The generals marched, with jaws set, along the ranks. Avitus, with barely a nod to his junior officers, singled out the men he deemed would be more of a liability than a help in battle and reassigned them to tasks in the supply chain or repairing weaponry.

No matter how weary they were, the soldiers grew two inches taller as the generals passed. Even the coward, Sangibanus, straightened his spine.

Sola

The road from Chateaubleau to Provins
Roman Province of Lugdunesis
18th September 451 AD

The tall woman walked alone. She wore a cape of midnight blue, drawn up closely to the base of her neck, and a capacious hood that hid her face. There were no carts or coaches going in her direction so she forged her own path against waves of refugees. Ashen-faced, feet grimed by the road, they clustered in wordless groups. Loads shifted on haphazardly stacked waggons and chickens squawked in willow coops. Children whimpered on their mothers' hips and oxen lowed under the whip.

Sola, the blue-hooded woman, was heading from Paris to Reims – a nine-day trek that she'd finish in six – in search of her husband and daughter. The last she'd heard, Attila had besieged Orleans and it made no sense that these refugees were heading towards, not away from, the scourge of God. She asked the calmest of them whence they came. Most were fleeing Vertus, where Hun horses had devoured the grain harvest; or Epernay, where grape vines burned, or Metz, where ravens were picking out the eyes of corpses in the streets. But none came from Reims, her home.

For speed and safety, Sola cut across fields shimmering with unburned corn, but when she came to a tangled forest she had to return to the road. Smoke was trapped under sombre branches and dark tree trunks were girdled with knotted undergrowth.

Behind a thicket, about fifty paces ahead of her, crouched three ruffians. One worried at a torn sandal with a stick but looked up from time to time, on the look-out for their next victim.

He grunted to the others – "S'that a woman or a man?"

"A woman! Can't you see by the way she walks?" answered a rogue whose broken nose had set skewed to the right of his face.

"She's big," said a taller, thinner accomplice, "looks young."

"A bonus for us," the third one smirked, exposing a missing eyetooth. "We can take turns. Who's going first?"

"Your turn this time, isn't it?" said the thin one, who kept count of these things.

"What's a woman doing out here alone?" asked the skew-nosed leader.

"Maybe she isn't," said the brains of the pack. "I wager a man'll come round that corner soon." They leant forward, peering through the bushes, but no one emerged from the gloom.

"Reckon it's time to 'ave her then!" The leader leapt onto the road.

Sola paused for a moment, looked at each man in turn, a slight lift forming at the edge of her lips. Burgundian deserters, no doubt. Three was one more than she felt confident she could handle, but only one was heavily armed and that was with a primitive club. They all had knives in their belts, but none had a sword or a spear.

She stood her ground and looked the leader in the eye. "I'm not looking for trouble," she said in Latin, not sure whether they'd speak it, but hoping that using the imperial tongue would increase her stature.

"Shouldn't be out by yourself then," he sneered, fondling the ball of his club.

Sola kept her eyes on him but saw the others circle, like wolves, in her peripheral vision. She listened to their open-mouthed breathing as they took up positions, one three paces behind her, one in front and the other four paces away at forty-five degrees to her left. All so predictable.

"Please don't make me do this," she said.

The leader thwacked the end of his club up and down in the ball of his hand and shot a globule of spit from the corner of his mouth.

With her left hand Sola undid the bow that held her cape in place and it cascaded to her feet. She raised her chin and pushed her hair back from her face in a gesture that could be interpreted as an invitation but, in fact, denoted resignation. Then she took two steps forward to give herself room.

Her assailants focused on her exposed throat and the rise of her breasts.

"She's begging for it." The man on her left licked his chops.

"Grab 'er!" yelled the leader and they all rushed in.

The foul odour of rotten teeth clouded Sola's face as the man at her back closed grubby hands round her throat and his leader aimed his club at her forehead.

Like lightning, her right hand pulled her finely-honed gladius from the scabbard hidden in the folds of her skirt. Left hand locked over right, she swung the sword back over her head and with double-fisted force rammed it into the neck of the man strangling her. As fast as it had pierced his jugular, she pulled it out and in one arc the blade flew over her shoulder and spliced open the skull of the man with the club.

The third man pulled up short, gaping at the body with its scalp split open, and a stain spread down the front of his tunic. His eyes swivelled to the kneeling figure, who was grabbing at his own throat now, trying to stop the spurting blood from pulsing out, then he turned on his heel and ran for his life.

Her heart pounding and her wrists jarred by the impact of blade on bone, Sola watched him flee until he was out of sight. When she was sure that the vagabond wasn't coming back, she turned to look at the man gurgling behind her. He was still on his knees, clutching his neck.

She raised her sword above his hunched shoulders and, with both hands on the hilt, stabbed straight down through the flesh between his ribs to pierce his heart.

It was an act of mercy, not vengeance.

She'd never found pleasure in taking a life, despite her extraordinary gift for it, but since the first time she'd faced the choice of kill or die, she'd chosen to live.

Her name meant "she who walks alone, unprotected," and that was how the slave-trader had termed her when he'd put her on the block and knocked her down to the highest bidder. Her mother had called her "Sola" because it meant "unique" but the men who'd dealt in her flesh had never thought of that.

Her arm was shaking slightly as she looked for something in the woods to clean her sword. She wouldn't sheath it dripping with blood. Wiping it on the grass, she pulled out a small drinking flask and emptied all but a few mouthfuls over the blade. She was carrying nothing else that she could afford to sacrifice.

Her eyebrows furrowed. *I've lost my fitness, but still have my reflexes.*

Fifteen years had passed since Sola, a barbarian, had married a Roman magistrate. She'd thought then that she'd never have to kill again but times had changed and her old skills could not be set aside.

She picked up her cloak, which was splattered with blood but whose colour hid it, and fastened it at her throat. Needing to see and hear clearly on her way through these woods, she didn't pull up the hood.

At the next stream, she knelt to wash her gladius and fill her flask. Questions tumbled through her mind like rapids over the river stones. The refugees on the road had been heading towards Orleans, not away from it – so where was Attila now? And not one of those she'd spoken with had been fleeing from Reims. Had Attila massacred all its citizens?

Sola shivered. All around her was danger of every kind yet, since leaving Paris, she hadn't seen a single legionnaire. Would – could – the Romans defend Gaul or would they abandon her?

Her frown sharp, Sola corked the flask and stood up. She must find her daughter, Leonida, and Marcus her husband. Alert to the sounds of the forest, she strode forward. But her stomach was knotted with dread that, if she ever reached Reims, she'd find them both dead.

Accidental Battle

Pouans-les-Vallées
Roman Province of Lugdunesis
19th September 451 AD

"Four legions of Gepids, sir," reported a scout who'd galloped to catch Aetius at the head of his cavalry column, "under Ardaric's banner."

"Hmph," said Avitus who was riding at Aetius' side. Tough and audacious, Ardaric the Gepid was one of Attila's most favoured generals. 'Gepid' meant 'slow' in their language, but they were doughty warriors and heavily armoured.

"Their position?" asked Aetius.

"Five miles to the rear on the road from Mery. They're marching more slowly than we are so the gap is widening."

The breath hissed out between Aetius' teeth.

Avitus glanced sideways at his friend, sharing his frustration. Aetius' profile, more pointed than normal, reminded him of his favourite hunting hound. "You won't order us to rear march to engage them when Attila's up ahead."

"Obviously not."

Avitus scratched his chin. "They're no threat to us, but we've left our allies trailing behind us. The Gepids will gain control of the bridge over the River Aube before the Franks and Burgundians get there."

Aetius nodded. "You've always been keen to test your strength against Gepid armour. How many men would you need to hold that bridge against Ardaric's legions?"

Avitus smiled. "A cohort'll do."

"With only one cohort, even you can't stand long against four legions of Gepids."

"I only have to stand long enough for the Franks and Burgundians to catch up. They number ten thousand each. When they arrive, we'll have Ardaric and his Gepids trapped."

Aetius nodded. "Don't engage battle unless you have to. Attila'a our target, not Ardaric."

"As if I need reminding!"

"Happy for a Tribune to command the rearguard?"

"No, I'll command it myself," said Avitus, "I didn't spend all those months rounding up our allies to lose them now. Aegidius the Frank, is capable and Heva is brave but with Ardaric in charge of the Gepids, I want that bridge under my personal command."

"March a cohort back and secure it."

Avitus rapped his finger on the pommel of his saddle, "You need that cohort more than I do. Two centuries'll do."

"Only two centuries now?"

Avitus winked at him. "The bridge is narrow and the river's deep. In all that armour, those Gepids won't be swimming across. We'll be alright."

With an amused smile, Aetius shook his head. "Take whatever you judge yourself to need, but don't die young, my friend."

"It's far too late for that!"

* * * * *

Ardaric, the Gepid, quick-marched his infantry towards the bridge over the Aube. The sun was past its zenith but there was daylight enough to cross the river, cut across country and catch up with Attila when he pitched camp for the night.

However, as the bridge came into sight Ardaric caught the flash of sun on steel and ordered a halt. His eyes narrowed at the sight of Roman squadrons locking shields. Beyond their wall of steel, a forest of upright spears hid the bridge. Ardaric cursed in the names of his Nordic gods then ordered his scouts to find another route across the river. An attack on the bridge would funnel his men into a killing machine.

Half an hour passed before the scouts rode back with news that they could ford the river five miles to the west, near a hamlet called Pouans-les-Vallées, where an aspen wood stood on one side of a field that banked gradually down to slow-flowing water. The far side of the ford was marshy and dotted with ponds, but it was the best crossing they had found, and time was running out. Ardaric squinted into the lowering sun, ordered his horns to blow an about-face, then led his black-tunicked, mounted elite away from the solid footing of the road onto a sludgy band of grass. The infantry slid down the bank and snaked along behind them.

By the time they reached the ford, the afternoon was fading. Anxious to reach Attila before nightfall, Ardaric entrusted the infantry to the orders of his second in command, Gunderit, and cantered his cavalry across the ford and up the other side. The horses' hooves pulverised the banks, turning powder to mud, and the river grew wider as its banks subsided.

Massed in orderly cohorts behind lank banners, the Gepid infantry rested their shields on their greaves or leant on their spears, waiting for their turn to cross. Grateful that the blistering heat of the day was ebbing, they listened to birds twittering their evensong in the woods beside the meandering river.

* * * * *

From the vantage point of his saddle, Heva, Prince of the Burgundians, discerned the distant glint of late afternoon light on armour and sent riders forward to investigate.

"Gepid infantry, Sire, under Ardaric's banner," they reported, "fording the river century by century."

"Gepids," Heva's blood thumped at the name of the Burgundian's ancient enemies, "where's Attila's main force?"

"No sign of it, Sire."

"How many Gepids?"

"Three full cohorts plus five centuries, Sire."

Heva's hand tapped the hilt of his sword and he frowned in thought. Two years before, Gepids had massacred his cousins at Visili and he was eager to settle the score, but his troops were raw and he was reluctant to engage a force of over fifteen thousand when he had only ten.

At the sound of a whinnying horse he looked up. A Frankish messenger, covered in dust streaked by sweat, galloped up. "Hail Prince Heva! Aegidius, King of the Franks, bids you to confer with him."

Heva raised both brows. The Franks and Burgundians were enemies, with nothing in common but their fear of Attila and a fragile fealty to Rome. Heva turned for counsel to Haldor, his second in command.

Haldor's hair was so light it camouflaged the white strands at his temples but the lines at the corners of his eyes declared that he was ten years older than his prince. He clenched his fist, as if bringing it up under a Gepid jaw, and nodded encouragement. Heva spurred his horse towards Aegidius' column.

Cantering through the midst of Frank warriors, Heva was struck by their bald heads, naked necks and bare backs. Aegidius had decreed that only kings and princes royal could wear their hair long. All other men were ordered to shave the rear half of their heads and brush the rest of their hair into a fringe over their foreheads. They were unarmoured and carried neither bows nor spears but every man shouldered a short-handled, double-headed throwing axe. Only a handful of officers had horses from which they'd leap down to fight on foot.

Aegidius's own black locks hung long down his back. He addressed

Heva in Latin, their only common tongue. "The Gepids are trapped between us and the river. We join forces and attack."

Heva's eyes turned wolf-like at the prospect of vengeance. The black balls in Aegidius's skull flared in recognition.

"What's the plan of attack?" Heva asked.

"Plan?" Aegidius raised his sword above his head. "We charge now before they escape! You herd them down into the marsh where we butcher them."

"Fight in the swamp?"

"The Gepid armour will drag them under."

"Some of my men are armoured too," said Heva, "the swamp won't favour them."

"I'm not requesting your co-operation – I order it."

Heva stared Aegidius in the eye for a moment then looked away. The Frank was an experienced general, decorated by Aetius, and should be obeyed. But a wave of apprehension, beyond normal battle nerves, pervaded Heva's body. Turning Thunder's head back in the direction of the Burgundian troops, he spurred him to a gallop.

The stallion's heavy hooves struck up puffs of dust and Heva could feel the big horse's lungs working against his inner thighs. But the prince was deaf to everything except the sound of the wind as it blew past his ears and the throbbing of his heart against his ribs. Time was suspended and Heva hung inside a bubble of air, cut off from the rest of the world.

In contrast to his deadened hearing, Heva's eyes had sharpened and he could see every blade of grass on the sunburnt slope leading down to the mass of Gepid back plates; the rays of light bouncing in stars off their helmets; each leaf of every green tree stood out as if it were carved in stone. He saw all the subtle gradations of the sky, from azure to almost white, and wisps of stratus clouds, feathered ten thousand feet above his head. Then an image of Leonida at sunset flooded his mind and he saw blood-coloured light in her hair.

Coming close to his men, he looked along their shaggy line and felt overwhelming pity for them. They carried bows with which they'd normally hunt their supper and pitchforks with which they'd turn their hay. Their shields were fragile, made of stretched hide, and their swords had been fashioned from ploughs. Only a handful wore helmets and body armour, even fewer wore greaves.

He looked down the bank towards the massed Gepids. What they lacked in speed they made up for in training, imitating and excelling the Romans. Their shields were solid steel; they carried twelve-foot spears to repel cavalry and short swords with which to gut their enemies. They all wore helmets and greaves. If they foundered in the mud it would be due to the unfavourable ground not lack of training or discipline.

Heva cantered to the front of his ranks, but his mouth was dry and no orders came to him. The odds suddenly seemed preposterous. He high-stepped Thunder along the line in a manner that told the soldiers they had to straighten up, but he could neither find words of encouragement nor orders to shout. The men shared anxious glances, expecting more from their prince.

A blood-curdling battle cry went up from the Franks. Spinning their double-headed throwing axes above their heads, they spewed down the field towards the Gepid infantry.

At first the Gepid rear ranks panicked and waded into the river but with a series of sharp horn blasts Gunderit commanded them to rally. In thigh-deep water, they turned as one to face the attack. Their shields came up en masse just as the Franks, with a shrieking howl, hurled their double-headed throwing axes. The front row of Gepid shields split apart, heads flew, and corpses crashed, like felled trees, knocking down their neighbours. The weight of their armour held them under and the Franks hacked at their bodies till the river ran red.

Anticipating a Burgundian charge, Gunderit ordered the troops who were still on dry land to form squares. The soldiers on the perimeter knelt and braced their twelve-foot pikes while the row behind slid the tips of their swords over the tops of their oblong shields and locked them together in the Roman manner.

On the brink of the field, seeing no opening, Heva wavered. If he ordered his archers' to unleash their arrows they would plunge into the heads and backs of the unarmoured Franks. If they aimed only at the Gepid squares on the banks they'd bounce off uselessly against the shields raised in the time-honoured Roman tortoise tactic. He had neither cavalry nor artillery to break their ranks.

But a command was needed and needed now. Courage must suffice. He raised his horn to his lips and sounded the charge then spurred Thunder forward. Behind him the battle cry went up and the Burgundians surged down the field and smashed like waves against the rocks of the Gepid defence.

A steel breastplate protected Thunder's chest but he took two spears in his forequarters and one to his front leg as he smashed through the wall of Gepid spears. As the stallion stumbled into a fall, Heva leapt from his back. Landing heavily, he looked up and found himself alone. Without the weight of a warhorse to barrel them through, his men hadn't been able to pierce the wall of Gepid spears.

In the thick of his enemy, Heva threw down his shield and drew both swords.

Haldor and the bravest of his warriors could see Heva's helmet and the shoulders of his bright red tunic surrounded by Gepids and threw themselves into hand to hand combat, trying to cut through to him.

Heva raised his broadsword in his right hand and in his left a finer blade made for last-ditch struggles such as this. They rang out on his enemies' armour as he swung and slashed but the Gepids swarmed around him. Heva spun round to fight a man at his back, his helmet fell from his head and his blond hair flew out around him. He took aim at the eye-socket of an enemy helmet, but the Gepid smashed the edge of his shield up, halfway between Heva's shoulder and elbow, and the bone snapped. With only one sword left, Heva fought on – desperately searching over the heads of his foes for an ally amidst the enemy metal. Haldor's eyes met his and he rallied his men in a desperate push – but it was too late – in a storm of swords the Gepids dragged Heva down and he was swallowed from sight.

Thunder had struggled to his feet and was waging his own battle. With three spears trailing from his body he reared up. Driven by instinct to fight and flee, he kicked a path clear for himself and galloped into the woods on the side of the field.

When the Burgundian army saw the riderless charger dragging three spears behind him, they rose in a wave of grief to avenge Heva's loss and drove the Gepids down the field and into the river. But the Franks were fatigued and didn't give chase so many escaped.

The battle exhausted itself. Twilight loomed. Gepid, Frankish and Burgundian horns all blew their retreats. The Gepids waded their way to the far side of the river while the Franks regrouped alongside the Burgundians to set up camp for the night. In the dissonant peace of evening birdsong, both sides counted their dead.

Heva's officers recovered his body and Thunder's groom, Marco, dared the threats of the darkening forest to go in search of his horse. An animal trailing blood like that would attract wolves in the night.

Aegidius the Frank had lost half his warriors to the gods of the underworld and suspected that both the Gepids and the Burgundians had too. His bare back covered in other men's blood, he took stock then marched towards the Burgundian camp. He intended to commiserate with Heva but when he saw a wiry, dark-bearded man limping back from the forest with Heva's horse trailing behind him he realised the extent of the Burgundians' loss.

Haldor, now leader of Burgundian forces, rose from the side of a wounded man and marched towards Aegidius.

"Heva died with both swords drawn," said the Nordic warrior.

"I salute his courage," Aegidius replied solemnly.

"We will bury him here, where he fought, where he fell, with all his weapons."

"You will mark his grave?"

"No, not now." Haldor's face was grey with shock, exhaustion and disappointment. "When the wars with Attila are finished, I'll send men to recover Heva's body and take it back to his family in Dijon."

"That is wise," said Aegidius, "in the morning we must move on. Do you accept my command until we meet up with Aetius?"

Haldor shook his head in emphatic defiance. "We are Burgundian. I will lead our men until we join up with the Romans."

"As you wish," said Aegidius, "but you might do better under the command of an experienced field officer."

"Who are *you* to come into our camp tonight and talk to me like that?" Haldor snarled at the insinuation that Heva had been at fault. He drew himself to his full height and stood nose to nose with the Frank. Aegidius held his stare for a double beat then broke off.

"There's no call for anger," said the Frank, "I intend no criticism. You fought bravely and Heva died with both swords drawn. Together we march, the hour before dawn."

The two men saluted each other. Aegidius's over-muscled outline was black against the bloody dusk as he trudged away and left the Burgundians to their grief.

In the last of the daylight, Marco was on one knee, dabbing with a rag at blood oozing from Thunder's flank. With a short-bladed knife he dug spearheads out of a mountain of muscle that felt frighteningly flaccid under his hand. He'd hobbled the horse so Thunder couldn't kick and tethered him close to the pack mules to give him a sense of security, but Thunder stood inert, his head low, long and motionless, even when the knife dug deep in his wounds.

This morning there had been twenty horses in Marco's charge, now there were only seven, all wounded. They pricked their ears and sniffed the air for traces of herd-mates whose corpses rose in ghostly mounds on the scarred field. Marco, who shunned human company, had taken it upon himself to go out and finish off the ones who were too far gone to live.

"You mustn't blame yourself," said Marco, twisting the knife to dislodge the last fragment of metal, "it's not your fault. Heva made you do it. . . no, we can't blame poor Heva. It was those bloody Franks what got us killed. Fight the Gepids in the swamp – suited them, not us." Marco packed a poultice into the last of the wounds and rigged up a bandage around the horse's girth to hold it in place. "You'll have to perk up or you'll be tomorrow night's meat ration . . . As long as you can still be ridden, you'll have a chance. There'll be officers looking for a mount after losing theirs. I have to go now, but I'll be back to check on you."

Marco gave his eyes a wipe, not that it mattered as no one would be looking at him, and made his way to obey the desolate summons of a lone horn.

An honour-guard had formed up around Heva's corpse. They had dug a grave in haste, only a few feet deep. As softly as mothers place their newborn babies down to rest, the soldiers had laid out their prince.

They buried him with his two strong swords at his side, golden amulets on his broken arms and rings on his dead white fingers. The gems from a single one of them would be worth more than any of his men could earn in a lifetime of labour but no one would deprive him of them, such was their love. Heva's bright red tunic had died a muddy brown, sodden with blood. Yet his face was almost perfect, an image of himself but cold as marble, unmarked except for one blue bruise at the temple. His eyes were closed. He looked peaceful, much younger in death than in life, much smaller too. Prayers were offered to many gods, not only Christian, although Heva had been baptised; tears were hidden.

By the light of rush tapers the Burgundian lament wailed towards the heartless stars. A chorus of wolves howled in the forest. The last light of day was extinguished.

Hope

The Roman bridge on the road from Troyes to Reims
Province of Lugdunesis
Afternoon of 19th September, 451 AD

For a day and a half after her encounter with the bandits, Sola cut through fields and woods to intersect with the main highway between Troyes and Reims. The forests were silent and dark, as if birds dared not sing but, as light filtered through the last of the trees, she came to an open stretch of ground churned up by hooves. She stopped behind a grey-leafed bush and sniffed the dusty air. A double-headed throwing axe lay on the ground – thrown or dropped she couldn't say – and the horse manure was fresh. Leaving the cover of the bush, she bent down and ran her fingers around the outline of a hoof. Too big to be a Hun pony but unshod so not likely to be Roman. Gepid, perhaps?

She picked up the throwing axe, slung the strap diagonally across her back and was flexing her shoulders to make sure that the extra weapon wouldn't limit her movements when a battle cry went up in the distance. She spun round. Before her mind had time to quash her instincts, she answered the call to war, by sprinting towards it.

Through the trees, on the far side of the river a surging mass of armour came into view. Her heart pumping hard, she stopped and watched – *I'm not here for this, it's not my fight* – but her fist clenched at the sight.

She tried to turn away from the pull of Burgundians grappling with death, but the sight of a blond-headed man battling alone amidst a sea

142

of Gepid metal tore at her sinews. When she saw broadswords hacking at his armoured shoulders, she slipped the throwing axe from her back, spun it three times at arm's length and let it fly. It razored through the sky but instead of waiting to see if she'd hit her mark, Sola turned her back and set off at a run back through the forest towards the Roman road. When she reached it, she bent over, her lungs heaving, and waited for her pulse to settle to a steady pump, then set off again at a lope. By the time she arrived at the crossroads just north of the bridge over the Aube, she was barely sweating.

From a distance, she saw that the bridge was guarded by a detachment of Romans and this disorientated her. Did they not know that a battle was raging only five miles away?

From the cover of trees, she watched the camp. All seemed quiet. The soldiers were pitching camp and lighting fires, making no attempt to disguise their presence. Sola brushed off her cloak and walked straight up to the gate to seek asylum for the night,.

"Who goes there?" challenged a sentry.

"The wife of Marcus Ruricius, a Roman citizen," Sola pushed back her hood to show her face.

The guard's eyes opened wide at the sight of a lone woman. "You're a refugee?"

"No." With a long finger she smoothed a tendril of hair from her forehead, "I'm not running from anything. I'm going back to Reims in search of my husband and daughter. Would you be kind enough to take me to your commanding officer? The hour is late, and I need to rest for the night."

His mouth half open, the guard hesitated, nonplussed by her unabashed tone of authority. "Very well then. Please follow me."

He led her through rows of rectangular tents to one larger than the rest at the centre of the camp. He saluted the sentries at the door and asked for permission to enter the praetorium.

Sola waited outside, looking out into the dimming crepuscule, glad for the cool of evening. The conflict between the Gepids, Franks and Burgundians down by the river would be long over now, but what did it mean?

Ten minutes passed before a bare-headed officer, dressed in a general's uniform, strode out of the tent. He was much older than she'd expected. The creases at the corners of his bright blue eyes suggested he had a sense of humour but his mouth was tense. He folded his arms, muscled from a lifetime of wielding weapons, over the lion-rampant embossed on his breastplate and stood astride. Sola saw the scars of battle-axes, lances, arrows and picks, all healed on his thighs. In a voice that rumbled in his throat like a growl, he asked, "Your name, madam?"

"Sola. I am the wife of Marcus Ruricius, a town councillor of Reims."

"What brings you here?"

"I must go north in search of my husband and daughter." Not liking to be put on the defensive, she asked, "To whom am I speaking, sir?"

"My name is Eparchius Avitus." Their eyes met, then the general took a step back and ran an assessing look over her. She seemed a strange kind of woman – as tall as he was. The raised veins on her long, wiry arms, suggested she was an athlete. Yet she dressed like a Roman matron in a long tunic of white cotton and a travelling cloak. Her feline eyes kicked up at the corners and the fairness of her hair betrayed barbarian blood, but her Latin was perfect, albeit with a slight southern song to it. "You cannot go north, madam; the road is closed to all but the army."

"But I must."

"It isn't safe."

"I know, but that's irrelevant."

The general looked her up and down once more and his lip rose at one corner. Apart from her physical appearance, there was something else, indefinable, that set her apart from the females in his world. "You said that your husband was a town councillor of Reims?"

"I did."

Avitus turned away for a moment, pondering the magnitude of what he had to say. When he looked back his voice had softened. "Madam, I regret to inform you that Attila sacked Reims. He spared not one of the town councillors and massacred the populace."

Sola's heart stopped. Her body went hollow, as if a knife had cleaved her in two then scooped out the marrow of her bones. Yet, although her knees felt like water she didn't stumble. "Not one?"

"There's no doubt at all. I'm sorry."

Sola pushed the hair back from her temples. Her voice became thin. "Surely some people must have survived Attila's sacking?"

Avitus kept his eyes locked on hers and shook his head.

Sola tightened her cloak around her neck. Her body shook and she could hardly draw breath. "The women and children?"

Avitus looked away to a line of soldiers raising a palisade on the perimeter of the camp for a moment, wondering if she'd be able to withstand his response, then turned back to her. "Attila locked all the women and children inside the church and set it on fire."

"Burned them alive?"

He nodded, solemn-lipped.

"No one escaped?" Sola's eyes were wild, dark and liquid.

"No one."

Avitus watched as grief flooded her face, then she mastered it. He waited for her to weep or faint but when she didn't he felt he should tell her more. "I don't want to offer you false hope, but when we passed through Troyes this morning, there was a rumour going round that a lone girl had escaped on a stolen imperial courier horse."

Light flickered across Sola's features. "Did they say anything about the girl's appearance?"

"Not that I heard. You may ask my men for more details, but I'm afraid, madam, I've other matters to attend to." Aware that two centurions were waiting for orders, Avitus was about to turn away when

Sola reached out a hand and touched his forearm. He looked down in surprise then back into her eyes, so deep a blue that they looked almost black in the twilight. They, not her hand, held him in their grip.

"Do you know where the girl is now?" she asked.

"No, but I can see that you hold out hope that your daughter lives," he sighed. "In your position, I'd head south to Troyes. All lands to the north are in flames or ashes. There's nothing and no one left alive. Aetius and our allies are riding into that cauldron of Hades as we speak. We're a rear-guard and march to join him at dawn."

At the sound of Aetius' name, Sola felt as if a man twice her size had clubbed her on one temple and then the other. She lifted her hand from Avitus' forearm and, with steel will, steadied herself. "Flavius Aetius?"

"Yes, madam, Flavius Aetius, the magister militum."

"The golden-haired Aetius?"

Avitus smiled wryly. Had she heard him described that way or had she met the man? "Not that long ago, the eagle's hair was gold, but it's silver now. Do you know him?"

Sola's heart drummed fit to break her ribs. "I did, once. Long ago."

A thousand thoughts rushed through her head. Attila had killed her husband and Aetius was about to go to war. Would he want to know the secret that she'd kept hidden for fifteen years? Did she want him to? She drew a deep breath. "General, will you see Aetius?"

"Of course."

"When you do, would you please tell him that you met a woman called Sola who was searching for her daughter?"

Avitus raised his brows. Why would that interest the magister militum?

"And, if you can . . ." Sola looked down, the corner of one eyebrow flickering with stress, "please tell him that my daughter, Leonida, was born nine months after the Battle of Rimini."

When she looked up, Avitus saw both pain and strength in her eyes. "We're at war, madam. I can make no promises."

Sola worked to force the frown from her face and the tightness from her lips.

Avitus stepped away and surveyed the sentries on patrol, the soldiers digging ditches and raising the palisade for the night. All was in order. When he turned back, Sola had mastered her expression. "Sir, may I ask, what happened to Orleans?" she asked.

Avitus smiled and Sola saw the warmth that the lines at the corners of his eyes had promised. Then, to her surprise, he winked and said, "Attila invaded Orleans and set it alight, but we drove him out of the city, saved half the garrison and many of her citizens."

"Thank you. I'll take the road south in the morning." Part of her wished to head north with him, to find Aetius, to fight Attila, but that would never be. "I'd march through a thousand armies if that's what it would take to find Leonida, but it's clear from all you've told me that, if there is a survivor, the girl must have fled south to Troyes."

Avitus nodded. "It's the only possibility. I can't offer you an escort. We expect the Frank and Burgundian legions to be coming up on that road, if not tonight, then early tomorrow."

Sola smiled wryly. "I didn't come to seek an escort, general."

"I can offer you a tent and some food."

"Thank you. I spent last night bundled in my cloak in the woods and would be grateful for both." She had no fear of the wild animals but didn't want to be caught outside the camp by a troop of passing Franks.

Avitus' eyes followed her movements as she pulled up the hood of her cloak and turned to go. "You're not like the others."

"The other what?" Sola looked back over her shoulder, unblinking and transfixed him.

"The other refugees. They limp in, bleeding-footed, beseeching our aid. Some demand miracles. You strode in here alone and asked for nothing. How did you acquire that confidence?"

Sola's eyes flickered over the scars on his thighs. "I've had a hard life, general, which many have tried to wrest from me, but my wounds have all healed, as have yours."

"I bid you goodnight, madam." Avitus inclined his head slightly, as if in salute, then ordered an optio to set up her tent.

Sola watched the sentries salute and let down the flaps of the praetorium behind him, then she followed the optio to a space at the end of a row of bivouacs.

While two platoon-men laid out her tent and knocked in the pegs, she walked out to the last remaining gap in the perimeter palisade and looked across the plains to the dark shapes of trees that marked the meandering path of the River Aube. Everything was still, but Sola felt profound misgiving. Somewhere, beyond her field of vision, something of vital importance had gone gravely wrong.

As soon as the tent was up, she unrolled the blanket the men had left for her and collapsed onto it, grieving for Marcus, the only man who'd ever loved her for who she was. Never more could she run her fingers over his thighs and lift her lips to his. Never more would his laugh make her smile. The scent of sandalwood would be forever his, and it would bring tears to her eyes whenever she encountered it. Never more would her heart glow at his touch. She wrapped the blanket around her but couldn't stop shivering, and wept till her eyes were dry.

Unable to sleep, she listened to wolves howling from one stand of forest to the next. Her mouth, like her eyes, was dry so she sat up and found her flask in the dark. Nothing would bring Marcus back but tomorrow she would search for the girl who might be Leonida. It was all she could do.

Thoughts of her daughter brought back memories of a more distant love, never forgotten, whose wounds had taken long years to heal to clean, white, scars. Alone, in the dark, she tried to conjure an image of the greatest man alive, Flavius Aetius, as he'd been when she had known him. Aetius belonged to another life, a life in which she'd been the Empress Galla Placidia's body-guard.

She remembered the day she'd seen him, mounted on a snowy stallion with scarlet trappings, at the head of his household cavalry in Rome. The horsehair crest of his golden helmet made him look seven feet tall and she hadn't been the only one whose blood had rushed to her cheeks at the sight of him. The Empress and her two children – the boy, Valentinian III, in whose name Galla ruled the world, and his sister, Honoria, a spotty fourteen-year-old – had assembled on the palace parade ground to welcome him. The way Honoria's face blushed a blotchy red at the sight of Aetius had annoyed Sola, for she had worshipped him then.

She frowned ruefully at the memory of that spoilt little monster, Valentinian III, and the way Honoria and her friends had mocked him for his indolence and stupidity. As soon as Valentinian attained his majority, he avenged himself by declaring that Honoria must remain celibate. Honoria showed her brother what she thought of this folly by bedding her chamberlain. Her promiscuity obliged Valentinian to find her a husband and, out of malice he forced the boring old senator, Bassus Herculanus, on her.

Sola's fingers strayed along the frayed edge of the blanket and her frown deepened. Part of her wished she'd run a knife through Valentinian the day she'd caught him wringing the neck of a dove in the palace courtyard. If she had, perhaps Marcus and countless others would still be alive, for Valentinian's spite towards his sister had unleashed the catapults of war.

Imploring him to rescue her, Honoria had sent her ring to Attila and, although he hadn't an iota of interest in her, the Hun had claimed her as his bride and demanded half the Empire as her dowry. The ring had been tinder to Attila's inferno, and now the whole world would burn.

Sola put a hand behind her neck and lay down again. Had the ring really set the world ablaze? If she'd sacrificed her life by killing

Valentinian, would it have made any difference? Eyes wide open in the darkness, she reflected on what she knew of the Hun. Nations prostrated themselves at his feet rather than risk battle with him. The few who did resist, he obliterated. A born destroyer, he would lay the world waste. Only Aetius had the will to oppose him, no matter what the odds.

Sola sighed from the depths of her being. Aetius' touch had made her skin goose-bump when he'd pulled her into his chest, all those years ago, and kissed her under a sky of fiery stars.

Before she married Marcus, she and Aetius had been lovers in the night. She'd believed that he would spread his eagle's wings and that together they'd fly. But then came the Battle of Rimini, where, in hand to hand combat, Aetius killed Bonafacius, his only rival for the command of Rome's legions. Bonafacius' death left the Empress no choice except to appoint Aetius magister militum, and Sola's eagle had soared out of sight.

Part of Sola ached to find him, fight at his side and lend him her strength as she'd given him her heart. She wanted to raise her gladius next to his and smite down their common enemy, to protect Aetius and let him protect her. But that could never be.

And if she did find him in the heat of battle, in command of the field of war, would he want her there? Aetius had his army now, he held all the power an honest man could. With Marcus gone, Leonida had only her. Although Sola would never know for sure whether the daughter she'd born so soon after her marriage to Marcus was his or the eagle's spawn, it was Marcus who had resurrected Sola from heartbreak and Leonida was all that she could save of him now.

Buffeted by the shocks of the day, Sola was restless on the pebbles poking through the ground-sheet. It was only as her heavy eyelids closed that she remembered she hadn't mentioned the battle in the swamp to Eparchius Avitus.

Yet to sleep was no mercy, for she dreamed. A nightmare of Leonida tied to a stake in the middle of a burning field of corn, unable to move as the flames grew higher and closer, woke her in the dark. She sat up in a cold sweat, and reached for her gladius, then remembered where she was. *It was only a dream.* A dream, but reality made the nightmare pale.

Only when the wolves had fallen silent and the moon had waned did Sola find a moment of respite.

* * * * *

She rose at birdcall. It was still dark but all around her men were breaking camp and making ready to march at first light. In the distance, she heard the clank of legions already on the march.

She made her way to the southern gates and stood discretely out of sight as the sentries saluted their incoming allies. Aegidius swaggered in at the head of his bare-backed Franks. Behind them, led by a blond warrior riding a wounded horse, the Burgundians doggedly put one foot in front of the other. The freshness of their injuries and the grim but determined set of their lips told her they were the survivors of the battle she'd witnessed.

Anxious for any scrap of information about the girl who'd escaped Reims, she singled out a shy-looking infantryman with a smashed-in face at the rear of the ranks. As she spoke quietly and quickly to him in his native tongue his eyes lit up. Emphasising his own importance as a guardian of horses, he gabbled out a story about a girl and her Akal Teke. He told her the maiden had been alive and well when they'd parted but he didn't know what happened to her after that.

Sola thanked him and slipped out of the gates unnoticed, feeling as if she could run the whole twenty miles to Troyes on one breath, but dreading what news she might discover there.

In the days that followed she often wondered what her destiny would have been had she turned north, to the Catalaunian Plains, instead of south that day.

The Catalaunian Plains

Gaul

Dawn, 20th September 451 AD

Twenty miles northeast of the Roman bridge, centurions barked orders at the ranks to break camp. The bray of pack animals and ringing of mallets on tent-pegs overlaid the huff of collapsing canvas. Since the battle for Orleans, Aetius had hounded the Hun over one hundred and sixty miles of open country at a crippling pace, but his soldiers readied themselves for another day's chase without a hint of complaint.

In full battle armour, Aetius was dictating orders to half a dozen equites outside his praetorium when, over the helmets of his infantry, he saw Avitus' lion rampant standard appear. He mounted up, a smile flickering at the corners of his lips. "You're early."

Avitus thumped a fist to his breastplate and saluted. "I've ridden ahead of the rearguard. They'll be here by the third hour. Aegidius is with them, dragging the remnants of the Franks and the Burgundian third legion behind him." The twinkle left his eye. "They've lost half their men."

"They deserted?" asked Aetius, fearing the worst. The last thing he needed now was for the Franks or Burgundians to change sides.

"No, nothing like that, but between them they suffered over seven and a half-thousand casualties in a skirmish with the Gepids last night. To ensure there's no more foolishness, I posted a century of Romans to their fore and another at their rear."

"A battle with seven and a half thousand casualites can't be termed a 'skirmish'. Gepid losses?"

"At least ten cohorts, but Ardaric's black-shirts weren't engaged. They'd already forded the river and struck out across country to join Attila."

"How did the battle start?"

"Aegidius decided to fight the Gepids in a swamp, five miles from the bridge over the Aube, and convinced Prince Heva to join the attack."

Aetius frowned.

"Heva was killed," said Avitus.

Aetius' eyes darkened. "His loss will be felt throughout Gaul."

"You thought highly of him?"

"Heva came to the Praetorian Prefect's house, while you were away raising an army of Goths. A noble young man, I remember him well. Whether it was deliberate or not, Aegidius has eliminated one of his future rivals for control of our northern provinces."

"I see." Avitus looked out, over the heads of the infantry. "We're ready to march."

Aetius nudged his stallion round and surveyed his legions. Row upon row of steel-shouldered soldiers had formed up behind the scarlet banners of their centuries. At the head of each legion, perched high on the aquilifers' standards, eagles glittered. Beyond the infantry, to the fore and the flank, cavalry horses jangled on their bits. Aetius raised his fist and signalled to his trumpeters to sound the advance.

As one, the cohorts marched forward and shook the earth.

Attila's Camp

The Catalaunian Plains, Gaul
Dawn, 20th September 451 AD

To the east and south of Epernay lies a grassy plain, one hundred miles long and sixty miles wide. It's gentle ground, green, except when burnt by a long dry summer, smooth and flat.

The sun rising at his back, Attila scanned the horizon, searching for the cloud of dust that haunted him. On every day's march, it grew taller and thicker but, as morning light tipped over the hills onto the plain, the line between earth and sky was still sharp and clean.

Attila turned his horse and squinted into the rising sun, towards the plains of his birth, and was confronted by mountains. His stomach knotted and bile rose to his mouth. The flat expanse of the Catalaunian Plains was the last ground in Gaul that favoured his battle tactics. Hills were a death-trap.

Mounted at his side, Ardaric the Gepid frowned. "The men are exhausted and so are the horses. Every night, the smoke of Roman campfires draws nearer."

Attila scowled. He'd never imagined that Aetius could drive his mongrel army this far and fast. "There's smoke, but no flames. They can't catch us."

Ardaric knew better than to argue with the scourge of God, but the evident lie enraged him. "Enough! This plain favours us."

Attila spat and yanked at the bridle, startling his horse. His eyes following the long trail of plunder waggons behind them. They'd journeyed through the night, but still couldn't catch up with him. "I'd rather burn those waggons than leave my spoils to that Roman cur."

The Gepid clenched his teeth and his eyes followed Attila's back along the trail of waggons. His share of that booty would be lost if Attila burned them. "Then we must fight, before Aetius has a chance to capture them."

Attila spat from the corner of his mouth. From under glowering brows, he then slowly surveyed the plain. "Here we make our stand. Order the waggons off the road, along with the artillery carts, and form a circle."

Ardaric's lips curled upward. He saluted then cantered off to relay the orders.

When the Gepid had gone, Attila spurred his horse to his tent. Inside, rage over took him. He kicked a table from its feet, knocking a copper bowl of water across the goat skins on his floor. *Kysaghan's guts! – What's Aetius doing? We outnumber him ten to one. In the first dust of battle, those louse-infected Goths will change sides and join my Huns.*

Attila stamped on the bowl until he flattened it, then paced. A line of sweat broke out on his upper lip as he pulled at the wisps of his beard. With an evil glint in his eye, he barged out through the tent flaps and shouted – "Summon the augur!"

Two soldiers in scaled armour and pointed helmets ran off to do his bidding. Attila sat on a wooden throne by an unlit fire and brooded.

His soldiers came back, dragging a bleating sheep. Behind them, the hem of his long black robes sullied by the dust of four days' panicked ride, followed the shaman. He bowed low to Attila. While the soldiers knocked the beast off its legs and flipped it onto its back, the shaman lit the fire. The flames cast shadows on his hook-nosed face as he took the sheep's muzzle in his hand and pulled the neck back. With one quick swipe of his knife, he slit the soft fur of the lamb's throat. When the jugular stopped spurting and the body went slack, he sawed the blade down through the pelt and hooked out its

155

entrails. While the bloody mass congealed on the ground, he raised his eyes towards a blank blue sky and muttered an incantation.

Attila worshipped no gods, except himself, but was superstitious. He'd always felt that some dark force gave him strength and protected his personal interests. Today, something in his bones told him that the message from the gods might not be all that he wanted and he should keep it to himself. Only a handful of bodyguards were present to witness the shaman's performance.

While the augur babbled incomprehensibly, Attila stared in silence at the entrails on the ground. His close-together, beady-black eyes peered with apprehension past the splayed nostrils of his long, flat nose. The shaman stirred the guts with a long baton dipped in blood then his eyes narrowed to slits and ridges radiated between his brows.

"What? What do you see?" asked Attila.

"I see the biggest battle the world has ever known, here, today . . . hard fought."

Attila hurried the prophecy on with his hands.

"One of the enemy leaders is killed," said the shaman.

"Aetius?"

"I cannot see the name." Sweat ran down the augur's neck.

"Look harder! Is it Aetius?"

The shaman heard a dangerous tilt in Attila's tone. "It is not the will of the gods to reveal the name to us now. Perhaps they will tell me later."

Attila raised his hand, as if to slap the shaman. "What good are you and your predictions if you can't even tell me the name!?"

Despite his ire, Attila wasn't going to kill him. The shaman was his trusted advisor and through his mouth the gods had predicted his greatest victories. The Hun slung his thumbs into the belt of his tunic, his head hunched between his shoulders. "Come back in an hour and try again."

"Very well, sire." The shaman bowed so low that his black plait grazed the ground. Still bent at the waist, backed away for half a dozen steps before daring to stand. His robes tangling around his ankles, he walked as fast as he deemed permissible from Attila's presence.

Attila, his brows thunderous, paced around the smouldering campfire on the short, bandy legs of a man who lived his life in the saddle. Cursing the name of Aetius, he looked skywards, to see if any eagles were circling.

His eye lit on a solitary mountain, the only high ground within a mile of the camp. From the plains, it rose into an escarpment shaped like a wave about to break. Two-thirds of the way up there was a plateau and from its rear edge, a cliff-like ridge jutted up to the summit. With gnarled knuckles, Attila tugged at his beard. The hill was shaped like a pair of shoulders with a head in the middle, the chimera of Greek myth. It shadowed the plain.

He called for Sky Hawk. The young horseman led his pony by the reins and knelt before his warlord.

"Stand up," barked Attila, "secure that high ground. I'll order a cohort of Ostrogoths up behind you but take that mountain now."

The First Hour

Aetius, mounted on Achilles at the head of his army, watched a blazing orb rise above the grey horizon into a cloudless heaven – the portent of another blistering day. Galloping towards him, four scouts were kicking up dust-clouds. As they came closer the bronze medallions on the cross-bars on their horses' chests caught the light and the riders punched the air. They reined hard in front of him and saluted.

"The enemy has drawn up his waggon-train and formed a circle, Sir!"

Without a flicker of expression, Aetius spurred his charger from a standstill to a canter and followed the scouts to a rise. Avitus pushed his helmet forward and set off after them with Sidonius and seven other equites at his back. Through dusky morning air, they looked out on Attila's makeshift fort.

"You've done it!" exclaimed, Avitus, his blue eyes bright. "You've cornered the scourge of God!"

Aetius permitted himself half a smile. "The rat's dug himself a hole, now let's see if he has the courage to come out of it."

"A detachment of Hun cavalry is headed up that escarpment," said Avitus. "We must put a stop to that. Sidonius! Get Ecdicius – and two turmae – now!"

In less than a minute, Ecdicius thundered up with sixty-four centaur-like cavalrymen in a phalanx behind his flying-horse banner.

"Take that hill before the enemy does," ordered Aetius, "hold it at all costs."

The ground trembled as Ecdicius galloped off.

"It's a race to the top," said Avitus, as the dust settled behind the horsemen, "and the Huns have a head start."

"Yes, but we need the high ground. We'll fight this battle from that mountain, not on the open plains as Attila wants. We, not the Hun, dictate the terms of our engagement."

Aetius turned to his officers and ordered a century of mounted archers and a vanguard of infantry up after Ecdicius. Then he turned to the commander of the artillery and ordered balista up the hill: forty arrow cannons and fifty semi-automatic scorpions. The double chain-driven scorpions were mounted on metal tripods and loaded automatically from magazines of metal bolts.

Watching the race between the Huns and his son, Avitus frowned. Attila's Ostrogoths were closing in on Ecdicius from behind. "I can't see any mule tracks up that escarpment. It'll be a challenge to get the balista up."

Aetius gave Avitus a look that said *another statement of the obvious.* "We'll belay it up the cliff face. Nothing we haven't done a thousand times before."

Avitus surveyed the plains where rows of metal-shouldered warriors ranged further than the eye could see. They were forming up into cohorts and legions, darkening the yellow grass. "This is not just another war. In all history, there's never been a battle of this magnitude, and there'll never be another. Look at the scale of it!"

"It's the war of two worlds," said Aetius.

Avitus smiled ruefully. "To win may take more than we've got."

"Then every man must give more than he has."

Avitus was watching Ecdicius gallop straight towards the cliff face. "As usual, you expect us to accomplish the impossible."

"And, as usual," Aetius looked over at Theodoric's white charger at the head of a column of Goths, "you achieve it."

Ecdicius had arrived at the foot of the hill. The Huns were halfway up on the opposite side. Avitus' eyes sparkled at the compliment but his voice was gruff. "Our boys have a steeper climb but the distance is a slightly shorter. The race will be a close and the Ostrogoths are closing in from behind." Avitus frowned at Aetius, willing him to order the rest of the ala up to reinforce his son, but Aetius shock his head. "We need calvary on our wings."

Avitus clenched his teeth and watched as one of Ecdicus' turnae whirled back, formed a wedge and shattered the Ostrogoths.

Aetius raised his arm and ordered the trumpets to sound a steady forward march. The distance between the generals and the mountain slowly narrowed as they watched Ecdicius' horses power off their hindquarters and up the escarpment. Sky Hawk had seen them too and his men, who'd already been climbing at a canter, were bent over their horses' necks, flailing at them with their whips.

Ecdicius, leading the charge up the mountain, barely touched the spurs to the sides of his mount but it leapt upwards with spirit and courage. At a gallop, Sky Hawk swooped sideways on his saddle, drew his bow and took aim. He fired out three arrows in one second before the fourth caught Ecdicius' stallion in the throat. The horse screamed and rolled forward over its legs.

One of Ecdicius' bucellarii had seen the threat and was already at his side. Ecdicius grabbed his hand and, without touching the ground, pounced directly behind his saddle. Another soldier galloped up with a mount who'd lost its rider, Ecdicius reached out for the reins and leapt onto its back.

In his camp down on the plain, Attila cursed the name of every demon in hell as he watched the do-or-die battle for the high ground. The Romans were first to the summit but Sky Hawk and the Ostrogoths charged and charged again to dislodge them before they could reinforce their position. The battle became a dark, swirling whirlpool fought on all fronts. Attila cast a searing scowl at the augur and ordered another detachment of Ostrogoths up behind the first.

The Romans main body was quick-marching now, advancing in well-drilled unison across the plain. Avitus, Aetius and the tense-faced ranks squinted upwards at the conflict on the escarpment.

"They're giving us a fight for it."

"Yes, but we're going to win that one." Aetius, turned away from the struggle on the hill to look behind and check the disposition of his troops. "Order battle formation. I need to talk to you and Theodoric first, then we'll summon Sangibanus."

"I'm not sure how much use that'll be," said Avitus.

With precision, Aetius moved his legions forward. Leaving nothing to the discretion of Aegidius, he sent scouts to ride his orders back to the Franks and Burgundians who were lagging behind in a way that made him question their will to fight.

Suddenly a cheer roared up from the Roman infantry. Stumbling and skidding down the face of the escarpment, Sky Hawk and the Ostrogoths were in full flight. Edicius' sure-footed cavalry gave chase while Roman archers took up their positions on the summit of the three-headed hill and the first of the scorpions was belayed up the cliff-face.

Avitus' face split into the proudest of grins.

The Third Hour in Attila's Camp

Attila's waggon circle on the Catalaunian Plains
20th September 451 AD

"Fuck it!" swore Attila as he smashed the goblet of wine he'd been gulping into the ground and stamped it under the heel of his boot. A dark red stain soaked into the dust.

The augur's face blanched. He was expecting the worst. The heads and guts of three dead sheep were lying in a tangled mass around his feet. The buzzing of a growing circle of flies above them was the only noise in the aftershock of Attila's curse.

"Why can't you tell me who the fucking dead leader will be?!"

"The gods will not disclose it, sire."

"Is it Aetius?"

"It may be."

Attila grabbed the augur by the cowl of his gown and pulled his face to within six inches of his own. "Could it be *me*?"

The augur's stomach retched in Attila's rancid breath. "That doesn't seem to be the meaning of the omens, my Lord. I see an enemy leader falling."

"Get out!" shouted Attila hurling the man away and drawing his sword. "Fuck off! I don't need to hear your donkey shit!"

The augur steadied himself, bowed to the ground then walked away as fast as the shreds of his dignity would allow. The Hun had started waving his scimitar wildly around his head – at no particular target – and the soothsayer praised a dozen gods that it hadn't taken his head off.

Attila's officers stood mutely in a circle around him.

"What are you all gawping at? Are you ready to go out and fight?"

"Everything is battle-ready, Sire," the Ostrogoth king said quietly, keeping his eyes lowered, "we've been standing with our weapons whetted since the first hour of the day."

"Good! Now *fuck off!!* I'll summon you when I want you!"

With wooden faces, the officers saluted and retired.

Attila sat down on a stool outside his tent, brooding over his destiny. If it was going to be Aetius who met his death, then it would all be worth it. But the augur hadn't satisfied him that he, Attila, wasn't the leader at risk.

The Fourth Hour on the Roman Hill

Roman headquarters
The three-headed hill above the Catalaunian Plains
20th September 451 AD

Monumental as statues, Aetius and Avitus sat mounted on their warhorses and surveyed Attila's camp from the vantage point of the hill where they'd triumphed. Next to them, mounted on a sturdy grey charger, sat a fearsome warrior, Theodoric I, King of the Goths. A thick, black beard protruded from under the helmet that encased his face. His eyes were hidden in behind two narrow slits but, as he turned, they caught the light. In his right hand he held a viciously tipped spear. Long swords hung on either side of his armoured thighs and the fanged-heads of wolves on the shoulders of his cloak snarled in the wind.

Next to him, Avitus looked down on the waggon circle where Huns swarmed like ants. "Still hiding in his hole. Thinks that if he stays there long enough, we'll come down and attack."

"He should know us better than that," said Aetius. None of the veteran commanders would throw away his men's lives by giving Attila's archers the chance to pick them off from inside his barricade.

A dust-caked messenger reined in beside the allied leaders. "The Franks and Burgundians have taken up position."

Aetius dismissed him.

"We're at full strength and in battle order now," said Avitus.

"Another statement of the obvious." Aetius' eyes were moving over the massed troops of the Roman, Goth and Alani forces who'd been in battle formation since the second hour of the day. They stood in perfect lines, with the bottom edge of their oblong shields resting on the ground and eyes forward, sweltering under the beat of a vicious sun.

"The sun is at its zenith, but there's no sign of Attila," said Theodoric, "soon it'll be too late in the day to take the field."

"He'll come," said Aetius. "Summon Sangibanus."

In order to stop the Alani from running away at the first whiff of battle, Aetius had wedged them between the Romans on the high ground and the Goths on their flank, in the centre of the front line.

Sangibanus trotted up, looking trimmer than he had at the fight for Orleans, with only a slight stretch of leather straps holding the front and backplates of his armour together. He'd already sent a messenger up to Aetius with the suggestion that it was too late in the day to commence battle and that the Alani should withdraw, but Aetius had replied with a curt refusal. Nonetheless, upon receiving the summons to meet the generals on top of the hill, Sangibanus' hopes of retreating without being obliged to fight had risen again. Theodoric and Avitus stared at him hard as he pulled to a halt and raised an arm in salute.

Aetius spoke. "I've put you and your troops in the middle of our line for several reasons, Sangibanus. After your failure to defend Orleans, Attila will expect you to be feeble in battle. He'll strike the Alani first and attempt to shatter you."

Sangibanus' face fell.

"Like a rising storm," said Aetius, "his cavalry will trot in circles, just beyond the reach of your bows. When their war-cry goes up – a keening scream that strikes terror into the demons of Hades – don't waste your arrows, they'll still be out of range.

Attila's trumpets will sound the attack and the outside edge of each swirling mass will peel off at the gallop, straight towards you. The rest will follow. They'll target a short stretch of your line – perhaps two hundred yards wide – but that miserable handful of men must endure and stand firm. Take cover behind your shields and hold your fire. At two hundred yards out, the Huns will swing round and gallop parallel to your line, the archers turned sideways in their saddles – they'll fire, reload, fire – again, again, again. Each Hun carries sixty arrows in his quiver and can fire ten of them off faster than you can count to five."

Sangibanus' head hunched between his shoulders.

"Sit tall," ordered Aetius. "Twenty thousand arrows a minute will hail down on your line and even when the Huns turn and gallop away from you, they'll keep firing over their horses' rumps. When the first wave wheels off to reload, return fire, but beware that the second will be on you now. Your men will fall, but your line must never break."

Aetius' lips hardened and his words shot out like bolts of scorpion fire. "If you break, Sangibanus, your name will be remembered forever as a synonym for cowardice".

Sangibanus shrank back in his saddle.

"These are my orders," said Aetius, "when Attila attacks, you *will* fall back but your line must *never* break. If you fall back he will give chase to divide and overwhelm our forces with his superior numbers. If you fail, he'll win this battle and the world will be doomed. If you hold the centre, the Romans and Goths will trap Attila in a pincer movement."

Aetius clenched his fist, as if crushing the Hun in it. A cool breeze lifted the stifling heat for an instant and he stared Sangibanus in the eye. "I expect every soldier who serves Rome, whether born Roman or not, to fight like a Roman. Do you understand the importance of your orders?"

"Yes, Sir."

"Dismissed."

But Aetius knew that Sangibanus understood nothing at all. The man was of a new generation, a generation that didn't believe in absolutes.

When Sangibanus had trotted downhill, Theodoric leant forward. "The Alani will rout. Sangibanus knows nothing of battle."

Avitus winked at his erstwhile enemy. "But you and I do."

Theodoric didn't smile but turned to Aetius. "You told Sangibanus nothing of what happens after Attila's archers have scythed his lines, that they'll charge and dismount, battle-axes in hand. . ."

"Didn't want to frighten him." Aetius turned aside and ordered the cohort of new recruits to march down the hill and position themselves in the centre of the Alani line.

They had no experience, but the magister militum, half-barbarian by birth, put his trust in Roman blood.

* * * * *

In the centre of the cohort of new recruits, Brutus and Quintus were sweating with nerves. Waiting, in full battle armour, since an hour before dawn, the day already seemed endless. Yet their stomachs heaved when they heard they were about to march down to the field of war.

Quintus' nose had peeled and revealed pink skin that made Brutus think of a boyhood summer, only a year ago, when they'd swum in the river near home and lain naked on the grassy bank to dry. But the memory seemed to belong to someone else, a boy who'd died or never truly existed.

"Remember all that digging we did on the march up here?" asked Quintus.

"Them blisters!"

"Thought that was hard, but I'd give my eye-teeth to be back there now."

"You an' me both," said Brutus, "an' there's nothing I wouldn't give for one of them ditches we dug to be out there, between us an' the Hun horse."

"Attention! About face!" barked a centurion. In unison, the troops turned away from their headquarters and faced the plains.

"Sheep singled out and sent to the slaughter," Quintus mumbled between the cheek plates of his helmet, his face a ghastly white.

"March!"

The cohort stepped forward, away from the relative security of the three-headed hill towards Attila's plains.

"Battle can't be that bad," said Brutus, but every fibre of his body tensed with terror and his voice pitched high.

"No veterans to fall back on," said Quintus, "nothing but us an' them auxiliaries."

"A motley bunch of barbarians if ever I saw one."

"Of doubtful loyalty."

"At least the Alani are in the front row."

"That's no consolation," said Quintus, "that gov'nor of theirs would've thrown open the gates of Orleans if us Romans hadn't stopped 'im. First sight of the Huns an' he'll bolt. Any case, auxiliaries always go into battle before us regulars."

Brutus peered between the shoulder-plates of the men ahead of him. On the other side of Sangibanus' wobbly line, half a million battle-hardened Huns painted the plain black to the horizon.

At first, the clank of Roman armour brought fear to his heart for he knew that each step brought him closer to death but, when the last of the centuries fell in and joined the downhill march, the aquilifer raised the legionary eagle. It was the first time since Brutus joined up that the gilded bird of prey had led the legion out of camp. Although he couldn't see the aquilifer's face, the red plumes of his helmet streamed out behind him like a horse's mane as he set a fast but measured pace, reserving what he could of the legion's energy for the imminent fight.

Concentrating on matching the aquilifer's pace calmed Brutus and the thunder of a whole legion marching in unison began to make him believe that he was invincible. He focused on keeping in step with his cohorts and vowed that he'd never let them down.

When his century took its place behind the thin Alani line, Brutus had his first close view of Attila's waggon circle. Shoulder to shoulder with Quintus, he peered between the helmets and spears in front of him and saw the tips of Attila's bows aimed at him and his friend. A red mist descended over his mind and the urge to slice his way through Attila's barbarians rose like lust in his loins, so palpable that his mouth watered for the taste of Hun blood.

The Fourth Hour in Attila's Camp

Attila's waggon circle on the Catalaunian Plains
20th September 451 AD

"Get the augur!" bellowed Attila.

A bodyguard scurried off and returned with the shaman who bowed to the ground, but kept out of reach of Attila's scimitar.

"Come here, come here," said Attila with a smile that exposed long, yellow, rodent-like teeth. He spread his arms wide as if welcoming a friend.

The gesture did nothing to stop the augur's knees from shaking but he had no choice except to edge towards his master. Attila put his arm around his shoulders and pulled him down under a sweaty armpit. Crouching sideways to fit, the augur feared that Attila was about to strangle him.

"No need to be nervous! I'd never hurt you." Attila swiped away a swarm of flies and pushed the augur's head lower over the heap of intestines. "I just need you to take a closer look at the auspices again before I make a decision."

The augur's eyes fixated on the pile of entrails at his feet. He stared at the complex mass of twisted guts and tried to hear them speak. But the harder he struggled to interpret them, the more they looked like nothing but the bloody waste from an abattoir, black with flies, and already starting to smell of rot under the early afternoon sun. Attila stared with him. "Now, tell me what you see this time."

The augur's throat went dry. "It's hard to discern the message, sire.

The situation is complicated. . ."

"No, no, my friend," Attila cajoled, in a voice as sweet as carrion flesh, taking his arm off the augur's shoulder and beginning to pace around the mess on the ground. "It's not as hard as it seems. All you have to do is take it step by step. Let's start at the beginning, this dead commander you told me about, does his name begin with an 'A'?"

The augur was past pretending that he could see anything at all and was terrified that the Hun was about to draw his sword again. Although Attila's voice was calm, his eyes were darting crazily from side to side.

"Now that you ask me to look at it that way, sire, things do seem simpler . . . Yes, I do believe that the name might begin with an 'A'."

"That's good, you're getting somewhere." Attila drew back thin lips and exposed his rat-like incisors. "Now, concentrate, is it Aetius or Avitus who dies?"

The augur felt the demons he'd conjured up to help him serve Attila breathing down his neck. His hairs stood on end and he felt compelled to tell the truth. "I'm afraid, great lord, that I cannot see that clearly, but. . ."

A sharp right jab to his jaw split open his lip and loosened his bottom front teeth.

"You idiot! *You idiot!!* My name begins with an "A", you son of a donkey!" Attila screamed, drawing his scimitar. "Get out! Get out before I take your head off!"

The shaman hitched up his tunic and ran this time.

Attila withdrew to his tent alone and thudded down onto a stool, next to a bed bedecked in an elaborately embroidered quilt.

He brooded.

The fact was he had no choices left. Aetius had ridden him down, relentlessly, in a way that Attila had never believed anyone in the world was capable of. He, Attila, was the mightiest, swiftest general on earth. He had conquered all nations, subjugated the Ostrogoths, the Gepids and countless others. They were nothing but slaves, vassals, grovelling at his feet. Yet Aetius ... who the fuck was Aetius, a Roman half-breed, to create an alliance of his enemies? When had the Goths, Burgundians and Franks ever ridden out under a Roman eagle? Never!

Attila pulled at his beard. He still couldn't believe that it wasn't a clever trap on the part of Theodoric to lure Aetius into battle then turn on him and help Attila put an end to all he stood for.

Suddenly, Attila broke out in a cold sweat. Above the sounds of the camp he heard the whining voice of his brother, Bleda, whom he'd murdered to steal his half of the Hunnic Empire. Bleda who, in times of trouble, haunted him – not a comfort but a curse. The ghost of Bleda was telling him that he was wrong to go to war. Attila put his hands over his ears and yelled – "Be silent!" but the whining persisted. He stood up, wild eyes circling the tent. There was nowhere inside that an assassin or spy could hide. "You're dead!" he said to empty space, "and I alone rule. All that was yours is now mine."

Yet the boast was hollow, for he was imprisoned inside his own camp. He had half a million warriors at his disposal, but there was the crux of the problem – half a million mouths to feed and horses to water, in the middle of the sun-scorched plain, where there wasn't a drop to drink nor a crumb to eat except what his men carried with them. Sooner or later, he'd have to come out and there'd be Aetius, like a cat outside a mouse-hole. Attila's gut boiled with hatred. *There's nothing to fear, they're outnumbered. The Alani will break at the first glimpse of a cavalry charge. The Goths, Franks, Burgundians, Bretons and Saxons – they'll all rout, or better still, join me and grind the Romans into the dust.*

Attila stood up, cursed and cursed again. He had no choice but to break out, so he planned his battle tactics. He'd pitch like against like in this fight: heavily armoured Gepids against the Roman infantry; Hunnic and Ostrogoth cavalry against Theodoric's Goths. His Hun forces would attack that fat fop, Sangibanus. At least the barbarians would fight in a way he could anticipate, not like Aetius with his endless tricks.

Attila wiped sweat from his brow. Despite his bravado, his hand shook. He revisited the insane image of Roman cavalry charging up a cliff face on the three-headed hill. The augur's prophecy unsettled him. He'd take as many precautions as possible with his own life – stay in the centre, well back from the front line and surround himself with his bodyguards.

Attila said no prayers seeking guidance or salvation. He made no sacrifices in the hour before battle. His eye rolling back and spittle at the corners of his mouth, he threw aside the tent flap and snarled orders to his vassals to get into battle position.

The Fifth Hour on the Roman Hill

Roman headquarters
The three-headed hill above the Catalaunian Plains
20th September 451 AD

Avitus, standing next to his standard-bearer on the three-headed hill, watched the Roman cohort moving into position on the plain. *Well executed, as it should be.* A rare wind lifted his banner for a moment so that his lion rampant flew side by side with Aetius' eagle.

Sidonius was at hand, taking Avitus' dictation. The sun was west of its zenith and for him, as for all the men, the wait before combat was dragging. Slaves walked down the lines, refilling water flasks while the ranks checked are rechecked their weapons. They were anxious to know when battle would engage, but Aetius was giving nothing away. Eager to distinguish himself in battle, Sidonius was disappointed Avitus had assigned him and seven other equites to a long, metal bench on which they'd transcribe and disseminate the generals' orders. He'd tried arguing that he should be in the thick of the battle, but Avitus had been adamant he didn't want Papianilla left a widow as well as fatherless. The command station would be the last position to be taken by the Huns.

Sidonius marched back to his post with Avitus' orders. As he approached, he saw his seven fellow equites standing in a circle, listening intently to a decanus. A man in his prime, the decanus had a full head of jet-black hair and a closely shaven jaw. He wore a breastplate embossed with an eagle and the studded leather skirt of the elite troops. His face was calm but stern.

The equites were at most twenty years old and all were aristocrats. They stood with their armour on the ground next to them and most had let their thigh-length, maroon tunics fall from their backs and drape from their belts in the heat. Their scarless shoulders were broad and well-muscled, bronzed by the sun. Behind them, their twelve-foot anti-cavalry spears were stowed in perfect order in a rack, their freshly whetted tips white-hot in the sun. Red and black pennants hung limply down the sides of the polished shafts, waiting for the winds of battle to blow them to life. The equites listened in absolute silence to the decanus, their heads slightly bent, weight on one leg more than the other, and their arms crossed.

Sidonius noticed a pair of soldiers from another cohort, dressed in rough blue tunics, looking askance at the equites and their shiny new equipment that screamed "privilege" as they marched past. Although the blue boys would have spent hours checking the rivets in their pila, their spears wouldn't be new but picked up from old battlegrounds and straightened out to be thrown again.

As he approached his group of equites, Sidonius raised a hand above his head to show that he was carrying a general's orders. The solemn soldiers looked up, jaws set with untested confidence. The decanus, without any of the usual formality between an officer and his men, was farewelling them. The equites pulled their tunics up onto their shoulders, picked up their armour and took the orders from Sidonius then sat at their bench and wrote as fast as their hands could move.

Sidonius took his place at one end of the table. Seated, he could no longer see the generals on their steeds but he could make out their standards, hanging limp under the beat of a leaden sun. A constant stream of runners brought Aetius' written orders back to him faster than he could transcribe and relay them off down the lines.

From other directions, written requests from the allies kept firing back at him – clarification – latest information – changes to Attila's position – to which Sidonius replied on his own initiative. Then came a more difficult question, the Burgundians requested thirteen horses for their officers. Feeling a twinge of guilt that he'd forgotten to pass on Heva's message to Aetius, Sidonius wrote back asking why they couldn't supply their own mounts. The dinner where the black dwarf had appeared in Lyon had been less than three weeks ago, yet it felt as if decades had passed.

The troops Heva had led into battle at Pouans-les-Vallées had joined the rest of their tribe under the leadership of his elder brother, Gundobad, and his father, King Gundioc. They replied that they didn't travel with reserve mounts for anyone.

Thirteen horses wouldn't normally be difficult to find from the Roman reserves, but it wasn't up to Sidonius to decide such matters under battle conditions. He hastily wrote out a note for Ecdicius who was in command of the cavalry.

Reading it, Ecdicius shook his head. The gruelling one hundred and sixty miles chase from Orleans had been raced at the pace of the Hippodrome. Without respite, his horses had gone straight into the thrash of battle and a third had been killed or wounded. He clenched his jaw, determined to avenge the death of his own stallion on the escarpment, then wrote to Sidonius – *We can spare the Burgundians nothing.*

When Sidonius sent the answer down the line the Burgundian reply ricocheted back – *Without horses our officers cannot lead their men into battle.*

Sidonius frowned, scribbled out two copies of the message and sent one to Ecdicius and the other to Avitus. Avitus' reply arrived a second before Ecdicius' second refusal – *Tell Ecdicius to find three horses for the Burgundian general and his two alternates.*

Ecdicius singled out three mounts, giving away no star performers but making sure that those he did accord the Burgundians had stamina. Haldor the Burgundian dismounted from Heva's warhorse, Thunder, who'd been bleeding profusely all morning, and passed him down the line to an officer who was neither on the wing of his division nor the centre of the front line. The horse had little left to give and couldn't be relied on to withstand an enemy charge, but he'd get what use he could out of the dying charger. Tears welled in Haldor's pale blue eyes when he read the Roman reply, but he squared his shoulders and told his officers that they would run on foot ahead of their men into Attila's cavalry.

It meant certain death, but not one of them flinched.

The Sixth Hour in Attila's Camp

Attila's waggon circle on the Catalaunian Plains
20th September 451 AD

The sun glanced off Attila's helmet and flashed over the faces of the chieftains and warriors who thronged around him. Bows slung over their shoulders, quivers bursting with arrows, battle-axes and swords on their baldricks, they were transfixed by his performance. His eyes rolled back in his head, showing their whites instead of the irises. He raged from side to side in front of a mountain of horse saddles he'd ordered to be collected and stacked up on the ashes of his campfire. His blood turned to acid and fizzed through his veins, the jugular visibly pulsating, and the slash of his scimitar hummed in his vassals' ears. Although it was broad daylight, ten men holding flaming torches stood at his back. Attila's peroration was coming to its climax.

Here you stand, after subduing the world! War is your custom! You have conquered all except the Roman union of discordant races before you! Now it is their turn to die! It is our right to glut ourselves on vengeance! Despise them!

Look – even before our attack they are smitten with terror! They seek the heights, they seize the hills and fear a battle in open fields. You know how feeble a Roman attack is! While they are still gathering in order and forming one line with locked shields, they are paralysed by the first dust of battle. Attack the Alani, smite the Goths! They are cowards, all! Seek swift victory in the spot where the battle rages. Cut their sinews and their bodies will collapse, gouge out their bones. Let your fury burst forth! Show first your cunning, Huns, then your deeds of arms!

If you are wounded, exact the death of your foe in revenge! If you are not wounded then revel in the slaughter of your enemies. No spear can harm you if you are destined to live and there is nothing you can do to avoid Fate if it is your time to die. Why would Fortune have made the Huns victorious over all other nations unless it was to prepare us for the satisfaction of this conflict? Slay Aetius!

Attack! Attack! They are not bold enough to attack us. I will hurl the first spear!

Attila stopped pacing and dropped the pitch of his voice to a low menace. His bloodshot eyes narrowed under lowered brows.

If any one of you can stand at rest while Attila fights, he is a dead man.

As he pronounced the last words, the men holding naked flames behind him threw their torches into the pile of saddles doused with axle grease and they exploded into a pyrotechnic frenzy.

Inflamed by Attila's words, the Huns jumped on their horses and jostled shoulder to shoulder as they raced out through the main gate and galloped in circling whirlwinds onto the plain.

Attila wasn't at the front of his army. He placed himself carefully in the centre of his most trusted bodyguards where nothing Roman was likely to reach him.

It was late afternoon. His fear for his life had led him to delay the battle until an hour when most armies would have withdrawn from the field for the day but now it would rage.

The Sixth Hour on the Roman Hill

Roman headquarters
The three-headed hill above the Catalaunian Plains
20th September 451 AD

"I still live in hope that Attila will burn himself to death," said Avitus', whose blue eyes danced as he observed the bonfire flaring up in the centre of the Hun encampment.

Aetius wasn't listening. The battle wouldn't be over before nightfall and they would have to fight in the dark. He and the fifty-thousand troops who held the vantage point and looked down from the eagle's nest were silent as Attila's horsemen streamed out of the waggon circle and kicked up tornadoes of dust.

Down the lines, coiled Roman horns, as wide as a man's spread arms, blasted out the order to advance. The aquilifers raised their eagles, gilded eyes and hooked beaks glittering, and marched. Behind them flew the blood-red banners of every cohort and its centuries. In perfect rows, steel breast-plates blazing in the afternoon sun, warriors raised their shields as one. Borne on by the spirit of war, they took fateful first steps towards the enemy.

As still as a stone god, Aetius sat on Achilles' back, breathing slowly and deeply. The horse snorted and jangled at the bit, his front hooves planted squarely on the edge of the ridge and his ears pricked forward. Aetius held his right arm motionless above his head, fingers straight, while his army marched to the beat of his heart. At the perfect moment, with the precision of a razor, his hand sliced down to his side, the horns sounded the charge and his men bellowed the roar of war.

Theodoric, who'd been cantering his white charger along his lines, heard the horns, swung his head round and spurred him into a charge towards Attila's flank. Down thirty miles of allied lines, the kings and princes of the alliance rallied their men and followed his lead.

Feeling older than the hill on which he stood, Avitus marvelled at the sight of wave upon wave of fighting men flooding the plains. Attila's hordes stopped circling and charged straight towards the Alani front line. Watching for the moment of impact, Avitus prayed under his breath for his troops on the battlefield –

O Mars, ye god of war, steady their blood and strengthen their swords.

The Seventh Hour

Brutus and Quintus stood shield to shield, in the centre of their cohort, in the centre of the Alani front line, in the centre of the Catalaunian Plains. They didn't need an officer to tell them that they were placed at exactly the point where Attila would focus his attack.

A trumpet sounded and the two thin rows of Alani in front of them dropped to their knees behind their shields, dug the blunt end of their anti-cavalry pikes into the ground and braced for impact. Behind the impenetrable wall of spikes, Brutus' nerves might have subsided had the kneeling of the Alani not exposed a clear view of coverless brown ground, parched as a desert, and a black horde of Hun horsemen with bows drawn storming towards him. Ochre-coloured clouds rose from their horses' hooves and drowned the stark blue sky.

The Hun battle-shriek went up – *what in Hades is that?* and Brutus' blood curdled. He wiped dust from his eyes, unable to believe what he saw. In only seconds, the demons would be on him. His body shook but there was no time to think before his centurion ordered –

shields above heads –

and the first wave of three-pronged arrows hailed down. He felt their growing weight on his scudus. When the drumming stopped and the order came to face front, arrows prickled it, thistle-thick, but when he shook the scudus hundreds more fell at his feet. Over the flat edge of his upright shield he saw Attila's horses had closed the distance to one hundred yards. The Huns were shouldering their lances, picking their targets – and he was one of them.

"*Weapons at the ready!*" yelled the decanus and Brutus dug in the hobnails of the boot on his back foot and raised his spear to his shoulder, his eyes ranging in search of a target he thought he could hit amongst the galloping frenzy. From under the brow of his helmet he glimpsed Quintus' ashen face at his side.

"If we die today, we die together," said Brutus, "I'll stay with you – no matter what."

Quintus screwed up his eyes, tearing from the dust, and nodded in reply as he balanced the weight of his seven foot pilum over his shoulder and listened for the order.

"*Throw!*" shouted the decanus and a storm of steel and wooden shanks with pyramid tips shot forward over the Alani. Some found their marks in the chests of Attila's mounts or the thighs of their riders – but nothing slowed their howling advance.

"*Lock shields!*"

A wall of metal banged into place.

"*Draw swords!*"

– *and prepare to die* thought Brutus.

From behind him, the Alani archers started firing. Arrows whizzed over his head but only a few of the front row of Huns fell to the ground. Again Brutus heard the order "*Shields above heads*" and in confusion struggled to get his up before the sky turned black and a barrage of arrows from the Roman artillery cannons on the three-headed hill soared over him. They culled hundreds of Huns this time – but still the horsemen, pointed helmets and lances flashing, kept coming, the gaps left by the fallen instantly filled. Brutus heard officers shouting but the clamour of galloping drowned out their words and only the buglers could pierce the din.

"Shields forward!" sounded a horn and Brutus swung his scudus

down and anchored its edge with his foot then laid his sword blade
flat on the top of it.

Through the quarter-inch gap between the top edge of the shield
and his helmet he watched the Huns churning towards him. Leaning
sideways from their saddles they let volley after volley fly. Two Alani
pikeman fell dead and rolled back against his shield. With gauntleted
fists, the rest gripped the shafts of their spears for grim death and leant
their weight forward. *Surely neither beast nor man can break through
this forest of steel.* But the Hun horses didn't baulk and kept hurtling
towards him. Behind them, riding out of the clouds of dust the first
wave kicked up, came more men than he could ever have imagined.

Then *crash!*

The edge of Brutus' shield slammed into his helmet and shoved
him down onto his back knee. He tried to keep his balance but a hoof
nearly took out his eyes as a horse jumped clear over the spear wall and
smashed a gap between him and Quintus who spun through the air
then thumped to the ground. The horse stumbled but found its feet.
With a bloodcurdling shriek, a Hun his black plait spinning round his
shoulders, slashed a scimitar through the neck of the recruit next to
Quintus.

Brutus saw Quintus struggling to unlock his shield from the dead
man's, whose face had been sliced half away, but couldn't help as he
pushed himself up before another wave of cavalry thundered out of
the dust. He hunched armoured shoulders up against the backplate of
his helmet and ducked the swing of an axe then deflected the Hun's
scimitar with a sweep from his gladius. The Hun spurred his horse and
leapt forward into battle with the next row of Romans. By the time
Brutus braced himself for the next attack Quintus was back at his side,
his shield up and sword at the ready. Blood streaked his face and his
eyes were wild.

There was no more thinking after that, just the frenzied clash
of metal on metal and flesh on flesh combat, the screams of horses

and men whose lungs choked with dust. Barely able to hear their centurion, they did their best to follow his orders until halfway through a command his voice stopped. The decanus rose in his place and continued yelling over the screams and clamour of war until the sun was dimmed by the dust on the horizon and his hoarse voice called out – *"Every man for himself."*

Blinded, choked and labouring with exhaustion, Brutus and Quintus stood back-to-back and slogged on. As daylight faded, the battle paused for breath and Brutus, hoping that it might be over, listened for a horn to sound the retreat. But the horns were silent and, through the murk of war, he could hear the clash of weapons. His arm ached so much from the weight of his shield that he let it down and quickly looked around to try to see what was happening.

The dust was so thick he didn't see the Hun coming. The speed of the enemy's horse drove his spear deep into Brutus' left thigh, sending pain such as he'd never known flaring from his leg to his brain. He fell to the ground, one hand clasping the gashed muscle, the other holding his shield over his body – expecting to die, but the Hun charged past.

In seconds, Quintus was on his knees next to him. He grabbed the wooden shaft of the spear with both hands. Brutus met his eyes and nodded. Quintus knelt on the injured leg and pulled with all his force but the spear wouldn't budge and Brutus roared with pain. Through streaming eyes he looked over Quintus' shoulder and saw pointed helmets, scimitars and hatchets hacking their way through the gloom towards them. *"Stand up!* They're behind you."

"I won't leave you!"

"Get up or we're dead!!"

Quintus shot a glance over his shoulder and in one movement whirled to face his enemies. Charging into a thicket of scimitars he yelled – *"Die!!"*

Brutus fumbled for his gladius and tried to stand but his leg buckled. He sucked his bottom lip over his teeth and bit down on it,

185

took the shaft of the spear in his left hand, held it as closely as he could to the ripped flesh, then smashed his unwounded shin up against it. The rod cracked but didn't snap. *You bastard* – screamed Brutus then smacked the shin back up again. He levered down on the shaft, all the veins in his arms writhing as he held his breath and pushed with all his force. Suddenly the wood snapped. Avoiding contact with the splintered six-inch stump protruding from his flesh, Brutus untied his sword belt. Quick and tight, without looking too closely, he knotted it around his thigh. Pushing up from his good leg, he grabbed his shield and ploughed into the fight. With two quick slashes of his gladius he slit the throats of one Hun and gutted another. Slash and stab, slash and stab, parry, slash and stab.

No orders, no rest, no reinforcements. Not a word could be heard over the clangour of metal, the grunts and screams. But Brutus knew that, hidden in the fog of battle, every man in the line, was fighting beyond his limits, just as he and Quintus were. It would go on that way all night – until they all lay dead.

The Eleventh Hour

Battle of the Catalaunian Plains
20th September 451 AD

Aetius, mounted on his warhorse streaked with sweat and blood, watched a blazing orb sink below a grey horizon, the portent of a merciless night. The dying sun coloured the dust clouds thick and red. His lips were set in a hard line, his brow creased. For every man on the field, this fight to the death would be fought in the dark. But there was no choice. He would never abandon the field to Attila, never.

On all sides of the three-headed hill, centurions repeatedly ordered their ranks to reform behind tattered standards and charge. But the Gepids in their armour and the Ostrogoths on horse had cut through to the top of the escarpment and the Romans were growing ever more weary.

In short bursts, Ecidicius' cavalry trumpets blasted commands above the clamour of war. In bone-crunching agony, his knees smashed against those of the enemy as he rode them off. Horses pushed shoulder to shoulder as he leaned out of the saddle to slash at armoured Ostrogoths. Again and again he charged, but he didn't have the numbers to push the enemy far before risking being encircled or leaving his infantry defenceless.

While the cavalry battle raged, officers on the ground rotated the men on foot in their lines. Each row fought until the troops could no longer lift their weapons, then the row behind stepped up and fought in turn until those men too became too fatigued to fight. Rotating the lines kept up momentum, but progress was being made in inches, not yards.

From the summit of the hill, the magister militum scanned the battle lines. He pulled out the scarf he wore between his neck and the edge of his armour and wiped sweat from his face then tucked it back in between his flesh and his metal. His eyes scanned far and wide, then close at hand, as he calculated the importance of every discernible detail. The Burgundians, avenging Heva's death, were holding up well under the leadership of Gundioc and Gundobad. The Franks weren't orderly but they were doing what they were supposed to do, killing the Huns. Despite the crushing cost of lives, the Bretons were holding their line, as were the Saxons, more seafarers than soldiers but vicious when crossed. He'd always known the Alani would be the weak point.

"Ye gods! Can you believe that anyone could be so *incompetent!*" he exclaimed to Avitus who'd seen him sitting still on the hill and hacked his way across the mêlée to see what was worrying him. "What does Sangibanus think he's doing?"

Down on the plain, Sangibanus' horse was pirouetting on the spot, drawing his men into little eddies around him that opened up gaps between the Alani line and the Roman cohort at the centre.

"I suppose he thinks he's leading his men," said Avitus. "It could be worse, he could have given way at the first charge. The line has held for over four hours. He's doing his best, it's just not worth much. What a shambles!"

"He's leading them in circles," said Aetius grimly, "creating the worst of all outcomes." The front line had turned into a "w" shape, with the Roman cohort in the middle rapidly becoming an island as the Alani caved in on either side. The Roman commander had ordered his men to form a square, a defensive position where they'd fight back to back until the last one fell, which would be in only a few minutes as there were fewer than two hundred left and Attila had focused his cavalry on them. "They'll be massacred to a man. Our boys should have fallen back with the Alani, but they're holding their position."

"Trying to set an example." Avitus turned away and searched the immediate battleground for the clipped red curls of Aetius' favourite subordinate. "Where've you sent Marjorian?"

"Ostrogoths took that spur," Aetius' eyes signalled a bloodbath halfway up the hill, "he's in the thick of it."

Avitus frowned and searched his own ranks for a senior officer he could spare to go down and stiffen up the Alani resistance. All his men were in hand-to-hand combat with Gepid black-shirts who'd broken through the Roman perimeter. The Ostrogoth cavalry thundered in raging waves to push the Gepids forward. Fifty paces away, Sidonius and his fellow noblemen turned over the metal camp table on which they'd been transcribing orders and reinforced it with supply boxes to form a barricade.

Avitus turned back to his lifelong friend, the greatest general that Rome had ever known. "Only you can do this. Get down to the front line – fast as you can."

The field commander's lips tightened. "I need a torch-bearer." He looked over towards the equites, deciding which of them to take with him. His eyes swept over Sidonius, who looked up from the barricade as if he felt an angel of death passing over him.

"Take one of the wounded," said Avitus, "that one over there, he can't stand to fight but he can ride." He called and the boy hobbled over. "We have a job for you. I'll give you a leg-up." Avitus himself helped the boy onto the horse.

"Stay close at hand and look after yourself," Aetius said to the tousle-headed youth as he fell in behind. "Give me one torch now and carry two spares." The general pushed the long metal handle of the first torch into the back of his sword belt.

Avitus couldn't help but smile at the sight. "Careful with that or you'll set the plumes of your helmet alight."

"I'm not Attila – I rely on my sword, not fire – but in the dark we all need a light to follow." He pulled up the head of his horse. "Will you be all right up here, alone, old man?"

"You know I will, or you wouldn't be leaving. Now get out of here, they need you down there." Avitus winked and managed a smile for Aetius and the young equites as they cantered round a mêlée of men then disappeared in the growing gloom.

They were barely gone when an Ostrogoth horn blasted another charge. Avitus gritted worn teeth in his bulldog jaw and settled his weight forward onto his thighs and the balls of his feet. *This is my style of fighting – hand to hand, relentless, foot to foot, sword against shield, methodical, rotating the ranks to keep them fresh. Move only forward – never retreat. I've been doing this for half a century. No one else on this battlefield – the largest the world has ever known – can boast that! If the Gepids want my post, they'll have to fight uphill for it, every step of the way, and at the top they'll face me. I'll never give an inch. If the gods of war will it, I'll die defending this hill.*

Down on the plain, the Huns swooped in repeatedly on the folding front line, first shooting arrows from a distance, then returning with their spears to skewer the Roman allies, next regrouping to charge anew with long swords drawn before dismounting to finish off the remnants with their hatchets. Attila hid amongst his bodyguards in the middle of his line.

Aetius arrived at the front and was rallying the Alani, who were fighting in terrified clusters, to form up into ranks and close the gap between themselves and what was left of the Roman cohort. His young torch-bearer had lost his life to a spear through the throat only halfway down the three-headed hill.

Aetius tied the reins of the equites' horse to a pommel of his saddle and galloped along the line to where Sangibanus was floundering. Aetius pulled up hard and Achilles reared, frothing at the bit.

"You know, Sangibanus, it's getting boring having to rescue you like this."

At the sound of Aetius' voice, Sangibanus stared into the murk as if he'd heard a spectre. Sweat was running in rivers down his dust-caked face and his armour was spattered with blood. He had deep wounds to both his legs and his sword arm was shaking from fatigue not fear.

"Your performance is improving," said Aetius. "If you put your energy into pushing forward instead of riding in circles you'll make headway. Remember that pincer movement I told you about on the three-headed hill?"

Sangibanus looked at Aetius as if he'd never heard the words "pincer movement" and had no idea what they might mean.

Aetius didn't blink. "Let me make it very simple for you, just do what I say and don't think for yourself. See that star?"

Sangibanus was gasping and couldn't form words to answer. He raised his head and wheezed an inaudible "Where?" while his bloodshot eyes searched for light through the dust. Aetius pointed and when he saw that Sangibanus had found the planet said – "Drive forward in that direction. If something gets in your way, go through it! Keep going until there are no more enemies in front of you, or you're dead."

Gaunt with exhaustion, Sangibanus' face sunk even further. Aetius turned a commanding eye on his inferior.

"Tonight is the night, Sangibanus. We fight till the end." Spurring his horse in the direction of the Roman cohort, he called back over his shoulder, almost kindly. "If you reach for the stars, you may never touch them, but you'll end up in a better place than you started from."

With his gladius held high above his head and the riderless horse behind him, Aetius spurred Achilles along the broken Alani line, crying out to the haggard men on foot, the injured, the dying – "We fight till the end!"

When he arrived at the beleaguered Roman square, he pulled a wounded warrior up onto the riderless horse. Immediately aware that the eagle had fallen, through the dust of the mêlée he sought out the aquilifer and found him crouched on one knee, head bowed. The aquilifer's knuckles showed white through the blood on his hands as he struggled to hold the legionary banner upright.

Seeing that he was mortally wounded, Aetius bent low from the back of his horse. "You've done all you can. Give me your eagle. It will fly high and your spirit with it."

Dazed by loss of blood, through blinding pain and the grit of battle, the aquilifer looked up. Dark red streaks ran from his lips but their corners rose. "Flavius Aetius. I was waiting for you." Aetius closed his fist around the standard and the aquilifer released his eagle. Aetius raised it against the darkened sky and the aquilifer's eyes followed it, then his last breath hissed between his lips and he collapsed.

Aetius turned to the men struggling behind him. "Form up! Arrow formation! We storm their centre."

In an endless torrent, Attila's cavalry thrashed down on them but the Romans rallied behind their eagle. When they were settled and ready to charge, Aetius positioned himself at the tip of the arrowhead and steadied his mount.

* * * * *

From the vortex of the hand-to-hand struggle on the three-headed hill, Avitus glanced down to the plain to gauge which way the battle was turning and glimpsed Theodoric at the head of a massed Gothic cavalry charge. The Goth, having seen that the Roman cohort was a shrinking island in a sea of Huns and the Alani front line was about to break, was attacking Attila's flank.

In the fading light, Avitus could see Theodroic's white charger at the head of the cavalry column, appearing then disappearing in the dust the ground coughed up. Avitus felt, rather than saw, the thud of impact above Theodroic's heart. The horse disappeared for a moment. When it emerged from the clouds and pounded on across the front of the charging phalanx, Avitus couldn't see if Theodoric was still on its back.

His breath caught in his throat, then he let out a deep sigh with the thought. *Time to see what young Thorismund is made of.* There was no respite for more than that.

As Theodoric fell, the last centurion on Avitus' flank of the defensive square took a axe through the jugular. No junior officers remained to step up and take his place and the primus pilus, the next most experienced warrior, was coughing blood. From his vantage point atop his horse's back, Avitus surveyed the surrounding mêlée. Sidonius' overturned desk had become his new last defence. Roman and Gepid bodies had heaped up before it and, in spiked boots, the Gepids were clambering over their own dead towards the desperate pack of young equites.

Avitus looked over the rest of his ranks. On all sides, almost all the officers lay in twisted mounds of dead. He bent down and pulled his lion standard from the ground where his soldiers had anchored it, balanced it against his shoulder and raised his sword above his head, then spurred his stallion across the front line. Foamed sweat blew from its flanks as it lowered its head and stretched fatigued legs to full length. With one hand, Avitus held aloft his lion rampant and it unfurled in the galloping wind, with the other he felled his enemies. His voice boomed at battle strength as he rallied his men, then pounded back across his lines to his point position.

Perspiration streamed down his face as he sat back in the saddle and scoured the plain for the silvery plumes of Aetius' helmet. Night was rolling in across the battlefield and he couldn't make him out. Avitus turned back towards his cohorts. Their energy was ebbing faster than the sun. The mere threat of imminent death wasn't enough to keep them on their feet. He needed to do something to help them find more inside themselves than they believed they had.

Putting the reins in one hand, he slid from his horse's back. A crazy thing to do for a man of his age, he knew it. Aetius had told him not to dismount but instinct told Avitus that his men needed to see him fighting on foot alongside them.

He looped the strap of his general's helmet tightly across one of the pommels of his saddle. "Escape", he murmured to the horse as he slapped its rump, hoping that the loyal steed would run from the carnage on the mount. Then he dropped to one knee beside the body of a dead centurion. With thumbs covered in blood, he gently closed the man's eyelids. "You won't be needing this now," he said to the body as he undid the centurion's helmet and pushed it onto his own head, then he rose up. "Let's go find out just how tough Gepid armour is." Standing straight, with the blood-red mane of the helmet flaming round his head, he addressed both the living and dead.

"I make an oath to you all: I'll die before I let Attila take this hill."

He glanced over the mass of seething swords clashing around him to where he'd last seen Sidonius and his equites defending their makeshift barricade. A dozen Gepids were trampling their own fallen and surging over the top. The last three of the equites stepped up to face the slit-eyed helmets and tried to push them back but the Gepids had the advantage of weight and numbers and bore down with merciless ferocity.

Sidonius became submerged in the struggle and lost from sight. Avitus raised his sword and roared at a squadron to follow him. The men fought to form up behind the horse-hair mane of the centurion's helmet.

Avitus looked back to the barricade and saw the last but one of the equites fall but breathed with relief as Sidonius and one other knight rose up, still fighting with all their might. Sidonius threw aside his shield and, with sword and dagger drawn, pressed his attack. Avitus' chest clenched when he saw it, knowing it to be the desperate move of a man who had nothing left to lose. Suddenly, Sidonius became the only man amongst the hundreds of thousands on the field of war to matter to him. He glanced back over his shoulder to see how many warriors had managed to follow him, wanting eight at least to match the Gepids' ten, but glad enough to see six, then raised his sword and pointed it towards the overrun barricade. "*Charge!*"

Astonished at his own speed, Avitus' boots crunched into the ground and his legs were young again as he slashed his way towards the boy who was his daughter's future but oh, so much more than that. His sword arm moved as if it weren't his own, mechanically lethal, each cut and thrust so well known that he didn't think, just hacked. Breath rasping his windpipe, his legs began to ache and his heart pounded so hard he thought it would explode or stop, but he never took his eyes off Sidonius' black-curled head, now helmetless. The equites had fought well before they fell, taking six of ten Gepids but four remained and were beating him back. A blade slashed down and Sidonius' last cohort fell, leaving him alone to face the attack.

Avitus threw his weight forward, his legs running as they had when he'd been a lad on the field of his gymnasium and claimed every record on the track. He pushed aside warriors as if they were straw. Twenty yards left – fifteen – ten – then relief, the last five opened up as clear ground. Sidonius raised his gladius and brought it crashing down at a Gepid neck – but it struck metal, not flesh, and the blade snapped.

The Twelfth Hour

The Battle of the Catalaunian Plains
20th September 451 AD

In any other battle, when the light faded each army would sound the retreat, but not this. The fate of the world hang in the balance.

As night fell, Aetius' trumpets blasted out their orders for the combined forces to commence their pincer movement against Attila. When his men were as ready as they could ever be, the Supreme Commander of the Allied forces pulled the torch from his sword belt and struck a spark from his fire-steel. The flame flared then steadied. A drawn sword in his other hand, Aetius raised it high, spurred Achilles to a gallop and bellowed, *"Charge!"*

While the Roman and Alani ranks attacked Attila's left flank, Thorismund led his column of mounted Goths against Attila's right and Theodoric's cavalry charged his centre. The Burgundians and other allies pushed beyond their limits and surged in behind on foot.

Midnight

The Battle of the Catalaunian Plains
20th – 21st September 451 AD

In a whirlwind pursuit through the black of night, Thorismund chased his enemy right through the main gate of Attila's encampment. A mass of hands dragged him from his horse and a scimitar slashed open his scalp before his bodyguards could reach him.

* * * * *

"Christ!" Brutus cried out, as he swung his sword wildly at the length of an arm he could barely lift and decapitated an unseen victim – "I've killed my best friend!"

* * * * *

I should never have expected them to be able to keep up, thought Aetius as he leant forward in his saddle and smote the Huns engulfing him. To create courage and momentum, he'd led the charge at a gallop but his army had been left behind and he was alone in the swirl of Attila's lines.

* * * * *

I hope someone survives to write a record of this, thought Sidonius as his sword shattered on a Gepid shoulderplate.

* * * * *

I've lived a long and interesting life, thought Avitus. With both hands on the hilt, he rammed his gladius through a Gepid breastplate, *to die fighting in hand-to-hand combat in the fiercest battle the world has ever seen will be a fitting end.*

* * * * *

"Fuck! I've got to save myself!" Attila cursed as his bodyguards routed. Caught in the pincer movement of the Gothic cavalry and Roman forces, he yanked his horse's head round, dug his spurs deep into its bleeding flanks, and fled.

Dawn

The Catalaunian Plains
21st September 451 AD

To the east and south of Epernay lies a plain, one hundred miles long and sixty miles wide. It is gentle ground, green except at the end of a long dry summer, smooth and flat.

It was here that Attila made his stand.

Dawn's graphite light sketched its lines and drew a lunar landscape. The field's smooth skin was pustulated by mounds of bodies, twisted, alone or lying in mountainous heaps, men and horses. Bleak and black. But the rivers ran red.

When the counting was done, they numbered 165,000 the warriors who died in that desperate fight of one day and one night.

Spare a thought not only for those who rode to war by choice but also for those who didn't, slaves and steeds, living blood, sinew, nerve and flesh, who suffered and perished for causes that were never their own.

Dawn brought the first wind of autumn. It passed over the plains, sweeping up the spirits of the dead. The massed ghosts of fallen warriors were aghast at their own numbers.

In the centre of the plain a wizened wisp of smoke rose from the empty heart of Attila's camp.

On top of the three-headed hill, Sidonius and one lone infantryman were clearing bodies from their barricade. The young nobleman's warm, but blooded, hands shook as they closed around the icy wrists of the last corpse. The trooper took the ankles and they carried it to a flat patch of what had once been grass and laid it at the end of a row of corpses.

"I'm thirsty, sir," said the gregarius, wiping his forehead.

Sidonius straightened up, searching for a medical post or supply station but couldn't find one. "Thank you for your help, you're free to go. Dismissed."

The gregarious saluted and walked towards the eagle of his century, picking up and shaking every water flask he passed.

Sidonius was looking from one sunken corpse to the next, thinking that, only yesterday, their faces had been plump with life, when a dark-haired figure leaning on a spear limped out of the dawn mist. With a start, Sidonius thought for a moment that the warrior in a blood-drenched tunic was a phantom. The square, clean-cut face was askew and so badly bruised that he barely recognised the decanus who'd addressed the equites before battle. The decanus' jaw was so far awry that he couldn't speak but the hand that clasped the back of Sidonius' neck was reassuringly warm. Tears edged from the corners of their eyes as they stood for a long moment, in silence, together. Then the decanus saluted the dead, inclined his head to the sole survivor and departed.

Sidonius' poet's hands were stiff and bruised, the knuckles swollen. He set to righting the wreckage around him, searching through boxes of stores, strewn in all directions, for some pens and ink, but it was futile. He turned over the equites' battered table, stacked boxes below its broken legs and sat down at one end. In the mournful light, he looked along the dented stretch of empty bench and heard the laughter of ghosts. He dreaded going back to his tent for he knew he'd find eight neatly rolled blankets and carefully stowed packs that his friends had planned to come back to. It would be his duty to sort out their possessions and write euphemisms to their mothers about how their sons had died. One image chased another in his mind but all were equally horrible.

Shaking with exhaustion and shock, he left the bench and slumped down on the ground, his head in his hands, reliving the moment that his sword had shattered on a Gepid shoulder plate and he'd believed himself dead.

Were it not for the red mane of a centurion's helmet appearing at the Gepid's back and Avitus, roaring like a lion, swinging his sword through his enemy's neck, Sidonius would have been laid out with his friends; saluted by the broken-jawed decanus; grieved for by Papianilla; his life unlived. All that he was born to be would never have been. His children unborn; his life's work undone; the course of his love for his wife unrun.

At the rattle of a sword belt, his head shot up and he reached for his gladius. But it was Avitus marching towards him, his back forever stiff, one foot lifting not quite high as it normally did. The black plumes of his general's helmet ran over the top of his head and down his back. Under his arm, he carried the centurion's helmet with its red horsehair crescent running from ear to ear. Sidonius pushed himself to his feet and saluted.

"You're wounded?" Avitus saw the pallor of his face and feared that he was bleeding internally.

"Nothing serious, sir, just flesh wounds. But I owe you my life."

"Think nothing of it, you fought well and deserved to survive."

"Nonetheless, sir. . ."

Avitus waved him quiet. "I've a mission for you. Take this helmet and find its rightful owner, that we may bury him with full honours."

Sidonius looked at the helmet and then at the tangled dead. His stomach heaved. It'd take time to muster the willpower to go rummaging amongst the mangled bodies. "Will that be all, sir, or are there orders you'd like transcribed?"

"No further orders for now." Avitus pushed the helmet into Sidonius' hands. "I believe we owe that centurion a debt of honour."

Sidonius' eyes welled with tears of exhaustion and anger. "Excuse me, sir, but is *honour* what war is about?"

Avitus raised his grizzled eyebrows. "Only the young can ask such questions." Seeing the pain in Sidonius' face, he let out a long breath. "Sometimes the only answer to force is greater force. War is about killing that man," he stabbed his finger at Attila's camp, "before he kills me." He looked down at the bodies lying near to them. "Your friends were aristocrats, too young to have families. Perhaps it could be said that they died for the honour of Rome. But the common soldiers who gave their lives last night were trying to save themselves. The reason they fought was to stop Attila from burning their homes, raping their wives, slaughtering their children and eating the stock they'd worked so arduously to raise."

Avitus looked over to the eagles in the distance and his voice deepened. "I've made war for fifty years and held enough dying men in my arms to know that those who're lucid as their life runs out speak not of honour, but of people and places they love, or of wrongs they wish forgiven. No one utters the word "eagle" with his last breath." He stepped in front of Sidonius, put a hand on his shoulder. "What did you fight for?"

"For Papianilla, mostly, and for you, sir."

The general shook his head. "You didn't need to fight to please me."

"And also for Rome, for all it stands for, for law and liberty"

"So much the better."

"How've you stood it so long, all this killing, the senseless waste?"

Avitus saw the anguish on his son-in-law's face, the furious incom-prehension. He turned his own hands palm upwards. They where stinging, raw and bloody. The callouses of fifty years' combat had been ripped off. "Sit down, Sidonius, and I'll tell you where it all began."

They sat together on the bloodstained ground. Avitus removed his helmet and put it on the grass next to the centurion's. "When I was only fifteen years old, I was sent to my first posting, a regular bit of guard work along the River Rhine. Nothing unusual about that. I was keen to get away from home and prove I was a man. Avoid being whipped by my tutor for misquoting Virgil! And everyone knew that it would be a quiet post, the river kept the northern border safe.

But on New Year's Day, 410, the Rhine froze solid, became a bridge. In their tens of thousands, barbarians flooded across it. Our border posts weren't designed for that. One or two boatloads at a time wasn't a problem, but whole armies? Not up to that!"

"So what could you do, sir?"

"Not enough, son, not enough," said Avitus, looking into the far-off distance. "I was atop a watchtower, striking my fire flint in the frozen wind and setting the brush warning bales alight. Up the fires shot, one after another down the line. When I'd finished, I looked out across that snow-bound world. Hordes of barbarians were marching across the river, and there –" he pointed, as if he could still see something – "alone, in their path, was a young woman trying to fish through the ice. A tiny girl was holding a stick in place while the mother raised her mallet to strike. The woman heard our horns, dropped it, grabbed her child's hand and ran. Made it to some snow-covered bushes and dug themselves in. I thought they'd be safe there, but when the main barbarian body had passed the woman dragged her daughter out. Who knows what she was planning to do – run home to her family I suppose – with never a thought for the Goth rearguard.

The leader kicked his horse into a canter and, run as she might, she hadn't chance. But she never let go of her little girl's hand. I remember that. Not until the Goth's sword sliced her head off."

Sidonius, swallowed hard. "What happened to the child?"

"The brute pulled her up by her hair and threw her over his horse's withers. Carried her off and left the mother's headless body soaking into the snow. More than that, I'll never know, but, over the years, when I've had moments of doubt about our Empire and asked myself what I'm fighting for, I think of that mother and child."

Sidonius shivered. "That's what started your defence of the innocent?"

"I vowed to do whatever I could, no matter what the price, and I've held to that." Avitus ran a hand over his red-rimmed eyes. "I'm an old man now, and today we've defeated Attila, the scourge of God, – mad and evil to the marrow of his bones and the greatest threat our civilisation has ever known. Now, it's time for me to go home and live out my final years in the peace for which we've paid so dearly." Avitus' lips lifted at one corner and he squeezed Sidonius' shoulder. "I'll watch you make my daughter happy and my grandchildren grow." Then the smile faded and his eyes became wistful. "But I understand your grief and anger, we've all lost friends today."

Sidonius looked sideways at him. "The magister militum, sir?"

"Last I saw of Aetius, he was headed down from our hill to lead our troops from the front line. There's been no sign of him since. Nor of, Theodoric . . ." Avitus looked down and shook his head. "Of all the allied leaders, only Gundobad the Burgundian has reported in. Good soldier, Gundobad. Solid." Avitus' knees cracked as he pushed himself back to his feet and put on his helmet. "In all my years, I've never seen carnage like this. It's up to you and I to finish what we started and bury our dead with honour, for their lives paid for our future. While I get the army in order, go find the body of that centurion."

"How will I recognise him, sir?"

"There won't be many centurions who've lost their helmets and he isn't far from here. From what I recall, he had well-ordered features. His eyes will be shut; my thumbs closed them."

They saluted then Sidonius watched Avitus' square shoulders march in the direction of the legionary eagles grounded on the ridge of the escarpment. Behind them, battered ranks of men were hammering in the standards around which they'd rallied in the darkest hours of battle and forming up behind them again. But many were standards still missing, down on the plains, in the grips of men who'd died defending them.

Sidonius walked over to a group of bodies and started pulling them off one another. Frowning, he was thinking *I must work for peace without death* when a cheer went up from the men assembling near the ridge. He looked up from his grisly task and his spirit soared at the sight of Aetius' plumed helmet and broad-shouldered silhouette cresting the summit on his warhorse, Achilles. Another cheer went up when a second horse appeared, ridden by a warrior with a bandaged head whom Sidonius barely recognised as Theodoric the Goth's son, Prince Thorismund.

Aetius had fought his way alone through a sea of Huns in the night. He'd cut through to the far side of the Hun phalanx, killing countless numbers of the enemy, but seen no traces of his own army in the dark and had spent what was left of the night with his allies in the Gothic camp.

Thorismund, his bound head still dripping blood, was worried about where his father was and Aetius had suggested that Theodoric might have become separated from his men, as he had, and found refuge in the Roman camp.

* * * * *

From a distance, all appeared to be still inside the Hun circle, but behind the smouldering waggons, the shattered survivors of the largest army the world had ever known were sheathing their weapons and preparing to flee. Defeated, the Huns huddled behind their barricades in fear that the Romans would charge and finish them off completely.

Sky Hawk wasn't amongst them. Neither he nor his mountain

pony would ever pick their way back up the razor ridge on the path back home. The saddle bags of booty, with which he could have made himself headman of many villages, would be shared between the Romans and their allies. His bones and his horse's would be subsumed in the soil of the Catalaunian Plains.

And where was Attila?

The warlord who had sought to rule the world was laid out on the embroidered bedspread in the airless silence of his tent.

No one came near him.

Brutus Wakes Up

Under a great weight, in abnormal darkness and cold, Brutus' eyelids opened.

His spirit was hovering above the pile of dead that buried him but, on seeing the hosts of demons and legions of shocked ghosts on the plains, decided to remain in the realm of men. His anima pushed itself back into Brutus' body then urged his flesh to make an effort. Its wounds didn't have to be fatal, but if he lay there doing nothing it wouldn't be long before an optio arrived and, with a quick jab from a short sword, put him out of earthly suffering.

As the anima reconnected with his flesh, Brutus saw a speck of light above him. At first it seemed to be at the end of a long tunnel but then it shot into focus only inches above his pupils. His lungs rasped in a ragged breath. In a moment of rising panic, he engaged his right arm and hand and pushed upwards, shouldering aside the corpses crushing him.

He struggled up onto one knee and vomited then fell forward and rolled onto his side. Cold and covered in coagulating blood, he looked down and saw that someone had tied his sword belt as a tourniquet around his thigh, but he couldn't remember who it'd been. Below the belt, a splintered shaft of wood stuck out of an ugly, blackened gash that seeped blood.

Brutus found he had to concentrate to make himself breathe.

He sucked in air that smelt faintly metallic. His mouth was dry as ash, his throat burning. Slowly, he articulated his neck to survey his surroundings. Blurred vision crisped and his mind started to sharpen.

All was quiet except for the flutter and chirp of birds picking their way through the eyes of the dead. Dozens, perhaps hundreds, of bodies were scattered like broken dolls on the blood-soaked soil around him. There wasn't one living man nearby. The battle was clearly over and he'd been left behind. He couldn't tell whether the grey light was dawn or dusk and had no sense at all of where he was.

Another wave of nausea rolled up and he dry-retched. He was cold, cold to the core, but beyond shivering, and this worried him. Was he already dead? His stomach heaved and a sword-like pain shot through his torso, telling him that he still, just barely, belonged to the living.

He ran his hands over his body. The shaft of pain radiated from a stab wound just below his right rib cage. It felt as if someone had rammed a burning poker through the hole and, via his entrails, into his groin, but it wasn't bleeding. A good sign. He found four sword wounds, one near his hip, another at the junction of his neck and shoulder, and two below his bottom left rib. The front-plate of his armour had been detached from the back and pushed aside in the conflict but, by luck or fate, had kept his heart, lungs and liver covered. His head was swollen and misshapen. When he looked down he saw that every inch of his body was covered in purple and red bruises, and much of it was oozing blood.

He turned his head, searching for danger, before rolling onto his hands and knees and levering himself up. Everything hurt, yet he manoeuvred to standing position with surprising speed. He swayed on his feet but his pulse pushed hard to get blood to his brain and he didn't fall. He tried to raise his shield arm and was surprised to find that he couldn't. The shoulder wasn't dislocated but every muscle around the ball of the joint had ripped off. The shield was nowhere to be seen.

He could barely swallow and couldn't find his water flask. On wobbly legs, he made his way over to three dead men and pulled each of their flask off their belts, squeezing and shaking them in search of a drop of water, but all were dry.

What to do next?

He steadied himself up, searched for his sword and found it grasped in the livid hand of a yellow-faced Hun who'd died trying to extract it from his stomach. Brutus overcame his revulsion and jerked it out of the corpse. It was hard to do for the man he'd killed was stiff with rigor mortis, but Brutus felt an irrational need to have that particular sword, not another, although plenty lay scattered on the ground around him. His mother had scrimped for years to buy it so that he could join the legion and he wasn't going to leave behind everything it meant to him.

His mind turned to home and cold sweat broke out all over him as it flashed back that he might have killed his best friend.

"Quintus!" Dead silence.

"*Quintussss!*" Brutus' hoarse voice broke off into a racking cough that spat up blood and ran a blade of fire down the wounds near his ribs.

"Quintus?" The call echoed off the armour of a heap of dead, as if a messenger was asking each body in turn his name, but none could answer.

Brutus staggered in a circle with a ten-foot radius, looking for a trace of his lifelong friend, praying that he and Quintus had been separated in the dark. If Quintus hadn't been right next to him then it couldn't be his head that Brutus had cut off.

Just as he started to convince himself that he had not killed Quintus, his eye was led to a white object twelve feet away. He stumbled over to it and fell to his knees. The sunburnt nose had turned black. Blind eyes accused him and Brutus screamed "NO! No! no . . ." then collapsed face forward onto the ground, sobbing tearlessly, unable to breathe.

His anima wasn't happy with this. Brutus needed to get up and walk; he needed to drink and forget those who were beyond human help. Take a grip on his own life.

Nudged by his spirit, instinct levered him back to his feet. One foot moved ahead of the other in the direction of a river he remembered crossing the day before, full of battle lust, when he hadn't known what death meant.

His foot stuck in the mud at the edge of a quickly flowing stream and, at last, he started shivering. The banks of the river had been dry before the fighting began and its waters just a trickle, but as he knelt to drink he saw a tide mark of crusty brown residue. Bits of human being lay like jetsam on the banks. The water was red, red with blood and gore, but he gulped it down.

When he'd slaked his thirst, he rolled onto his back. Every atom in his body yearned for sleep as he watched the pale green sky turn blue.

So it was dawn, but dawn of which day? Why was no one moving? Being the sole survivor of a battle, like life in the legions, wasn't what it was cracked up to be. He would've wept if he could but his eyes were parched.

From far in the distance, sounds arose that frightened him. Wailing, ululating shrieks and the thunder of horses galloping. He rose to his knees to try to see what the cause was, but couldn't, so crawled to a mound of dead soldiers near the river. They provided cover for their brother as he leant his weight on their bodies and peered across the plains.

Far away, he could see thousands of warriors racing across the plain as if the fires of Hades were at their heels. There was no enemy in front of them, no enemy behind, but they were at full gallop, as if charging into battle. At first Brutus thought he must be hallucinating, but suddenly they turned in a tight arc and started to circle, circle, circle, bellowing out grief and anger, around nothing that he could see from so far away. These were the death rites reserved for a king, but which king Brutus couldn't guess.

Were they Roman or Hun allies? It made no difference. Whoever they were, they'd loosed the gates of hell and let the demons out.

Brutus dragged himself on top of the bodies, searching for an escape from this pandemonium.

Behind him he saw the thorny crown of Attila's camp with a pall of black smoke in its centre. It filled him with abhorrence.

Above him, the rising sun struck the gilded eagles perched atop the Roman hill. They shone bright, like a lighthouse in the night. Brutus couldn't actually see them but felt as if they were turning all-seeing eyes in his direction, summoning him back to the aerie, their piercing talons reaching out to pluck him up.

But Brutus could never find the strength to climb way up there again. Roman eagles flew far too high for the likes of him; they demanded more than a man should ever give. Eagles were birds of prey.

He turned his back and walked the other way.

Victory

Roman headquarters
The three-headed hill above the Catalaunian Plains
21st September 451 AD

Aetius' eyes had sunken deep into grey sockets. Dawn etched lines on his bloodless face. The skin sagged, dehydrated by excessive physical effort. To find the resources it needed to fight through the night, his body had cannibalised itself. Muscles devoured muscle. But exhaustion did nothing to diminish the nobility of his bearing. He was the victor, the man who had saved the world from Attila the Hun.

From time to time, the Gothic prince, Thorismund raised a hand trembling from fatigue and wiped trickles of blood from his temples. He was a full thirty years younger than Aetius, but battle had hollowed him out to the same degree. Grey-skinned and emptied of resources, it would take months for him to recover. The Goth studied Aetius' noble profile, high cheekbones and gaunt face. The sun was rising and dazzling light reflected off Aetius' helmet as he turned his head and surveyed the plains that he alone commanded. Thorismund had never known a man like him and never would again.

The veteran, Avitus, stepped forward with arms outstretched and pulled first Aetius then Thorismund into his bloodied breastplate. Avitus' body had long ago been reduced to nothing but sinew, muscle and bone and he looked no more wizened than usual, but his thighs trembled with exhaustion and his shoulders ached. For a long moment, the three men embraced then Avitus clapped them both on the back and stepped out to arm's length. "I feared the worst when you didn't come back last night!" He looked Aetius up and down and judged that, although he was covered with blood, almost all of it was Hun.

"I feared the worst when it seemed our army had been swallowed up behind me." Aetius removed his helmet and held it at his side.

"Is my father with you?" Thorismund asked Avitus.

Avitus' face was grave. "We haven't seen him since yesterday. He's not in your camp?"

The Goth shook his head. "He didn't come back, but the field was so deep and wide and the battle such turmoil that it didn't surprise me."

"Some of his phalanx came up here with ours this morning but he wasn't amongst them," said Avitus, his eyes deep and dark.

Sombre silence, then Thorismund spoke. "I must scour the plains."

The three men surveyed the enormity of the task. For mile after mile over the length and breadth of the battlefield, bodies were mountained on top of each other, so thick in places, so high, that there was no place for living men to walk amongst the dead.

"Don't worry, son," Avitus put a hand on Thorismund's shoulder, "no matter how hard the task, we'll find your father, have no doubt. It may not be much help, but the last time I saw the old rogue he was leading the charge into Attila's flank. I'll send a century down to help with your search."

"Thank you, but no. We Goths will find our king."

"As you wish." Avitus raised a straight arm and pointed towards the heaps of bodies that best located where he'd seen Theodoric's horse stumble. "Start your search there, where I saw him at the head of his cavalry."

Thorismund nodded and the generals saluted each other. Unspoken grief stood like a spectre between them. Thorismund mounted his charger and pointed its nose downhill, not knowing whether he was a king or still a prince, but hoping for his father's sake that it was the latter.

"So, this is victory," Aetius said, surveying the desolate plains of death. "We stopped Attila."

"He still lives, I hear."

"Breathing but beaten. Beaten forever. He won't live long. Attila is not our problem now, it's how to stop Thorismund acting on the realisation that we've finished off our common enemy and they no longer need their alliance with Rome. There are three Goths for every Roman here. We're all too tired to fight against those odds today. Our men gave more than their all to vanquish the Hun."

"You'll come up with a solution," said Avitus, although he couldn't see one himself, "you always do, no matter how impossible the situation."

Aetius paced to and fro before answering, "I'll advise Thorismund that he must leave the field and hurry to secure his throne in Toulouse. We'll send his share of the booty down there after him."

Avitus chuckled. "You think he'll accept that?"

"Can you think of any better ideas, old man?" Aetius ached with fatigue.

"No."

"Well, then, I'll talk to him as soon as he gets back."

Deep silence overcame the two friends as they looked out from the summit over the remnants of horses and men. The bland face of the plain had been contorted into a screaming and scarred grimace.

"Without Theodoric, we couldn't have won," said Aetius, "even with him, victory was by a hair's breadth. And we owe it to you that he came and fought for us." Aetius fell silent for a moment then asked, "Tell me, how did we win?"

Avitus let out a long breath. "Remember that, from up here, we could see nothing at all after sunset, but reports this morning tell us that we were hammering away, trying to get enough momentum to fold the Gepid and Ostrogoth lines back on themselves, but making little progress. Then the charges led by you, Theodoric and Thorismund's cavalry, turned the tide of war. When the Hun saw that he was caught in your pincer movement, he broke off and scuttled back to hide in his hole." Avitus put his hand on Aetius' shoulder, turned and looked him in the eye. "Much though you praise Theodoric, and he deserves our praise, you must remember that none of us could have done any of this if it weren't for you."

With half a smile, Aetius shrugged off the compliment. "I left my men so far behind I couldn't see what was happening to them."

"What in the name of Mars made you think they'd be able to keep up with you?" Avitus' eyes crinkled with humour.

"We needed momentum to break Attila's line. Monstrously outnumbered, speed was our only answer."

"Not everyone can move at the pace of a demi-god. You have Sangibanus to thank for leading the Alani through behind you."

"Ha!" said Aetius, breaking into a full smile, "Sangibanus followed his star."

"I don't know what got into him, but, in the thick of war, he finally shaped up."

For an instant, Aetius looked happy, but only an instant.

Avitus frowned. "Our men gave their all, but gone are the days when Rome's Emperors led their armies into battle. Valentinian left us to save his world while he frolicked in Ravenna with his catamites."

"No point in being bitter about that," said Aetius, "the Empire lives on, and that's what matters. Our children have a future."

"It's good to have you back," said Avitus, "I was starting to worry that I'd be left in charge of all of this." The two men clasped fists, then Avitus winked at Aetius. While he marched off to bark orders at junior officers, his eyes darted from side to side, looking for signs of Theodoric.

A long hour passed before Avitus' heart leapt at the sight of a man wearing a two-headed wolf-cape wading up the hill on foot. But just as he started to run forward to embrace his old friend, he saw that the figure was taller and thinner than Theodoric. Sighing from the bottom of his lungs, he marched solemnly forward to greet the new king of the Goths, Thorismund, who was wearing his father's bloodstained cloak and whose face had aged ten years in one day.

"We've found my father."

"A great man. I'll miss him," said Avitus, his eyes welling. "I never imagined that he'd leave this earth before me."

"He was a valiant warrior," acknowledged Aetius, who had seen from a distance that it was Thorismund and come to comfort him.

Avitus knew better than to fold the young man into his arms and share his grief. Neither of them could afford to release the beasts of exhaustion and emotion.

"He was struck above the heart by a spear but that wasn't what killed him." Thorismund wiped away blood from his forehead. "The blow knocked him from his horse and his own cavalry trampled him. They didn't know what they'd done." The Goth shook a clenched fist at the sky. "We must attack Attila now and avenge my father's death!"

Aetius reached out an arm and shepherded Thorismund aside. "Come with me, to my tent, and we'll talk about that."

Oh, dear, thought Avitus as he watched Thorismund gesticulating wildly, *now Theodoric's gone, these Goths will be a problem.*

Forty minutes later, Thorismund stormed back past Avitus as if he couldn't see him but Aetius strolled out of his tent with a smile on his face. "It's alright."

"Doesn't look that way."

"The Goths will hold Theodoric's funeral rites on the plain, opposite the Hun gate. I've convinced Thorismund that we have no need to waste further lives on destroying the vermin – Attila is already dying although he might not know it yet. I told Thorismund he has to get back to Toulouse and secure his kingdom against would be usurpers. Our victory avenges his father's life. And I promised that I'd send half the booty down after him."

Avitus nodded. It didn't sound the most convincing of plans, but it appeared that Thorismund would follow it. "When will we celebrate our victory?"

Aetius half smiled and bowed his head. "When we've buried our dead, the grieving is done, and Attila dies in his own blood."

"Or burns himself to death," said Avitus.

The crisis past, Aetius mounted Achilles and walked him alone to the crest of the three-headed hill. The horse pricked forward his ears and planted monumental hooves square, but his eyes, the colour of molasses, sagged with exhaustion.

The illustrious Flavius Aetius, *magister militum, vir illustris, dux et patricius*, Aetius, the victor, looked down over the field of combat that he alone commanded. His face was calm, his lips set evenly, upturned at the corners, but his skin clung to his bones and his blood-shot eyes had sunk into his skull. He surveyed a carnage so vast that even he, the colossus of his age, could not comprehend it.

Perched on the ridge behind him the legionary eagles spread out their wings and called out to their lost offspring, preening in the sun of a new day.

Theodoric's Wake

The Catalaunian Plains
21st September 451 AD

The survivors raised Theodoric's trampled body on a funeral pyre. Cavalry keened out Gothic grief in whirling circles around it, then reined to a halt and formed three sides of a square. Clouds of dust settled silently over horses and men. Through a gap left open facing Attila's camp, the dead Theodoric stared down his enemy.

His warriors' feet hovered before each step as they slow-marched in time to the deep beat of a funeral drum past the body. At the front of the column came the new king, Thorismund, blood seeping through the bandage under his crown, followed by his brothers, Theodoric the younger and Euric. The kings and princes of the Bretons, Franks and Burgundians marched behind them, along with Sangibanus, who limped badly but whose armour now fitted.

Many were the missing. Haldor, who'd fought bravely but in vain to rescue Heva, was gone, as were the thirteen other officers of their legion who'd survived the Gepid battle at Pouans-les-Vallées the night before facing Attila. Aetius was absent, busy dealing with what needed to be done, not just for the present but for a better future. To allow his allies time to cry their hero heavenwards, he kept watch from atop the hill soaked in Roman blood.

Wearing his father's twin-headed wolf-cape, Thorismund addressed the mourners. When he'd finished his oration, the air hung still and silent for a breath, then the heavy shudder of troops slow marching in unison shook the ground.

Avitus, the horse-hair plumes of his helmet bristling, led a Roman honour guard straight down the slopes of the three-headed hill to fill in the open side in the funeral square. The allies saluted then closed ranks, their backs turned with contempt towards Attila's camp. Thorismund invited the Roman to speak. The troops looked up in shock and awe at his broad outline, red cape held and the mane on his helmeted head.

Avitus stepped forward and took his place next to the body of his old friend, his old adversary, in heavy silence. He looked out over the massed veterans, their armour a sea of metal that reached to the foot of the escarpment, then beyond, to the legionary eagles, and above the eagles to a wide blue sky. Then he looked down at Theodoric.

In fifty years of fighting, Avitus had seen innumerable dead, but even so, he recoiled from Theodoric's battered face. It didn't resemble his friend. The bones protruded too far and a frown of concentration creased his brow, as if, at the last instant of his existence, Theodoric had been trying to decipher the incomprehensible. The face was shadowed by fear. Theodoric had seen no loved ones coming to greet him into the afterlife and this troubled Avitus. He reached out and touched the ironstone beard, as stiff as wire, then heaved a sigh. His heart spoke rueful words – *All our arguments, all our plans for a peaceful and happy future, are futile now – such is the mockery of death.*

After a solemn moment, Avitus raised his chin. His throat rumbled as he projected his voice out and over five thousand men:

"Here lies the body of a great man, a formidable enemy, a powerful friend! A great king who gave his life that the world might live! Were it not for Theodoric's sacrifice, the civilised world would have ended here yesterday.

He didn't need to join us in battle. A lesser man would have cowered in the south, but Theodoric, leaving no rear guard behind him, made a forced march of a thousand miles to purge the world of Attila.

Until the end of time, the civilised world will owe Theodoric its freedom. It's our duty now to honour what he died for."

Avitus looked down again into the trampled face and caught a glimpse of his friend. He drew a gravel breath and dropped his voice.

"This is the warrior whom first I knew as a lad of just sixteen. His father asked me to tutor him in the arts of Roman warfare. I watched the youth grow to be a king. No nation could hope for a better leader – full of wisdom and courage. If we turned over his body we'd find no scars on his back for Theodoric fought from the front foot. No warrior was his equal.

His spirit has departed this realm, and we're left with the lifeless husk. An irretrievable loss." Avitus looked up. "But, instead of this corpse, cold and spiritless, I see Theodoric's passion, shrewdness and life-force. How hard he laughed! He mocked me often enough. Whenever I arrived outside the walls of his kingdom, he'd ask if I'd brought an army with me. Sometimes I had, more often I had not; the last time I stood before them, it was in search of one. Regardless of why I came, he opened the gates, his heart and mind, and let me in."

Avitus let every atom of air depart his lungs as his eyes looked at the faces of the Goths standing around the square.

"I am no orator, just a plain soldier. There's nothing that I can say that will do your dead king justice.

Theodoric never convinced himself that there was an afterlife, but I pray this morning your king has woken up somewhere else, surprised to find that he was wrong to doubt that heaven holds a place for men like him. When the day comes for you and I, who conquered Attila, to leave this earth, I trust that Theodoric will welcome us again."

Avitus threw back the red folds of his cloak and raised both arms towards the sky. "A great spirit has departed the earth. Farewell, my friend."

The Goths, who stood at attention listening to Avitus, forgot the pain of their own injuries. They forgot that their comrades had fallen at their sides, that they'd lost friends, fathers, sons and brothers. They didn't even pay much heed to his words. But what they did remember, till the day they died, was that the great Roman general – unvanquished warrior, pillar of the Empire, a man of arms who'd fought fifty campaign seasons – did nothing to hide the tears running down his cheeks when he spoke with love of a Gothic king.

Lost

B rutus made an effort to orientate himself but he was no navigator. He was used to following the crisp commands of officers on straight Roman roads. Getting from one place to the next had never required any thinking on his part, just physical exertion and obedience. He'd grown up in a small village and had never been anywhere before joining the legions. To struggle on alone, unbuoyed by camaraderie and without direction, daunted him.

The spear stump in his thigh made each step agony. He limped, looking over his shoulder for fear of attack, and wondered if he should try to make it back up the three-headed hill. In the distance, he saw a ray of sunlight glance off the gilded feathers of legionary eagles atop their standards on the escarpment. But Brutus had struggled on far enough now that if he tried to retrace his steps he'd have to pass Attila's camp. A trickle of hunched figures on horseback was ebbing out through its gates, staining the plains like blood from an open wound, and he didn't want to take his chances against them.

He sat down and, with all his force, pulled once more on the shaft of the broken spear. Stifling a scream, he twisted it and watched as it moved a merciless quarter of an inch. Closing his eyes, he bit through his bottom lip, grasped the stump and gave it one more tug. Without warning, the shaft shot out.

After the first blast of agony had passed, Brutus grinned down at the broken wood in his hand with tears of relief rolling from the corners of his eyes. But when he turned the shaft round in his hand, only half the spearhead was attached to it. He bawled out in rage and frustration then collapsed over his knees.

Minutes passed while he sobbed in abject misery. The shooting pain from ankle to hip was intolerable and he could do nothing to stop it so he tightened the tourniquet and pushed himself back up to his feet.

In agony, barely able to move, he decided to cling to the banks of the wandering river for both cover and water. It'd lead somewhere, eventually to the sea, albeit not in a straight line like the roads that always seemed, in and of themselves, to know where they were going. All he had to do was stay alive, find something to eat and drink. If soldiers approached he'd lie down and pretend to be dead until they'd passed.

Brutus didn't think of himself as a deserter. He was a survivor.

In a sullen manner, he slogged one foot in front of the other through his longest day, trying to block unwanted hauntings from his head. Few miles had been covered by the time the sun started to fall in the sky. Faint and shivering, his body became feverish. Although he didn't know it, he'd been walking in a south-westerly direction.

As a ridge of hills eclipsed the last light, the precarity of his situation began to obsess him. If the Romans found him, he'd be taken outside the camp and stoned to death for desertion. If barbarians of any type fell upon him, he was too badly injured to defend himself and would face death at their whim.

Even if he didn't cross the trail of another human being, he'd make easy pickings for the predators of the night. Nor did he have any way of keeping himself warm. He couldn't light a fire and had neither cloak nor blanket to cover himself. His armour was no defence against dying of exposure. Every time he stopped moving, the cold cut through him and he had to push himself on again in a delirium of pain and exhaustion.

He was at the point of giving up, lying down and dying when he turned a bend in the river and saw a skein of grey rising in the distance. It wasn't the smoke of a burning village, nor of a passing army, but the thin plume of a campfire lit by someone who didn't want it to draw attention. Friend or foe? Brutus knew he had no friends left in this part of the world but also that he had no choice except to seek the help of another human.

As he came closer to the smoke, the squat outline of three small stone, thatched huts emerged. They crouched near the edge of the river on a plateau of brown grass just high enough to avoid the spring floods. Round, with ramshackle walls, little more than heaps of uncemented rocks, they had no windows and only one door each, so low that he'd have to bend at the waist to get through. Without chimneys, smoke escaped through the thatch. Their innards would be coated with soot. Although primitive, they had an air of semi-permanence and, in the dried mud in the middle of the huddle of huts, a communal cooking fire flickered.

Each step Brutus managed towards them sent a flare of pain from his groin to his ankle and every breath sent a knife from under his ribs up through his neck. His aching back was stiff as a rock but he staggered on towards the hovels.

As he approached them, two childish figures came running out, the first a dark-haired boy with a spear on his shoulder. A few yards behind him galloped a girl, with a head of hair that looked like matted sheep's wool, brandishing a longbow. A withered leather quiver of arrows that looked like a hand-me-down from an older brother bounced on her shoulder as she raced to catch up with the spear-bearer.

Brutus tried to smile. They couldn't be more than eight years old and he had no fear of them, but then the boy drew back his arm and launched his missile. It landed harmlessly several feet short of its target. Brutus would have raised his hands in surrender but his left one was still paralysed and he had no energy left to lift the other.

The girl shot off an arrow that whizzed past his ear. Brutus kept on walking. In less than five seconds the girl fitted another to her bow and pulled the cord tight behind it. Brutus wondered if she was a Hun bastard as she stopped running, stood one foot forward, and took aim at his heart. Her hand was steady as she waited for him to come close enough for her shot to be accurate.

Ye gods! After all I've been through, I'm going to be killed by a child!? Brutus turned himself side on to minimise her target and waited for the arrow to pierce his ribs. *Let's make it quick!*

Just as she was about to let the arrow fly, a raucous call rang out behind her but she didn't lower her weapon. The shout was abrupt and louder the second time.

"Arno! Sissa!"

The girl dropped her bow to her side.

Brutus saw a blob of a human being hurrying towards the children. For someone so short and bulky, the creature moved fast. As the pyramid-shaped figure drew near, it pulled them both behind itself, unmistakably maternal.

Across a distance of fifty feet, mother and wounded warrior appraised each other.

The woman had a square jaw, a thin, down-turned mouth and ragged straight hair chopped off bluntly at shoulder length. Her chin jutted out in defiance of all comers and her biceps were impressive.

Through suspicious eyes she observed that the intruder was gravely injured, young, pale and losing blood. Nothing she couldn't handle with one arm tied behind her back. Nonetheless, she picked up her daughter's bow and took aim at the pupil of his right eye. Brutus was spent and put up no defence.

The woman jerked her jaw in the direction of his sword which he removed from its scabbard and let fall at his feet. Then she gestured again at the dagger at his belt but this was asking too much and he shook his head.

Her lips twitched upwards. A warrior, she thought and didn't insist; she'd simply shoot him if he made a wrong move. "Get his sword," she ordered the boy, Arno, who darted up and back like a dog and dropped it at her feet. She eased the string of her bow and jerked her head in the direction of the stone encirclement.

Brutus moved forward – *Where are the men in this camp?* – then he collapsed like a sack, unconscious at her feet.

The woman's name was Didra and her character more than made up for what she lacked in looks. Her heart was honest, her mind sharp and her bird-like eyes watched everything from under thick brows. When the men were away and she took command, her villagers ate well and were as warm and as safe as they could be.

Didra looped strong arms under Brutus' armpits while Arno and Sissa each took a foot and manhandled him into the primitive ring of stone huts. Gaggles of onlookers, who'd learnt to expect the worst from any situation, watched warily.

Didra and the children laid Brutus next to the campfire. She straightened him out and looked him over more closely. Gently, she put fingers into his wounds to see how deep they were. Instinct told her that the ragged flesh hid something buried. Near the middle of his thighbone she felt splinters of wood and let out a hiss. "Fetch a knife, Arno. Sissa, you put your hand on either side of the wound and hold it open."

Arno handed her an iron blade cross-bound by leather to a wooden handle. Sissa grimaced but did what she was told. If Brutus had been conscious while Didra dug her knife around the embedded spearhead, he would have been screaming.

Her face split into a smile as she levered out the last fragment. Arno held out his hand for it and she pinched a fold in her tunic, wiped the blood off and placed it on his palm.

"I want to see it too!" said Sissa, "I did the hard part."

"It's mine, not yours," said Arno, but he let her touch it.

Didra turned stern again. Brutus' skin was grey and glistened with a dew of sweat. His forehead burned. Reluctantly, she sacrificed some of the tribe's honey to make a herb poultice and stuffed it into his wounds. She would do what she could for him, but the outcome was beyond her control. Looking at him, she could tell that his body had sucked all of its energy into its vital core. Everything else was superfluous. His breathing was steady and slow. The battle for life was being fought silently, invisibly, deep inside and only time would tell whether death or regeneration would win.

The Burgundian Castle

Dijon, Capital of Burgundian Gaul
23rd – 25th September 451 AD

S ola had walked or run for three days straight since finding out the girl who'd escaped Reims had ridden towards Dijon. The shoes she'd bought in Troyes had given her blisters so she'd left them on the roadside and walked barefoot. Although the paving was in good order and her spirits high, a thousand tiny stones and thorns had bruised and cut her soles. She longed for a cart or a merchant with a pack animal to pass and offer her a ride, but the road was eerily empty and it was late in the day.

She had been sleeping in the wild and avoided the refugees who crossed her path. Animal predators held no fear for her but she didn't want to encounter humans. At worst, they'd try to rob, rape or kill her. At best, they demanded help. She could offer her strength to protect a fellow traveller, but not for long. One of them could match her pace and she wouldn't slow down with Leonida lost and needing to be found.

Sola had reached a long, straight stretch that led to the northern gate of Dijon when she heard clattering hooves and marching boots behind her. She turned and saw a cohort of men, war wounded and weary, approaching from the distance. Pulling her midnight hood around her face, she took cover in a stand of trees to watch them pass.

First came the scar-faced King, Gundioc, riding a wounded charger, and at his side his eldest son, Gundobad, a rugged looking warrior. Between them they led a riderless horse whose coat was drab, with weeping scabs spotting its forequarters and a gash in its chest.

Behind them trooped soldiers on foot, not one uninjured. Some marched as if they belonged to another world, muttering to departed friends. Weary though they were, Sola knew they were the victors. She waited until they'd passed then dusted down her cape and set off again.

In Dijon, she went first to a cobbler to buy herself a pair of kid slippers, then to the public baths where she purified her body and bandaged her swollen feet. Usually the baths were a lively meeting place, but today they were empty. The whole populace was at the forum, both celebrating the return of its veterans and grieving for those who'd never come home.

Even in her new shoes it was painful to walk. Although reluctant to go to the forum filled with soldiers returning to their loved ones, she had to if she wanted to find information about her daughter. Besides, she was ravenous with hunger.

She wolfed down bread and cheese from a street vendor then set about asking questions. She'd anticipated it would be difficult to trace Leonida and was astonished to find that her daughter was famous in Dijon for having been betrothed to the city's hero, their beloved Prince Heva, the owner of the riderless horse.

Joy lifted Sola to the peak of a wave but the knowledge that Leonida had suffered another terrible grief on top of the death of her father dashed her to the bottom. More desperate than ever to find her, Sola overcame the pain in her feet and took long, quick strides to the gates of the Burgundian castle.

The gates were guarded by eight staunch sentries, chests crossed by baldricks heavy with swords, who crossed their pikes to bar her way. Although she spoke to them in Burgundian they scoffed when she told them her daughter had been betrothed to their prince. One of the watchmen feinted at her with his spear and told her to be off but Sola remained, like a stone sentinel, fuming but powerless, at the corner of the bridge over the moat. A feline wildness lit her eyes as she studied every cranny in the walls of the fort, trying to work out a way to scale them when it got dark. But without an accomplice inside or proper equipment she concluded that she couldn't.

The sun set and slaves lit torches in iron sconces. When the watch on the gates changed, the outgoing guards told the newcomers she was crazy and laughed at her as they marched away.

Despair was on the brink of overwhelming her when a carriage drawn by matched black horses slowed down to cross the drawbridge. She stared into the shadowed interior and, in the flicker of torches, caught a glimpse of a square-jawed face, both imperious and kind. Sparkling eyes met hers and suddenly the passenger leant out the window.

"You're the woman who was looking for her daughter at the bridge over the River Aube. Did you find her?"

Sola recognised Avitus and her heart lifted. "No, sir. I've heard that she's inside this castle but the guards refuse me entry."

Avitus looked from the disarray of her long blond hair to the raggedness of the hem of her chiton and felt her desperation. "Are you sure you're not imagining this?"

"Perhaps I'm imagining that you've been kind enough to stop, but nothing else."

Sola never, ever, cried in front of anyone, but torchlight glowed in the tears that filled her eyes and Avitus saw them. "I cannot tarry, but I'll ensure that my servant makes enquiries. Stay where you are and he'll come back with an answer as soon as he has one."

With that, the sentries snapped a salute and Avitus leant back into the dark interior and crossed the bridge.

Her heart pounding against her ribs, Sola pulled her hood over her head and prepared for a long wait.

The moon was rising by the time two footmen arrived to usher

her past the sentries and into the main courtyard of the fortress. From there, Sola followed the swishing skirt of a lady-in-waiting into the queen's private apartments. Ragnahilde, the wife of Gundioc, wasn't present, but her attendant opened the door off the peristyle and let Sola into a comfortable, square room with a flagstone floor.

As her eyes adjusted to the light of a single candle, Sola saw her daughter curled up like a baby in the womb, clutching her coverlet and crying as if the world had ended. In one bound Sola was at her bedside and Leonida's slight arms clasped her neck.

Through Leonida's juddering sobs Sola made out the words, "Mumma, Heva's dead."

* * * * *

When the full moon had outshone the stars, and Leonida had cried herself to sleep in her mother's arms, Sola got up and walked out of the room, leaving the door open wide enough to hear her child's ragged breathing. The cool flagstones soothed the burning pads of her feet as she stepped into a covered walkway, one floor above an interior courtyard, whose arches mimicked Roman taste but whose proportions jarred. Placed in pairs, they were narrow and their stone pediments looked like brows raised over horrified eyes.

Sola looked down into a courtyard where men stood in clusters, clinging to companionship in the moonlight. She could tell from afar that they were talking of battle, lives lost, acts of courage that had been in vain. Sometimes they pointed to where a spear had entered an arm or grazed a neck, or bent to adjust a bandage that encircled a leg. With dazed eyes, they put arms around one another's shoulders and laughed in a fragile way. They relived nightmares with a sense of disbelief, surprised at being reunited with their friends and living when so many – too many – were dead.

Beyond them, through the windows of the main hall of the castle, yellow candlelight exuded a warmth from which Sola was excluded. She watched, feeling an immense distance. Heva was dead and neither she nor Leonida could be of any interest to the Burgundians.

Suddenly her spirits crashed. No longer on a quest that made her fearless, she felt aches and pains in every bone of her body. Alone, her husband gone, she prayed that the curse of solitude that had plagued much of her life wouldn't blight her child.

Sola imagined their return to Reims, to the burnt out ruins of what was once the home she'd shared with the only man who'd ever loved her for who she was, not what she could do for him. Alone, she would build a new life, not only for the sake of her daughter but also out of a cat-like curiosity that gave her a need to explore whatever was around the corner, despite the long struggle ahead of her and Leonida.

Wind blew through the courtyard, chilling her spirit. She shivered and walked back into Leonida's room, shutting the door behind her. Feeling that she couldn't lift a foot another step, she lowered herself as gently as she could onto the edge of the bed. The roughness of Leonida's breathing pained Sola and she wanted to make the world right for her, but there's no way to revive the dead.

In the dark, Sola lay still for lonely hours, listening to the muffled sounds of a life in the castle that she didn't belong to. The watch changed before, at last, a sleep as profound as death overcame her.

* * * * *

The first cock's crow found Sola already awake. She sat on the edge of the bed in the dim light and watched Leonida breathing smoothly, deeply at rest. There was a soft knock at the door and Sola opened it to a slave-girl holding a bowl of hot water and a warm drink of mead and honey which she gratefully accepted.

The same maid returned an hour later with a message from Queen Ragnahilde requesting Sola to pay her a visit in her private chambers.

"Can you find me a mirror and something clean to wear?" Sola asked. The girl came back a few minutes later with only the mirror. None of the clothes of the other women would be sufficiently long or broad enough in the shoulder. Sola washed her puffy eyes and face, did her best to tidy up her hair and edged her new shoes back over her blisters.

Leonida was still sound asleep.

"Would you please be so kind as to come back and wait here till I return?" Sola asked the slave, "I don't want my daughter waking up alone this morning after all she's been through."

"That will be a pleasure, my lady."

The maid led her downstairs and diagonally across the exterior courtyard. It was bustling with new energy in the morning light. Men whistled and joked as they unloaded supplies and trundled them away on handcarts or their own backs towards the cellars and storerooms. They were emptying a waggon-load of swords that had been collected after the great battle, throwing the weapons in a relay chain to the door of the armoury. King Gundioc and Avitus were talking earnestly on the city ramparts but were keeping half an eye on progress below in the courtyard.

The man on top of the sword cart interrupted his rhythmic throwing when he saw the two women crossing the line of his relay chain, but his first receiver was unaware of their presence and tossed the last sword on over his shoulder without looking. It would have knocked the maid hard in the head if Sola's right arm hadn't swooped in past the girl's body and caught the hilt with one hand. She did it by reflex, not thinking for a second of the impression her gesture might make on the people in the busy courtyard.

The maid thanked her profusely as Sola nonchalantly tossed the sword on to the next man in line, as if it weighed nothing.

The incident – over in a second – caught Avitus' eye.

"Did you see that?" he asked Gundioc.

"What?"

"The way that woman caught and threw that sword."

"No, I didn't notice . . . " the king carried on with his train of conversation, but the sight of Sola catching and throwing a sword like that had set Avitus thinking. There was something as familiar as it was astonishing in the way she'd moved. She'd done it with the ease and alacrity of a gladiator – a glad-i-a-tor! His eyes pivoted to take another look as Sola moved with speed and grace across the forum, ducked her fair head under a low castle doorway and disappeared.

When she'd come to his camp at the Roman bridge he'd found her unusual, but he'd been preoccupied with the coming battle. But now that he'd seen her move like a man in the arena, a memory surfaced that took him back to an extraordinary afternoon, some fifteen years before, when Pontius had just been beginning to get seriously rich and had organised private games in honour of the Empress Galla Placidia in Nimes. It was illegal for women to fight as gladiators, but Pontius had always had a prurient interest in female flesh and was putting on entertainment that he promised would be unique.

To mark his gratitude to Avitus for having evicted the Goths from Narbonne, Pontius gave him a ringside seat next to the Empress, and from there Avitus had seen Sola fight. As Pontius had promised, it hadn't been an ordinary duel of man against man, nor woman against woman. What they'd seen that day, they'd never seen before and would never see again.

Avitus looked at the iron-bound door closing behind Sola and the maid. Perhaps he was mistaken, but if not, he'd love to speak to her, at least once, if only to ask her how she'd done it . . .

"Have we finished up here?" Gundioc could see that Avitus wasn't listening any more.

"No, please continue. I leave for Lyon in the morning and we need to conclude our arrangements," replied the general, who was still staring at the door with a far-off look in his eyes.

* * * * *

Inside the cool, half-darkness of the castle, Queen Ragnahilde sat in a cavernous chamber with coloured tapestries draped over its stone walls. In comparison with Roman frescoes and marble, the Burgundian throne room was rough and cold but burst with ostentation.

The queen was of middle-age but her face still carried the discernible landmarks of having been a spectacular beauty in her youth. Her heavy-lidded eyes were the same dark brown as the long coils of her hair, dyed with sage and indigo, and her freckled skin still clung to her cheekbones. She fastened her lavish red tunic at the waist with a bejewelled belt and her arms and fingers were laden with rubies and garnets. She didn't rise when Sola entered the room but gave her an assessing stare, inclined her head and invited her to sit on a cross-legged chair next to the throne.

"My lady-in-waiting informed me that you arrived to reclaim your daughter last night," the queen said in accented Latin. "I was curious to meet you. Heva put Leonida in my care two weeks ago and I've found her to be a gracious and polite young woman, yet full of spirit. She wasn't born noble, but she has a noble nature. I did not at first approve of her engagement to a prince but her natural grace and intelligence won me over."

"Thank you, your majesty, for your kindness towards my daughter." Sola hid her irritation at Ragnahilde's condescension. "I share your grief at the loss of your son."

"Heva and Leonida seemed to love each other deeply, although they had so little time together. He was my stepson, but I feel his loss as if he'd been my own." Ragnahilde grazed a tear from the corner of her eye. "I understand that Attila killed your husband during the sacking of Reims?"

Sola nodded.

"Who is your daughter's guardian now that her father is gone?"

Sola hadn't yet thought about that but the queen's question prompted her to realise that Leonida had neither uncle, nor brother nor trusted male friend who could fulfil the role of guardian. "We have no close male relatives. I will be Leonida's guardian."

"But you're a woman."

"I'll apply to the courts to be declared in charge of my own affairs, sui juris, with the legal rights of a Roman citizen."

Ragnahilde raised an eyebrow. "I doubt that the courts will extend that status to the widow of a provincial magistrate."

"Perhaps not often, but I believe that my husband put measures in place to protect our interests."

"That may be, but you'll have to find an advocate who's prepared to take your case."

Sola sighed; she wasn't ready to worry about such things. But the queen was right, she had to hurry back and stake a claim to her husband's property before one of his distant cousins turned up to enforce a lien over it. "Do you mind if I ask, your highness, why our affairs interest you?"

"Before I answer that, am I right to assume that your husband was a man of property?"

Sola didn't like the queen's intrusive questioning but inclined her head.

"I expected no less." Ragnahilde stood up and walked over to a narrow window that looked out from the exterior castle wall across the town of Dijon to green fields and forests beyond.

Sola's nose twitched at the scent of rose and sandalwood that the queen left in her wake. Ragnahilde was slim, but not shapely, and shorter than the average Burgundian woman. Sola deduced that she was Frank by birth.

Ragnahilde stared into the distance for a few minutes. The crown prince, Gundobad, had been smitten on sight by Leonida and had asked the queen to intervene on his behalf but it didn't please her to do so. She returned to her throne and sat down. "Would you and your daughter care to stay a few days in Dijon before leaving for Reims?"

Sola was tired and irritable. It sounded as if, before discarding Heva's betrothed, Ragnahilde wanted to check whether the girl could serve some other purpose in her game of thrones.

"I'm deeply honoured by your interest in my daughter, and on another occasion would be delighted to bring her back to Dijon, but we must return to Reims immediately."

Ragnahilde was relieved that Sola had declined the invitation. "I bid you good day, that is, unless there's something I can do to help you on your way?"

"There is one thing, your highness." Sola stood up to go. "I need to buy a horse."

An expression of disdain marred the serenity of Ragnahilde's countenance. "I don't deal in horses, but I'm sure that a woman like you will be able to find someone who does."

Sola left the queen and went back to Leonida's room. When the maid told her that her daughter was peacefully asleep, she wasted no time and went in search of the stables to find the horse with a golden coat that Leonida had told her had saved her life.

When Leonida had arrived at the castle, the master of the king's horse had been quick to requisition Lightning and give her a lowly mule in return, but Lightning had bucked off and bitten every man who'd mounted her and when faced with the whip had simply sat down on her hindquarters, like a dog, and refused to move. No one had ever seen a horse sit like a dog before and the stableboys feared that she was possessed by a demon and wanted her disposed of quickly.

If Sola hadn't come asking for her, the Burgundians would have tried to sell the horse back to her rightful owners, the Romans. But the Romans would have required a written receipt, in triplicate, and made sure that the taxman had the details. Sola's offer of a purse full of silver coins with no questions asked was a welcome alternative.

If securing Lightning for Leonida was been surprisingly simple, finding a horse for herself was the opposite. Amongst the near-dead nags the Burgundians would consider parting with, only Thunder showed the slightest glimmer of potential, but his bones stuck out, his shoulder wouldn't stop bleeding and he kept knocking the scabs off his wounds as if even he wanted to put an end to it all. Marco, the groom, had been ordered to put the warhorse out of his misery, chop up his body and feed it to the king's hounds.

Sola had seen both animals and men recover from worse injuries than Thunder's, but only rarely and only when they had a will to live. Nor was Thunder her style of mount. He was broad-framed and if he ever recovered he'd need oats and hay that would be hard to find in a land incinerated by Attila. From the look of him, Sola feared her sore feet would get no immediate relief. But the horse had been Heva's and if she didn't try to save it Leonida would never forgive her.

Using a mounting block, she threw her leg over Thunder's wide but bony ribs. At first his ears went back and his back sagged, as if he resented her weight. She sat still for a minute then gathered up the reins just enough for him to sense that she expected him to pay attention. Thunder opened his eyes and lifted his head, sensing this was a rider he could trust.

Sola let him feel the full length of her thighs down his sides. When his ears went forward, she knew he felt safe and gently closed her calves around his belly. He took a short step, followed by a longer one. Sola smiled, knowing that her feet would find some respite.

New Beginnings

House of the Praetorian Prefect
Lyon, Roman Capital of Gaul
September 452 AD

"There you are chook," Petrina, the midwife, cooed as she handed Papianilla a bundle of swaddling clothes and put her own hands into the small of her aching back, "she's the most beautiful baby I've ever seen – and I've seen thousands of 'em."

The labour hadn't been easy but compared with when the midwife had dragged Sidonius into the world, twenty-two years earlier, it'd been quick. Only twelve hours and the little girl was a first child. Petrina watched the love flow between mother and baby. It was for these moments that she lived and she'd double the sacrifices to her favourite gods tonight.

Papianilla cradled the infant and stroked the down of fair hair that crowned her head. She named her Rosea and couldn't believe the tiny marvel bundle in her arms. The new baby's first visitors were its grandparents.

Avitus arrived, his blue eyes dancing. He inclined his pate over the baby's head and extended a gnarled forefinger. Rosea opened out the tentacles of her tiny hand, as fine and soft as a sea anemone, and closed them on her grandfather's calloused digit.

"Look at that! She has a strong grip!" Avitus looked across at his daughter with a smile that could light the darkest night. "Birth is the greatest miracle of all."

Papianilla glowed with pride. "I'm so happy that you're pleased! I was worried you'd be disappointed that our first child isn't a boy."

Avitus' smile dimmed for a moment as he contemplated his daughter's words. "There was a time when I would have wanted the first born to be a boy, but I've grown wiser. I've a greater respect for women now than I had in my youth. The world has changed, and women can't count on men to do what they ought to anymore. It took me a long time to realise that, but now I have, you don't need to worry I would have preferred a grandson. All that matters is that the baby is healthy and well loved."

Sedulla didn't share Avitus' new found liberalism. As she bent to kiss her daughter goodbye she whispered in her ear. "Don't worry, dear, the next one will be a boy."

Her mother's words deflated Papianilla's happiness. Sedulla had the knack of making even the most remarkable achievement appear inadequate.

As Avitus and Sedulla left, Sidonius ushered in his parents. Andromeda proclaimed that Rosea truly was the most beautiful of babies and Honorius deduced from the way the baby looked around the room that she had inherited the Apollinari habit of taking stock of the world. On top of that, he could almost have sworn – although he knew such a thing to be impossible in a new born – that she had smiled at him.

Death of Attila

To the East and South of Budapest lies a plain that stretches out to the Ukraine. It is gentle ground, green except at the end of a long dry summer, smooth and flat.

It was here Attila met his death.

In the months since his defeat on the Catalaunian fields he'd been slinking off towards his roots. After his allies had gone home to their various fiefdoms, Aetius was left with only the phantom of an army but still harried him every inch of the way. As is often the case with retreating armies, Attila's soldiers sickened.

The Hun had many wives already but more of any commodity was always better in his eyes and, as his prowess waned, a young girl called Ilica caught his eye. Her pubescent beauty was the talk of her tribe. She dreaded being wed to Attila but had no choice in the matter. The ceremony was enacted and a great banquet held at which the ogre drank to excess.

Behind her embroidered veil, in her flowing red silk wedding dress, Ilica was led to the bed-chamber with her husband. She was twelve years old and he was over fifty. With a drunken fist, he banged a thick iron door bolt into its catch, cursing as it nicked his knuckle, then spread-eagled his body on the marriage bed, undid his belt and put his hand between his legs.

"Take off your clothes."

Ilica shuddered with fear and revulsion.

"Strip naked!"

She did her best to smother her sobs as she fumbled with the lacings of her bodice. Her face was hidden by her veil so Attila couldn't see the terror in the sloped almond eyes that staring out through it. The sight of his bloated features, his teeth that stank of rot, and the way he drooled and groped himself made her stomach heave. If the door had been open she would have fled and braved the consequences.

"Faster!" he snarled, his voice slurred by alcohol. He pushed himself up onto an elbow to watch.

The girl's fingers shook so uncontrollably that she could not untie the cords of her gown. Her sobs became audible to Attila and his pulse sped with the rush of power. His blood coursed harder and faster through his arteries, then his nose started bleeding.

"Fuck!" he swore, collapsing back down on the coverlet, expecting the blood to stop. He was too drunk to get upright again, and, all of a sudden, he couldn't be bothered with this snivelling child. He'd claimed her as his property in front of his men and that was all that mattered. Didn't need or care to consummate the marriage. Nor would he be capable of the act after drinking so much.

In a growing pool of blood that drenched his pillow, Attila lost consciousness.

In the morning, when their master didn't appear, his guards became suspicious and broke down the door to his chamber. Inside they found the girl, sobbing behind her veil, and their leader dead.

His men took his body out and buried him with ceremonies befitting a warrior king. But no one wept for the Emperor of the Huns, the almighty Attila, the scourge of God. No one except Ilica, and that was out of fear she'd be accused of her husband's murder and that the devil would come back and haunt her.

Back Home

After the great battle, Sidonius wrote poems about loss and death, searching for answers that eluded him. Guilt haunted him, for his friends had perished but he had lived. Often he dreamt that he was packing their possessions when the tent flap lifted and they stepped in, smiling in the sunshine. They were alive, and it was real to him, but when he reached to embrace them his arms passed through their bodies and their faces faded to skulls. Papianilla was his only comfort. In the dark, he'd hold her warmth close and spread his fingers over her rounded belly, grasping for the flutter of new life.

He yearned to bring peace to the world without resorting to arms but before Avitus' example he felt inadequate. Months passed before Sedulla, through her connections at court, arranged a diplomatic posting for him and Sidonius found his voice and his vocation. In constant communication with the outside world, it was he who announced the news of Attila's sordid demise to his family.

Avitus' eyes sparked and he smiled, half-bitterly. "I always hoped that Attila would burn himself to death, but drowning in his own blood is a fitting end."

"What happened to the girl, Ilica, who married Attila?" Papianilla looked pale. She was halfway through her second pregnancy and vomiting morning, noon and night.

"One of Attila's older wives accused her of murdering him," said

Sidonius, "but no one believed her, and Ilica went safely home to her parents to start a new life."

"I'm glad."

"Aetius must be ecstatic." Sedulla wondered whether to suggest a feast to celebrate the Hun's death but decided against what could be a breach of etiquette.

"If he is, he won't boast," said Avitus. The veteran general sat in the circle of his family, looking from face to face. They had gathered to celebrate Rosea's first birthday and only Ecdicius was absent, away at Aetius' side. While no one was gloating over Attila's death, there was a palpable sense of relief. Avitus held out his arms to his granddaughter. "Come sit on my knee, Rosea."

"Look at that," said Sedulla, "she's only one but she can already climb onto her grandfather's lap." Despite making secret pagan sacrifices and extravagant donations to the newly built church in pursuit of a grandson, Sedulla was growing proud of Rosea.

"And talk," said Avitus with a wink. It warmed Avitus to see his family happy. Sedulla had been waiting for thirty years more than she'd expected for her husband to return to "normal life". In times gone by, the retirement age had been forty-five, then reduced to forty in an effort to attract more recruits, but it had always been up to Avitus to decide when he'd retire from the legions. While he missed the camaraderie of the camp and the sense of purpose war had given him, seeing Sedulla glow and act like a young girl in his presence was an unexpected compensation for the new quietness of his life. This quietness he would have called tedium if it weren't for the pleasures of fishing in the lake at Avitacum and watching his family grow.

He pondered the glory of Aetius, a general without equal, the shield that sheltered the Roman Empire. Aetius, never able to let down his guard. The blood-swilling Attila was dead, but the Vandals, Sueves, Goths and countless others were an ever-growing threat. With the weak and vacillating Valentinian Emperor of Rome, only Aetius kept the barbarians at bay.

Avitus passed Rosea to Papianilla then walked over to Sedulla and put a hand on her shoulder. "If it isn't too primitive for you, my dear, I'd like to light a fire of my own tonight. My enemy has fallen and I shall not mourn him but I'd like to roast a goat on a spit under the fig tree over there. Burn every trace of the Hun from our lives and raise a toast to Aetius, who killed him as surely as if he'd thrust a sword through his heart. We've endured long years of war, and it's time to celebrate."

Sedulla nodded. She would have preferred a proper banquet, but if one roasted goat would satisfy her husband, she'd see that he had it.

When the bonfire was sending sparks up into the branches of his ancient fig tree, Avitus sat in its warmth and raised a glass of spiced wine to Aetius and Ecdicius. He wondered where the magister militum and his son had pitched camp that night. Aetius would know by now of Attila's death, but would he celebrate? Avitus hoped he would hold a feast for all the veterans of the great battle, for they deserved to be honoured. He frowned, staring into the embers and thinking of all the friends they'd lost.

He tossed a log onto the fire. Flames shot up, reminding him of Attila's pyrotechnic display just before the Huns spun out of their encampment onto the plains. He saw Attila's face twisting in the flames, the slanted eyes glinting with blood-lust, and once again Avitus felt not fear, but revulsion. Revulsion for the evil that was Attila the Hun.

Avitus grunted. Burning would have been a more fitting end for him, but it was satisfying to think of Attila choking in a glut of his own blood. Avitus hoped the devil had known fear at the end, but the only thing that mattered was his obliteration.

He bent his head in a prayer to all the gods – couldn't risk leaving any of them out – *never, never, let such evil come to earth again.*

A Byway Brawl

The road from Clermont to Avitacum
Province of Auvergne, Roman Gaul
May 454 AD

Sidonius left the hillside city of Clermont basking in dawn light and set off at a leisurely pace towards his home at Avitacum. The rolling meadows surrounding the city were lush, new leaves sprouted on the trees, and his horse took the rise and fall of the road with an easy gait. Although it was late spring, the sleeping volcano brooding over the plains of Auvergne, Puy-de-Dôme, was covered with snow. The Temple of Mercury crowning its summit was a black oblong against sunlit white.

Sidonius was smiling, eager to see his baby son after two weeks away in Lyon on family and diplomatic business – although there was not much of a distinction between the two – and to hear the new words Rosea would have learnt. His heart flipped at the thought of taking Papianilla in his arms, kissing her, and leading her to bed. She'd been sick through almost all of her second pregnancy and had shown scant interest in him, but now that the birth of her son was three months behind her and the breastfeeding had been handed over to a wet nurse, her ardour had returned.

He came to the junction on the edge of the dappled forest where he'd leave the main road and follow the slope down to the shore of his lake. The turn-off was marked by two boulders, as tall as a man, that stood on an open patch of grass big enough to graze a goat. He was singing to himself when his horse suddenly whinnied and shied.

Brutus, carrying a spear and wearing only a shabby loincloth, leapt out from behind a boulder and snatched the bridle. The horse showed the whites of its eyes and raised its head but Brutus yanked viciously down on its mouth.

Sidonius surveyed his assailant with disdain, but not one iota of fear. "What do you think you're doing?"

Brutus' surly eyes glared up from under thick, black brows. "If you want to pass down this road, you pay my toll."

"This is an imperial Roman road paid for by the taxpayers of Gaul. Unhand my horse."

There was something about the arrogance of the pompous young Roman in his clean white clothes that got up Brutus' nose. "You not only have to pay the toll, you have to hand over your money as well."

The horse whinnied and tried again to pull up but Brutus dropped his spear and used both hands to keep it from rearing.

A rush of violated wrath surged up through Sidonius. He was armed with a gladius and it occurred to him to use it to swipe off the troublemaker's head but it was against his code of honour to use a weapon against an unarmed man. The highway robber was about his own age and, although he was broad-shouldered and heavily set, Sidonius decided to dismount and teach the beggar a lesson.

As far as Brutus was concerned, his attack was a justified struggle between the haves and the have-nots. The knight clearly had more than his fair share of the good things in life while he, Brutus, had nothing and he was up for the scrap. As Sidonius swung his leg over his horse's hindquarters Brutus grabbed his foot and dragged him under its belly. The horse, bred for the saddle not battle, bolted, its hooves narrowly missing Sidonius' head.

Sidonius landed hard on his back. Brutus brought back his boot and aimed a skull-splitting kick at his head but Sidonius blocked it with crossed forearms and kicked his own boot up into Brutus' gut.

Brutus staggered backwards then crashed in the dirt. Sidonius leapt to his feet and waited, fists raised, for his attacker to stand up.

With the ballistic force of a battering ram, Brutus launched himself off one knee into a flying tackle but Sidonius sidestepped it. Brutus hurtled past his target and smashed onto the ground but the impact did nothing to slow him down. He twisted through a summersault and back up onto his feet. Sweat beaded his brow. This robbery wasn't going as easily as he'd thought it would. He spat, raised both fists and jogged his weight forwards and backwards.

After several feints, Brutus strick out with a hard right jab followed by a leg sweep. The Roman blocked the punch and jumped the outstretched leg. Brutus let fly a knock-out left-hook but Sidonius ducked and it glanced off the side of his forehead. The fight found its rhythm and the Roman patrician and the former legionnaire slugged it out, blow for blow.

Half an hour later, both gasping for air, their blackened eyes met in the realisation that neither of them was going to win. Scowling, they drew back, put six yards between them, and, as if by mutual agreement, dropped their guards. Noses bleeding profusely, they bent over, hands on knees, spitting blood. Their eyes warily flicked up from time to time on the look-out for surprise attacks but, when nothing had happened for more than a minute, both slumped down onto the roadside verge. Sidonius looked down at the grass-and-bloodstained mess that had been his pristine white travelling tunic and started to laugh.

Once he'd got his breath back, he stood up, recovered his hip-flask from where it'd been thrown during their struggle, and offered his sparring partner water.

Brutus grabbed the flask and took a swig. "Fuck, that hurt!" He wiped his mouth. "Where'd a stuck up patrician like you learn to fight like that?"

"The same place you did." Sidonius looked pointedly at the dirty bandage that Brutus had tied around his uninjured right forearm. It was commonplace for army deserters to hide their legionary tattoos behind false wounds. He searched Brutus' puffy face, wondering if he'd known him on the Catalaunian Plains, but was unable to place the grubby features and shaggy beard.

"I thought that the likes of you didn't do military service," said Brutus, "the likes of me do all the fighting."

"It's true that the patrician class is exempt from serving in the army but that's never been my family's tradition. The last time I had to fight was against a platoon of Gepids who took the lives of all the equites alongside me."

Brutus' face darkened and he hung his head.

Sidonius filled the silence with a question – "You . . . deserted?"

"The past is my business, not yours."

Longer silence. The two young men were beginning to feel embarrassed by their cross-class camaraderie.

"I'd best be going." Sidonius rose to his feet.

Brutus said nothing. His face had drained of colour and he'd subsided into melancholy.

Sidonius watched him. There was something likeable about the lout, something worth saving. He ran his eyes over the bulk of his frame, leaner than it should be, with a jagged purple scar the length of one thigh. "Look, I'm not going to pay a toll or anything stupid like that, but is there anything that I can do to help you?"

"Like what?" Brutus sneered.

"I don't know, give you some money or something?"

"Never say no to money!" Brutus' wounded pride pushed him to refuse, but he'd learnt to swallow it since leaving the legion.

"Here, take half of what I have," Sidonius pulled two silver coins out of a pouch hung from his belt, "our fight was a draw, so you deserve no more than that."

Brutus snatched the coins from his open palm, bit one to test it, then slipped it into his loincloth. It was as much as he'd have earned in a month in the army. He could eat and buy a gourd of wine. "Why're you giving your money away, are you that rich – or plain stupid?"

"Neither. I'm normally careful with money. Don't ask me why, I'd like to help you."

"Pity's a luxury I can't afford," said Brutus sourly.

Sidonius walked off to catch his horse who was grazing on small shrubs under the trees. He didn't mount up but led it back to the roadside. Brutus was still sitting on the grass, as if dazed. "Are you alright?"

Brutus looked up. "Huh? You barely touched me!"

"I didn't mean it that way."

"Are you a do-gooder monk, or somethin' ?"

"I'm a diplomat." Sidonius straightened up the remnants of his cloak. "I guess that our paths won't cross again, but my name is Sidonius Apollinaris. Don't ask me why, but I'm willing to be your friend."

"That's a rash offer. There's broken things that even rich men like you can never fix, and I'm one of' em."

"You're too young to be so bitter. How old are you?"

"How the fuck would I know? When I was born no one wrote it down. But I was old enough to convince the recruiting officer that I was nineteen and ready for war."

"I'm twenty-three. I fought under Aetius against Attila."

Brutus said nothing.

"What's your name?" Sidonius asked. "You remind me of someone."

"Why'd I tell you my name? So you can report me to the imperial army and get me arrested?"

"I must go," Sidonius brushed himself down, "people are waiting for me."

"Well, good for you that you've got a home and family to go to."

"I live not far from here, down that road, in a villa called Avitacum. If you need something – an introduction, I don't know, something –

come down and ask for me."

"Have a nice ride home then." Brutus slouched on the grass, watching the Roman's back disappear into the green folds of trees that curtained the road. He wondered what the fuck all of that was about but was glad to have the coins tucked away in his loincloth.

Fishing

Papianilla no longer believed that Apollo drove his chariot across the sky, but she'd been watching the sun travel the heavens and knew that it was the sixth hour of the day. Shadows were lengthening on the lawn and although Sidonius had promised to be home before noon there was no sign of him.

She wasn't the only one waiting for him. Avitus had come to visit and was bursting with momentous news that he wouldn't share with his daughter. Instead, he'd taken himself off with a fishing rod to the lakeside and told her to send her husband down to join him as soon as he got home. From this, Papianilla knew that the matter was political or military. It irked her that her father thought he had to protect her from such things, but Sidonius would tell her everything later so she didn't make a fuss.

When, dishevelled and with a black eye, Sidonius did at last dismount in front of the portico Papianilla flew into his arms and kissed the bruises on his face. He put his hands around her waist and cradled her close.

"Baguadae?" she asked, worried that there were bandits on the road.

Sidonius nodded. "It's nothing but a few bruises. No harm done, but it was close to home. How are the children?"

"They're fine, everything's fine, but my father's here waiting for you with some urgent news. He's in his favourite fishing spot and asked me to send you straight down."

"Has something happened to your mother?"

"No, of course not, she's as tough as army boots."

"Did he say what the news is about?"

"He gave nothing away."

Sidonius kissed Papianilla fleetingly on the lips then set off down the lawn. She watched him go and worried that they didn't have enough staff to guard the roads as well as the house and wished that he hadn't walked away before discussing how they could protect their home, Sidonius found Avitus sitting on a sawn-off tree stump, looking out over the lake to a spot well beyond his cork float. The old soldier didn't stir when greeted. Sidonius sat down silently on the grass and waited to be told what was happening.

Avitus turned sharp blue eyes on him. "You have to leave for Toulouse in the morning. Thorismund's been assassinated."

"By whom? He was young, strong, and noble. Who'd assassinate such a king?"

"He had enemies, plenty of them, jealous men who wanted his crown. It could have been a cousin or the new arrivals from Spain, but, most likely it was Theodoric, his younger brother who killed him before he could father a son."

Sidonius could feel cold wrath brewing inside Avitus. Thorismund's cavalry charge had been critical in the victory over Attila. "It's a travesty that a murderer carries his father's noble name. How did Thorismund die?"

"He was being bled by a physician to treat a wound that had festered since the Catalaunian Plains," Avitus looked out beyond his cork float again, "left arm strapped to the bed to raise the veins. When a band of nine assassins attacked, Thorismund grabbed the only weapon to hand – a three legged stool – and fought for his life. Killed seven before the last two got him." Avitus' shoulders slumped over his fishing rod. He gave the end a twitch, then let it settle back on the still water. "He was a great warrior, just like his father."

"And a friend to Rome," said Sidonius.

Avitus raised the tip of his rod again and tightened the line. "We know nothing of this new Theodoric. He was never destined to be king. But he's your age. I want you to go to Toulouse and befriend him. Find out what kind of ally – or enemy – he'll make."

"You ask nothing more than that I make a study of him?"

"Make him like you," Avitus perused his son-in-law's face, "usually you're good at that." That subject closed, he became less pensive. "You've been in a fight. Bagaudae?"

"Yes, on the road not far from here."

Avitus grunted and called Sidonius by his nickname. "The future worries me, Sollius. Who'll defend the Empire when my generation's gone? Warriors like Aetius, Ecdicius and Marjorian are few and far between." Aware Sidonius might read the absence of his name from the list of military heroes as a slight he added, "That's why we can't waste men like you on the army, you're more valuable forging treaties for us. We need allies, but the right kind, those who share our values and aren't just after the spoils of war."

Sidonius was mollified. "I'll see what I can do in Toulouse."

"Write to Agricola, not me," Avitus instructed, "I'm almost sure the Emperor intercepts my correspondence, fishing for evidence of a conspiracy to depose him."

"I'll do as you ask."

Sidonius stood up and walked with a slow step back up the closely clipped lawn to the villa, wondering how he could explain his imminent departure to Papianilla.

Avitus returned to his fishing. He was bored by retirement; it didn't suit him.

Theodoric II

Toulouse, Capital of the Gothic Kingdom, Southern Gaul
September 454 AD

With one foot resting on the stretcher of a lion-pawed desk, Sidonius stared into space, spinning his stylus between finger and thumb. Since dawn, he'd been dashing off sentences on wax tablets only to erase them with the stylus' flat end. He was searching for the perfect words before committing his report on Theodoric to parchment and sending it to Avitus.

A shaft of westering light picked out dust particles dancing in the air between the window and his desk. It hit the cut and polished edge of the crystal inkwell that his father had given him to celebrate his graduation from the school of rhetoric. Sidonius rubbed his eyes and yawned then stretched back in his chair. He turned the inkwell and light exploded into a rainbow of blues and yellows from its edges. The crystal felt cool and smooth, satisfyingly heavy. A fine channel ran around the top so that the ink would drain back into the well when he tapped the excess off the nib of his pen. A single word of Sidonius' full name was chased at the foot of each faceted face: Gaius-Modestus-Sidonius-Apollinaris. He wasn't fond of the two adjectives – it was tempting the fates to be referred to as "happy" and "modest" – and preferred to be known simply as Sidonius, or even "Sollius", to his friends.

He turned the crystal round so that only Sidonius and Apollinaris remained visible and ran his forefinger over the letters, slender but ending with strong serifs. The engraver had spared no effort in perfecting them. Although Sidonius wasn't yet twenty-five, he found himself hoping that the words on his gravestone would be carved as cleanly. *Too much thinking of the end, when I've yet to write the beginning.*

He picked up the pen Papianilla had given him to celebrate their first wedding anniversary. The shaft was made of ebony, as full of potential as a sorcerer's stick. A fine twist of gold snaked round the lower fifth of the wand. Its coils formed a cartridge that fed ink into a nib mimicking a swan's beak. A pair of open wings formed the top end of the wire. Papianilla had chosen the motif in homage to the pairs of birds that glided over the lake at Avitacum. They symbolised life-long love. Sidonius had told her that they reminded him of her.

He dipped his nib into the carbon-black, tapped the nib and hovered for a second. The letter was, as Avitus had requested, addressed to Agricola.

You have begged a description of Theodoric, the new Gothic king. . . he began, then stopped, regretting the word "new". The letter might be intercepted and he didn't want Theodoric's spies inferring any criticism. Better not to say "new" when that might be read as "illegitimate".

Sidonius rubbed his forehead, aware that what he chose to omit from his letter would have as much significance as what he put into it. He decided to start with something straightforward, a physical description of the man whom nobody had taken much notice of up until he'd murdered his brother.

He is in height above the average man but below the giant. The nose is finely aquiline; the lips are thin and not enlarged by any distension of the mouth. Every day the hair springing from his nostrils is cut back . . . That detail would let them know that Theodoric was romanised. *His shoulders are smooth, the upper and forearms strong and hard; hands broad, breast prominent, waist receding . . . the sides swell with salient muscle, the well-girt flanks are full of vigour. His thighs are like hard horn . . . Before daybreak . . . he prays with assiduity, but, if I may speak in confidence, one may suspect more of habit than conviction in this piety. . .*

Theodoric was a heretic, a follower of the Arian branch of Christianity that preached that Jesus was not divine but just a man of extraordinary faith. Arianism had been outlawed in favour of Catholicism fifty years ago but the Goths refused to understand that being an ally of Rome entailed conforming to her moral code.

Sidonius continued with his portrait: in his daily business, the king is protected by armed nobles and his guards in their animal skins; *there is either sensible talk or none* in his chamber hung with silk or linen draperies. After he has eaten, he will string his own bow, considering it unmanly to let anyone else do it, and join the hunt. He asks you what you would like to see him target. *You choose and he hits.*

Sidonius had cultivated Theodoric's friendship. The treaty that had dammed hostilities between the Romans and the Goths for over twenty-five years could still hold back the rising barbarian tide. He admonished himself that he wasn't writing a history but a wave of melancholy fell over him.

He blotted the ink, rolled the scroll and sealed it before walking to the window. In the forum below, Goths dressed in colourful linens were bustling about daily life yet everything bright and beautiful or glittering with glory seemed suddenly fragile. Latin was spoken less and less in the Empire. Barbarians, incapable of building a straight road or wall, flooded in bringing their contorted aesthetics and superstitions with them. On every sea voyage, the Saxons, who shaved their hair to halfway back their heads, threw one in ten of their prisoners overboard and felt self-righteous about it. Aetius had defeated Attila, but what was the future of civilisation now?

Sidonius tried to reason himself out of his morbidity. *Theodoric will support Rome, as his father and brother did; Aetius is invincible in battle; I'm the father of a son and daughter already. The next generation to lead Gaul is born.*

But he could not reason away the feeling that he was teetering on the edge of an abyss. Before the cliff crumbled and he pitched into blackness he wanted to capture the magnificence of Rome. These days would never be seen again and demanded descriptions as iridescent as a peacock's tail. He wanted to capture their glorious shimmering before night rendered men blind. He reached again for his pen, this time to write a poem.

Bagaudae

After the Battle of the Catalaunian Plains, when the lost and wounded Brutus staggered into a circle of hovels and Didra saved him, he unwittingly became part of a gang of bagaudae.

As Rome's power waned, the bagaudae had erupted like acne across the face of Gaul. They were vagrants, both Roman and barbarian. Some were villains, others simply dispossessed and, from time to time, they started insurgencies that were quickly suppressed by local governors.

Shepherding a handful of rustled sheep and a couple of stolen cows, the former farmers amongst Brutus' gang had either lost their homes to the taxman or seen them scorched by Attila. Yet they clung to the belief that they were men of the land and, when melting snow turned streams to rivers, they moved their stock to summer pastures on the volcanic plateau around Clermont. Brutus moved with them.

It rained every day, the bagaudae huts leaked and he wallowed in mud. He began to long for a tightly roped tent with seven squadron-mates who all knew better than to tamper with his things. He missed the square meals dished out in the legions but couldn't see a way of joining up again. Not only was he a deserter, which alone would warrant death, but he'd killed one of his own cohort. Whenever he remembered Quintus, he felt the weight of grief compress his chest.

The baugaudae leader, a thug named Brandag, had modelled himself on Attila but was incapable of organising an assault on even small defended villages. Instead he resorted to theft and highway robbery, although the word "highway" was an overstatement, "byway" was more apt. Important highways were still patrolled by Roman forces or, in federal territories, were under the protection of allied warlords so Brandag's bagaudae were limited to unstrategic routes.

After his brawl with Sidonius, Brutus returned to camp with a black eye and a dent to his ego. He hid his two sestertii in his loincloth and told Brandag that he'd run into a Roman patrol but managed to escape. If any of the gang suspected Brutus had something of value they'd steal it while he slept. Living with bagaudae entailed constant deceit but, fortunately for Brutus, he lied as easily as he breathed. Nonetheless, he thought himself superior to them and when Brandag boasted that he'd held up a priest, stolen his *Bible* and sold it to another priest in the next town Brutus barely hid a sneer of contempt.

For three days after his encounter with Sidonius, Brutus found himself wandering back to the fork in the road leading to Avitacum. On the fourth day, he turned down the alleyway of trees towards the villa, despite knowing it was a dead end and there'd be no traffic for him to hold up.

Under the cover of a broad-leafed forest, the route wound down to the edge of a green-blue lake. Brutus took a drink from its water then stood up and stared across at the limestone villa on the opposite bank. He turned and walked ten steps back up the road, but feeling sick and hopeless at the thought of returning to the misery of bagaudae life, he turned towards the lake again. With desperate eyes, he stared at the white façade of Avitacum. Its stone wings stretched out either side of the doric columned portico as if welcoming him in.

Seizing his courage in both hands, he set off round the shore towards it. In the hope that no one would stop and question him, he skirted around the back of the house to the stableyard entrance, but when he reached it a wave of nerves ran up through his stomach and he was about to sprint back the way he'd come when two guard dogs started barking. A stout slave woman, holding a broom across her body as if it were a staff, came out and called them to heel then yelled out -

"What business have you 'ere?"

"I . . . I've come to see a friend of mine. . ." Brutus stammered.

"What's 'is name then?"

"Sidonius Apollinaris." As the words left his lips, Brutus heard how ridiculous he sounded.

"The master?" the slave woman guffawed.

"Yes," Brutus improvised, "he invited me."

"'E's not 'ere," the woman smirked as she looked him up and down, "you'll 'ave to come back another day." She gave the air a poke with the shaft of her broom as if shooing away a cat.

Having nothing left to lose, Brutus got cocky. He put on a smile and asked in his best Latin, "Would it be possible to see the mistress in his place and give her the message I have for her husband?"

The woman stopped smirking. Messengers of all sorts came and went unexpectedly when the Aviti were in residence and it was *just* possible that Brutus might be one of them. "Who sent you?"

"I can't tell you, it's confidential."

"Wait 'ere a minute." She took her broom with her, lest he steal it, and told the dogs to stay then headed off into the house. Brutus would have run away but as soon as he moved both dogs growled and raised their hackles so he stayed put.

The slave found Papianilla on the flagstone terrace outside the library and explained that there was a visitor looking for the master.

"Do we know him?"

"No, I've never seen 'im before, my lady. He's rough, but he's Roman."

"In that case, please send a boy down to the lake to tell my father that a man who says he's a messenger is here to see him."

The slave-child ran back with instructions from Avitus to send the messenger down to the lakeside. Avitus preferred to greet his correspondents out of earshot of the house. Even at Avitacum, he couldn't be sure there were no spies amongst the staff.

Brutus' stomach was leaping but he'd decided the best thing to do was bluff it out. He pulled his shoulders back and advanced down the lawn.

Avitus didn't get up from the log he was sitting on. The float of his line lay still on the lake. He turned his head and sized up the young man striding towards him. False bravado, a black eye and a badly swollen jaw. Would probably lose some teeth. Avitus was proud of Sidonius, sure it was he who'd landed that punch.

Brutus' grubby brown tunic finished halfway up his thigh and he wore neither cloak nor helmet, so Avitus could see both the gladius hilt protruding from a home-made leather scabbard hanging from a plaited hide belt and the short dagger strapped to his ankle. A soldier once, but a man of no rank.

Feeling the scrutiny of the old man's eyes, Brutus arrived at the lakeside and realised that he had absolutely no idea what to do next. By instinct, he pulled to a halt three yards in front of the fisherman and gave a legionary salute.

Avitus took in the scar of a deep wound that was visible on Brutus' pumped up quadriceps. It was a wound of war, the kind of injury that would have killed most men, and he surmised that there were other scars hidden by Brutus' tunic but the young man still moved well. "Which legion did you belong to?"

Brutus hesitated to incriminate himself but knew it would be impossible to deceive the old fox. He'd given himself away with his salute and the conspicuous dirty bandage on his forearm. "The Twelfth, sir.'

"Cohort?"

"The seventh, sir." Brutus was annoyed with himself for concluding each answer with "sir".

"The seventh cohort saw hard fighting against Attila," said Avitus, "were you with them then?"

"Yes, sir."

Avitus looked sternly at him. "My son-in-law came home with a black eye three days ago. Said he'd been attacked by a bagaudae vagrant. You, I assume."

Brutus was sweating and wanted to run away before Avitus had him arrested, but his feet had sunk roots into the ground and he couldn't make himself move.

"It seems most unlikely," continued Avitus, "that you're the bearer of an imperial message. So what was it that brought you to our lake today?"

A lump swelled in Brutus' throat. "I don't know, sir. I just came."

"You need help?"

Brutus stayed dumb.

"Of course you need help – you're a deserter." Avitus twitched at a bite on his fishing line. "If you want my help, you'd better tell me your story, and quick, before I have you seized and executed."

"I didn't mean to do it," blurted Brutus. "It was an accident."

"What was an accident?"

Brutus didn't understand why he couldn't move his legs and flee. As if confessing his sins to a priest, he opened his mouth. "I was blind in the dark. By mistake I killed the man next to me. He was my best friend." Brutus' eyes glistened. "In the morning, there was no one around. I was wounded and couldn't get back to my legion." Brutus stood staring at his own dirt-encrusted toes. In the fight with Sidonius, he'd stubbed the big one and the nail was black. The ankle strap on one of his sandals was broken and he'd tied it on with twine.

Avitus gave him a moment before asking, "Is that what you want to do, get back to your legion?"

Brutus chewed his lip. He didn't know what he wanted, but he knew he did not want to go back to killing people. "No, it's too late for me to go back there now."

Avitus stood up and looked out at the lake for a moment, adjusting his fishing line and turning his back to Brutus, both to give the deserter a chance to abscond and to signal his disgust at his lack of fibre.

But Brutus' feet still anchored him. He was as incapable of moving as a craft with no wind. Rudderless. Nowhere to go, and no means of getting there. Desperation overwhelmed him.

After a couple of minutes' quiet contemplation, Avitus tested the tension on his fishing line then turned around and spoke. "The seventh cohort of the twelfth legion was nigh annihilated the night we destroyed Attila. There weren't enough survivors for the seventh to be kept together and form an independent cohort, so they were dispersed and transferred to different legions. For all that anyone knows, you might've been sent to Spain, Italy, or somewhere else in Gaul, for the last three years. It's unlikely that anyone would bother checking the records of a gregarius. Things aren't as black and white as you might think. If you really wanted to unmask your arm and take your place as part of the imperial forces again, it's quite possible that I could arrange it for you."

Brutus stood staring straight ahead, not sure if he could believe the old man, afraid of joining the legions but also afraid of dying with a knife in his ribs after a failed bagaudae robbery.

Avitus stroked his clean-shaven chin, watching Brutus' expression change from fear to confusion, then asked, "Do you have any idea who I am?"

"No, sir. I was told to go down to the lakeside and give my message to the fisherman sitting on the stump of a tree down there."

"So much the better. I have contacts in Lyon who might be willing to help you, but you'd have to be prepared to face up to all aspects of army life again. Despite your injuries, you're able-bodied and will be exempt from nothing until you work your way up."

"Sir, if I go back they'll stone me."

"Not if I tell them not to, they won't." Avitus sat up straight with one hand on his thigh. His deep contempt for cowardice moved his lips to a sneer as he looked at Brutus. "It's right to stone deserters, they deserve no better; their cowardice endangers their brothers-in-arms and undermines our Empire. Nonetheless, if I believe what you tell me, you didn't desert in battle. You fought it out to the end but found yourself injured and detached from the little that was left of your cohort. With a leg wound like that," Avitus gestured at the purple scar eight inches long on Brutus' thigh, "you wouldn't have been able to march up to headquarters. I'm surprised you lived."

Avitus looked back at his fishing rod. The wound was an evil one, and the boy seemed to be worthy of a second chance, but intuition told him that there was something awry with Brutus. "I'm not prepared to take a risk on a man like you, just like that. If you're serious, come back to see me here in three days' time and we can make arrangements for you to resume your life in the legions. If you're not here then, I'll treat you as an outlaw. Now go, and leave an old man to a quiet afternoon's fishing before he regrets taking an interest in your welfare."

"Sir, if I may ask, will you tell me who you are?"

"No. You owe my passing concern to the fact that my son-in-law gave you his name and told you where he lived. That and the fact that you had the nerve to come here today and speak with me in his absence. Now, leave me to my trout and carp and go make your mind up before I change mine." Avitus pulled in and then recast his line.

Three days passed then Brutus came back and Avitus, not without misgivings, found him a post in the Lyon garrison.

Lion's Paw

When an invitation to attend the consecration of the new cathedral at Reims arrived, Sedulla leapt at the opportunity to go beyond her normal round of country life in Auvergne interspersed with political hobnobbing in Lyon. Christianity offered a restrained alternative to the sensual excesses of her youth and she believed that it had rewarded her donations and prayers with the birth of her grandson.

Avitus had at first been reluctant to attend but was growing bored of fishing and no longer being part of any military action. When it occurred to him that all of Reims' leading citizens would be invited to the ceremony including, perhaps, the fair-haired widow of the former town councillor, Ruricius, he agreed to accompany his wife.

Still under reconstruction after being ransacked and burned by Attila, the city of Reims was a building site. The cathedral would take decades to finish, but it was roofed in and could accommodate a thousand citizens.

Christianity had started out as a fashionable fad but had become the Empire's official religion. Although Avitus would never openly admit it, he found little to like in its *mea culpae* and unending sermons on penitence. In the old days, at a feast of Mercury, Jupiter or Venus one could expect good food, dancing, bright colours and carousing followed by whatever came naturally. Roman religion was a celebration of life in the present, not some continual self-abnegation in the hope of life after

266

death. Christianity seemed to be all about denying the pleasures of the flesh whether they be food, sex or wine. Feast days were few but fasts were every week. Christianity didn't suit Avitus, but in these troubled times the populace were flocking to it.

Avitus wasn't alone in finding the service to consecrate the cathedral was dull and long-winded. When he nipped outside the cathedral to escape the tedium of day-long pontifications he found other men, sitting in the shade of colonnades of the cathedral cloisters, playing checkers and dice. He joined the young ones in a ball game or two but was frustrated to find that he wasn't as fit as he used to be and had to sit down and take a rest. In his youth he'd excelled at that sport, along with all others.

Avitus had scanned the faces in the crowd inside the church in search of a tall, blonde woman but hadn't been able to pick Sola out. Perhaps her husband's contribution to the city had already been forgotten and she hadn't received an invitation. Curiosity spurred him to ask his fellow checker-players if they'd heard of her.

It turned out they had. Sola was notorious for having insisted on her daughter's rights to her deceased father's property. A second cousin, from whom Ruricius had borrowed money, had made a claim, but Sola had paid an advocate to contest it and the court had found in favour of Leonida. This was not to the checker-players' liking as it set a dangerous precedent, but the magistrate who gave the judgment had reasoned it so thoroughly in Leonida's favour that there was nothing anyone could do to overturn it. Although Sola had found other ways to compensate the cousin, the success of a half-barbarian woman against a Roman citizen had set tongues wagging.

On hearing the story, Avitus hid his smile. *His girl*, as – for no reason whatsoever – he'd started thinking of Sola, had again proved her mettle. He tut-tutted mock disapproval of her legal successes but decided that, rather than going back into the church and enduring three more hours of hymns and psalms, he'd pay Sola a visit.

Her villa was only a few blocks away from the cathedral and quite distinctive – *you won't be able to miss it, well worth a look, rebuilt from the ground up, quite an eyesore* – said his confederates.

Avitus glanced at the sundial on the wall near a door of the cathedral to make sure he wasn't mistaken as to the hour then ambled off, humming a tune and casting his eye over the new buildings springing up in the city centre. He was sure that he'd have no trouble identifying Sola's home as he'd been told it was the only one in the whole of Reims with elephant-repelling spikes studding its bronze gates.

He found the house hidden behind a high wall with tall, arched gates that indeed could repel an elephant attack. A grin spread over Avitus' face. He knew his military history: Hannibal had passed through Gaul on elephants five hundred years before and a detested Roman governor, by the name of Ahenobarbus, had used war elephants to conquer Avitus' own Arveni ancestors, during the consulship of Manilius and Carbo. Ahenobarbus had offended Avitus' ancestors' in their defeat by parading through the streets on elephant-back. The citizens of Reims could laugh at Sola's architectural taste, but Avitus warmed to her for it.

The elephant spikes sent a frisson of expectation through him as he stood at her gates, nose to nose with a door-knocker cast in bronze in the shape of a lion's head. The lion's lips snarled back to expose sabre-toothed fangs so realistic that Avitus could almost smell the carnivore's breath. Beneath its maleficent jaw hung a life-sized paw, claws fully extended. He extended his hand, its back criss-crossed with the scars of fifty years' combat, raised the paw and let it fall with a reverberating thud. A servant immediately slid open a small hatch to see who was summoning him. Recognising authority when it came calling, the slave unbolted and swung wide a pedestrian gate that screeched on its hinges and Avitus strode in.

"Is your mistress receiving visitors?"

"I'll make enquiries. May I ask who is calling?"

"Eparchius Avitus."

The slave scraped a low bow in recognition of the illustrious name, backed away and showed Avitus into a small ante-room.

In less than half a minute, Sola stalked in. Her hair was loose about her shoulders but held back from her face by a silver circlet and her white linen chiton fell to just above her ankles. Avitus noticed her fine leather sandals and elegant feet.

"An unexpected pleasure." Sola looked around for Avitus' wife. It wasn't the norm for men to call alone on single women unless the women were known to be loose. A frown crossed her face.

Avitus inclined his head in a bow. "The pleasure is mine, madam."

"May I offer you some refreshments in my office? You'll have to excuse the disarray, our home is still under construction."

He followed her into a well-proportioned room with high ceilings and glazed arched doors that gave onto a courtyard planted with jasmine. The golden light of afternoon streamed through open shutters. A simple fountain played in the centre of a round pond. Birds darted in and out of the water, drinking and washing in its shallows before flitting back into the branches of flowering trees. Avitus looked around in surprise. "You've created a haven of peace behind your warlike facade."

"Thank you." Sola moved towards a desk on which wax tablets, a stylus and scrolls of parchment were stacked. She'd spread open architectural drawings and used glass globes to weigh down their corners.

Amidst the peaceful elegance he noticed a jarring note – the sword belt at her waist. "Was that your husband's gladius?"

"No, it's mine. I've had it for many years."

Avitus grunted. "You know how to use it?"

Sola made a sound that was halfway between a laugh and the sound of a horse snorting. "One never knows these days when one might have to defend oneself."

Avitus' pulse sped up. He looked harder at her long, well-muscled arms and legs and wondered how quick she'd be with a weapon. Feeling suddenly playful, he moved his hand towards the hilt of his gladius but before he'd touched it Sola had drawn hers.

"I see you're an expert," he said with a smile only half felt. She stood with her sword held in a double-handed grip, tip up, her knees slightly bent – a stance from which a fast man could gut him in one-hundredth of a second.

He opened his arms wide to indicate harmlessness and took a casual step to the side so that he'd have time to draw his own sword and parry her strike if he had to but made no other move to defend himself. "Is this the welcome you give all your guests or is it reserved for those who help you find your child?"

Sola smiled in return. "Didn't you seek a demonstration of my swordsmanship?"

"You've convinced me! I need see no more," he said with a smile. He would have loved to spar and test her skills but, after the ball game at the cathedral, didn't want to risk even playful competition with a woman who was, indeed, a former gladiator. His heart still pumping fast, he circled her. "When you came to the Roman bridge during the wars with Attila, I thought you unusual but didn't remember then where I'd seen you before. Now I've worked it out – Nimes, fifteen years ago, a senator called Pontius put on some private games. Do you remember the event?"

With a sigh, Sola sheathed her sword. A wave of sadness washed the light from her face. "How could I forget?"

Avitus nodded, waiting for her emotion to pass. "You risked your life in the arena."

"And won my freedom." Sola ran a hand back through her hair then looked him in the eye. "You know that I was once a slave?"

"I didn't, but it makes no difference to me. I was greatly marked by your courage, strength and speed." His gaze voyaged over the tall, athletic woman, her blond hair whitening at the temples, her eyes so dark a blue. "I am not mistaken, am I, it was really you?"

Sola turned slowly away from him. Holding the front of her chiton over her breast with one hand, she undid the clasp on her left shoulder.

The linen tumbled to her waist, baring her back.

Avitus' eyes widened then shone with tears. Four long, white scars scraped across her scapula and below them, on the rib behind her heart, was the circle of a puncture wound. He held his hand out over the marks, fingers and thumb spread, and saw that the lion's paw dwarfed his own. "Let me help you." He picked up the corner of the fallen chiton.

She reached her fingers over her shoulder to take it from him and the weight and warmth of his hand lingered on hers. She fastened the clip and turned to face him.

"I remember the way you addressed the Empress," said Avitus.

Sola smile wryly. "It wasn't the traditional *We who are about to die salute you.*"

"No. If I remember rightly, you said, *For you, O Romans – I will never die!*"

"You were the only dignitary who understood me. I spoke in Burgundian."

"My Burgundian is limited, but I saw your spirit." Avitus looked into her eyes. "I would never have believed what you did to be possible, if I hadn't witnessed it – the most incredible feat. Could you tell me how you survived such ill-matched combat?"

Sola sat down behind her desk. Her lips formed a bow of cupid but she shook her head. "There are some things that I never speak of. That day is amongst them." Her reply hung in the air like the last note of a melancholy ballad.

"I understand," said Avitus, "I've memories that I never share, memories of war and death – grief. But let's not be morbid. Tell me, how's your daughter, what's her name again?"

"Leonida. She's as well as can be expected after suffering the loss of both her father and her betrothed."

"I see," said Avitus, sensing that on this subject too, Sola was unwilling to speak. "Then tell me about yourself. How did you become a gladiator when it's no longer legal for women to fight in the arena?"

Again Sola let out a sigh, but this man had been kind and helped bring her daughter back to her. "If you have time to listen, please sit down. I'll send for some food and drink. What would you like?"

"Nothing, thank you, except a glass of water." Avitus helped himself to one from a pitcher on a tripod then sat down opposite her, "since I've left the army, it's become too easy to overeat."

"What brought you to Reims today?"

"The consecration of the new cathedral, but that can wait. Something more personal – instinctive – has drawn me to your home."

Sola studied his face, square jawed, hook-nosed, leathered by years in the saddle. The lines of his life were drawn across his forehead, around his mouth, fanning out like a peacock's tail from the corners of his eyes. Eyes so blue they brought a laughing brook under a summer sky into the room. But this man had killed for a living, as had she. "Perhaps you were just bored by the church service?"

Avitus laughed, liking her better by the minute. "That as well. I know that there's nothing I can say to make you trust a man like me, but I'd be honoured if we could talk. I'd love to know the history of a woman like you. In my experience, you're unique."

Sola blushed. "How much time do you have?"

"The service will drone on for another two or three hours at least. As long as I'm back before it ends, no one will notice that I've escaped."

"Are you sure you don't want anything to eat?"

"Certain."

Sola stood up, walked to an open window and watched a jewel coloured bird drink from her fountain. "I don't know where I come from, although it's surely north of the Rhine for I do remember crossing that river as a tiny child, cradled in my mother's arms and hidden in the dark under a pile of putrid deer pelts. A Roman patrolman stopped the boat and searched it, but their stench put him off and he didn't uncover us.

After that, there were happy times, until one bitter winter when the roads were choked with snow and no food could get through. We were starving, so my mother bundled me up in rabbit skins and led me down to the frozen river. We were trying to hammer a hole through the ice to fish when Roman border guards sounded the alarm and all the way down the banks of the Rhine the flames from brush warning bales flashed up. Red, so red against the pale grey sky."

Avitus' eyes widened and he sat on the edge of his chair, his heart thundering.

"We ran, my mother and I. But it was no good." Sola's face went white and she closed her lips, no longer full and smiling, but thin and downturned.

Avitus raised a hand. "You don't have to tell me what happened. I think I witnessed it."

"*You* saw it?" Sola's eyes darted towards him, her heart pounding.

"My first posting as a lad was on the Rhine border. Meant to be a punishment if the truth be told – I was an athlete, not a scholar, and my father sent me off to the army to teach me the virtues of Virgil over the tedium of garrison life, but I'd been looking forward to it. It was a chance for adventure and an escape from the lashings of my schoolmaster. I was only fifteen but thought myself a man.

The Rhine shouldn't have been any trouble at all – capture handfuls of refugees if they tried to take a boat across the border, but no real fighting. On another day, it could've been me who stopped your boat and lifted the deer pelts. The Rhine kept us safe from any invading force. Until the coldest night of my life – New Year's Eve, 410, when the river froze solid."

Sola's eyes darkened.

"I was on watch the next morning," said Avitus, "lit those warning bales myself. I was calm, did it faster than you'd ever think possible, although the fire-steel was covered in ice and slipped in my grip. The captain ordered us to form a perimeter around the top of the watchtower and draw our bows but the enemy never came within range. My arm started to shake from holding the bowstring taut, and my fingers grew numb with cold. My eyes were focused on the barbarians, seeking a target, when I saw them – a lone woman and a small child, right in the path of the invading Goths." Avitus looked sideways at Sola before continuing. Her eyes were far away. He let out a sigh then went on. "A horseman cantered forward and killed the woman then slung the child over his saddle."

Sola let out her breath, ran a hand through her hair, and turned away from him.

Avitus hung his head. "It's been my everlasting regret that I couldn't save that girl and her mother."

Sola buried her face in her hands, letting her hair fall forward to hide her silent tears and her body shook with stifled sobs.

Avitus stood up, walked through the arched door into the courtyard, and left her time to grieve. He'd never forget the sight of that Goth on horseback gathering ground on the young woman, who clung to her daughter's hand while she ran, until the brute had swung his sword. Nor could he forget the Goth dragging the child up by her hair and throwing her across the neck of his horse. Avitus' eyes too welled with tears at the thought of what that orphaned girl must have lived through.

Silent minutes passed before he heard Sola sniff, get up and pour herself a glass of water. He waited till she'd sat down on one of a pair of sabre-legged chairs that looked out on to the pond then he went back into the room and sat on the other one.

"I'm sorry." His hand covering hers on the ebonised arm. "If there'd been more of us, then perhaps we could've sallied out and fought, but we were only a dozen on my watchtower and the Goths were thousands. I volunteered to ride out through the snow and pass on the call for reinforcements. They never came but our legions rebelled and we waged war against the barbarians." His hand closed around her fingers. "That was the beginning of everything for me, my whole career. You should know that, to me, you and your mother were worth fighting for."

Sola turned ocean-deep eyes on him. "Thank you; thank you for doing all you could."

He nodded then turned away so she could wipe an escaped tear from her cheek. "You still haven't told me how you became a gladiator."

"Another day, perhaps. But for now, I can tell you that I was sold as a slave and learned to fight to stay alive."

Avitus nodded. "No mean achievement, to become a gladiator. You must have worked very hard."

"I did."

"I didn't mean to cause you pain today. If it's any consolation, you should know it means more than I can tell you to learn that the little girl I saw abducted not only survived but became a great warrior, a beautiful woman and a loving mother."

Tears welled again in Sola's eyes. She'd told her deceased husband about her past but to share it with someone who'd witnessed the horror gave her the sense that, for the first time in her life, she'd been truly understood.

Avitus rose to go.

"Will I see you again?" Sola asked, looking up at him.

"I'd like that," Avitus smiled, "but you must know that I'm loyal to my wife."

Sola hadn't meant it that way and her face flushed.

"I see that perhaps I flatter myself," said Avitus with a wry smile.

"Not at all, sir," she rose too and offered him her hand in dismissal, "it's been an honour to meet you. I'll remain forever in your debt for the help you gave me in finding my daughter and for all the years you fought to protect others like me from what I suffered."

"And I will remain forever grateful to you for giving meaning to my life – my whole life – as a soldier," said Avitus.

Her eyes held his. "I've never met such kindness as yours, all the more remarkable given that, at our first meeting, you were facing Attila the Hun and, at our second, you had just fought the bloodiest battle of all time. I'm surprised you even noticed me."

"You're impossible to forget." Avitus bent to kiss the back the hand she held out to him on a strong, unbending wrist. His eyes rested on the veins that ran up along her forearm. Warrior's veins, the result of years of wielding a sword. Ruefully he smiled, wanting to kiss those as well but forbidding himself.

Sola walked with him through the cool of her ante-room, her heart still beating fast but with a new sense of peace, then she beckoned to the gatekeeper who opened the pedestrian entrance and bowed to their guest. Avitus turned back and waved in a way that looked like a salute then, to Sola's surprise, winked. Her lips widened and showed her straight white teeth, then she winked back.

She looks so young when she smiles, just a girl again, thought Avitus, then turned away.

Sola stood still, watching until his blood red cloak had disappeared.

Back in the cathedral, Sedulla had been becoming increasingly irritated as each minute passed. She'd expected her husband to abscond halfway through the service – he'd never been one to sit still – but the liturgy was drawing to a close and if he wasn't back soon it would cause her monumental embarrassment to leave unescorted and make small-talk alone with the new bishop and city dignitaries.

Just as the priest started intoning a solemn *Nunc Dimittis* she heard Avitus excusing himself for stepping on her neighbours' toes. *He never could pass unnoticed*, she thought as he sat down and ignored her reproving look. She raised an eyebrow. There was something different about him, a new – no, an old – fire in his eyes. He'd been bored and restless since his retirement but today he exuded his former vigour. Sedulla doubted that the consecration of the cathedral had brought it back.

Papianilla's Dream

Avitacum, Province of Auvergne, Gaul
454 AD

"Your trout was delicious," said Papianilla to her father.

Avitus licked his lips and patted his stomach. "It put up quite a fight."

His daughter smiled and sat next to him on the terrace. She looked out across the lake to the cleavage of Avitacum's hills. "The sunset is magnificent."

The water turned to molten gold. Above her head, the sky was royal blue, but lower down it shaded to green then merged into a band of red and orange behind silhouetted mountains. Small stars started to light up like glow-worms. Papianilla pulled a woollen palla round her shoulders as the sun fled and the temperature suddenly tumbled. A chill wind blew up from the surface of the lake, now dark and sombre. She sighed and shivered.

Avitus' brows creased as he looked at his daughter. "You look pale, have those children been tiring you again?"

Since his grandson, Apollinaris, had been born Papianilla lacked energy and it worried Avitus. He could not bear to lose his only daughter to the slow, lingering infection that stole so many young mothers from their families.

"No, they're no trouble at all. We have plenty of help and it's good that Nona has lived long enough to see her great-grandchildren. She keeps an eye on the housemaids and nurses. The children are safe and well cared for as long as Nona is here."

Avitus was watching the stars coming to life, one after another. The planet Venus, usually brightest and earliest of them, seemed to be missing from the panoply. Wrong time of year for her, he supposed.

"It's not here," Papianilla said, out of nowhere.

"Venus, you mean? I was just thinking the same thing," he smiled at his daughter.

"No, I was looking for the comet, not Venus," Papianilla shivered again. "Last night I had a dream, so vivid that I thought it must be real. You and I were sitting together here, looking at a sunset just like this, but there was a bright comet that arced across the sky. Its silver-gold tail streaked out behind it, so clearly that I was sure that we'd see it this evening. It was spectacular and I wanted to watch it with you tonight."

"There's no comet that I can see, nor have I heard from the astronomers that one is on its way," said Avitus gently, worrying about his daughter.

"It was such powerful dream. I really believed that it meant a comet would come today. Its tail was bright as a sickle under a harvest sun."

"What happened in your dream?" Avitus asked. An image of the plumes of Aetius' helmet streaming out behind him as he rode flickered across his mind.

"It stopped flying straight across the sky and its tail flared out, like a horse's in the wind, and arced into a curve. Then it plummeted towards the black earth. I was afraid of what would happen when it crashed."

"What did happen?"

"I don't know. I woke up before the impact." Papianilla tightened her palla around her shoulders.

Avitus placed his gnarly paw over his daughter's white hand and patted it.

Three days later an imperial courier arrived.

Sedulla's Sources

Avitus had worked his way up from the roots of the army and Sedulla – born an aristocrat and impeccably well-connected – saw it as her duty to protect her sometimes guileless husband from the vipers' nest of politics. Discreetly proud of her network of spies, her blood turned cold when one of them, a faceless slave as invisible to his masters as a piece of furniture, brought her news that Avitus must know.

Her hands trembling, she hitched up the hem of her silken chiton and, with a basket of apples on her arm, set off down the lawn to his fishing spot.

He looked up with a smile, surprised to see his wife bringing him something to eat herself instead of sending a slave.

"May I have a seat?"

"Of course, my dear." Avitus vacated his tree stump. "What a pleasure it is to see you here."

Sedulla set the basket on the ground. From under slightly sagging lids, she scanned the lake and surrounding grounds. There was no one in sight and the chirrup of cicadas would drown out what she had to tell him. He was wise to choose such a place to meet his messengers. "I've heard rumours which I must pass on to you before it's too late."

Avitus, now standing at her side, kept his eyes on his fishing float.

"Our Emperor, Valentinian . . ."

"That idiot! What now? I hear his mother's ghost tortures him every night – and long may Galla haunt him!"

"Indeed, since he assassinated her, he's known to rant at her shade, whom he alone can see or hear, as if she were there haranguing him in return. But what I have to tell you is worse."

"Who's next then?"

"Your friend, the magister militum."

Avitus' eyes shot wide and he looked carefully at his wife. "That can't be right! Not even Valentinian would be stupid enough to kill Rome's saviour. Aetius' name alone holds the Vandals at bay and the populace worships him."

"My source was present at a game of dice between Valentinian and Petronius Maximus."

"Maximus – I might have known – another nobody, jealous of Aetius. Joined the civil service because he didn't have the balls for the army."

"Despite what you think of him, my dear, Maximus is the most decorated nonmilitary citizen of Rome. And yes, you're right, he's rabid with jealousy since Aetius has been elected to his fourth consulship, the only man who ever has."

"An honour that Aetius unquestionably deserves."

"No one can deny that Rome owes him even more than that, but Maximus is bilious with envy. Valentinian's eunuch of the bedchamber, Heraclius, was also in attendance when the Emperor and Maximus played dice."

Avitus frowned. "Dissolute, useless, vapid – Valentinian and his eunuchs! When he's not debauching honest women, he's debauching slaves."

Sedulla stood up and put her arm around Avitus' waist, looking out as he did towards the fishing line dipping tranquilly into the lake. She laid her head on his shoulder, knowing they looked the epitome of a loving couple, still happy together in the autumn of their years.

"My spy tells me that Petronius Maximus said . . ."

Petronius Maximus Plays Dice

Rome, Italy
September 454 AD

A tall, urbane man, with hair elaborately quiffed upwards from his forehead then plaited in rows across the back of his skull, sat hunched over a checkered board and rolled his dice. A double six.

"You're in luck tonight, Maximus," said the Emperor opposite him, sulking.

Petronius Maximus gave him a sly smile. "It must be the presence of a demi-god that brings me good fortune, Caesar. Here," he pushed the dice towards Valentinian, "I owe you my luck. Pray, choose your move."

The Emperor removed two of his opponent's pieces from the board then rolled again as if it was still his turn. His eunuch, Heraclius, plumped up a striped silk cushion and slipped it behind his master's back. Valentinian leant back, perusing Maximus. Since, on his sixth attempt, Valentinian had succeeded in assassinating his own mother, Maximus had been constantly in his ear. Tonight the subject was Flavius Aetius. "When mother was with us, Aetius never caused any trouble."

The white under Petronius Maximus' irises showed as he looked up from shaking his dice. "There were times that she doubted him, Caesar."

"But that was mother," said Valentinian, "she trusted no one, not even me."

Petronius Maximus knew full well that Valentinian had poisoned the woman whose wisdom had secured his throne and his Empire. "Galla Placidia was a trial to you, Sire. But Aetius is the real threat now. Not only is he master and commander of all your troops, but today the assembly of the people elected him to a record fourth consulship."

Valentinian frowned. He had no interest in the work of governing the Empire, that had been his mother's job, but since she'd gone the comitia centuriata had become a nuisance.

Maximus saw his annoyance and fanned its flames. "The crowds are jubilant. They sing Aetius' praises in every tavern, as if he were divine – which, of course, only an Emperor can be." He leant forward and paused for effect. "Loved by his men and respected by his enemies, Aetius is poised to seize your throne."

Valentinian's fish-like eyes darted from side to side as if he expected Aetius – supported by Galla Placidia's ghost – to march into the room and usurp him right then and there.

Maximus nodded at Valentinian's discomfort. "It's time to get rid of the magister militum."

Valentinian bit his lip. "If Aetius were gone, who'd defend me from the barbarians?"

"Attila is dead, Caesar, you can do without Aetius now."

"You jest," said Valentinian, flicking his fringe back from his forehead, "the Huns are beaten but the Vandals, Sueves, and Goths are at my throat."

"There are other ways to protect ourselves." Maximus had expected this. "I'll build a great wall – and nobody builds walls better than me, believe me – a great, great wall."

"And how can we pay for that?"

"I'll make the barbarians pay for it."

"But how?" asked Valentinian.

"I just will, Caesar, trust me. Together we'll make Rome great again."

"And even if you did build a wall, who'd kill Aetius?"

Petronius dared to poke a finger into the Emperor's chest. "You, sire."

Valentinian sucked in his breath so fast he choked. Heraclius rushed forward with a goblet of wine mixed with water. Valentinian had never picked up a sword in his life. When his coughing stopped, he whispered to Maximus. "And how in Hades could I do that?"

"It will require cunning, Sire, not force, and you have proven yourself to be full of cunning."

Valentinian took that as a compliment and crooked a finger for Heraclius to pour more wine. Maximus watched lamplight slither over the slave's oiled shoulders and chest then rolled his weighted dice. "Double sixes again, Caesar. A good omen."

Valentinian wiped a sweaty hand over his lips. "You must give me proof of your loyalty. Words will not suffice."

"Whatever you wish, Sire." Petronius Maximus had made sure to profit from his public offices. "I'm very rich."

Valentinian licked his lips. "Your wife."

Maximus' eyes bulged. He kept his voluptuous young Carisa under lock and key, only bringing her out to display on public festivals or at private parties.

"Send her to me – tonight," drooled Valentinian.

"Tonight? I'm afraid I cannot do without her, sire."

"I understand," said Valentinian, settling back in his chair, "that's how I feel about Aetius."

Petronius retrieved an unloaded pair of dice from the folds of his toga and rattled them in cupped hands. Perhaps, if he lost the game to the Emperor and Heraclius kept pouring the wine, Valentinian would change his mind. With a self-deprecating smile he let the dice fly. "There, oh mighty Caesar, you've beaten me – again."

"So I have, and now I claim my prize."

Maximus' pulse lurched out of time and beads of perspiration burst out above his lips.

Valentinian saw them and smirked. "Your signet ring."

Petronius Maximus kept his eyes lowered as he tugged it off his porcine digit. Never had he felt such loathing for another man but he swallowed it.

Valentinian cast a smug glance at Heraclius then wrapped his podgy fingers round the ring. "Leave us, Maximus."

His guts churning, Petronius Maximus bowed and walked backwards.

* * * * *

In her dressing chamber in the grandest villa in Rome, Carisa applied shards of shining mica to the lids of her clear, green eyes and cochineal juice to her lips. Her husband had sent his signet ring and a command that she attend the Empress Eudoxia immediately in the palace. The invitation flattered and excited Carisa, for Eudoxia was not only married to the Emperor but descended from another, while Carisa was plebeian by birth.

A maid coiled Carisa's thick black hair round the perfect curve of her forehead, placed a pearl circlet above it and draped a gossamer thin palla over her mistress's shoulders. "A litter has arrived to collect you, madam."

Carisa inspected her attire in a mirror and adjusted the pearls in her hair, then walked down the marble peristyle to where a litter and four swarthy slaves awaited. A Nubian giant pulled back the curtain and helped her in. Valentinian had cut out the bearers' tongues so they couldn't tell of what they saw but the widening of the Nubian's eyes and the swelling in his groin told Carisa what he thought of her. She pulled her palla over her face and stepped in then pulled the curtains tightly together behind her, her stomach a flutter of nerves.

The Nubians set her down inside the palace gate and two purple-crested body-guards led her to the Emperor's private apartments. It was the third hour of the night, the palace was quiet and their boots rang out in the colonnaded peristyle. They opened double doors and Carisa stepped out of the torchlight into a room lit with oil lamps, their wicks turned low. She looked around for her husband and Eudoxia but, as her pupils dilated, she saw that she was alone with Valentinian. The guards backed out with a cackle, the Emperor locked the door.

Three hours past before the key turned again. Carisa pulled her ripped palla over her bruised breasts and crashed her way past the guards. Tears sparkling with mica streaked down her face as she ran from one pilastered doorway to the next, back down the peristyle towards the gates, until she found her husband. Maximus was squatting over his dice in an ante-room, as if nothing were amiss, but when he saw Carisa he leapt to intercept her before she could make a scene. Lips thin and cruel, he gripped her arm and pushed her back towards the entrance.

"He raped me!" Carisa screamed, shaking with shock and rage, "He raped me while you sat by playing dice. You let him do it!"

The senators playing dice with Maximus sidled away.

"He raped you? I don't believe you, my dear, you're imagining things."

Carisa's tears abruptly stopped as a new horror rose before her. "*You* planned this."

"Don't be ridiculous, you're hysterical." Petronius Maximus looked over his shoulder at the senators and raised his brows to say that she was crazy as he pushed her round a corner, out of sight.

"I hate you, I *hate* you," she hissed.

"You're making a drama out of nothing." He gripped her arm so tight that bruises rose in the shape of his fingerprints.

"I'll hate you till the day I die!" Carisa struggled to shake off his hold.

Petronius' voice was unnaturally calm, his lips curled in a mocking smile. "Hate me for the rest of your life if you will, it won't be for long."

Fear gave her strength and Carisa broke free, put her hand to her throat, and ran at full tilt to the mutes' litter. Seeing her dishevelled state and the bruises on her arm, the Nubian hurried her in and set off at a trot to her home.

* * * * *

The next morning Petronius Maximus called on Valentinian and found him smirking. *I've never known such an odious man.*

"Have your ring back, Maximus, I have no further use for it."

"It's yours sire, my gift." Maximus didn't want to touch it now that it symbolised humiliation to him.

"No, really, I insist," said Valentinian, "I want to return to you that which is yours." He yawned and stretched. "I didn't get much sleep last night."

Maximus' blood became bile, hating Valentinian more for the fact that he'd tossed Carisa aside than for the fact that he'd taken her in the first place. But he feigned a sickening smile. "And Aetius? Have you had any further thoughts about the magister militum?"

"I believe we have," said Valentinian turning a simpering eye towards Heraclius.

* * * * *

For the remaining two weeks of Carisa's existence, Petronius Maximus couldn't bring himself to touch the Emperor's cast off. He consoled himself that the sacrifice of his wife's virtue had put him one move closer to the imperial diadem but visions of Valentinian with his wife tormented him. Day and night he plotted how to be rid of him. *And when that dissolute fool is dead, I'll take his wife to my bed.*

In order for Maximus to be free to marry the Empress Eudoxia, Carisa would have to meet with an accident. He didn't want her soiled beauty anymore so that would cause him no regret. A simple fall from the balcony outside her bedchamber would suffice. No one would ever know if she'd jumped or been pushed. He imagined her splattered body being found by slaves who wouldn't dare to ask any questions and congratulated himself on the infallibility of his plans.

It would soon be the third anniversary of Aetius' conquest of Attila. The notion of killing that great man on such an auspicious occasion would appeal to Valentinian's vanity.

An Asteroid Hits Earth

The whole known world
21st September 454 AD

Sometimes, the fall of a comet triggers the end of an age. Taken alone, the impact might be survived but coming on top of centuries of stress it heralds extinction. When the jealous Emperor assassinated Flavius Aetius the earth shook, tilted and spun a different way. Where a star had shone, there was blackness.

Sidonius wrote, *the disfigured left hand has severed the healthy right*.

For what imagined slight no one could guess. With impeccable loyalty, Aetius had served the Empire for over thirty years. Never out of the saddle, never flinching in the face of overwhelming odds, never demanding reward.

When an imperial messenger arrived at Avitacum and placed a parchment scroll into Avitus' hands, the veteran general took it into the library and locked the door. The news knocked the wind from his lungs. He staggered to a sabre-legged chair whose legs bowed and creaked under the weight of his grief.

Alone, alone and unmoving, Avitus sat with his head in his hands as the sun god rode his chariot from one side of the sky to the other. *Now we have a real problem, there's no one alive who can take Aetius' place ...*

When Sedulla heard the news, for once she was silent. Even she could find not one disparaging comment to make about Aetius, a man whose only weaknesses were virtues taken to excess – courage that made him take unreasonable risks; loyalty so unshakeable that he was never suspicious of the Emperor he served; love taken to such extremes of self – sacrifice that, in the end, he hadn't taken care of himself. No, Sedulla had nothing to say about Aetius, but prayed that God might rest his noble spirit.

Papianilla knocked on her father's door but he didn't open it. Her babies, too young to understand, grizzled. She regretted that they wouldn't be old enough to remember the mighty and good Aetius. She put her ear to the library door but her grandmother, Nona, pulled her away. "Leave your father alone with his grief."

A week passed. Avitus' meals went cold on his doorstep and no sound was heard from inside the library. "I wouldn't be surprised if this killed him," Sedulla told her daughter.

Papianilla turned round eyes towards the dark wooden door, but she couldn't conjure an image of her father dying, not even out of grief for his closest friend.

Sidonius was in Toulouse, paying court to Theodoric II, when a grey-faced messenger was ushered into the council chamber. The knight bowed and held out a scroll. The king read it in silence. Theodoric's face drained of blood then he rose to his feet, raised both arms to shoulder height and called for silence. His courtiers' faces lengthened as he read the news. When he'd finished, he looked out over their hung heads and found his people were now shorter.

Grown men wiped tears from their beards. Many had marched

to battle behind Aetius' banner. For them, the magister militum had defined what being a warrior was. Some had been close enough to the front line to have seen the white-gold plumes on his helmet and his flaming torch as he led the charge that crushed the Huns.

Theodoric glanced across at Sidonius, as if to ask what he should do next, but the Roman, like the Goths, had tears on his cheeks. Clutching the scroll in his fist, the king turned on his heel and left the court. He needed time to calculate the consequences of the magister militum's death.

Sidonius watched Theodoric leave. He knew that, in the interests of diplomacy, he should follow him but he hadn't the heart for it.

When Aetius had first ridden to rescue the Empire, Sidonius hadn't yet been born. For the whole of his life, Aetius had stood for what it meant to be Roman and he was grateful to have known the privilege of riding in his shadow.

Not only kings, but nations, had come when Aetius called. Yet, great though he was, he'd also been merciful. Sidonius smiled at the memory of the quirk at the corner of Aetius' lips when he'd spared him punishment for escaping camp. The magister militum had understood.

Tears welled as he remembered the sight of him reining in Achilles, who was foamed with sweat and whose nostrils flared, and shouting over his shoulder to Avitus, "Will you be alright up here alone, old man?"

Without him, would any of them be?

The Disfigured Hand

Sedulla sat with her daughter in the ladies' drawing room at Avitacum. Summer had faded away and the evenings would have been cold if slaves hadn't built up the furnaces for the central heating. Warm air flowed under the floors and up pipes through the walls into the ceiling. The evening was clement, but both women were shivering.

"In thirty years I've never seen your father like this."

Papianilla, who rarely dared show physical affection to her parents, took her mother's hand and rubbed her thumb over its raised blue veins, noticing for the first time that Sedulla was aging.

Surreptitiously, Sedulla wiped tears from the side of her nose, removed her fingers from her daughter's clasp and made a show of rearranging the pins that held her hair in an elaborate bun.

"How did they kill him, Mama?" Since hearing the news, Papianilla had been longing to ask her mother how anyone had managed to kill the invincible Aetius. She trusted Sedulla's spies to know the truth.

Sedulla looked haggard. "Valentinian invited Aetius to a banquet in honour of his historic fourth consulship and the third anniversary of his victory over Attila. He insisted that Aetius remove his weapons and leave his body-guards at the gates, then asked him to go over some army accounts in private. The eunuch, Heraclius, with whom Valentinian is unnaturally close, attended them.

Aetius was seated at a table with his back to Heraclius when the eunuch pulled a meat cleaver out from under his cloak and buried it in the back of his neck." Disgust wrinkled her Sedulla's lips. "Then Valentinian jumped up and sank a gladius into Aetius' throat. It was the first time that coward has ever held a sword."

Papianilla shuddered. "But *why*? Without Aetius, barbarians will overrun the Empire."

Long lines ran from the corners of Sedulla's mouth to her chin. Her lower lids were crimson. "To say that Valentinian is vile is an understatement. The man is beneath despicable. Since murdering his mother, what little mind he had, he's lost. He's surrounded by sycophants and schemers and is too stupid to discern what's true from what's not."

Sedulla paused, staring at the frescoes on the other side of the room, but not seeing them. Her mind was ticking through what she'd heard from Rome, trying to make a connection between the story she'd heard about Petronius Maximus pimping his wife and Aetius' death. "Petronius Maximus was responsible for this. Aetius was everything that Maximus could never be. This is his first move in a plan to wear the imperial diadem himself."

"Then none of us is safe?"

To hide the rising tide of fear she felt for her family, especially for Avitus, Sedulla endeavoured to sound stern. "You need to be aware of how ungrateful the world can be, of the viciousness that stalks successful men and women. An inferior makes himself feel superior by destroying those who are greater than himself." She frowned then put her glass down on the table, as if moving a piece on a checkerboard. "But the game isn't over yet. The Empire still has your father, your husband and your brother."

Papianilla's eyes widened and her voice went thin. "That doesn't sound like enough people to save us from the barbarians."

"There are one or two others – Marjorian, Aetius' second in command, for instance."

"Is that all? Is there really no one but *us* left to save the world?"

Sedulla pursed her lips and Papianilla felt a pit open in her stomach.

* * * * *

For two full weeks, Avitus remained locked behind his double doors with grief as his sole companion. At first, he refused to believe that even the vacuous Valentinian could make the strategic blunder of killing Aetius; but disbelief passed and the gulf of a loss so great that Avitus didn't know how to combat it opened beneath him. Tears coursed the hollows of his beaten cheeks. He'd quench them and square his back only to have them well up and flood again. He paced the room, or lay on a scroll-ended sofa staring at the ceiling, trying to solve the whole world's problems.

While his mind churned over the consequences of the Emperor's evil, his heart replayed thirty-five years of images of Flavius Aetius, his friend. Aetius, Aetius . . . always Aetius . . . the one man who could always be trusted to do the right thing, to grapple with any challenge or setback with easy courage and genius, to achieve the impossible.

Avitus remembered not only the relentless chase over the plains in hunt of Attila but other battles where Aetius had marched or ridden, without food or rest, for days and nights on end. Always first into battle, no matter how dangerous the odds. Through bravery, skill or sheer genius, Aetius, his armour splattered with blood, was victorious. Avitus regretted that they'd never had time to celebrate together. There'd always been dead to bury, allies or enemies to outwit and no time to rest.

Another image came to Avitus and he sat up, grasping his stomach as if he'd been stabbed. The thought of Aetius, the greatest hero of his age, being cut down from behind by a eunuch with a meat-axe brought bile to his mouth.

When, on the fourteenth day, Avitus pushed wide the oak doors of the library, a new fierceness in his eye made Sedulla reel backwards two steps. Grief and vengeance were graven on his face. What alchemy was at work in her ancient warrior?

He called for food and, while his wife and daughter picked at their plates, devoured a haunch of beef. When he'd chewed the marrow from the bones, he strode from his dining couch to the terrace that looked over the lake.

Sedulla followed him, his favourite scented oils in her hand, planning to anoint his feet as she so often had when he'd come home blistered or wounded from war. "Come sit with me, let me massage your soles."

Avitus tried to smile but could not. Standing legs astride, he turned his back to the sinking sun. "We will avenge him."

The Emperor's Archery Practice

On a sunny morning, the Campus Martius was an island of green amongst the terracotta rooves of Rome. Purple-grey hilltops painted a monumental backdrop to the temples and tombs that made the Campus the holiest of holy places but left ample room for chariot races, archery, and cavalry practice.

A decanus shooed away a group of boys kicking a ball next to a field where ringed targets were set out for the Emperor's archery practice. Six months had passed since Valentinian and Heraclius had assassinated Aetius.

The decanus took his place in the ranks of a century of men who stood at ease, shields resting on their greaves. The purple crests of their helmets marked them out as the Emperor's bodyguards but they slouched with boredom, guffawing over last night's drinking stories. Tediously late, Valentinian and Heraclius ambled up on matching dapple-grey geldings. The centurion ordered his men to attention.

Heraclius' tunic barely covered the top of his thighs. He'd oiled his eyelashes and dusted them with kohl and his hair was unguent with frankincense. The Emperor dismounted first and ran his hand lingeringly down his eunuch's shaven calf. When Heraclius jumped down from his horse the hem of his skirt flounced up and gave his master a glimpse of soft buttocks. Valentinian couldn't resist slipping his hand up the tunic and squeezing one of them. His guards stood motionless and stony-eyed in the still of morning.

"A perfect day to shoot off my arrows," the Emperor simpered.

Heraclius tittered. The centurion rolled his eyes at the decanus but his men stared straight ahead.

The partners in murder were sauntering, arm in arm, towards a row of youths waiting with Valentinian's bows already strung for him when, from opposite sides of the field, Thraustila and Optila, two of Aetius' personal cavalry, converged on them. The first breeze of morning rifled the horse-hair crests of their helmets as they drew their swords and quickened their pace. Valentinian's guards remained motionless.

Thraustila rammed his gladius to its hilt in Heraclius' guts. Valentinian's jaw dropped in horror and his mouth moved like a gasping fish as his lover folded to a heap on the ground, his white tunic flooding red

Optila balled his fist and made a quick jab to the side of the Emperor's head. He wanted Valentinian to look at him and know that it was *he*, one of Aetius' own, who was about to kill him, he who was prepared to die for this moment and be remembered for all eternity as the man who avenged the greatest general the world had ever known.

Gaping, Valentinian turned towards him. Optila pointed the tip of his gladius at the Emperor's throat, watched the face drain white and lips tremble. He held the insipid eyes just long enough to be sure that the Emperor had recognised him. Valentinian tried to shout *Seize him!* But emitted only a wordless squeal and his guards didn't move a muscle.

Optila rammed his gladus through the Emperor's neck and felt the body become a dead weight on his blade. He held it at arm's length, watching Valentinian's blood course over his hand in weakening spurts, then shook the corpse from his sword and tossed it to the ground.

A cheer went up from the boys playing football but oblivious athletes further away on the Campus Martius continued to throw their shot put and discus.

Optila and Thraustila wiped their blades on the Emperor's silken robes then stood straight and sheathed their swords, expecting the inevitable consequences of regicide. But the centurion ordered his men to salute and when the avengers marched from field the guards drummed the hilts of their swords on their shields and sent up an earsplitting cheer.

Optila and Thraustila marched directly to the Senate House. Jaws resolute and eyes brimming with pride and grief for Aetius, they saluted the column near the door that thanked him for saving the Empire. Then they squared their shoulders, looked up at the bronze panelled doors, thirty feet high, opened them and marched into the cavernous gloom within.

After they explained to the senators that they'd assassinated Valentinian and the catamite who'd helped him destroy the greatest man in Rome, Petronius Maximus rose to the rostrum to deliver a loquacious speech he'd prepared in advance. A gloat of satisfaction infused him as the Senate replied by offering him the imperial diadem.

Of Messengers and Men

Sidonius rented a villa near the Gothic castle in Toulouse. The floor of the ante-room was decorated with a mosaic of Hermes, the messenger god, and on Hermes' mouth stood a man with a dark beard and head bowed, as if the god was spitting him out.

"Sit down." Sidonius extended his arm towards a bench on which petitioners usually waited to be granted an audience. "May I offer you some refreshments?"

"Thank you, sir, just a glass of water would be more than adequate," said the visitor, although his stomach, aslosh with nerves, was empty.

"Your letter of introduction says that you're a merchant by the name of Amantius who plies his wares amongst men of learning on the routes to Marseille, Lyon and beyond. My classmate, Magnus Felix, recommends you highly." Sidonius ran his eyes over the merchant's cloak, which was bordered with embroidered stags and of good quality.

"Thank you," said Amantius, who carried with him samples of parchment he hoped might be of interest to the diplomat, "I trade those routes and many others. May I show you my wares?"

Sidonius indicated a table on which to lay them out.

Amantius took his time, making sure that everything was displayed to its best advantage, then stepped back.

"May I?" asked Sidonius. Amantius nodded and Sidonius took sheets of parchment between his thumb and fingers, feeling for quality.

He held a page up to the light of the window. "Do you have a wife and children who suffer from your absences from home?"

"I have no family apart from a brother, sir. My parents have departed this world and the life of a travelling merchant isn't conducive to marriage."

Sidonius picked up another sample and made a show of studying the grain. "And do you have an opinion on the state of Gaul and our new Emperor?"

Amantius, acutely attuned to every nuance and where a piece of silver might be earned, asked, sotto voce, "Is it the parchment that interests you, my lord, or . . . other services?"

Sidonius gauged the reaction in Amantius' honey-coloured eyes as he said, "I'm looking for someone I can trust as a messenger. A person who will arouse no suspicion on the roads."

The eyes widened minutely then feigned indifference. A diplomat like Sidonius had access to imperial couriers, not to mention three other classes of postal service. "The messages must be sensitive, my lord, if they cannot travel by public means."

Sidonius nodded. "Sensitive, and often urgent." If he'd misjudged Amantius, the merchant would be able to earn himself a pretty sum by denouncing him to the Emperor's informers.

"To whom would I be expected to deliver them?".

"Quite often to members of my family, people I trust. But if they fell into the wrong hands the consequences could be severe. Their safe and discreet delivery is a matter of life and death."

"Who might be interested in these messages, besides their intended recipients?"

"The Emperor, Petronius Maximus. His advisors. Perhaps the Goths and other barbarians."

"I see," said Amantius. Were the Goths and the Aviti plotting to undermine and usurp the power of Rome? A man caught carrying such messages would be tortured to the last drop of his endurance then put to death. "It'd take a fortune to convince a messenger to take risks like that."

Sidonius hid his disappointment. "And what fortune might it cost to send a message from here to my father-in-law's estate near Clermont in under a week?"

A slight frown crossed Amantius' forehead and he tugged at his curly brown beard. "If it were a man who regularly bought my finest parchments and belonged to one of the most respected families in Gaul who asked me, and the recipient was Eparchius Avitus, I might consider carrying the message to be a matter of honour."

The corners of Sidonius' lips relaxed.

"When Aetius was alive," explained Amantius, "he kept the main roads in Gaul and beyond clear of bagaudae and barbarian raiders. All Rome does now is levy taxes and confiscate our property if we can't afford to pay them. Your wife's family, the Aviti, and your own, the Apollinari, are two of the oldest and noblest in Gaul. You're Romans of the highest rank, but your roots are here with us. Petronius Maximus cares nothing for Gaul, but you do."

Sidonius smiled broadened. He wasn't yet sure that Amantius wasn't a double agent, but there was something intense in his features and sure in his voice that made Sidonius warm to him.

Amantius smiled back. "Yes, someone like me would be prepared to risk his life simply because he wanted what was best for his homeland."

The men shook hands, then Sidonius' voice became solemn, "How good is your memory? The first message I'd like transmitted must be memorised and recited word for word."

"I've an excellent memory, my lord."

"Then tell Avitus *your friends are ready to march to save the Empire. They wait only upon your word.*"

Amantius swallowed – *save the Empire but not the Emperor* – a treasonous distinction. But he nodded assent. "That's a simple message. It means nothing in particular. Even under torture, I'm sure I wouldn't be able to remember who asked me to carry it, nor the words themselves."

"When can you leave?" asked Sidonius.

"Dawn tomorrow." Amantius adjusted the folds of his cloak on his shoulder, worrying that perhaps he'd been too hasty in his decision. "Now, regarding my fine vellum here, do you find it to your liking? I could drop off my merchandise tonight and pick up payment this evening, if that would suit your lordship?"

"I'll pay you now." Sidonius singled out three samples of the best quality and put three silver coins in his hand, five times what the parchment was worth. "Can Gaul rely on you, Amantius?"

"Without the slightest doubt," Amantius slipped the coins down the front of his tunic, "but there's one detail I'd like you to know about me before I leave."

"That is?" Sidonius' chest clenched with the thought that the meeting might have been a trap.

"I'm Jewish."

Sidonius grinned with relief. Jews were a distrusted minority who usually kept their identity hidden rather than be reviled as "Christ killers" but Amantius' religion could be an advantage to his mission. No one would expect him to be in the confidence of Christians.

Sidonius reached out his hand and clasped the Jew's in his.

An Old Soldier Does Not Fade Away

Avitacum, Province of Auvergne, Gaul
April 455 AD

Amantius had just delivered Sidonius' message to Avitus and was trudging back up the road from Avitacum, trailing his pack mule behind him, when a horse thundered at full-tilt downhill towards them. He leapt from the road, his stomach churning, as an imperial messenger raced by.

Was I a fool to take this mission? The inscrutable old general had listened attentively, but said not a word, then placed a solidus in Amantius' hand and dismissed him. The gold coin, that had seemed outrageously generous only twenty minutes ago, suddenly felt flimsy.

While Amantius flicked his switch on the mule's rump and climbed back onto the road, Sedulla was lowering herself onto a cross-legged stool opposite her husband on the terrace at Avitacum. Her pulse too was beating at a brisker than normal pace as she watched Avitus fiddling with his fishing lures. His pensive but detached expression told her his thoughts were elsewhere.

"It's a busy morning," she said, "first a travelling merchant arrives and you cloak yourself in the library with him, then only minutes later an imperial – " Avitus dropped his lures on his lap and looked up, his eyes sharp – "courier is at the door."

Avitus was already on his feet. "Why didn't you tell me sooner? Show him into my library at once."

When, half an hour later, Avitus had made sure that the courier had cantered back up the road and out of sight, with an enigmatic smile he went out to the terrace where Sedulla was waiting for him.

He plumped up his cushions and took his time to sit down, then looked her in the face. "It appears that Petronius Maximus has belatedly realised he needs military men to avoid the obliteration of our Empire. He's called me out of retirement to take Aetius' place as magister militum."

Sedulla raised an eyebrow and her lips hardened. "Maximus made a fatal mistake when he broke off his engagement to Geiseric the Vandal's daughter and took Valentinian's widow, Eudoxia – by force – to his marriage bed. I expect you're about to tell me that the repudiation of his daughter has incited the Vandal king to attack Rome. And Petronius Maximus expects *you* to save *him*?"

Avitus smiled. Sedulla's sense of the triggers and brakes in political life had always impressed him. "Geiseric has already taken Sicily and Corsica and is marching on Rome, but I believe that Aetius' death played a far greater role in his decision to invade than Petronius Maximus' repudiation of his daughter."

Sedulla leant forward and took her husbands' sun blotched hand in hers. "You won't go, of course."

Avitus patted the back of her hand and gave her a wink. "But of course I will."

Sedulla's face blanched. Her voice pitched high. "You can't mean that."

"I've accepted the call to arms," he said, more gently.

Sedulla's mouth opened as she drew in a breath that would have whimpered had she not turned it into a cough. She stood up and walked to the edge of the terrace, tears rising in her eyes. After all these years she'd thought that, at last, she'd come first – not the army, not duty, not yet another war! But . . . she calmed herself. A wailing woman would only push Avitus away. She turned back towards him, her face a picture of composure although unusually pale.

"Far be it from me to question either your judgment or your loyalties, but are you happy to leap to the command of the man who brought death to Aetius?"

"Now, my dear," Avitus answered, a wry rise at the corner of his lips, "you know full well that there's a world of difference between accepting an imperial position and leaping to the command of the Emperor."

"You used not to make such distinctions." Sedulla had believed that, after a lifetime together, she knew her husband inside and out. Above all things, he'd always been loyal. So what was this?

"Times change, Sedulla. Petronius Maximus is not just another loathsome man who's killed to wear a crown. He's weak and out of his depth. No match for the Vandals. The future of the world is again at stake. If I don't, who can save Rome?"

"Marjorian," said Sedulla, each syllable dropping like a stone from her lips.

Avitus, stood up and paced with his hands behind his back. The name had hit its mark. Marjorian, who'd been Aetius' second in command, might have been a better choice. He was young, almost as brilliant a general as the man at whose shoulder he'd learned the art of war. Although he and Aetius had been close for many years, their bond had been loosened, if not broken, before the great man's death when Marjorian had become a suitor for the Emperor's daughter, to whom Aetius' son was already betrothed. Aetius had sent Marjorian to a cold and dismal place, far off in the northern reaches of the Empire, to get him well out of the race for her hand. It would indeed have been possible for Maximus to have offered the post to Marjorian. But he had not.

Avitus stared out over the placid face of his lake. Perhaps Maximus simply believed him to be the superior general and knew he had influence with the Goths whom he could, perhaps, recruit to come to Rome's aid against the Vandals. The Goths had never forgiven

Geiseric for sending his Gothic princess wife back to her father with her ears and nose hacked off.

Avitus felt Sedulla's eyes following him and turned back to the woman who'd always stood at his side. "It's done now. I *am* the new magister militum."

Sedulla rose to speak but he held up a hand. "Let me finish. For reasons of my own, I'd planned already to go to Toulouse and parley with the new Theodoric." A hard glint appeared in Avitus' eyes. "But, I can assure you, my dear, that neither the Gothic king nor I will make haste to rescue Petronius Maximus from the fate to which he's condemned himself. It'll take time to muster our troops and our march over the Alps will be slow. The Vandals will reach Rome ahead of us."

Comprehension dawned on Sedulla's face.

"When Rome falls," continued Avitus, "Petronius Maximus will suffer the consequences."

Sedulla's hooded eyes grew wide and a smile rose at the edges of her lips. She'd never suspected her husband – "a plain soldier" – to burn with imperial ambitions at this stage of life, but this new ruthlessness impressed her. "You'd let the Vandals loot and sate their lust in order to be rid of the Emperor?"

"I could never be accused of leaving Rome to her fate." Avitus lowered his chin, "but I will not sacrifice the only military means that the Empire has left on a futile defence. Nor will I ever bend my knee to that piece of slime, Petronius Maximus, who's done more to bring the Empire to her knees than any blood-swilling barbarian.

When the time's right *I* will free Rome from Geiseric and rebuild the Empire from the ground up." An image of Sola's newly built fortress with its anti-elephant gates in Reims came to Avitus' mind. He squared his jaw. "Rome will be stronger than she's ever been before."

Sedulla's smile faded to a frown. Doubt churned her innards. As much as she admired his determination and ambition, Avitus was a soldier, not a politician. To oust the Vandals from the city would be trouble enough. Perhaps – with careful planning and luck – he could achieve that. But at what price? And even if he lived through the battles, they would be only the beginning of the challenges he'd face. Her mind, always fast, snapped all the conclusions into place. "You'll die if you attempt that."

Avitus' face sagged. "Thank you, my dear, for your encouragement."

"I mean it. This isn't a quest for a man your age. You owe it to your family to stay here in Gaul, where we'll all be safe. If you go to Rome, it's not your own life alone that you jeopardise but the very survival of our dynasty."

Avitus shook his head and turned away. *What dynasty?* Sedulla stood up and clung to his forearm. "Don't go. I beg you, don't. Let the Vandals loot Rome – it makes little difference to us here in Gaul."

Avitus took another long look at his wife, the frown that radiated between her brows, the pointed chin and fading chestnut hair. The fear in her eyes. "You've always dreamed of being Empress, Sedulla. Why this change of heart?"

"It's all too late," she grasped his wrist with both hands, her nails digging into his skin, "don't you see this is all too late for us?"

Avitus nodded. "What I see is that you believe it to be that way." Gently, he unwound her fingers and stepped off the terrace onto the lawn but her trembling lip stopped him from walking away.

"You need more time to think about this," called Sedulla then swallowed her tears and fell quiet, knowing that the more she protested, the harder would become his resolve. "Please don't go," were her last words, then she put a hand to her mouth and disappeared into the house.

Avitus rubbed a hand over the marks she'd left on his forearm, then strode off down the lawn towards his fishing log on the bank of the lake. Perhaps his wife was right; the risks were too high, he was too old to take up another fight and should leave the mission of saving Rome to younger men. Perhaps.

But who and where were these younger men who could save Rome? Marjorian was under the influence of the barbarian schemer, Ricimer, who'd infiltrated court circles and couldn't be trusted. And the more Avitus dredged his way through the military ranks, the more he knew that he alone had the skills it would take to break the Vandals' back.

Deep in debate with himself, he walked along banks where weeping willows blew like hair in the wind over rippled water, Sedulla's words echoing in his ears – *you'll die.* Throughout their marriage she'd too often turned out to be right.

When he rounded a bend and his log-stump came into view, the spectre of a tall, hooded figure standing next to it stopped him in his tracks. A rush of alarm shot up his spine. He was armed only with the dagger he wore strapped to his ankle and an assassin had infiltrated Avitacum.

But the figure turned towards him and pushed the midnight-blue wool of her cloak back from her blonde-white hair. "I've come to talk to you."

Avitus kept his distance. "It's not a good time."

Sola looked down at her hands for a moment then back up at him. Her ocean-blue eyes locked with his lighter ones. "No, Avitus, I have to talk to you now. Rome will soon be in ruins."

"Now it's you who's stating the obvious."

"I've been thinking. The man who murdered your friend is on the imperial throne. The Vandals have already taken Sicily and Corsica and with Aetius gone there's no one to stop them conquering Rome." Sola drew a deep breath. "Except you."

"Is that why you came here? To tell me to muster my allies and march on Rome?"

"Isn't that what you were born to do?"

"Not according to Sedulla – my wife. She thinks our time has passed."

Sola bowed her head, then looked up, running a hand back through her hair. "But you know it's not. Your time is about to come." Then she turned and started to walk away along the lake bank.

"Sola," called Avitus, "how'd you know to find me here?"

"The whole of Gaul knows that you've retired to Avitacum."

"But how did you know I'd be here, by the lake."

"I didn't, but I thought that if I were to choose a spot to fish, this'd be it."

Avitus smiled and raised a hand in farewell, stronger for the fact that she believed in him. Watching the billowing of her cloak as she walked away, a question came to him. "Sola."

She turned and stood looking back with eyebrows raised.

"Aetius?" he asked.

Her eyes filled with darkness that could have been longing or could have been grief and he knew she'd never answer him. Avitus nodded then raised his hand in the way he did to her, half wave, half salute.

Sola's lips opened to show her white teeth and her long legs stretched out into a march, but she took only a few paces before calling back. "It's an honour to know you, Avitus. You'll defeat the Vandals, but keep safe, my friend."

The next day, the household slaves sniffled as they stood in a line to say goodbye to their master outside the fluted doric columns of the portico. The coachman held the reins to the four matched stallions that pulled the immaculate black carriage with gilded lions rampant on each corner of the roof.

Avitus pulled his wife into his shoulders and stroked the back of her head and, for once, despite the watching eyes, she let him. Then he held her out at arms' length and his eyes caressed her slightly drooping lids and the feathered lines on her cheeks. Just as he had every time he'd gone off to war, he wondered if he'd ever see her again and tried to inscribe her features on his memory. Then he kissed her lips and stepped up, disappearing into the darkness of his carriage.

The driver clacked the reins on the back of the leading horse, set its nose in the direction of Theodoric II's court, and metal-rimmed wheels ground through the gravel. Avitus waved farewell through the window but his face remained inscrutable as he headed south.

The Precipitous and
Slippery Peak of Office

Rome, Italy

31st May 455 AD

Only seventy-eight days did Petronius Maximus survive as Emperor of the Western Roman Empire. Perched on the precipitous and slippery peak of office, his head swam beneath the diadem of power. When the Vandals attacked Rome the army, the populace and the vigiles fled. Flamboyant in their purple plumes and elaborate armour, his overpaid bodyguard did not rise to Rome's defence. Petronius Maximus, abandoned and swamped by the crowd, struggled alone to make his way out of the city. A man less vain would have thrown off the purple toga, but Maximus clutched his across a flab of white belly and yelled for the crowd to make way.

A single soldier, dressed in the unembossed armour of Rome's trusted cohortes urbanae, was chasing a handful of looters out of an arcade when he heard his cries for help. Petronius Maximus nearly wept with relief when he saw the guardsman lay off and turn in his direction.

Ursus, who'd defended Orleans, had a scar that slashed from forehead to chin. His eyebrows had never grown back after Attila's attack and half his face was covered in crinkled pink skin. At the sound of the Emperor's voice he blinked and looked twice then forced his way through the swill of plebs towards the purple toga bobbing in a seafoam of homespun.

Arriving face to face with the Emperor, he searched the sweaty white features and sagging jaw, struggling to equate this panicked spectacle with the man wearing a laurel wreath whom he'd last seen mounted on a pristine white horse inspecting the troops. Then, sure that it was indeed Maximus and not a decoy, Ursus drew his sword.

"Good man," gushed Maximus, "save me!"

Ursus' jaw hardened and his eyes turned cold. *"Never!"*

Rising up tall, like the bear he was named for, he plunged his blade into the Emperor's chest. The body crumpled and Ursus raised his bloody sword above his head. "For Aetius!"

The crowd stopped running from the Vandals, let out a cheer then swarmed around him. Rabid with rage at the Emperor who'd brought ruin to Rome, their hands snapped onto Maximus like the jaws of dogs fighting over a corpse. They ripped the body limb from limb and hurled the fleshy fragments into the yellow swirl of the Tiber.

A Letter to Felix

Rome, Italy
21st September 455 AD

Sidonius' pulse raced with both excitement and fever. He'd drunk contaminated water on his journey to Rome, his head was aching and he had to get back to work on a poem he was going to read at Avitus' coronation. But he couldn't resist dashing off a letter about his voyage, over land and sea, to his friend, Felix. When the master of rhetoric at their school in Lyon had whipped Virgil into the pair of them, he and Felix had compared their stripes from the cane and dreamed of seeing the eternal city for themselves one day.

Sidonius lifted Papianilla's ebony pen from its box and leant his arm across a sheet of Amantius' parchment. He hesitated for a second, quelling an urge to retch, but determined not to let Felix down.

My dear friend, Felix,

I write to you from Rome.

In late May, I was near Arles with my father-in-law, raising an army of Goths to march with him to save Rome, when news arrived that Petronius Maximus been ripped apart by the populace while fleeing the Vandals.

The Goths promptly declared Avitus Emperor and the Senate in Rome ratified his appointment on August the fifth. Instead of racing precipitately to his coronation, as a lesser man might have, Avitus spent a month consolidating his position in Gaul then marched over the Alps. We were prepared to make war but the Vandals fled before Avitus' advance.

Our journey, across three legendary mountain ranges and ten rivers about which songs were sung, took only forty-two days. Avitus could have marched faster were it not for the Goths, who did their best but slowed him down. And so here I am, riding side by side with the new ruler of the world, a man whom I've known and loved from the day I was born.

Nothing matches the excitement of counting down the last fifty mile-markers – taller than a man and thicker than the column of a temple – on the Via Aurelia. Even from a distance, Rome imposes herself on the landscape. First, one sees a smudge of smoke from the hearths of the world's biggest city, then market gardens, villas, temples, cemeteries. The roads are lined with tombs that vary from the modest to the monumental. We passed a family picnicking amongst the graves of their loved ones until a wind blew up and sent the ashes from a nearby cremation over their dinners.

On the twenty-first of September – the first anniversary of Aetius' death – we passed through the row of upright white stones that mark the line Romulus drew with his plough to define the city limits. The Porta Capena, the gate through which Rome's legions marched to conquer the world, came into sight, built high enough for a triumphal parade of elephants to pass through.

I'm sorry, but I must leave off this letter for, at Avitus' side, I am to lead the imperial procession into the Hippodrome. A crowd of two hundred thousand waits to welcome us and I must prepare a speech in his honour.

Keep us in your thoughts as you are always in ours, Farewell.

The Aviti Arrive

Crowned by a laurel wreath and dressed in full battle regalia, Avitus drove a quadriga of four matched white stallions along the Via Triumphalis to his coronation. For the first time, he'd draped a purple cloak over the shoulder plates of his armour. Sunlight dazzled the onlookers as it struck the lion rampant embossed across his gilded breastplate. Avitus looked down into awestruck faces that saw in his muscled arms and greying head the image of Jupiter, the greatest of gods. From time to time, when he saw a child, he'd give it a wink and smile at the parents.

Sidonius, dressed in a spotless white toga hemmed with gold, rode on his left and Ecdicius, wearing a silver helmet with a crimson horse-hair crest and a scarlet cloak, on his right. They raised their hands to the cheering crowd who saw in them two demigods.

"Redemption! Redemption!" yelled a toothless man waving a straw hat and Avitus grinned at Sidonius who called down to the peasant – "Have no fear for the future, our arrival marks the beginning of a new imperial dynasty."

* * * * *

From the terrace of a palace whose walls fluttered with hawk-like flags, Ricimer the Sueve watched the procession with a different slant to his eyes, Ricimer stared at his enemies, the Goths, riding in Avitus' wake. They were looking around at the city's treasures and defences as if taking an inventory of their prospective possessions. Ricimer plucked a lemon from an ornamental tree and crushed it in his fist. The juice dripped like blood between his fingers then he hurled the split skin onto the helmet of a passing Goth. The warrior glared upwards, saw only a shadow outlined against the sky above the parapet and rode on, but Ricimer's glare followed the procession to the end of the Via Triumphalis. *Welcome to Rome, Eparchius Avitus. Your reign will be short.*

* * * * *

Avitus wrapped the reins of his quadriga around his right forearm and pulled it wide to turn the lead horse through the gates of the largest stadium the world had ever known, the Hippodrome. The crowd cramming the rows of stone seats that stepped up each side of the Circus Maximus, rose like the boiling crest of a wave to applaud him.

Avitus' blue eyes sparkled under the lion's crest on his gold helmet as he reined his horses and took the turning post. The stamping feet of the audience rolled like thunder from one end of the stadium to the other. With a smile that erased the lines from his face, Avitus raised his right arm to salute the populace and two hundred thousand voices yelled to burst their lungs: "Caesar! Caesar! Caesar!"

The Emperor reined his quadriga to a halt and ascended the marble steps of the podium. Sidonius and Ecdicius followed at either shoulder. On her throne, under a vaulted roof held aloft by towering columns, Sedulla was waiting for him. The myriad folds of her scarlet chiton were hemmed with gold-threaded embroidery and her hair was tightly crimped behind a crown so heavy it made her neck ache.

Coiled brass horns an arm span wide let out a blast that echoed down the walls of the stadium. Before the blast tapered off a giant water organ drowned it out. The organ held a stormy chord then cut into abrupt silence.

Avitus rose to the podium. A roar of approval went up from the stands for this aged soldier, the opposite of that brainless fop, Valentinian, or the detested Petronius Maximus who, in only seventy-eight days, had let the Vandals rape Rome.

Avitus stood with his arms outstretched until the crowd hushed. His gravel-toned baritone was quiet, at first. He spoke with gravity, methodically, like the plain soldier he knew he was. The crowd leant forward on their seats, straining to hear him. Then, in a rumbling crescendo, his voice rose to the bellow that had carried his orders over the din of the bloodiest battles the Empire had ever known. It raised the hairs on the arms of his audience and set the air afire.

He promised stability, security and freedom behind the shield of his alliances and his fifty years' battle experience. But little did it matter what he said, it was the man he was and the fact the Vandals had fled him that counted. The populace felt safe.

When he finished speaking, the audience leapt to its feet in a frenzy of acclamation. Arms spread wide, Avitus acknowledged their applause then signalled the crowd to be seated. He dropped his voice from the pace and roar of rapids to the calm of a quiet river and promised, "Together, we will make Rome's future more glorious than her past."

Another round of cheering went up then Avitus took his seat on the imperial throne. The crowd sat back down on stone-stepped benches and the applause faded out.

In the Emperor's shadow, shivering with nerves and fever, Sidonius rose to speak. The air was so still that the senators on the podium could hear the rustle of his robes and the crackle of parchment as he smoothed his papers down on the rostrum. At first, the crowd shared the young man's nervousness but, with diction as crisp as the folds in his toga, he told them that Avitus, although old, would make the Empire young and strong. He thanked his allies, the Goths, and promised an end to the

Vandal lootings and the return of safety, freedom and power. By the time he'd finished the crowd was whooping with enthusiasm for his eloquence.

Papianilla took Sidonius' hand and squeezed it under her palla as he returned to his seat beside her. He glanced over at Sedulla, who was smiling, and knew that his speech had been a success.

To the right of his imperial parents sat Ecdicius, the warrior-son of a new Emperor who, in time, would pass on the diadem to him. When the family rose to deafening applause and left the stage, he felt the energy of pure potency infuse his body. Brutally handsome, he left the crowd in no doubt that he could have whomever and whatever he chose. Ecdicius' libidinous lips didn't need to form words to proclaim his virility. Men bowed and women reached out to touch this god of war as he strode past dignitaries and ambassadors from every nation.

The Aviti retired to the imperial palace, surrounded by terraces studded with cypresses, that looked out from the Palatine over the six other hills of Rome and the River Tiber.

Sidonius lowered himself onto a sofa, stretched out his legs and put a hand over his eyes. Slaves had rearranged the room to show it off to its best but it was half-empty as the Vandals had taken all the furniture and treasure they could carry. Although Sidonius' mind was basking in the afterglow of the rapturous reception his speech had received, his body ran hot and cold with fever. He'd kept going long enough to perform in front of the crowd but now the spectacle was over fatigue hammered him and he wanted to sleep for a week.

Ecdicius felt no such fatigue. He stood tall in his uniform with a glass in his hand. "I propose a toast, to my father – the Emperor!"

Sidonius dutifully pushed himself up and drank. "To Avitus."

"And another, to my brother-in-law, Sidonius, for the speech he wrote about our achievements."

Although he was expected to toast Ecdicius in reply Sidonius felt as if someone was stabbing a dagger at the back of his eyes. He mustered a smile but dizziness overcame him and he plunked down on the edge of his sofa again. Ecdicius laughed and patted him on the shoulder.

Papianilla and Sedulla were seated on a pair of chairs next to a tripod laden with scented candles. Bergamot and jasmine competed with the tang of nearby cypress trees. Papianilla flushed with pleasure at her brother's toast but frowned with concern when Sidonius sat down without returning his compliments. She was about to get up and go over to him but Sedulla put a hand on her arm. She had news she wanted to be the first to tell her daughter.

"I have it on very good authority that the Senate will erect a bronze statue, between the Latin and Greek libraries in Trajan's forum, in honour of Sidonius. There is no greater an accolade for a young poet than that." Sedulla smiled and she lifted her hand from her daughter-in-law's forearm. "Now you may go to him."

Papianilla threw her arms around Sidonius' neck then leant into his cheek and whispered, "I'm so proud of you."

Later, when the excitement started to die down, Papianilla retired to the nursery to settle the children to sleep. Her infant son was grizzling at his nurse but her daughter, Rosea, was exploring her new territory and pouted when her mother lifted her up and tucked her into bed. Papianilla was sure the little girl would try to sneak out and listen to the adults as soon as she left the room. She kissed her children good night then went back to the terrace.

Sidonius was still lying on his couch while Sedulla sat in an ivory throne that she'd brought from Gaul, looking out over the lights of Rome. As a young girl, she'd never dared to dream of becoming Empress – she knew that such grand ambitions usually took generations to come to fruition – but here she was, thanks to Avitus. She had exceeded her own expectations. Not for the first time, she congratulated herself for having cut off a previous engagement when Avitus, a young general then, had appeared at her father's house and asked for her hand.

And Avitus, what did the Emperor Eparchius Avitus feel now that he wore the imperial diadem?

His shoulders were heavy with the weight of the world. He was missing Aetius. This was just the first step in rebuilding the Empire, and he dreaded what an inspection of the city's resources would reveal in the morning. Looking at the sparseness of furniture in the Emperor's apartments, he felt foreboding in his bones. The Vandals had spent more than a month looting Rome before fleeing his advance. There wouldn't be a solidus left in the treasury or an ounce of grain in the horrea.

Ecdicius, still dressed in parade uniform, was pulsing with belief in his own prowess. "Will you come down to the city with me and celebrate?" he asked Sidonius.

Papianilla shot a look at her husband. He wasn't well and she didn't want to be left alone while he went off into his man's world to do things she did not like to imagine. She wanted to sleep with her head on his heart, listening to its beat.

In truth, Sidonius wanted only to be with Papianilla. His stomach and bowels were upset and the throb in his head was getting worse. "Not tonight, Ecdicius."

"Come on! You used to be up for fun and adventure. What's happened to you?"

"You celebrate, brother, for both of us. I'm happy to stay here and savour a moment's peace before we throw ourselves back into the fray in the morning."

Ecdicius took his leave of his parents and set off into the town with half a dozen bodyguards in tow. He wouldn't make the mistake Aetius had of assuming, because he was strong and well-loved, that he was safe.

"We'll start at Pontius' palace," he told his companions, "he can be counted on to put on a good show." Pontius had remarried and, now that her father had become Emperor of Rome, had conveniently forgotten Papianilla's rejection of his proposal.

Ecdicius left five of his bodyguards at Pontius' gate and went into the palace with only one young officer, Industrius, whose discretion he could count on. Torches flamed at every yard along the wall and braziers burned bright with intoxicating incense.

They reached the private apartments where twinned Nubians, almost seven feet tall, with the neck and shoulders of oxen but effeminate jaws and protuberant lips, swung the bronze coffered doors aside for them. Ecdicius and Industrius left their cloaks and swords in the custody of two nude, but bejewelled, eunuchs and walked through to the main salon. The eunuchs' semi-tumescence swung pendulously against their thighs as they ushered them in.

As Ecdicius' eyes adjusted to the relative darkness, he could see that the party was in full swing. Plates were piled high with oysters and grapes from Pontius' estates, wine was being served undiluted and girls, naked above the waist, gyrated their buttocks in time to the beat of drums and the throbbing of lyres. There wasn't a single respectable woman in sight but the room was replete with perfumed courtesans with painted faces and transparent saffron veils. These were not just common whores; Pontius had chosen Rome's finest, male and female.

One of the Adonis-like youths had jumped up on to a table and was dancing on it, naked except for thin black leather straps that he'd tied around his chest, wrists and ankles. He had placed oil lamps around his feet and their glow highlighted the contours of his body, gleaming with a fine layer of sweat. Full on frontal, he masturbated as those who were not otherwise occupied stared. His hand moved faster and faster as the drum beat sped up and his hips thrust to the rhythm.

Ecdicius scanned the room for opportunity. Industrius had already joined a four-way knot of limbs and lips. Looking round, Ecdicius could barely recognise Pontius, who had a girl on top of him moving up and down to try to get some stiffness into his limp penis. Pontius was getting older and had been drinking too much. Another naked girl had her thighs astride his face. Fortunately for the rest of the party Pontius was being attended to behind a gauze curtain that screened his corpulence from the pulsating athleticism in the rest of the room.

By the time Ecdicius' head turned back to the beginning point the masturbating boy was no longer standing on the table but lying on his side. One man had his cock in the young man's mouth and another was fucking him from behind. The boy looked as if he was enjoying it. One of the oil lamps had spilled and a thin line of fire ran from one end of the table to the other but was burning no one.

As far as Ecdicius could see, all the girls were already taken and for a moment he thought that perhaps he'd be better off making his choice from the plebs celebrating in the streets outside when a couple, dancing to a sensuous, slow song in one of the alcoves, caught his eye. The man was tall and built like a gladiator, the woman, whose bare back was turned towards Ecdicius, had a nipped in waist and a long gossamer skirt that draped from a wide metal belt over her rounded hips. He noticed that the belt had a loop at the back to which a chain or rope could be attached. One of her legs was wrapped around the man she was embracing and its bare calf and ankle promised Ecdicius that if she turned round the rest of her body would be voluptuous. She wore sandals with thin leather straps and a metal cuff around one ankle. Ecdicius noticed that, like the belt, it had a lock to which a chain could be attached.

The man was probing his tongue into her mouth but his eyes intercepted Ecdicius' stare and without unlocking his lips from the courtesan's he raised his hand and signalled him to join them. Ecdicius came up behind the girl without seeing her face, slipped his hands into the heat between their two tight bodies and explored her nipples. His penis rose hard against her buttocks. She started dancing between the two of them, without a word being said, her breasts one minute pressed up against one muscled chest, the next against the other, driving them both into a frenzy of lust. Her lips were full and she smelt fresh. Ecdicius wanted to feel her mouth on his cock. He thought of manoeuvring her into the same position as the boy on the table and letting her dancing partner go first at the other end but then he realised that he was in no mood to share. He was the most desirable man in Rome and he didn't want to compete with anyone else for a woman's attention. He broke off for a second and whispered a word in her partner's ear. The young man's eyes hardened but he knew who Ecdicius was. With as good a grace as he could muster, he disengaged and left Ecdicius alone with the most sensuous girl in the room.

They didn't talk. Ecdicius led her through one of the gauze curtains, bent her over a cushion and thrust hard into her from behind, fast and furious, just for the release of it. All he wanted was a woman, any woman, into whom he could empty his balls.

When he'd come he pushed her head down to his groin. Her luscious lips and velvet tongue knew exactly how to pleasure a man. Other girls pushed the curtains aside tentatively and ventured in but he raised his hand to send them elsewhere, they would only be a distraction. This girl was expert, her breasts soft and heavy. He roped her thick hair round his hand to move her head at the speed he wanted. He didn't feel like joining the orgy, he wanted to exploit every aspect of one woman, no matter how nameless, no matter how temporary. He spent hours with her and by the time he tired he'd bruised her every orifice.

When he'd finished with her, she looked up at him with swollen lips, a glimmer of hope in her eyes as if expecting more, believing she would become his mistress, that he'd started to care for her.

Ecdicius looked down at her as if she were an alien object, not a human being. He noticed for the first time the tattoo on the back of her hand that marked her forever with the stigma of a slave. It repelled him. He had no interest in her, nor in fact in any of the other couplings in the room.

Satiated, he made his way out of the alcove and looked around again. Somehow the participants in the orgy had been transformed from attractive to merely ordinary. No one was spectacular enough to arouse his desire. Suddenly he'd had his fill for tonight of naked bodies contorting around each other. They looked sordid. He didn't see himself as one of those men, going at it like animals. It was all too easy, they came here for sex they knew they would get because it had been paid for. He wanted more than that. He wanted a challenge, not a whore.

He retrieved his cloak and sword, told Industrius that he could stay as long as he liked, and headed home, not to the imperial palace where he suddenly felt self-conscious about showing his face, but to the army barracks where no one would think the less of him for having glutted himself.

When he was alone in his room he wondered why he felt empty. Normally a night of revelry would have left him grinning. Something had usurped his pleasure. When he thought about it, he realised that it was the new role his father's Emperorship had forced on him. No more was he an all-conquering soldier with the right to a warrior's booty. He'd become a role model. His life was no longer private and he was too important to be seen consorting with prostitutes. This was supposed to be a Christian Empire and he would be expected to marry an aristocrat or a foreign princess to build an alliance.

As he lay on his side in the Spartan barracks, trying to get some sleep in the hour left before the sun came up, he realised that something more was missing than just his erstwhile freedom.

He felt the need to love and to be loved in the way his sister loved her husband. But he was a slave to his destiny. *Marriage and a family can wait* – thought the twenty-five-year-old as he drifted into slumber, *the army is my bride.*

Empty Vessels

On a bank of the Tiber, at the foot of the Aventine Hill, Avitus and his entourage had come to the end of their tour of the Emporium district. In times of peace, merchandise from the Empire, China, India and Africa rushed into Rome through this port but sea wars with the Vandals had reduced it to a trickle. A failure to dole out free grain to the populace was the fastest way to start a riot and, on his first day as Emperor, that was the last thing Avitus wanted so he'd come to inspect the state of supplies.

The old man tried to remain optimistic as he approached the Horrea Aggripina, the last of the warehouses on his list. The building appeared to be intact and fully functional, its exterior concrete walls neither broken nor blemished. But, as he, Sidonius, their guards and scribes entered the courtyard their footsteps echoed and Avitus' stomach sank.

The warehouse was possessed of a cavernous emptiness. Massive doors had been levered off their hinges on each of the storage chambers and either hung, like drunks leaning against a wall, or had given in and collapsed to the ground. Inside each compartment the floor of fine amber brickwork laid in a herringbone pattern, normally hidden by grain, met walls forty feet high that rose to coffered ceilings. For the sake of thoroughness, Sidonius told his clerks to enter every room and record its lack of contents on an inventory list.

Avitus stood in the main courtyard, giving orders for the doors to be replaced, and waited for Sidonius' scribes to complete their futile search. The base of the statue that used to honour Neptune stood blatantly naked at one end of the courtyard. The sea, just across the road from the warehouse, hadn't risen up to protect its god when the Vandals had wrestled him from his plinth and manhandled him into their ship.

From the far side of the courtyard, Sidonius shook his head as he read through his scribes' reports and Avitus felt again the leaden weight of the world descend on him. He was all-powerful, yet perilously powerless. With every storehouse a black, hopeless hole, Rome would starve.

So had it been with the Treasury, the rooms of state, and even his own bedchamber, all ransacked. All the statues and valuables looted by barbarians.

Sidonius came to his father-in-law's side. "We couldn't have got here fast enough to head the Vandals off and prevent this, no matter what we'd done."

"Perhaps not," Avitus replied but in his head he was making unduly harsh comparisons between himself and Aetius. "Even if we had, we'd only have kept Petronius Maximus on the throne a few more months, and lost lives doing it. The Treasury would still have been emptied, but by him and his cronies instead of the Vandals."

"Exactly," said Sidonius. "Please stop blaming yourself – it's a miracle we got here at all and that the Vandals fled our advance. Even Aetius couldn't have marched faster than we did over the Alps."

Avitus attempted a wan smile for his daughter's fine young husband who was always kind, no matter the circumstances. "Grain is critical. I'll put you in charge of it." He wanted to be rid of the logistics and knew that he could trust Sidonius to deliver an honest solution rather than using the crisis to divert money into his own pocket.

"It would be my pleasure," said Sidonius, with an obliging smile but feeling a wave of panic. The Vandals controlled Sicily and Northern Africa, the only two places that could furnish the requisite volume of grain. *Does he think I'm Jesus Christ and can feed five thousand people on five loaves of bread and a few fishes? Except that this is worse, for I have a country of millions to feed on nothing at all.*

Avitus stated the obvious. "We'll have to fight Geiseric to reforge the supply chain or there'll be no grain." Then he put a guiding hand on Sidonius' elbow and walked a few steps further away from the attendant scribes. Keeping half an eye on them, he continued in a quieter voice: "We have to look at this as an opportunity, but the Vandals are not our only enemies. As long as Ricimer's in Rome, we're in danger; I'm sending him away to battle the Vandals."

"You'd put our army in the hands of a barbarian? A man whose father was a Sueve and mother a Goth?"

Avitus looked glum but determined. "We have to convince him to work with us. The prestige of a Roman command still means something to newcomers like him. If I put him in charge of the strike force against Geiseric, it may assuage his lust for power. And much though I distrust Ricimer, he fought alongside Marjorian under Aetius' command. There's no better pedigree than that."

"Couldn't you give the command to Ecdicius instead?" Sidonius asked in a voice as tart as lime.

"Ecdicius is a cavalry commander. The Vandals fight at sea. Ecdicius' time will come, but not yet, and I need the men I trust in Rome. More importantly, I want Ricimer gone."

"Ricimer's an Arian Christian, not a Roman Catholic." Sidonius was clutching at straws.

"Do you think I care about that," thundered Avitus, "only the army counts. We have enough problems without inventing complications."

Sidonius wiped his brow, searching for a better way to articulate his concerns. "Ricimer lusts for power."

Avitus tugged at his purple toga as if it was strangling him. "They all lust for power. I'm simply channelling that lust into something that supports civilisation instead of destroying it."

Sidonius hung his head. He'd never known Avitus so irritable. The sense of humour that had made facing a crisis with him bearable had abandoned him. Every move bore a mortal risk.

Ricimer Returns

The shipping lanes stayed closed throughout Ricimer's campaign. Rome grumbled on an empty stomach. On the last, long hot day of August, Sidonius watched the hours on his water clock subside and wiped sweat from the back of his neck. Hungry and angry, a crowd had gathered in the Coliseum, making ready to riot. Sidonius' sandals clacked frenetically as he paced, hoping for news that the Vandal blockade had been lifted but preparing himself to face the crowd empty-handed.

A courier came in. "General Ricimer has broken the Vandal blockade, sir. Two grain ships have come into port."

Sidonius grinned. "Summon my lictors."

Eight stout lictors brandishing rods beat back ragged men who shouted at Sidonius as he walked the streets to the arena. He mounted a box and announced that the blockade was lifted with his normal persuasive eloquence but instead of the cheers he expected was met with grumbling undertones and heckling. As soon as he told the crowd that grain ships had arrived men scrambled out of the exits towards the port.

Sidonius was left standing in the centre of the ring, a bitter taste in his mouth. Centuries of handing out grain to the populace had created a monster. As he stepped down from the box, a new despair filled him. He took Nero's crytoporticus back to the palace on the

Palatine Hill, shaking his head as he walked up the cool, half-buried passageway.

Safe within the palace walls, he went in search of Avitus and found him standing, shoulders hunched over a stack of scrolls on his desk. The old man looked up from the chaos of his papers. "Demands for help from all corners of the Empire, a litany of complaints and problems, no solutions." Sidonius saw the furrows on his face and his smile faltered but he forced it back. "Yet I have good news for you. The crowd in the coliseum dispersed without any violence and tomorrow Ricimer will return to Rome."

"You're glad about that? I doubt it. You detest Ricimer."

Sidonius again stopped his lips from dipping down at the corners. "Personal enmity must be set aside in the Empire's interests."

Avitus began to pace, one white-knuckled hand clasping the other wrist behind his back. "On the field of war, we defeated the Hun, lost 165,000 men and saved the world. But now barbarians infest the inner sanctum of Rome's power. It's the enemy within who's most dangerous now."

"Your confidence in Ricimer's military ability was not misplaced."

Avitus shook his head. "I had Ricimer report to me this morning. He won a decent victory over the Vandals on the southern coast of Sicily at Agrimento, and a decisive victory at sea off the coast of Corsica. Destroyed three-quarters of Geiseric's fleet."

"Yet you're unhappy about that?"

"Damn it all!" Avitus banged the desk. "He says he didn't have the means to push an attack into the Vandal stronghold of Carthage. But of course he did! And even if he didn't think he could defeat Geiseric, he should have pursued him just the same. If it'd been me on the field of war, I'd have pushed my advantage after Corsica and besieged Carthage until it fell or I died trying. But not Ricimer."

Sidonius hung his head. "So, the Vandals still control northern Africa – our grain and our taxes."

Avitus nodded. "But it's not just that – it's *Ricimer* who's the problem. Marched in here behind his black hawk banner, as if it were a legionary eagle, then stared at me with that insolent look. Saluted alright but sat down before I offered him a seat. He's a schemer. Came back because it's Rome he wants – for himself, not its people. Demanded that I appoint him Field Commander of the Imperial Army in Italy."

Sidonius' jaw dropped. "But you didn't?"

"What choice did I have?" Avitus rubbed his brow. "He's brought the army back from the wars against the Vandals, paid the soldiers a share of the booty they captured – never asked my leave! We need that money. The people need that money. But now he's bribed the army I can't count on military support."

"You put a barbarian in the second highest military post in the entire Empire?"

"His victory had to be recognised or he'd have turned the troops against us."

Sidonius frowned. "The army loves you, Avitus."

"The army loves the man who paid them to drink away the spoils of war."

Sidonius shook his head and opened his arms, as if pleading. "Why didn't you appoint Marjorian instead of Ricimer. He's Roman, you could trust him."

Avitus' face was grey. "I'm no longer sure of that. Marjorian is the Commander-in-Chief of the Imperial Guard, but he's close to Ricimer and grows closer every day."

A premonition of disaster clawed an icy nail down Sidonius' spine. "Promoting Ricimer will increase his standing with the Senate."

"Yes, but even Ricimer knows that a full-blooded barbarian will never wear the imperial purple. That's why he needs Marjorian. With his illustrious Roman ancestry, Marjorian *could* make a stab at usurping me. He's a brilliant young general, Aetius' most talented protégé. I do my best to keep separate him from Ricimer, but it's beyond me."

Sidonius fell quiet. It was too late to argue. Silence hung heavily then Avitus asked, "How many grain ships came in?"

"Just two, but more will follow."

The Emperor's frown deepened. "The Senate's grumbling that my Goths eat too much."

Sidonius held his tongue.

"You agree with them?" asked Avitus.

Sidonius had spent nearly a year struggling to find the bare minimum with which to feed Rome's hungry mouths. It'd been impossible not to notice the Gothic bodyguards guzzled whatever they wanted while Rome's own children starved. If he didn't tell his father-in-law the hard truth, who would? "It's a matter of fact, not opinion, that the Goths consume an enormous share of our sparse resources."

Avitus' shoulders caved in and he slumped into a curule chair. "The Senate's pushing me to send them home, back to Gaul. What d'you think?"

"I suggest we think on it for a week or two and see how many more grain ships sail in."

Avitus looked up from under sagging lids. "I don't want to be left in Rome with Ricimer's dagger pointed between my shoulder blades and no one I can trust at my back."

"You can't put your trust in the Goths, they're mercenaries."

"The Goths have never let me down. They don't change loyalties on the spin of a coin."

Sidonius raised his eyebrows.

"Alright," said Avitus, "there were times they pushed the limits, but in a crisis they always took my side. Took me thirty years to build that bond. You know how slow and obdurate they are, quick to anger, suspicious of anything new. If Marjorian took the throne they'd rebel." Avitus saw Sidonius' confusion. "The last wars with the Goths were before you were born, but they eviscerated Gaul. I've spent my whole life fighting to protect the peace."

Up until that moment, Sidonius had never understood that Avitus' objective, all the years he'd been at war, had been peace, not power.

Avitus pushed up from the arm of the curule chair and levered himself to his feet. Sidonius heard his knees crack and it pained him to know that the old man was finally becoming ancient.

"Let's give it time," Sidonius repeated, "let's see what happens now the shipping lanes are open."

Sidonius took his leave and walked past beggars holding out their palms for alms to his home at the foot of the Palatine Hill. He frowned in thought. No one could deny that the Goths were big, hairy, ate too much, smelled and got drunk. Their height, bulk and aggressive brandishing of weaponry made them look more like an occupying force than the defenders of Rome. Aristocrats and plebeians alike detested the sight of barbarians dressed in animal skins and horned helmets patrolling their city. But if the Goths went home to Gaul, Avitus would be vulnerable to the vagaries of the army's loyalties.

* * * * *

A month passed. A trickle of ships arrived at the Roman port but, after the first wave, it dried up. Word spread that the Empire had no money to pay for grain and traders were increasingly unwilling to risk pirates and the Vandal navy. Pressure mounted to send the fodder-hungry Goths back to where they came from.

Sidonius sweated on his march up the steep path from the forum to the palace. Summer was over but temperatures had failed to fall. He turned away from emaciated plebeians who glared as he passed, as though they'd rip the toga from his back.

Avitus' Gothic guard opened the doors and Sidonius sat down

to wait on a creaking army campaign chair in an ante-room. He leant the back of his head against the wall and studied the coffered ceiling, then the pilasters carved in coloured marble around the room, admiring the workmanship. They were part of the subtle ostentation of an Empire that had ruled the world. Sidonius wondered if the people of Rome, used to tyrants who plated their palaces with gold, would respect a caesar whose only interest was to save them. Could a good man rule in such a vipers' nest?

The door to the Emperor's private chamber opened and Avitus, looking even older than the last time Sidonius had visited, signalled him in. Sidonius shut the door behind them. The two men stood at arm's length in the centre of the room.

"I've come to a decision," Avitus said, "I must send the Goths home."

Sidonius looked at his feet, not knowing what to say.

"You've done your best," said Avitus, "to find food for the populace, but they're spoiled. Whatever we give them, they want more. Hand-out after hand-out. They're not like us, they never learned to fend for themselves."

Avitus turned away, his hands on the sides of his head, as if blocking out a sound, then threw them up to the gods and stared at the ceiling. "We haven't a single solidus, not even a shaved down nummus, in the Treasury. The people will rebel unless I send the Goths away. They ripped Maximus to pieces with their bare hands and threw his remains into the Tiber. They'll do the same to us." Avitus paced in circles while Sidonius waited silently.

In a voice as dark as a coffin's lid, Avitus concluded. "It's not my own end I fear. I'm old. I've fought hard and lived well. It's the spectre that succeeds my death that haunts me. I lie awake at night watching the moonlight wax and wane on my ceiling – even the moon sleeps, but I cannot. If I fail in this task, if I cannot feed my people, the best that Rome can hope for is Marjorian as a puppet Emperor, his strings pulled by Ricimer the barbarian."

Sidonius stood still while his father-in-law paced from one end of the room to the other in a long and heavy silence.

"I've had time to watch Ricimer," said Avitus. "He's as ruthless as Attila but more cunning. His manipulations are subtle and he's cruel." Avitus stopped perambulating and looked Sidonius in the face. "I didn't fight to save Rome so she could be usurped by a barbarian warlord. I fought for what she stood for, before the rot set in."

Sidonius was hesitant to ask the question that had been bothering him. "How will you pay the Goths to leave? They outnumber us. They won't leave without a reward."

"You think I haven't already thought of that?" Avitus flashed back angrily, "but before I tell you how, I want to get one thing straight: I'm not paying the Goths out of fear, nor for any other reason except that I said I would and, as long as I've lived, I've never broken my word."

Sidonius bowed his head. Avitus had lived by his principles and it was for his integrity as much as his valour that the Goths had supported him. "I never meant to imply any criticism, sire, I apologise if I offended you."

In days not long gone by Avitus wouldn't have been so sensitive, but having to deal with the machinations of the Senate had changed the way he heard things. "The Vandals stole everything that could be transported," said Avitus, "only statues too monumental to be moved remain."

"You can't pay the Goths with statues," said Sidonius.

"No, so I am going to melt them down and turn them into coins."

Sidonius was struck in equal proportions by admiration for Avitus' ingenuity and by the tragedy of the Roman Empire having to melt down its heritage to bribe barbarians. But if the Goths stayed, the people starved; and if they went, Rome and her Emperor risked being ripped to pieces; it had happened before. "So it comes to this, does it?" he asked, with a thought for his own newly erected bust between the Greek and the Latin libraries. "We destroy the culture we came to rescue?"

The outer edges of Avitus' upper lids had folded over his eyes, no longer bright, but bleached and watery. He stared at his son-in-law, answerless.

"So bitter is the irony." Sidonius turned away to hide his tears.

Statues Melt

Rome, Italy
September 456 AD

Sidonius had dragged his feet to the forum as if there were a ball and chain fettering each ankle. It was less than a year since he'd ridden into the city believing he was starting a new imperial dynasty, and now this. The Goths' bearded faces were avaricious as they hurried about their task, missing nothing from towering monuments to the tiniest plaques.

Sidonius swallowed back acid tears. The moment of ecstatic pride he'd felt the day his bronze had been mounted in its place – the moment he'd believed his legacy would last forever in the very heart of civilisation – had been only three months ago. But today he'd come to watch his newly minted image toppled from its plinth, rough handled by the Goths, loaded into a waggon and carted to the smelting house.

How quickly that moment of glory had passed, and how visceral was Sidonius' pain as he witnessed the destruction of memorials to heroes – military, artistic, literary, athletic – who had made Rome great. He held his jaw square and forced himself to watch. He was the Emperor's son-in-law and must set an example of fortitude and loyalty, regardless of his own feelings.

Would anyone remember him? His face had been rendered in life-like detail, a face in the full pride of its youth, but now it would become anonymous in a barbarian's swine-skin purse. How ironic that the currency would melt his image into that of Avitus. The Emperor,

336

who'd given him so much in life, would deprive him of immortality.

The forum buzzed with spectators, like wasps swarming to sting. In purple-fringed robes, senators and patricians watched, outraged and incredulous as either their own edifices or those of their illustrious ancestors were thrown into Gothic handcarts. The pride of Rome, its patrimony, despoiled before their eyes. The travesty was made worse by the fact that the demolition of their heritage had been ordered by an Emperor of their own election in order to pay his barbarian henchmen.

Throughout Rome the massacre of symbols and insignia took place. The massive bronze bull in the cattle market was finally slaughtered; gods and goddesses too great to be destroyed by the Vandals were taken to pieces and melted down. Sacrilege.

In one afternoon, with one action so pragmatically and honestly motivated, Avitus lost the support of his peers, his citizens, and dismantled his power base.

Thirty Years Was Not Long Enough

The Emperor's private apartments, Rome, Italy
September 456 AD

The Vandals had looted the Emperor's private apartments but gilded Corinthian pilasters still climbed twenty feet between marbled floors and coffered ceilings. The gods and nymphs of legend soared in bacchanalian excess, beyond the touch of mortal woe, but the music had stopped. An old man and his wife sat face to face, clasping hands, on folding army issue stools, oblivious to the joyous dance above their heads. All was quiet. The doors and shutters were closed; the light dimmed; but the scent of an ancient cedar tree outside the windows filtered into the room.

Since Avitus and all but a skeleton army had left Gaul, bands of bagaudae had been making trouble on his private estates. Avitus used this disarray as his excuse to send Sedulla and his grandchildren home. She did not want to go.

"So you're sending me away, old man, in your hour of greatest need?"

"I am, wife, it's for the best."

"Why? You really think it's safer to send me to Gaul to face the bands of bagaudae rabble alone than keep me at your side?" Although Sedulla's voice was steady, there was a fearful edge to it.

"The tragic truth is, that it is." He squeezed her fingers gently then passed his hand, crisscrossed with scars, over his brow as if to wipe away the strain. His eyes were dimmed with sadness as he looked at

338

his wife, reminiscing to the very first day they'd met.

He'd been so impressed by her! She was tall, handsome rather than beautiful, intelligent, as haughty as an empress in waiting. He was of average height, and although his family was well respected they didn't have the airs and graces that marked them out as aristocrats. Sedulla had a grandeur about her, even when she was only twenty. He'd come courting at the age of forty, planning his retirement from the legions at the normal age. They'd known thirty-two summers since then and she'd never given him any reason to regret choosing her as his partner in life.

He looked at her tenderly. Her chestnut hair was streaked with grey which she, unlike other aristocratic women, chose not to hide. He took a lock of it between his thumb and forefinger and caressed it fondly. In his eyes, she didn't seem a day older than she had all those summers ago. They'd moved in tandem through time.

He said softly, "I don't know if these things matter to you or not, but you might like to know that since the day we were wed I've never touched another woman."

Sedulla blushed. She'd often wondered if she had been the only one, but had never dared to hope, in a society where orgies were the norm and prostitutes of every description trawled the streets, that her husband, a warrior, could have remained loyal to her. To alleviate the intensity of the moment she joked. "Since the day of our wedding? I note that you say nothing about the night before!"

"The night before as well! Fidelity from before the wedding vows? Now that really would have been ridiculous."

The old couple laughed, unaware that it would be the last laugh they'd ever share.

When the laughter stopped, Sedulla felt tears rolling from the corners of her eyes. She wiped them away as she spoke. "I don't understand why you are sending me away when you need me most."

Avitus patted the back of her hand with his gentle paw. "You've always said that family, not the Empire, matters most. But I've sacrificed my life to the Empire. I don't want to sacrifice the lives of my family as well. Take our grandchildren to a place you can keep them safe," Avitus paused and smiled tenderly at his wife, "I know you, the bagaudae are no real threat to you, you'll sort them out. The nest of snakes that is Rome is much more dangerous."

The old general sighed then continued. "Until this point in my life, despite all the assassinations I've seen, the barbarity of mankind, I've never really understood how lethal jealousy can be to the innocent. To kill Aetius was insane – insane beyond belief! – but now we're here in Rome, I can see the same thing could happen again. It's quite possible, probable even, that to further his personal ambition, someone will kill not only me or you but our children and our children's children. I'm not prepared to risk little Rosea's life, nor the baby Apollinaris. Take them far and keep them safe. They are the future."

Sedulla's lips were thin and drawn. "Yet you're quite happy to ride out to war with Ecdicius at your side and leave Papianilla here with Sidonius?"

"I'm a realist," her husband replied, "we can't do without fighting men like our son, and Papianilla will never leave Sidonius' side. She'll want to keep the children here, but in the end she'll come round to letting you take care of them for her. She'll stay with her husband till the end of his days, of that I'm sure, as you would with me, if I let you ... but I cannot let you stay with me now."

Sedulla rubbed her eyes. She knew there was nothing she could say or do to dissuade her husband from his chosen course of action. Avitus had spoken and it was his considered opinion. Once he'd given a matter thought and made up his mind, neither man nor God could move him. "Very well. We'll do as you wish." She found it hard to say what came next for it sounded final, as if all hope was lost. "Thank you, Avitus my darling, for all you've done. For making me Empress. You've always been my one and only love." She reached out and ran her fingertips over his high cheekbone; pressed her palm to the caved-in side of his face; tucked the heel of her hand under the strength of his jaw and relished its warmth. They'd grown closer, year after year, known each other better, loved each other more, knowing that the other one was always there. Her eyes met his and she was surprised at the unquestioning love she saw in them, a love that was at least as powerful as her own for him. "No one else could have, or would have, done all that you have done. All your life, you've fought for what's right."

"I wasn't alone," said Avitus, "you were always there, in my heart. You and my cohorts. You and the innocent I fought to save."

Sedulla wiped her eyes and tried to smile. "Thank you for being you, and for the amazing journey together that our life has been. I wouldn't have missed a minute of it."

Avitus stood and lifted her to her feet. He pulled her close into his chest so that she couldn't see the tears welling in his eyes. Once she took the carriage in the direction of Lyon, he doubted he would ever see her again. The Alps would lie between them, along with greater barriers, less visible but insurmountable.

"I'm glad you're here with me," he kissed the top of her head before gently pushing her to arm's length, "but I have to get on with what we started and must say goodbye to you now."

Last Walk Along the Tiber

Rome, Italy
September 456 AD

Sidonius stood alone on the Sublician Bridge, at the upstream end of the cattle market whose traders' energy had become stagnant when their bronze bull was liquidated. The River Tiber dragged languidly past the market gates.

It was less than a year since the Aviti had ridden triumphally into Rome, full of hope and belief in the future, though it may as well have been more than a century for all the relevance that moment had now. Sidonius had just left Avitus alone in the Emperor's throne room where the old man had told him that he and Ecidicius must follow Sedulla back to Gaul and raise an army to replace the Goths he was sending home.

Sidonius caressed the Sublician's wooden rails with tender regret. It was the oldest bridge in Rome. On these slats, the hero Horatius had defied the king of Tarquin's Etruscan soldiers when they had tried to destroy Rome's nascent Republic. In those days, the bridge had been made entirely of wood so that it could be dismantled to stop enemies from advancing across the river. The timber piles had been replaced by stone, but the values which had founded first the Republic and then the Empire had rotted all the same.

Sidonius crossed to the river's western bank. The Tiber was coming to the end of a journey that had started in the Apennine hills, flowed past Narnia, then down into the Plain of Latium. Its waters were the colour of wheat, full of silt, as it wove its way through the city. When the wind blew from the wrong direction the stench of tanneries assailed his nostrils. Carrion birds cawed in the distance.

Sidonius put a hand over his nose and walked over the Aemilian Bridge, back to the more fashionable, eastern side of the river. As he wandered past the walls of the Theatre of Marcellus he looked up at the stylised masks carved between each of its arches. Their distorted faces portrayed tragedy, comedy and satire. Surely he was living them all at once?

Yet, despite his pain and anxiety, at a quiet time of day like this, when the brick was honey-brown in the afternoon sun and pigeons clustered and cooed on terracotta-tiled rooves, the eternal city still exuded magic.

Sidonius found a peaceful spot on the bank of the river, knelt and cupped a handful of Rome's blood in his palms. He watched the reflected light on its tilting surface for a moment, then drank, knowing that the taste of the Tiber would never leave his mouth.

The Fall of Ravenna

Italy

17th September 456 AD

Avitus stood, his head bowed, reading the inscription on the base of Aetius' column in front of the Senate House. When he'd finished, he looked up to the peak of the obelisk and straightened the folds of his imperial purple toga. Then he walked through sepulchral doors into the chilled air within and was enshrouded by lethal silence.

As far as the senators were concerned, since Avitus had taken over as Emperor he'd done nothing for them. He'd appointed his favourites from Gaul over the heads of the Italian aristocracy and fed his army of barbarians ahead of the plebs. Now he'd added insult to injury by melting down their monuments. Although, less than a year ago, he'd saved them from the Vandals, the senators were nigh unanimous that the general from Gaul and his Gothic friends had to go.

Avitus' eyes adjusted to the half-light and he surveyed the senators' faces, as stony as the benches on which they sat, seeking a smile or nod of encouragement. In the absence of either, he walked on creaking knees to the rostrum and delivered a ponderous speech in which he called for austerity and unity. When he'd finished, the senators sat as stiff as their starched white robes. Avitus' heart drummed three beats in his ears before the audience gave a muted round of applause. Without another word, he turned and walked out into the daylight. *Time to leave the jackals to their howling.*

344

In the week that followed, he moved his administration from Rome to Ravenna, taking with him the bare minimum number of bureaucrats needed to keep the cogs of the Empire turning and his most loyal generals. The nobly named Flavius Julius Valerius Majorianus Augustus, more briefly termed "Marjorian", Commander-in-Chief of the Imperial Guard, was not one of them.

Majorian and Ricimer had become friends when they'd fought together under Aetius in the days when Romans and Goths had been enemies. Ricimer dropped oily words on the embers of Marjorian's discontent and blew them up into outright revolt. Together, Marjorian and Ricimer led their troops north against Ravenna in pursuit of Avitus, planning to depose him.

Avitus left Ravenna's defence in the hands of Remistus, a Gothic general, and headed through northern Italy towards Gaul in search of reinforcements. Marjorian besieged the city and it fell on September the 17th. After some debate whether to garrotte Remistus, (for he was a barbarian), or behead him, (as he was a Roman general), Ricimer and Marjorian had him marched outside to the foot of the city walls and run him through with a sword.

When an imperial messenger caught up with Avitus, not far from the town of Piacenza, with the news that Ravenna had fallen the Emperor called for a pen and paper. Seated at his campaign desk, sweat trickling down the ravines on his face, he dashed out a note, folded then sealed it with red wax. He ordered the courier to ride with all haste and deliver it to a woman called Sola, who lived one block north of the cathedral, behind elephant repelling walls, in Reims. There was a lion's paw knocker on her gate.

Taking much longer over his next letters, Avitus wrote to Ecdicius and Sidonius on the subject of raising Gallic reinforcements and referring, obliquely, to things that they should do were he not to make it back over the Alps alive.

He didn't have the heart to write to Sedulla yet. Nor to his daughter.

They would hear what had happened soon enough. No need to add to their worries.

Where were his allies, the Goths, for whom he'd melted down Rome's heritage? Theodoric II had taken his tonnes of bronze coins and used them to pay for a war against the Ricimer's tribe, the Sueves, on the Northern Coast of the Iberian Peninsula. When Avitus' call for reinforcements reached him, he ignored it.

Double-headed Throwing Axes

S ola's face split into the rare arc of a smile.

She'd just finished a fifteen-minute bout with her daughter in which she hadn't unsworded her at all and had only twice been in the position to slit her throat. Leonida was making progress.

From the moment she'd thrown her a gladius, the girl had grabbed it with both hands and poured all of her anger at the world into her attack. Sola immediately saw that Leonida had inherited the warrior spirit and would advance on any target, no matter how much bigger or stronger it was than she. The knowledge brought a wry smile to her face. Such courage carried its own risks; sometimes to wait or withdraw was the better strategy, but so much easier to teach Leonida when to rein herself in than to instil bravery into someone naturally timid.

Another week of practice at this rate and Leonida would be more than competent with a sword and they would move on to dagger and spear. And Sola was enjoying herself! It was years since she'd picked up her weapons just to train, not to kill, with a purpose that brought her joy.

She'd found a stash of Frankish double-headed throwing axes, set up bales of straw as targets and was having fun decimating them. It wasn't often she had the time or place to practice with such weapons without attracting unwanted attention. As each of her axe-throws sliced the straw bales shorter and shorter, Sola stepped back to increase her range with a sense of satisfaction as she refined her technique. But she didn't let Leonida try her arm even when the girl begged her for a turn. It wouldn't be safe to put a double-headed throwing axe into the hands of a beginner.

The week in Troyes had given her time and reason to reconnect with her daughter. They'd started by visiting the family who'd looked after Leonida when she'd passed through the town with Heva. That was pleasant enough, but they had little left in common. Sola was no longer married to a magistrate and the fourteen-year-old girl who'd given Leonida her dress and boots was now a nineteen-year-old mother of two. Nonetheless, the family made Sola and Leonida welcome.

Rather than stay with them, Sola had borrowed a centurion's house in the Roman barracks. This exceptional favour had been granted courtesy of Marco, the old groom who now held the position of "horse doctor". All but a skeleton garrison were on the march to Lyon and from there over the Alps to join Avitus. Marco hadn't gone with them as he was lame himself and had sick horses to tend. He obtained leave for a day to ride out to Pouans-les-Vallées with Sola and Leonida to look for Heva's grave, but he too had been defeated by the way the field had been levelled by ploughing. Despite cascades of tears and heart-rending sobs from Leonida, they abandoned the hunt.

Sola was so fully occupied with thoughts for Leonida and her training in Troyes that a week passed before it occurred to her that her household back in Reims might be starting to wonder where she was. She sent a message by first-class post to let them know that she and her daughter were safe and would stay away for at least ten days more.

When her letter arrived at her home after the fall of Ravenna, the gatekeeper frowned and sat down on his haunches, wringing his hat, tortured by the responsibility of the vellum that an imperial messenger had thrust into his hands. The day after delivering the letter, the courier returned, seeking Sola's reply, but had spurred his horse on as soon as the gatekeeper told him that the mistress hadn't been home.

Semi-literate, the gatekeeper could read enough of Sola's message to understand that she would prolong her stay in Troyes but he couldn't write a response. He conferred with the cook and she agreed to go down to the marketplace and dictate a note to a freedman who made his living writing for the townsfolk. This done, the cook consigned the reply to first class post. It would take three days for it to arrive in Troyes but with bagaudae on all the roads these days the official postal service was a safer choice than a travelling merchant.

The Bishop of Piacenza

Avitus sat alone in his praetorium at the core of his camp, midway between Ravenna and the Italian Alps. His tent was pitched on the axis of four internal roads that ended in open gates pointing north, south, east and west. The tent flaps were tied back with leather straps and the light of a westering sun filled it with a golden glow. Avitus would have preferred his doors to be laced shut but had left them open in order to give his men the impression of normality and confidence. Despite the warmth of sunlight on his weathered face, his whole body shivered. He pulled his prickly woollen army blanket over his shoulders but it made no difference.

At the ninth hour of the day, one of his scouts had ridden in with news that Marjorian had control of the road to the north of Piacenza, cutting off Avitus' only route to the Alps. It had been a shock. He couldn't work out how Marjorian had manoeuvred his army ahead of him without being seen, but since the young general had learnt his skills from Aetius he didn't question the accuracy of the scout's report.

Less than half an hour later, the commander of his own rearguard cantered up to the praetorium to inform him that Ricimer's army blocked the retreat to the south.

Avitus dismissed him then withdrew, alone and wordless, into the womb of his tent.

There he sat on a campaign chair, staring down the road through the open door to the camp gate that framed a view of the terracotta rooves of Piacenza. The name meant "a pleasing place of good omen". Above its walls, white clouds hovered in an azure sky. Humped green mountains sloped up from the town towards them. A straight grey road led from the tent out of his camp and on through scrubby trees to the city gate. Piacenza's walls were fortified. They glowed in the afternoon light. The town was close. *We could march in there tomorrow morning, hole up and hold out.* But Avitus was a man of action and neither hiding nor siege had ever come naturally to him.

He grinned wryly as he wondered what Aetius would have done. Outflank, encircle, crush – but it was too late for that. The only tactic left to Avitus was to make sure that the ground he fought on would favour his battle tactics.

He rose from his folding chair and walked out of the tent, past guards who saluted. He didn't acknowledge them with a glance or a smile as he usually would lest they catch fear in his eyes. Taking several deep breaths, he straightened his back and marched towards the northern gate. Keeping his pace unhurried, he walked twenty yards beyond it, clasped his hands behind his back and, from a grassy knoll, surveyed the surrounding terrain.

In the distance he could see the standards of Marjorian's legions, all in good order, fluttering in the wind. Too many of them. He stopped counting and walked around the perimeter to survey the road south. His stomach turned at the sight of Ricimer's black hawks, anchored across his retreat route, and his camp behind them.

Avitus walked back to the northern gate, his thoughts accompanied by the familiar drumbeat of the footsteps of guards patrolling the wooden boardwalk of the palisade.

So, this is the end, and this my funeral march.

He shook his head to clear his melancholy and sharpened up. Between his present position and the town stood an orchard. A small river meandered towards it then disappeared behind green-leafed

351

trees. Women and children carrying baskets were harvesting red apples. He'd send a messenger down to tell them to clear out before the fighting started.

In front of the orchard was a patch of flat ground, just the right size for the fight he had in mind. He decided to form up three sides of a square and use the orchard to shield his back. It would fragment any cavalry charges and provide cover for his wounded, for wounded there would be – too many. Marjorian was a brilliant young officer, and Ricimer, well, Ricimer was a barbarian and capable of limitless atrocity.

Avitus considered for a moment whether Ricimer would set fire to the trees and concluded that if he could, he would, but that his wounded could fight the fire by drawing water from the stream to the rear.

His gaze turned towards Piacenza's crenellated walls and lingered with longing on them, then he let out a sigh and sneered at himself. He'd never let overwhelming odds stop him fighting for what he believed in and he wouldn't start now. Taking refuge in Piacenza would mean slow but certain death.

He turned back into his camp and marched up the via principalis, his boots crunching in the grit. He forced a smile and words of camaraderie for his men but this time they averted their eyes from him. Bad news had travelled fast.

Summoning his officers to the forum outside his tent, with customary gruffness he ordered them to have the troops in battle order and ready to march before cock-crow. When they'd gone, he retired to his tent again and this time tied the doors shut. Unlacing his cuirass and greaves, he threw his armour onto waiting hooks, stretched out on his camp bed with his hands behind his head and fell asleep.

In the dark before dawn he woke with a stiff neck and sat up, feeling the ache of night dew in his joints. By the time a slave came in, carrying an oil lamp and a meal of bread, cheese and fruit, he was at his desk, scribbling squares and arrows to show movement around the stream and trees. But little did it avail him, for his battle position always ended up with his troops surrounded by superior forces and fighting in a square.

His face was greyish-white in the lamplight as he shaved with a long steel blade before a rectangular mirror. He glanced at the food but had no appetite, then strapped on his breastplate and greaves, planning to stride out into the dawning light. But he sat down again, running his fingers over the horsehair crest of his helmet, and muttered a prayer. He didn't know to which god – there were so many of them – but not the Christian one who'd have told him to surrender and turn the other cheek. He had a dragging sensation in his gut that he should have sacrificed a beast to Mars, but those days, the days of his youth, belonged to a different age. Nonetheless, he would have felt better if he had.

Putting his helmet on, he pushed back the tent flap. Outside his officers were waiting in a motionless row, faceless shadows against a sky turning green. White stars were fading fast.

My last dawn.

Avitus laid out the battle formation to them. It was simple. No need for a map. He explained that their aim was to cut a path through the enemy and capture the road north. Do battle against Marjorian. As light crept through the morning air, he saw fear and disbelief spread over their faces.

He turned to Marcellianus, tall and dark with a cleft chin, to whom he'd entrusted the command of the field. Marcellianus didn't cower or pale but gave Avitus a wink. They understood each other. Avitus smiled. He'd chosen him as his field commander for, at last, he'd admitted he no longer had the physical speed or stamina required. And Marcellianus was ready for it, eager to test his skills against his red-headed rival.

Avitus winked back at Marcellianus then stuck his jaw forward before addressing his men. "We do battle here today, not to die heroes, but to defeat the enemies of Rome. We must live and fight another day. What matters now is discipline and courage."

As the sun rose, he dismissed his officers. Looking up at the last of the fading stars then down across the rolling fields to the shadows of Piacenza, he didn't need an augur to tell him that the auspices were not promising. But Marcellianus was a brave and effective officer, a good man, and he trusted him.

In less than an hour Marcellianus was captured and beheaded. Full light revealed Avitus' square with its back to the apple trees and surrounded on three sides by Marjorian and Ricimer's legions. As fireballs hurtled over Avitus' head and set the orchard behind him on fire, he saw Marjorian galloping along his lines, his red hair flying. Romans killing Romans.

Fire took hold of the orchard and the screaming of his injured scorched Avitus' ears. Men in front of him were falling while Marjorian and Ricimer closed in. With the back of his red leather gauntlet, Avitus wiped the sweat from his brow and took a final look at his troop dispositions. Sheathing his gladius he drew himself tall and turned to his bodyguards.

"Lay down your weapons." To a man, they stared blankly at him. "Lay down your weapons and save yourselves. My capture is inevitable."

It didn't take long. Before noon Avitus found himself alone behind his captured lion rampant amidst a cohort of the enemy. The hissing of flames dying under water thrown from bucket-chains by peasants trying to save their orchard, and the groans and screams of his injured men, drowned out the debate that was raging between Ricimer and Marjorian, but from a distance Avitus watched them arguing.

Marjorian's thick shock of hair was aflame in the sunlight, his blue eyes as bright as Avitus' used to be. He wore a silver breast-plate embossed with the image of the sun god driving a quadriga across his chest and towered over Ricimer, who'd removed his armour and was leaning back in a leather-seated camp chair with his hands linked over the beginning of a middle-aged paunch.

"We'll spare his life but force him to abdicate," said Marjorian, "ordain him bishop of Piacenza and tell him to retire."

Ricimer rolled his eyes. "Avitus, a bishop? He'd never accept! No, he must not live. We behead him – now."

"If we do that, both Gaul and the Goths will rebel."

"Without Avitus, there'd be no one left to lead a rebellion," said Ricimer, unlinking his hands from his stomach and sitting up.

Marjorian's auburn eyebrows drew together. Bad blood ran between Ricimer's people and the Goths but that had to be set aside. Avitus had been a cohort and friend of Aetius, fought fifty years in the legions, and the noble Marjorian would never forget that.

Ricimer's lip twitched. This was the first time his young and malleable cohort had defied him. He rose to his feet and stretched his back, playing for time. "There's no need to argue. Avitus lost his way. He became the puppet of the Goths, advancing their interests over ours. It may not be what you want to hear, but it *is* his time to die."

"Let the old man go!" Marjorian thumped his fist down on the campaign table and it clattered to the ground. "Look at him, standing over there alone. He deserves to have a few years of peace at the end of a lifetime's service to Rome."

Ricimer didn't flinch as the table glanced off his greaves and bounced at his feet. He stood glaring in the direction of Avitus' lone, grey head surrounded by guards. "What old man?" Ricimer bared his teeth and snarled. "You see an old man over there, do you? I don't! I see an enemy. Given half the chance, Avitus will raise another army and come back to fight us. We need to kill him – *now*."

Marjorian looked down an aquiline nose at Ricimer. "If you don't give Avitus the chance to abdicate and retire into the Church, I'll order my legions to engage yours in battle – right here, right now."

Ricimer chuckled. Who would have suspected that Marjorian, the product of centuries of selective breeding, could be so devoted to a Gallic provincial? "Have it your way then. We'll let Avitus assume the bishopric of Piacenza and quietly fade away."

Marjorian grunted, not quite trusting him, but didn't want to let the moment of acquiescence slip by. "I'll tell Avitus now that his army must surrender to ours and we'll let him live."

Ricimer kicked aside the fallen table and sat down again. He steepled his hands beneath his chin and watched Marjorian's golden head cut a path amongst the guards' steel helmets towards Avitus. *You think that you've saved him, but my enemy must die.*

When informed of his choices by Marjorian, Avitus allowed himself to be anointed with oil as the Bishop of Piacenza. He'd always recognised reality when it glared him in the face. The fact that Marjorian was Aetius' protégé helped ease the moment of humiliation. He waited on bended knee in the church of Piacenza, making a pretence of praying, until he was sure that Ricimer and Marjorian had withdrawn their armies and marched well away. Then, dressed in his bishop's alb, he climbed into his carriage with its four rampant lions at the corners.

The driver cracked the whip and headed in the direction of Gaul where Avitus would raise a new army to march on Rome and cut it free from Ricimer's web.

Sola's Letter

As soon as she heard that a message from Avitus was waiting for her at home, Sola galloped north from Troyes with Leonida at her side. The house slaves had been watching out for them day and night and swung wide the elephant gates to hurry them in. Sola and Leonida slid from the sweating backs of their horses and a slave boy led their mounts to water. The gatekeeper went down on one knee and held out the imperial parchment, desperate to be relieved of responsibility. Sola thanked him, strode across the atrium into her office and locked the door before unravelling the scroll.

She read it once, turned the paper over to check there was nothing more to it, then read it again.

It was only one line long, a simple question – *"How did you kill the lion?"*

She sat down at her desk, no longer cluttered with architectural plans, and wrote her reply straight onto the back of the parchment.

"It was simple really, once I decided to do it. Courage, focus, reflex. I knew that I had to kill it before it killed me . . ."

She wouldn't have elaborated on the sword strokes to anyone else, but she went into every detail for Avitus, every shift of weight, the smell of the lion's breath, the gouges its claws made in her flesh, how they festered afterwards and the scars they'd left.

But she knew that the question wasn't what it seemed. He needed more than words from her. She'd heard about the loss of Ravenna, and knew that her friend was facing his last battle.

At the bottom of her reply, she drew in red, the colour of his gauntlet, two lions rampant facing each other with their paws touching. Avitus would know she meant that she was with him, his mirror image in spirit. Then she strode as fast as she could through the city streets of Reims to see the commander of the garrison and ask if an imperial courier was due. None was. He'd heard two days ago that Avitus had been defeated at Piacenza. Since then there'd been no news.

Sola sprinted back to her house, legs shaking. She took the stairs to her bedroom three at a time, barred the door and tore off the linen tablecloth that hid a trunk in the corner. With a key she kept on her belt, she unlocked it and pulled out a helmet and a tunic of fine chainmail. Unworn for twenty years, they still fitted her. She pulled her midnight blue cloak from a cupboard and threw it over her shoulders.

Pausing in the luminous air of her room to draw in a few calm breaths, she decided that she needed nothing more than a fast horse, her swords and the will of the gods to take her to Avitus' side and raced back downstairs.

Leonida, hearing the whirlwind of her movements, ran into the hallway – "What are you doing, Mama?"

"I'm riding to Piacenza to help Avitus."

Leonida's eyes opened wide with fear. "What's happened?"

"His army's been defeated."

"Then there's nothing you can do."

"Perhaps I can rescue him from his captors, or assassinate his enemies."

Leonida stared at her mother in disbelief. "But why?"

"He found you for me. And it's perhaps because of me that he is where he is. I urged him to rule although we both knew the risks."

"I'm sure he would have done it without your encouragement."

"Probably. But that changes nothing. He's a good man, and that's reason enough to try to save his life."

"You're not going," said Leonida, anger in her voice, "you're too old. I'll go in your stead."

Sola looked at her tall, willowy daughter, who had no idea what life held for her. "You're not ready yet."

"We can go together," said Leonida.

"*No.*"

Leonida swallowed. "Then take my horse. Lightning can't be caught, you'll be safe on her."

Sola's eyes filled with tears. Lightning meant the world to Leonida and no one else ever rode the mare.

"I'll saddle her up," said Leonida, "while you put your provisions together."

Sola disappeared into the kitchen. When she emerged from the shade of the villa into the glare of the courtyard with saddlebags draped over her shoulders, she found Leonida waiting with Lightning's reins in one hand. Despite her hurry to mount up and go, Sola looked twice at her daughter who had something of the vixen in her face.

Leonida held out the reins. Sola took a handful of mane and swung a leg over Lightning's back, but as soon as her weight was in the saddle the horse screamed and reared. The more Sola gripped her legs round its belly, the more it bucked until finally she let go and rolled off onto the paving stones. As she sat up, Lightning landed a front hoof directly on her right foot. A flaming rod of pain shot up Sola's leg. She crumpled forward, both hands on the swelling foot, and watched as blood flooded under her golden skin and turned it black.

Leonida rushed forward and went down on her knees beside her mother. "I'm sorry, I'm sorry, I didn't think she'd do that."

"It's not your fault," said Sola through gritted teeth.

"It is, I pushed a nail through her saddle blanket so that she'd buck and you'd think she was unrideable and wouldn't go – but I didn't mean for her to hurt you!"

"It might still be alright," said Sola, "run inside and get me the bandages I keep in the kitchen cupboard." Leonida disappeared and Sola lay on her back, propping her foot up on a planter box. When the girl came back with long strips of linen she pulled off her sandal and wound the material tightly round the bruising and swelling. The pain was excruciating, but she stood up on the other leg and tried to put her foot to the ground. Impossible. Her face fell. "It's broken. I can't ride. I can't fight."

"I'll find Avitus," said Leonida, who'd calmed Lightning and held her by the bridle.

Sola hopped to a stone bench and sat with her broken foot up, angry with her daughter and with herself. "Go then," she said, "but dress like a man." She pulled her chainmail tunic over her head and handed it to Leonida who slipped it on. It was the right length but far too wide for the girl. To Sola, Leonida looked like a child playing at being grown up. But someone had to go to Avitus, and it could only be her. "Pile your hair up under a helmet. Don't stop for anyone or anything. Speed is your best defence. If you find him, give him this letter and ask him if he needs you to ride a message to someone else. Whatever you do, don't join any combat."

Leonida picked up the bread, cheese and dried fruit that had been scattered from the saddlebags and loaded them along with a gourd of water. Sola took a small leather pouch of silver and bronze coins from around her neck and held it out to her. "Come here a minute."

Leonida sat down beside her mother, still holding her horse's reins. "I'm so sorry, Mumma, for your broken foot, and for Avitus."

"Don't worry about me; take care of yourself." With tears of frustration and love, Sola held her daughter tight then patted her back. "Off you go then, and godspeed."

Leonida stood up and used the pommels of the saddle to pull herself onto the horse's back. She looked down at Sola, who showed no outward sign of the pain she was suffering. "I don't understand why this is so important to you, but if it matters to you, then it matters to me. I'll find Avitus and give him your letter."

"That's all I can hope for. But at all costs, keep yourself safe."

Leonida nudged her horse forward and called for the gatekeeper to come and open the gates.

Still seated on the bench, Sola watched her daughter head out on horseback towards the city walls. What dangers awaited her, she could not know, but her eyes were bright with poignant pride that her only child was ready to go.

* * * * *

Lightning's familiar stride made Leonida feel free and light as the city walls of Reims disappeared down the road behind her. High on her horse, she seemed untouchable as they took the first steps in a journey of a thousand, thousand paces. The voyage across the Alps and seven major rivers would challenge even her Akal Teke.

Lightning's coat quivered and although she took the road at a gallop, it was more measured than her usual flight, as if she knew she needed to conserve energy for the alpine climbs. By noon of the fourth day after leaving Reims they arrived at the outskirts of Lyon. There the girl had to seek further news of Avitus. She dared not ride to the Roman barracks and ask outright, as her mother would have done, but went instead to find Petrina, the old midwife who was reputed to have connections to nearly everyone in Lyon.

If asked, Petrina couldn't have explained why she was unsurprised when she opened her door to a tall young woman dressed as a man holding a golden horse by the bridle. She exhaled slowly and stood with her hands in the small of her aching back, looking the stranger up and down. The reputation of her expertise had spread over three decades, and it wasn't unusual for girls in trouble to appear at her door, but a single glance at Leonida told her she wasn't pregnant.

Leonida asked for water for Lightning then tethered her and followed Petrina into the house, explaining that she had a letter from her mother to deliver to Avitus. Petrina had always been discreet and didn't ask why. "I have connections that can help. Come back at dawn tomorrow and I'll tell you whatever I find out."

Leonida thanked her then followed her directions to a livery stable and slept in the hay of Lightning's stall. As soon as the sky started to lighten, she made her way back through Lyon's cobbled streets to Petrina's house.

"Come upstairs and sit down," said the midwife, casting a look into the street over Leonida's shoulder. They settled down on a wooden bench and Petrina took Leonida's hand in hers. "Avitus lost a battle at Piacenza and has been deposed. No one in Gaul has seen him since. He hasn't yet crossed the Alps. Ricimer wants him dead. Any fool could see that, as long as there's breath in his body, Avitus will return to Gaul and raise another army."

"What should I do?"

"How important is this letter from your mother?"

"I don't know."

"It can serve little purpose now. It's November, the days are short and snows may fall at any moment. You shouldn't try to cross the Alps this time of year. What's worse, you risking running into Ricimer."

Leonida listened to the midwife but knew what Sola would do. "I must go."

Petrina frowned. She hunched her shoulders, trying to release the tension around her neck. *Why do people like this haunt me – the difficult, misplaced, the odd men out who have to get up and fight instead of chugging along with the flow of life?* "Alright, go if you must. There's only one road to Turin, it'd be hard to get lost, but let's make a quick offering to the gods." She unlocked a small cabinet on the wall and took out a horseshoe-shaped fire steel and a nugget of incense and handed them to Leonida. "You make the spark."

"To which god?"

"Mercury, of course." Petrina had been to church and listened to the priest blaming the world's misfortunes on Rome's sins. But even as she'd sat with her head bowed and her shawl drawn demurely round her shoulders she'd questioned his way of looking at things. Who could say that Rome's misfortunes weren't caused by the old gods' anger over being abandoned for this new one, Christos?

Together Leonida and the midwife watched the smoke from the incense rise and, for a moment, felt comforted.

Petrina kissed the girl on both cheeks, pulled her into the plump softness of a quick hug then released her. "Keep warm and come back before the snows fall."

A Church on a Hill

Leonida cantered southeast, across flat land, towards the foothills cradling Grenoble, the last major city on the Gallic side of the Alps. She slowed down as she approached the first mountain range, partly because Lightning needed a rest but also because she was on the lookout for signs of Avitus. A long, flat road cut its way through a gorge. The foothills were rugged mountains, daunting in themselves but only the little sisters of the sky-scouring range beyond.

Just before noon she came to the western gate. Delving deep to find courage, she asked the sentries for news of Avitus but they had none. She skirted the forum at a trot, avoiding the curious stares of onlookers who looked up as Lightning's hooves clattered past.

"Strange colour, that horse," said a man selling sheaths of corn from a handcart.

"And look at the legs on the lad riding it," said his neighbour, a spice trader, with a nudge of his elbow, "pity he's in such a hurry."

Leonida turned her nose up. Without dismounting, she let Lightning drink her fill from a fountain in the corner of the market place then rode out through the eastern watchtower gate. Crossing a bridge over a dry moat, she trotted onwards past a church atop a hill at a crossroads two miles beyond the city walls.

As soon as she left the church behind, Leonida was confronted by the mass of the Italian Alps. Walls of solid rock, purple, grey and black, blocked her view in all directions. Her stomach sank. Even when she tipped her neck backwards she could barely see the tops of the ragged white heads perforating the deep blue ceiling of sky. Tears pricking the back of her lids, she touched her heels lightly to Lightning's side and the horse lengthened her stride to a measured canter.

Steed and girl gathered themselves up for the alpine climb. Leonida was staring down the road ahead, wondering how best to tackle it, when a dark dot in the distance caught her eye. Quickly it began to take the shape of a carriage moving at a rapid clip downhill towards her. Her heart flew to her throat as a black coach accompanied by a squadron of outriders, four in front, four behind, took form. She reined Lightning to a halt and nudged her off the road.

It was him! It could be no other. The matched black horses' hooves were shod and polished, their coats gleamed with sweat yet they were still relatively fresh. Lions, carved and gilded, prowled forward on each corner of the roof as if about to leap.

Avitus had descended twelve miles from Bourg-d'Oisan, an alpine valley town, and the horses had traversed two mountain ranges already that morning. He was rejoicing to have arrived safely in Gaul again and was travelling so quickly that before Leonida had time to work out a way of intercepting him he'd galloped past.

In fear of losing track of him, Leonida turned back in the direction of Grenoble and shadowed the road from a discreet distance. She realised that she would have to catch up to him before he entered the city and became inaccessible, but had no idea of how to get past his guard. Mystified, but infinitely relieved, she watched the coach slow down then come to a complete halt two miles outside the city walls.

An old man descended and walked alone in the direction of the church on top of the hill. He posted his guards at the crossroads to keep a lookout in all directions so that he could go alone and pray in peace.

Leonida watched from a distance as the soldiers took up their positions and Avitus started walking up the narrow footpath meandering past a grove of trees to the summit then she then skirted around behind the woods to avoid coming into sight. She took her helmet off so that it wouldn't reflect the sun, thinking how lucky it was that Lightning's coat and her own hair would be camouflaged against the golden alpine tundra, then lay low on her horse's back as her hooves flitted over the ground.

Avitus' mind was absorbed in thought as he walked through the necropolis of white grave markers up to the church. He was in a hurry to make an offering to God to thank him for the safe passage he'd given him over the Alps; for having held off the snow; for the fact that he'd escaped Italy alive and was coming close to his homeland and would see his wife and family again. He chose the chapel instead of the big cathedral in town as he wanted solitude, not ceremony, to pray for guidance as to the best way to tackle the future.

A mounted figure suddenly appeared from nowhere at his side. Avitus jumped with a start then peered up against the noonday sun, which had not long cleared the mountain tops, at the unknown horseman. The sun illuminated a halo of hair that flowed around an oval face he couldn't make out. As he shielded his eyes, he saw what appeared to be a vision – a girl wearing a Roman cloak mounted on a long-legged, metallic horse.

She reined her mount to a halt and spoke. "I am Sola's daughter, Leonida."

Avitus' blue eyes sparkled with laughter at himself. "Of course you are! You had me worried for a moment, I thought you were a visitor from the next world come to take me. You have hair like an angel and you ride a horse that looks as if it's been gilded, like Nero's palace." He looked hard at her, seeing Sola in her features and something else that he couldn't quite place.

"Are you Emperor Eparchius Avitus?" Leonida asked solemnly.

"I am indeed."

"Then please accept this letter from my mother." Leonida pulled a scroll from deep inside the folds of her cloak, as if drawing it out from her heart, and passed it into the open palm Avitus extended to her.

"Thank you." He took it graciously. "Will you dismount and walk with me a minute? How is your mother?"

Leonida glided off Lightning's back to the old man's side. She was taller than he but sylph-like next to the breadth of his shoulders.

"My mother's well, thank you, except for a broken foot. If she could have ridden and fought she would have come to find you herself. She wanted you to know that."

Avitus nodded, his heart warmed by the thought.

"And yourself, Caesar?" asked Leonida.

Avitus chuckled again. "How am I? It's a fair while since anyone has asked me that! I'm well, my girl, I'm alive, for which I'm grateful. Being alive should never be taken for granted."

Avitus gave a hand signal that all was well to his men at the junction at the foot of the hill who'd noticed the appearance of a stranger next to their Emperor.

"Tell me about your horse," the old man said to the girl. Leonida did, then asked him about his team of four. Together, they ambled up through the necropolis to the church crowning the breast of the hill. Drawing in the fresh scent of evergreen pines, they looked down on the bare skeletons of deciduous trees picked out on the plain by a watery sun.

"Your mother is a remarkable woman," said Avitus, "not only because she killed a lion."

"Thank you, sir, she says the same of you. She told me that you found me after the wars with Attila."

"She would have found you herself, I barely helped."

"But she's grateful to you, and so am I."

Leonida began to wish that Avitus was the grandfather she'd never known. Avitus thought, with affection, that one day his granddaughter,

Rosea, might grow up to be a tall young woman as proud and pure as his new friend. From under grizzled brows he looked sideways at her. She was the image of her mother, beautiful and courageous, but red-haired instead of blond.

At first her golden tresses reminded him of Marjorian but then he remembered that, on the rare occasions he'd seen Aetius unshaven, his beard had been fiery. A quizzical light sharpened Avitus' eyes. He looked more closely and saw a resemblance he hadn't dared to hope for. His breath caught in his throat then his face mellowed. Sola walked alone in a dangerous world. Perhaps she'd reasoned that Leonida's life would be in danger if anyone suspected a connection to the magister militum, or perhaps there was no connection at all, but it comforted him to believe that Aetius might live on in this girl. He put a hand on her shoulder, feeling its warmth and resilience, and joy infused his heart.

But, above their heads, bruised clouds were gathering over the peaks of the Alps. Avitus' eyes darkened. "That storm looks ominous. You'd better make your way into the city before it breaks on us."

"You are not coming with me?" asked Leonida.

"Not just yet, dear, I need time to myself. Give my thanks to your mother for her letter and ride safely."

"She told me to ask you if there were messages you wanted to send to anyone."

"Thank you, but I'm almost home now. You ride on, keep yourself safe."

Avitus kissed Leonida on both cheeks then bid her good-bye on the steps of the church made of granite hewn from the bones of the Alps. Smiling, he watched her canter off down the hill, avoiding all contact with his guards as she bypassed the crossroads, and head across country towards Grenoble.

When he saw she was safely on her way, he sat down on the church steps to read Sola's letter. It was autumn, the early afternoon the air was still mild and the stones had gathered the warmth of the sun.

His expression changed as he followed Sola's words, at first frowning with concentration, then laughing and slapping his thigh with enthusiasm as she got further into her description of fighting the lion. He swung his arm, mimicking some of her sword blows, and when the moment came that she plunged her blade into the lion's chest for the final time, his own right arm jerked upwards as if he too held a gladus and was thrusting it into the heart of the beast.

"Ye gods!" he smiled with satisfaction, "What a woman! Perhaps I'll be able to convince Sedulla to invite her to dinner. She's someone I want to know better."

He carefully smoothed and folded the letter into four and placed it into the breast of his alb.

When Avitus had asked Sola to write to him about how she'd killed the lion he'd been feeling overwhelmed by the combined forces of Ricimer and Marjorian. It seemed to him then that a woman must have felt a similar terror when facing a lion. He'd wanted to know her strategy for defeating it. How did she put it?

"It was easy once I had made up my mind to do it . . . courage, focus, reflex . . ."

He'd been defeated at Piacenza but would rise again, he told himself as he unlatched the heavy wooden door and stepped across the threshold of the empty church. It was a damned nuisance that the Goths had chosen to go off and attack Ricimer's tribe, but he hoped that, when that bit of raiding was over, they'd come back to his side. In the meantime, he'd be safe here in Gaul.

Inside the church, everything was quiet and the air suddenly chill. In the early days, when Christianity was just catching on and he, like others, had converted because it was the thing to do if you were a Roman citizen with political or military ambitions, he hadn't liked churches. He'd preferred the open rows of columns and courtyards that formed the temples of the old gods. They seemed less gloomy and, on a feast day when a bull was sacrificed, if you hung about afterwards you could get a good slice of steak rather than a piece of dry bread and single sip of wine.

He would have liked to have somewhere he could go to pray and make offerings to all of the gods at once, as he did in the Pantheon in Rome, or at least those most important to him – Jupiter, Mercury and Mars. However, Christos had taken over and left him few choices of ritual when it came to seeking divine help. Churches had improved since Avitus' youth and he'd come to appreciate the subtleties of the religion as well. There was a lot to be said for loving your fellow man, as long as that didn't include the likes of Attila or Ricimer.

Avitus bowed his head humbly as he walked past the baptismal font. It was in one such that he'd been fully immersed for his christening. It was octagonal and three feet deep, filled only once a year – the Friday before Easter – to give pagans a chance at eternal life through Christ. In a church built of light grey granite, this font was surrounded by white marble paving stones locking into each other without a hair's breadth between them.

This church had changed since he last visited it on the way to Rome. It had been upgraded with a mosaic of the Christ clothed in gold about to ascend into a lapis lazuli sky. For once, Jesus didn't look as if he was suffering. There was peace in his eyes.

Avitus sat down in the front row of rush-seated chairs to pray. He sat, rather than knelt, on account of his sore knees and because he was alone and didn't have to worry about what other people might think. He intended to be there a little while at least. There was a lot to discuss with God.

First, he gave thanks for his safe escape from Italy, then for his health and that of his family. Then he started to ask for guidance in earnest. He also asked for forgiveness for all his sins, such as he saw them, and prayed that Roman civilisation would live on.

He lifted his head and looked around him. All was quiet. He could see from the way the sun had moved to shining through one window instead of another, that the afternoon was wearing on. He wondered if the storm he and Leonida had seen in the distance would pass him by on his last two miles to Grenoble.

He got up and walked to the altar. He was travelling with a small jewelled casket with gold coins inside it to give as an offering to the grand new church of St Julian, in the town of Brioude, in his home province of Auvergne, but he'd left it down the hill in the carriage with his guards. Otherwise he would have taken out a few of the coins and given them to this travellers' church, placed at a crossroads to give itinerants the chance to give thanks for their safe arrivals or ask for a blessing on their outward journeys. It was much humbler an edifice than the resting place of a saint and he would like to leave something for it, something for the ordinary people who voyaged through, living out their lives.

He bent down and removed his dagger from its sheath on his ankle underneath his bishop's alb. He'd never taken it out before except in moments of life and death hand to hand fighting, but this seemed a fitting place to sacrifice it. It had one gem encrusted in its hilt that would be worth a pretty penny and could do some good if left in the hands of the kind of priest he hoped was in charge of such a modest, but not insignificant, place.

He laid the dagger on the palm of one hand. A ray of weak autumn light, shining through an arched window onto the altar, lingered on it. Avitus turned the dagger over, so the ruby in its hilt sparkled, then sighed as he felt its warm metal leave his hand for the last time when he placed it on the altar cloth.

He needed to cheer himself up after parting with this lifelong treasure, so he sat down again and unfolded Sola's letter. Her daring and agility brought back his smile. The corners of his eyes crinkled in his leathery skin and when he finished he winked. Feeling as if he'd found a new lease of life, he rose and put on his cape. With a steady tread, he walked back down the aisle and pushed open the heavy doors on hinges that groaned with resistance.

As his eyes adjusted to the bright light outside the air was knocked from his lungs as if he'd run at full tilt into a wall of stone.

The entire church was surrounded by Ricimer's men, members of the barbarian's personal bodyguard, standing at arms behind Ricimer's black-beaked standards. The church walls had been so thick and he'd been so deeply immersed in his prayers that Avitus hadn't heard them arrive.

A century of guards, under the command of a Tribune, had drawn a perimeter around the churchyard and another was formed up in a phalanx in front of the steps. They were getting cold. The sun had slid behind the mountains. Ricimer's men had marched at the double all day and sweated under their armour. If Avitus hadn't stopped to pray, they wouldn't have caught up with him before he entered the protective embrace of Grenoble's city walls. Now a wind was blowing up and turning their perspiration into ice. They'd been waiting at the ready for almost two hours. Attila would have attacked and killed his prey directly but their commanding officer had served under Aetius and respected sanctuary. What's more, for once the Tribune was loath to carry out Ricimer's orders.

There was a moment's silence when all that could be heard was the mournful song of a nightingale in the distance and a whoosh of wind sighing through mountain pines. Then the Tribune stepped forward and saluted.

Avitus' eyes were steel-blue as he ponderously walked down the stone steps one by one until he stood eye to eye with the officer. "You've come to kill me."

"Those are our orders," the Tribune answered, his jaw tight.

Avitus could see that Ricimer's man had tears in his eyes. Every pore on his drained white face was visible and Avitus noticed each individual hair that curved in black eyebrows flecked with a single strand of white.

The Tribune called his men to attention then ordered a salute. With razor-sharp precision each man thumped his clenched right fist over his heart then, in perfect unison, raised his open hand in the direction of the glowering sky. They held the salute for a long count of ten then snapped their arms back down to their sides. There was silence again. It was the ultimate sign of respect for a legendary Roman whom they'd been sent to assassinate on the orders of a barbarian.

Avitus had his last laugh: "I suppose I should be flattered that Ricimer thought it necessary to send not one, but two centuries of men to finish off a lone, seventy-two-year-old man."

He paused a second then asked the Tribune for a statement of the obvious: "My guard are all dead, are they?"

"It was necessary to kill them. We offered them the chance to surrender, but they chose to fight to the death."

"Ah . . . they were good men, all of them . . . loyal."

The Tribune was becoming uncomfortable. The job he'd been given was painful enough without Avitus becoming more and more human to him by the instant.

Avitus sensed his growing impatience; the Tribune didn't want to look soft in front of his men. Avitus backed up the steps, one by one, scanning the ranks of armoured guards for an escape route. When he got to the landing under the portico he stopped.

What was it Sola had said? It's easy to kill a lion once your mind is made up. *Courage, focus, reflex.*

Avitus stood alone on the top of the stairs and drew his gladius. He held it with both hands locked on the hilt and stared out over the waiting soldiers. For a terrible minute, the officers and men held their breath. Surely the old man wasn't crazy enough to fight them? Surely he'd step down and bend his neck so that the Tribune could behead him?

In a movement too quick for the eye to see, Avitus inverted the sword and rammed it up below his own ribs. The perfectly focused point struck his heart.

He fell knees first onto the steps. Staring straight ahead into the space above the helmet of Ricimer's henchman, the light left his bright blue eyes, then the corpse fell forward. Blood trickled down one granite step to the next, and the next, in the way tears stream down a cheek.

The centuries let out their breath and their faces bleached white.

The lion was dead.

The Tribune walked in silence up the steps and bent down to take Avitus' sword from a hand that was still warm. If he removed it then the priest who'd find the body of his dead Emperor would assume that he'd been assassinated, not committed suicide. That would mean that Avitus could be buried on holy ground. Since the birth of civilisation there'd been a tradition that a commander surrounded by the enemy and facing certain defeat should fall on his own sword rather than be taken by the enemy. Avitus had done the honourable thing and his soul shouldn't be punished for it.

Lightning flashed followed by a rolling roar of thunder, then another. Outraged mountains reverberated them. Raindrops, so heavy and fast that they stung the back of the Tribune's arms, hurtled down in howls of disapproval as he disengaged Avitus' sword from his firmly locked fingers. The torrent turned the trickle of blue blood on the steps into a waterfall.

The Tribune handed the sword to an optio to clean and take back to Rome to show Ricimer that their job was done. He gave the order to about-face and quick march. The men were eager to escape the scene, every man among them certain he was damned for all eternity.

Author's Notes

"A brook flowing between low banks through the plain was greatly increased by blood from the wounds of the slain. It was not flooded by showers, as brooks usually rise, but was swollen by a strange stream and turned into a torrent by the increase of blood. Those whose wounds drove them to slake their parching thirst drank water mingled with gore. In their wretched plight they were forced to drink what they thought was the blood they had poured from their own wounds."

Jordanes, 551 AD. *The Origin and Deeds of the Goths*, translated by

Charles C. Mierow, on the Battle of the Catalaunian Plains

To research fifth century history is akin to navigating from one island to the next without a chart. While time has erased almost all the contemporary written histories, fragments remain and when one discovers them, suddenly characters and places that were only names, and sometimes not even that, spring up in all their vibrancy. But between these islets of information lie dark waters of supposition, rational deduction and intuition.

The events and main male characters in *Rivers Ran Red* are based on facts, in so far as the facts are known. Where there are competing versions of the facts I've chosen the one that I believe, on balance, is most plausible or most in keeping with the picture of the characters and events my research has led me to. At certain times on the journey, I've felt almost as if spirits from the past were guiding me, anxious that their lost stories be told, but I certainly do not claim to be an expert on the era let alone to be right. There is always an element of interpretation of what is known in history. One of the things that surprised in researching ancient history is the extent to which one academic theory builds on another without going back to original sources, and how much of what we think we know about the Romans is seen through nineteenth century British imperial spectacles. To try and remove this unconscious bias is one of the reasons I favoured contemporary and near contemporary accounts and histories over later ones when putting together this tale.

The journey of researching *River Ran Red* has been full of surprises and taken me from New Zealand to obscure locations on the far side of the world, long forgotten and far from the tourist track. Often research has reversed my preconceptions about characters and how life worked in ancient times. There are many instances of this, but perhaps the most important for this novel is that Attila did not at all fit my preconception of a heroic and brilliant plains general. Sources contemporary with Attila suggest to me that, if he were born today, he would be diagnosed as a megalomanic and psychopath. But Attila became a figure of myth (as it suited his would-be successors) within fifty years of his inglorious death and has been glamourised ever since.

In contrast, Flavius Aetius, the Roman field commander (magister militum) who opposed Attila, was, to paraphrase Edward Gibbon in *The History of the Decline and Fall of the Roman Empire*, the only major figure in ancient history about whom neither his enemies nor his allies had a negative word to say. Aetius, by all accounts, was an intelligent, noble human being as well as a superb warrior, able to ride for days without sleeping or eating and expert in every form of weaponry. It is said that when he called, not only armies but whole nations answered. The contrast between these two characters is reflected in the way I've depicted them, not out of artistic choice, for artistic choice would have made them both more nuanced, but out of the desire to tell things the way they were. History tends to favour the memories of those whose atrocities have shocked us. Hence Attila the Hun is still a household name but relatively few people have heard of Flavius Aetius. Yet to forget Aetius and remember Attila is akin to people in the future forgetting Churchill but remembering Hitler.

It astounds me that both the exact location and date of the Battle of the Catalaunian Plains, fought in 451 in northern France, in which history tells us 165,000 men died in less than twenty-four hours, have been lost and forgotten. There are two competing purported dates, one in June and the other in September, both in 451. Given that, in ancient times, the campaign season was the spring and summer months, and given that Attila had caused havoc over eastern Europe before arriving in the West, I've adopted the latter date as giving him time to get there with his army.

There are many competing academic theories as to where the battle site was. I felt it was so wrong that the location of the biggest and bloodiest battle of all Antiquity had been forgotten that I went to France, hired a car and visited the three sites that are, according to nineteenth to twenty-first academic historians, the most likely location of the carnage. It seemed to me that the topography would resolve the issue, as Jordanes (a sixth century historian, who based his writings on Cassiodorus' earlier history of events) had said: "The armies met, as we have said, in the Catalaunian Plains. The battle field was a plain rising by a sharp slope to a ridge, which both armies sought to gain;…" Of the competing modern sites, none conformed to this description, so I elected in the novel to assume that they all formed part of one larger battlefield and to prefer what Jordanes, Cassiodorus, Priscus and Sidonius Apollinaris have to say about the battle and the characters. Priscus was a fifth century diplomat and historian who met Attila the Hun in person; Cassiodorus' grandfather was part of a Roman diplomatic embassy sent to Attila; Sidonius was a prolific writer who was aged about twenty at the time of the wars with Attila and who started, but didn't finish a history of them (now lost). Cassiodorus is said to have based his history of the battles on eye-witness accounts taken from survivors. It seemed to me that these people, who were close in time and place to the wars with Attila, were a more reliable source of information than academics postulating their theories from a distance of 1500 years and in *Rivers Ran Red* I have relied on ancient historians rather than modern ones.

No one is entirely sure which barbarian tribes fought on Attila's side and which for the Romans. One person who died nameless is the prince whose buried weapons were turned up by a plough near Pouans-les-vallées in France in the 1840s. Academics have not hazarded a view as to which side of the conflict he was on nor which tribe he belonged to. Perhaps rashly, I've created the character of Heva around this unknown prince, made him a Roman ally (because a pair of gold tweezers were found with his remains and the Romans were fastidious about body hair when barbarians were not) and called him Heva because he was wearing a ring inscribed 'Heva'. After much research, I found out that 'Heva' meant 'life' in ancient Burgundian, so I have made him a Burgundian prince. Some academics have hypothesised that he was buried away from the battle site but I am not of this opinion as many horse-trappings were found in the same area and, while one may transport the body of a prince, in times of war one isn't likely to cart horse carcasses away.

While I have not contradicted any known facts in the novel, I have nonetheless used a certain amount of artistic licence. History says, for example, that the Romans and their allies won the battle by exerting a pincer movement on Attila and that there were no Roman regulars in Aetius' army, which he'd had to recruit from auxiliaries. The Romans were at one end of the line and the Goths at the other as Aetius had positioned his cowardly allies, the Alani, in between them so they couldn't desert. As I wanted the reader to experience the horror of Attila's attack through the eyes of a young soldier, I've placed fictional Roman recruits with the Alani. I have turned the folding 'V' of a pincer movement into a potentially disastrous 'W' with the Roman cohort holding out as the Alani cave in on either side. I have also fictionally made Sangibanus, the cowardly Alani governor (who did, in fact, offer to open the gates of Orleans to Attila) come through and be courageous in battle.

Not all in the battle scene is fiction. It is a fact that Aetius led his army personally from the front while Attila hid himself amidst his bodyguards and held back, despite his rousing speech to his men, which is quoted in *Rivers Ran Red* with only tiny modifications.

Another element of artistic licence is that I've portrayed Avitus as a humble man who worked his way up through the ranks before becoming Emperor of Rome. It's unlikely that this is the case as Avitus held high office as Praetorian Prefect of Gaul in 439. It is however, true that he was largely responsible for recruiting Theodoric I, King of the Goths, to the Roman side of the conflict with Attila. Despite much research as to how Avitus died, all I could find out is that he disappeared after being deposed as Emperor of Rome on his way to make an offering in a church in Gaul. His death I have fictionalised. The name of Avitus' wife is unknown so I made one up, but that of his daughter, Papianilla, is remembered and his sons really were called Ecdicius and Agricola. Sidonius Apollinaris was his real son-in-law.

History too often forgets working class men, slaves and women. Such is the case of the female gladiator who, according to 1st century Roman historian, Martial, killed a lion in the Coliseum in 80 AD. Martial didn't give the lion-killer a name, but her remarkable deed inspired the character of Sola.

Acknowledgements

Thanks first and foremost to James George without whom *The Last of the Romans* trilogy would never have come into being. With unparalleled generosity of heart and spirit he laboured over it with me, always providing counsel and support in times of need. His sense of humour and literary critiques are priceless gifts. Thanks also to Cloud Ink Press, in particular Dione Jones, Alana Bolton Cooke, Helen McNeil, Thalia Henry and Mark Johnson for their support, encouragement and diligence; and to Anna Gailani, copy-editor and Craig Voilich, designer.

Thanks also to my daughters, Christobelle and Mirella Grierson-Ryrie and Philippe Flagel, who all followed uncharted roads with me in search of fifth-century saints, sinners and battlefields. Thanks also to the many friends who have put up with my fascination with forgotten wars and weapons for their feedback and advice.

I would also like to acknowledge the writings of two men, long dead. The first is Sidonius Apollinaris, the fifth century poet who wrote down details that otherwise would be forgotten and who regretted having begun but never finished a history of the wars with Attila. The second is O. M. Dalton, the first person to translate Sidonius' writings into English, whose critique of him was so blistering that I felt bound to research Sidonius' life and defend him.

Bibliography

Anderson, WB: *Sidonious, Poems and letters with and English translation and introduction*, Loeb Classical Library online, first published in print in 1936

Ando, C: *Imperial Ideology and Provincial Loyalty and the Roman Empire*, University of California Press, c2000

Anonymous: *The Weapons, Armor and Tactics of the Fearsome Huns Which Dominated Europe and Asia*, Sept 2017, https://about-history.com/the-weapons-armor-and-tactics-of-the-fearsome-huns-which-dominated-europe-and-asia/

Apollinaris, S : *Panegyric on Avitus*, 456. https://www.cambridge.org/core/books/envoys-and-political-communication-in-the-late-antique-west-411533/hero-as-envoy-sidonius-apollinaris-panegyric-on-avitus/75F5E7DD49A535BDA17 BBB944C48AB67

Beard, M, North, J, Price, S: *Religions of Rome, Volume I*, Cambridge University Press, 1998

Brittain, Charles: *No Place for a Platonist Soul in Fifth-Century Gaul? The Case of Mamertus Claudianus*, in Mathisen and Shanzer

Brown, P: *Through the Eye of a Needle, Wealth, the Fall of Rome and the Making of Christianity in the West, 350-550 AD*, Princeton University Press, 2012, *The Cult of the Saints*, The University of Chicago Press, 1981

Burgess, R: *The Gallic Chronicle of 452: A New Critical Edition with a Brief Introduction*, in Mathisen and Shanzer
The Gallic Chronicle of 511: A New Critical Edition with a Brief Introduction, in Mathisen and Shanzer

Christensen, A S: *Cassiodorus, Jordanes and the History of the Goths: Studies in a Migration Myth*, Museum Tusculanum Press, Feb. 2002

Dalton, O M: *The Letters of Sidonius, translated, with introduction and notes*, 2 vols, Oxford University Press, 1915

Drinkwater, J F: *The Bacaudae of fifth-century Gaul*, in Drinkwater and Elton, *Fifth century gaul: A Crisis of Identity*, Cambridge University Press, 2010

Elton, H: *Defence in fifth-century Gaul*, in Drinkwater and Elton

Elton, H: (2014). Military Developments in the Fifth Century. In M. Maas (Ed.), *The Cambridge Companion to the Age of Attila* (Cambridge Companions to the Ancient World, pp. 125-139). Cambridge: Cambridge University Press. doi:10.1017/CCO9781139128964.011

Ernak, H: Hun Warfare, http://www.ernak-horde.com/Hun_warfare.html

Fanning, S: *Emperors and empires in Fifth-century Gaul*, in Drinkwater and Elton

Feeney, Denis: *Literature and Religion at Rome: Cultures, Contexts and Beliefs*, Cambridge University Press, 1998

Gibbon, E: The History of the Decline and Fall of the Roman Empire, Strahan & Cadell, London, 1776-1789, https://oll.libertyfund.org/titles/gibbon-the-history-of-the-decline-and-fall-of-the-roman-empire-12-vols

Gibson, Roy: *Reading the Letters of Sidonius by the Book*, in van Waarden and Kelly, 2013

Goldberg, Eric J: *The Fall of the Roman Empire Revisited: Sidonius Apollinaris and His Crisis of Identity* Published by the Corcoran Department of History at the University of Virginia. (Volume Thirty-Seven), 1995

Harries, J D: *Sidonius Apollinaris and the Fall of Rome*, Clarendon Press, Oxford, 1994
Sidonius Apollinaris, Rome and the Barbarians: A Climate of Treason? In Drinkwater and Elton, 1992, p298-308
Not the Theodosian Code: Euric's Law and Late Fifth-Century Gaul, in Mathisen and Shanzer, 2001, p 39-51
Sidonius Apollinaris, Rome and the barbarians: a climate of treason? in Drinkwater and Elton,1992, p 298-308

Heather, P: *The emergence of the Visigothic kingdom*, in Drinkwater and Elton

Heinzelmann, M: *The 'affair' of Hilary of Arles (455) and Gallo-Roman identity in the fifth-century*, in Mathisen and Shanzer

Hodgkin, Thomas: *Italy and her Invaders*, Clarendon Press, Oxford, 1885, p 535-553, Open Library on-line created 2008

Jones, A H M, Morris J, Martindale, J R: *Prosopography of the Later Roman Empire*, Cambridge University Press, 1971-92

Jordanes *The Origins and Deeds of the Goths*, 551, (Jordanes says he writes ". . . to condense in my own style in this small book the twelve volumes of [Cassiodorus] Senator on the origin and deeds of the Getae [i.e. Goths] from olden times to the present day." Translated by Charles C Miero, University of Calgary, https://people.ucalgary.ca/~vandersp/Courses/texts/jordgeti.html

King, C E: *Roman, local and barbarian coinages in fifth-century Gaul*, in Drinkwater and Elton

Kulikowski, M: *Rome's Gothic Wars*, in Drinkwater and Elton, 1992
The Visigothic Settlement in Aquitania: The Imperial Perspective, in Mathisen and Shanzer
Carmen VII of Sidonius and a Hitherto Unknown Gothic Civil War, ILA 1, 334-92

Kuppers, J: *Autobiographisches in den Briefen des Apollinaris Sidonius*, in M Reichel (ed.) *Antike Autobiographien, Werke – Epochen –Gattungen*, (Cologne) 2005 p 251-77

Liebeschuetz, J H W G: *Alaric's Goths: nation or army?* In Drinkwater and Elton

Livermore, Harold, (2006) *Twilight of the Goths: The Kingdom of Toledo, c.565-711*, Kindle edition

Loyen, A: *L'Albis chez Claudien et chez Sidoine Apollinaire*, REL 11, 1933, p 203-11

Maenchen-Helfen, J O: *A History of the Huns, Studies in their History and Culture*, University of California Press, 1973

Mathisen, R W, and Shanzer D: *Society and Culture in Late Antique Gaul Revisiting the Sources*, Ashgate, 2001

Mathisen, R W: *Roman Aristocrats in Barbarian Gaul: Strategies for Survival in an Age of Transition*, University Press of Texas, 1993
Fifth-century visitors to Italy: business or pleasure? in Drinkwater and Elton, 1992
The Letters of Ruricius of Limoges and the Passage from Roman to Frankish Gaul, in Mathisen and Shanzer
Dating the Letters of Sidonius, in van Waarden and Kelly, 2013

Meyers, Jean Persée: *Prolegomènes bibliographiques á la lecture des Panegyriques de Sidoine Apollinaire*, Vita Latina Année 2008 vol 179, p 77-86

Mratschek, Sigrid: *Creating Identity from the Past: The Construction of History in the Letters of Sidonius*, in van Waarden and Kelly, 2013

Percival, J: *The fifth-century Villa: new life or death postponed?* In Drinkwater and Elton

Priscus: At the court of Attila, circa 448-9, Translation by J.B. Bury (Priscus, fr. 8 in *Fragmenta Historicorum Graecorum*) http://faculty.georgetown.edu/jod/texts/priscus.html

Rees, R: *Diocletian and the Tetrarchy*, Edinburgh University Press, 2004

Reinach, S: *Sur une passage de Sidoine Apollinaire: Les pretendus volcans de la France central au Ve siècle*, in Rev. arch, p 127-34, 1916

Roberts, M: *Barbarians in Gaul: the response of the poets*, in Drinkwater and Elton

Romer, F E: *Sidonius Apollinaris and the Fall of Rome, A.D. 407-485*, review in American Journal of Philology, Volume 117, Number 4 (Whole Number 468), Winter 1996, p. 663-666

Rousseau, P: *In Search of Sidonius the Bishop*, Historia 25, 1976, pp. 356-77

Ruckett, Julia, Margareta, Maria: *Romans and Goths in late Antique Gaul: aspects of political and cultural assimilation in the fifth century AD*, Masters thesis, Durham University, 2011

Rutherford, H: *Sidonius Apollinaris Etude d'une Figure Gallo-Roman du Ve siècle*, J de Bussac, Clermont-Ferrand, 1938

Schwarcz, Andreas: *The Visigothic Setttlement in Aquitania: Chronology and Archaeology*, in Mathisen and Shanzer

Shanzer, Danuta: *Bishops, Letters, Fast, Food and Feast in Later Roman Gaul*, in Mathisen and Shanzer

Stevens, C E: *Sidonius Apollinaris and His Age*, Oxford Clarendon Press, 1933

Suetonius, G T: *De vita Caesarum, 121 AD*, (known as *The Twelve Caesars*), translated by Robert Graves, Penguin Classics revised edition, 2007.

Teitler, H C: *Un-roman activities in antique Gaul: the cases of Arvandus and Seronatus*, in Mathisen and Shanzer

Van Waarden, Johannes A, and Kelly, Gavin: *New Approaches to Sidonius Apollinaris*, Peeters, 2013

Van Waarden, Johannes A: *Writing to Survive Vol I*, Peeters, 2010

Wes, M A: *Crisis and Conversion in fifth-century Gaul: aristocrats and ascetics between 'horizontality' and 'verticality'*, in Mathisen and Shanzer

White, D E: *Tertullian the African: An Anthropological Reading of Tertullian's Context*, Walter de Gruyter Gmbh & Co, 2007

White, Heather: *Textual problems in the poems of Sidonius Apollinaris*, Veleia 27, 2010

Wickham, C: *Framing the Early Middle Ages, Europe and the Mediterranean, 400-800*, Oxford University Press, 2005

Wood, I N: *Continuity or Calamity: the constraints of the literary models*, in Drinkwater and Elton

Woolf, Greg: *Becoming Roman: The Origins of Provincial Civilization in Gaul*, Cambridge University Press, 1998

Zehetner, Dr S: *The Equites Legionis and the Roman Cavalry*, https://brewminate. com/the-equites-legionis-and-the-roman-cavalry/, posted Dec 29, 2018

Glossary

Aetius — Roman name derived from Ancient Greek "aetós", meaning "eagle".

Akhal Teke — one of the oldest breeds of horse, known for its speed, endurance, adaptability and intelligence. Akhal Teke coats have a distinctive metallic sheen that led to the nickname "Golden Horse".

Ala (pl. Alae) — Roman elite cavalry made up of several turmae (see over).

Anima — Latin word used to describe ideas such as breath, soul, spirit or vital force.

Aquilifer — bearer of the eagle standard in a Roman legion. The name comes from aquila, meaning eagle and fers from the Latin word for bringing or carrying. The eagle standard usually had upraised wings surrounded by a laurel wreath and was held aloft on a narrow trapezoidal base. It was the legion's most important possession and the aquilifer's position was one of enormous prestige. Losing the aquila was considered the greatest dishonor a legion could endure. This post had to be filled by steady, veteran soldiers, with an excellent understanding of the tactics of the legion. The aquilifer was paid twice the basic wage.

Bagaudae — (also spelled bacaudae) displaced peasants, farmers, former soldiers, bandits, both Roman and barbarian, who banded together in gangs from the third century to the Fall of the Western Empire. They occasionally organised themselves to rebel against local governors but were repeatedly suppressed. They were a symptom of late Roman economic and social decline.

Bucellarii	privately paid escort troops, sometimes comprising thousands of men, for either high ranking military officers or civil officials. They were a feature of the late Empire and could act as private armies. They provided the best cavalry in the 5th century Roman armies, and were often better armed and paid than the regular army.
Centurion	professional officers in command of groups of about eighty fighting men and twenty slaves, servants or orderlies, in the Roman army after the Marian Reforms of 107BC. Unlike common soldiers, they were allowed to marry while serving. Senior centurions could command cohorts or take senior straff roles in heir legions.
Chiton	a sleeveless shirt worn by Greek and Roman men and women, draped by the wearer and kept in place at the shoulders by brooches (fibulae) and at the waist by a belt. Excess material was pulled up over the belt in a blouson fashion. It was worn ankle-length at all times by women and either short or long by men.
Cohort	a standard tactical military unit of a Roman legion, though the standard changed with time and situation, and was usually composed of between 500-800 soldiers. A cohort is considered to be the equivalent of a modern military battalion.
Cohortes Urbanae	urban cohorts formed by the Emperor Augustus to counterbalance the power of the Praetorian Guard in the city of Rome and to serve as a police force.
Comitia Centuriata	Assembly of the people of Rome. The Comitia centuriata, in which the richest Romans were in the majority, elected the consuls.
Consul	was the title of each of the two annually elected chief magistrates who jointly ruled the ancient Roman Republic. Consuls served for only one year (to prevent corruption) and could only rule when they agreed, because each consul could veto the other one's decision. Consuls were elected to office and held power for one year. There were always two

consuls in power at any time. During the Roman imperial period, consuls became symbolic representatives of Rome's republican heritage and held little power and authority, with the Emperor acting as the supreme authority. Nonetheles, Romans considered the consulship the highest level of the cursus honorum (an ascending sequence of public offices to which politicians aspired).

crytoporticus	an underground tunnel leading from the coliseum to the emperor's palace on top of the Palatine Hill.
Decanus	the leader of a squad of eight legionaries (a contubernium) that lived in the same tent and the two support units/ servants of the contubernium. Roughly equivalent to a modern sergeant or corporal.
Decurion	Commander of a cavalry unit (turma) of 10 to 30 eques legionis.
Dux et Patricius	a title awarded to Flavius Aetius. Dux is Latin for leader and, later, duke. Patricius signifies membership of the ruling class of Rome.
Gladius	the primary sword of ancient Roman infantry, generally made out of steel. The blade was fine, about 5/16 of an inch (approx. 8mm) thick at the ridge near the pommel, and tapered to about 3/16" (approx. 5 mm)before abruptly coming to the tip in the last 3 inches (7.6 cm). It measured about 18 to 20 inches (46-51cm) and about 2 inches (5 cm) wide. Gladii were two-edged for cutting and had a tapered point for stabbing during thrusting. A solid grip was provided by a knobbed hilt, possibly with ridges for the fingers. Blade strength was achieved by welding together strips of steel, (in which case the sword had a channel down the center), or by fashioning a single piece of high-carbon steel, rhomboidal in cross-section. It weighed about 1.2-1.6 Kg (2.65 – 3.5lbs).
Gregarius	lowest rank in Roman army, means 'herd animal'. Equivalent to modern private.

Hades — ancient Greek god of the dead and king of the underworld. Name became synonymous with hell.

Horreum (pl. horrea) — a type of ancient Roman public warehouse. Although the Latin term is often used to refer to granaries, horrea were used to store many other types of goods.

Kysaghan — a Hun god of war.

Magister Militum — meaning 'master of the soldiers', the magister militum was a top-level military command used in the later Roman Empire. Used alone, the term referred to the senior military officer (equivalent to a war theatre commander, the emperor remaining the supreme commander) of the Empire. Greek sources translate the term either as strategos or stratelates.

Nummus — meaning 'coin', word is used to describe the low value copper or bronze coins issued by the Late Roman and Byzantine empires.

Optio — officer appointed by a centurion from within the ranks to act as his second in command. There was one for each centurion and were paid twice the basic wage. There were many other roles an optio could adopt. Stationed at the rear of the ranks in order to keep the troops in order, an optio enforced the centurion's orders, took over the centurion's command in battle should the need arise, supervised his subordinates and had a variety of administration duties. Equivalent to modern First Sergeant of Lieutenant.

Palla — ancient Roman mantle worn by women, fastened by brooches, it was similart to the pallium that men wore. It was rectangular instead of semi-circular as with the traditional toga.

Peristyle — a continuous porch formed by a row of columns surrounding the perimeter of building or a courtyard.

Pilum (pl. pila) — a javelin, generally about 2 metres (6 ft 7 in) long overall, commonly used by the Roman army. A pilum consists of an iron shank about 7 millimetres (0.28 in) in diameter and 60 centimetres (24 in) long with a pyramidal head.

Praefectus Castrorum — third in command of the legion. Generally he was a long serving veteran from a lower social status than the Tribunes whom he outranked, and who previously had served as primus pilus and finished his 25 years with the legions. He was used as a senior officer in charge of training a legion, though he could also command a cohort of auxiliaries.

Praetorian Prefect — the highest-level administrative division of the Empire. The prefects again functioned as the chief ministers of the state and the Emperor's territorial governors.

Praetorium — a general's tent within a Roman encampment. The general's war council would meet within this tent.

Primus Pilus — commanding centurion of the first century, first cohort and therefore the most senior centurion of a legion. The Primus Pilus had a chance of later becoming a Praefectus Castrorum. When the Primus Pilus retired, he would most likely gain entry into the equestrian class. He was paid 60 times the base wage. Primus Pilus were also paid more than an average centurion.

Quadriga — a chariot drawn by four horses abreast.

Scutum (pl. scuta) — Rectangular or oval shield made of vertically connected wooden boards with a small bronze boss which protects shield's handle.

Sestertius (pl. sestertii) — an ancient Roman coin. During the Roman Republic it was a small silver coin. During the Empire it became a large brass coin.

Spina — A low wall that ran most of the length of the Hippodrome (chariot racing stadium) and divided the course. Decorated with monuments and sculptures that could be tilted or removed to keep spectators informed of the laps completed by the racers.

Solidus — ancient Roman coin of nearly solid gold.

Stigma	tattoo.
Sueve	(also known as Suebi), the Sueves were an ancient group of Germanic tribes. Beginning in the 1st century BC, various Sueve tribes moved south-westwards from the Baltic Sea and the Elbe and came into conflict with Ancient Rome.
Sui juris	possessing full civil and legal rights to act in one's own capacity with out the consent of a parent or guardian, a right only rarely extended to women in Ancient Rome.
Tribune	second in command of the legion, (behind the legate).
Turma (pl. Turmae)	Roman cavalry unit of approximately 32 men.
Via principalis	the main transverse street, passing in front of the headquarters building or general's, in a Roman camp or fort.
Vigiles	the Vigiles Urbani (watchmen of the city) or Cohortes Vigilum (cohorts of the watchmen) were the fire-fighters and police of Ancient Rome.
Vir Illustris	meaning 'illustrious man', was a used as a formal indication of standing in late antiquity to describe the highest ranks within the senates of Rome and Constantinople.

Lightning Source UK Ltd.
Milton Keynes UK
UKHW011504070720
366155UK00004B/944